SOMETHING BRUSHED AGAINST THE LIVING ROOM WINDOW—

Vicki straightened. The large ground level windows of the basement apartment had always been a tempting target for neighborhood kids. She walked over and flicked on the floor lamp. With luck, enough of the brilliant white light would spill out into the night and she'd actually be able to see the little vandals before they ran.

She paused at the window, one hand holding the edge of the curtain, the other the cords of the venetian blind. This close, Vicki could hear that something was definitely rubbing against the other side of the glass. With one smooth, practiced motion, she threw the curtain aside and yanked the length of the blind up against its top support.

Pressed up against the glass, fingers splayed, mouth silently working, was her mother. Two pairs of eyes, an identical shade of gray, widened in simultaneous recognition.

The Vicki's world slid sideways for a second.

My mother is dead. . . .

Also by:
TANYA HUFF:

BLOOD PRICE
BLOOD TRAIL
BLOOD LINES
BLOOD PACT
BLOOD DEBT

****

SING THE FOUR QUARTERS
FIFTH QUARTER
NO QUARTER
THE QUARTERED SEA

****

SUMMON THE KEEPER
THE SECOND SUMMONING*
****

THE FIRE'S STONE

****

GATE OF DARKNESS, CIRCLE OF LIGHT

****

WIZARD OF THE GROVE

****

VALOR'S CHOICE

*Coming soon from DAW Books

BLOOD PACT

PACT

TANYA HUFF

DAW BOOKS, INC.
DONALD A. WOLLHEIM, FOUNDER
375 Hudson Street, New York, NY 10014

ELIZABETH R. WOLLHEIM
SHEILA E. GILBERT
PUBLISHERS

First Printing, November 1993

19   18   17   16   15   14   13   12   11   10

DAW TRADEMARK REGISTERED
U.S. PAT. OFF. AND FOREIGN COUNTRIES
—MARCA REGISTRADA
HECHO EN U.S.A.

PRINTED IN THE U.S.A.

For Mrs. Mac, who helped me through a rough time without having a clue of what she was getting into and never really got thanked. Thank you.

Thanks also to Michael Humphries of Wattam's Funeral Home in Picton, Ontario, who gave generously of his time and expertise.

One

"Mrs. Simmons? It's Vicki Nelson calling; the private investigator from Toronto?" She paused and considered how best to present the information. *Oh, what the hell* . . . "We've found your husband."

"Is he . . . alive?"

"Yes, ma'am, very much so. He's working as an insurance adjuster under the name Tom O'Conner."

"Don always works in insurance."

"Yes, ma'am, that's how we found him. I've just sent you a package, by courier, containing a copy of everything we've discovered including a number of recent photographs—you should receive it before noon tomorrow. The moment you call me with a positive ID, I'll take the information to the police and they can pick him up."

"The police thought they found him once before—in Vancouver—but when they went to pick him up he was gone."

"Well, he'll be there this time." Vicki leaned back in her chair, shoved her free hand up under the bottom edge of her glasses and scrubbed at her eyes. In eight years with the Metropolitan Toronto Police and nearly two years out on her own, she'd seen some real SOBs; Simmons/O'Conner ranked right up there with the best of them. Anyone who faked his own death in order to ditch a wife and five kids deserved exactly what he got. "My partner's going to talk to him tonight. I think your husband will decide to stay right where he is."

* * *

The bar was noisy and smoky, with tables too small to be useful and chairs too stylized to be comfortable. The beer was overpriced, the liquor over-iced, and the menu a tarted-up mix of at least three kinds of quasi-ethnic cooking plus the usual grease and carbohydrates. The staff were all young, attractive, and interchangeable. The clientele were a little older, not quite so attractive although they tried desperately hard to camouflage it, and just as faceless. It was, for the moment, the premier poser bar in the city and all the wannabes in Toronto shoehorned themselves through its doors on Friday night.

Henry Fitzroy paused just past the threshold and scanned the crowd through narrowed eyes. The smell of so many bodies crammed together, the sound of so many heartbeats pounding in time to the music blasting out of half a dozen suspended speakers, the feel of so many lives in so little space pulled the Hunger up and threatened to turn it loose. Fastidiousness more than willpower held it in check. In over four and a half centuries, Henry had never seen so many people working so hard and so futilely at having a good time.

It was the kind of place he wouldn't be caught dead in under normal circumstances, but tonight he was hunting and this was where his quarry had gone to ground. The crowd parted as he moved away from the door, and eddies of whispered speculation followed in his wake.

"Who does he think he is . . ."

". . . I'm telling you, he's somebody . . ."

Henry Fitzroy, bastard son of Henry VIII, one time Duke of Richmond and Somerset, Lord President of the Council of the North, noted, with an inward sigh, that some things never changed. He sat down at the bar—the young man who had been on the stool having vacated it as Henry approached—and waved the bartender away.

To his right, an attractive young woman raised one ebony brow in obvious invitation. Although his gaze dropped to the pulse that beat in the ivory column of her throat and almost involuntarily traced the vein until it disappeared beneath the soft drape of magenta silk clinging to shoulders and breasts, he regretfully, silently, declined. She acknowledged both his glance and his refusal, then turned to more receptive game. Henry hid a smile. He wasn't the only hunter abroad tonight.

To his left, a wide back in a charcoal gray suit made up most of the view. The hair above the suit had been artfully styled to hide the thinning patches just as the suit itself had been cut to cover the areas that a fortieth birthday had thickened. Henry reached out and tapped lightly on one wool-clad shoulder.

The wearer of the suit turned, saw no one he knew, and began to scowl. Then he fell into the depths of a pair of hazel eyes, much darker than hazel eyes should have been, much deeper than mortal eyes could be.

"We need to have a talk, Mr. O'Conner."

It would have taken a much stronger man to look away.

"In fact, I think you'd better come with me." A thin sheen of sweat greased the other man's forehead. "This is just a little too public for what I plan to . . ." Slightly elongated canines became visible for an instant between parted lips. ". . . discuss."

"And?"

Henry stood at the window, one hand flat against the cool glass. Although he seemed to be looking down at the lights of the city, he was actually watching the reflection of the woman seated on the couch behind him. "And what?"

"Henry, stop being an undead pain in the ass. Did you convince Mr. O'Conner/Simmons to stay put until the police arrive?"

He loved to watch her; loved to watch emotions play across her face, loved to watch her move, loved to watch her in repose. Loved her. But as that was a topic not to be discussed, all he said was, "Yes."

"Good. I hope you scared the living shit out of him while you were at it."

"Vicki." He turned, arms crossed on his chest, and frowned in what was only partially mock disapproval. "I am not your personal bogeyman, to be pulled out of the closet every time you think someone needs to have the fear of God . . ."

Vicki snorted. "Think highly of yourself, don't you?"

". . . put into them," he continued, ignoring the interruption.

"Have I ever treated you like my 'personal bogeyman'?" She raised a hand to cut off his immediate reply. "Be honest. You have certain skills, just like I have certain skills, and when I think it's necessary, I use them. Besides," she pushed her glasses back into place on the bridge of her nose, "you said you wanted to be more involved in my business. Help out with more cases now that you've handed in *Purple Passion's Pinnacle* and aren't due to start another romantic masterpiece until next month."

"*Love Labors On.*" Henry saw no reason to be ashamed of writing historical romances; it paid well and he was good at it. He doubted, however, that Vicki had ever read one. She wasn't the type to enjoy, or even desire, escape through fiction. "Tonight—it wasn't what I had in mind when I said I wanted to be more involved."

"Henry, it's been over a year." She sounded amused. "You should know by now that most private investigating consists of days and days of boring, tedious research. Thrilling and exciting life-threatening situations are few and far between."

Henry raised one red-gold brow.

Vicki looked a little sheepish. "Look, it's not my fault people keep trying to kill me. And you. And anyway, you *know* those were the exceptions that prove the rule.'' She straightened, tucking one sneakered foot up under her butt. ''Tonight, I needed to convince a sleazebag—who deserved to be terrified after what he put his wife and kids through—to stay put until the police arrive. Tonight, I needed you. Henry Fitzroy, vampire. No one else could've done it.''

Upon reflection, he was willing to grant her that no one else could have done the job as well although a couple of burly mortals and fifty feet of rope would have had the same general effect. ''You really didn't like him, did you?''

''No. I didn't.'' Her lip curled. ''It's one thing to walk out of your responsibilities, but it takes a special kind of asshole to do it in such a way that everyone thinks he's dead. They mourned him, Henry. Cried for him. And the son of a bitch was off building a new life, fancy-free, while they were bringing flowers, every Saturday, to an empty grave. If he hadn't gotten into the background of that national news report, they'd still be crying for him. He owes them. In my book, he owes them big.''

''Well, then, you'll be happy to know that I did, as you so inelegantly put it, scare the living shit out of him.''

''Good.'' She loosened her grip on the throw pillow. ''Did you . . . uh . . . feed?''

''Would it matter if I had?'' Would she admit it if it mattered. ''Blood's blood, Vicki. And his fear was enough to raise the Hunger.''

''I know. And I know you feed from others. It's just . . .'' She dragged one hand through her hair, standing it up in dark blonde spikes. ''It's just that . . .''

''No. I didn't feed from him.'' Her involuntary smile was all he could have asked, so he crossed the room to see it better.

''You're probably hungry, then.''

''Yes.'' He took her hand and gently caressed the inner skin of her wrist with his thumb. Her pulse leapt under his touch.

She tried to stand, but he pushed her back, bent his head, and ran his tongue down the faint blue line of a vein.

"Henry, if we don't go soon, I won't be able to . . ." Her voice faded out as her brain became preoccupied with other things. With a mighty effort, she forced her throat to open and her mouth to work. "We'll end up staying on the . . . couch."

He lifted his mouth long enough to murmur, "So?" and that was the last coherent word either of them spoke for some time.

"Four o'clock in the morning," Vicki muttered, digging for the keys to her apartment. "Another two hours and I'll have seen the clock around. Again. Why do I keep doing this to myself?" Her wrist throbbed, as if in answer, and she sighed. "Never mind. Stupid question."

Muscles tensed across her back as the door unexpectedly swung fully open. The security chain hung loose, unlocked, arcing back and forth, scraping softly, metal against wood. Holding her breath, she filtered out the ambient noises of the apartment—the sound of the refrigerator motor, a dripping tap, the distant hum of the hydro substation across the street—and noted a faint mechanical whir. It sounded like . . .

She almost had it when a sudden noise drove off all hope of identification. The horrible crunching, grinding, smashing, continued for about ten seconds, then muted.

"I'll grind his bones to make my bread . . ." It was the closest she could come to figuring out what could possibly be happening. *And all things considered, I'm not denying the possibility of a literal translation.* After demons, werewolves, mummies, not to mention the omnipresent vampire in her life, a Jack-eating giant in her living room was less than impossible no matter how unlikely.

She shrugged the huge, black leather purse off her

shoulder and caught it just before it hit the floor. With the strap wrapped twice around her wrist it made a weapon even a giant would flinch at. *Good thing I hung onto that brick . . .*

The sensible thing to do would involve closing the door, trotting to the phone booth on the corner, and calling the cops.

I am way too tired for this shit. Vicki stepped silently into the apartment. *Four in the morning courage. Gotta love it.*

Sliding each foot a centimeter above the floor and placing it back down with exaggerated care, she made her way along the short length of hall and around the corner into the living room, senses straining. Over the last few months she'd started to believe that, while the retinitis pigmentosa had robbed her of any semblance of night sight, sound and smell were beginning to compensate. The proof would be in the pudding; although she knew the streetlight outside the bay window provided a certain amount of illumination in spite of the blinds and the apartment never actually got completely dark, as far as her vision was concerned, she might as well be wearing a padded blindfold.

Well, not quite a blindfold. Even she couldn't miss the blob of light that had to be the television flickering silently against the far wall. She stopped, weapon ready, cocked her head, and got a whiff of a well known after-shave mixed with . . . cheese?''

The sudden release of tension almost knocked her over.

''What the hell are you doing here at this hour, Celluci?''

''What does it look like?'' the familiar voice asked mockingly in turn. ''I'm watching an incredibly stupid movie with the sound off and eating very stale taco chips. How long have you had these things sitting around, anyway?''

Vicki groped for the wall, then walked her fingers along it to the switch for the overhead light. Blinking away tears as her sensitive eyes reacted to the glare, she gently lowered her purse to the floor. Mr. Chin, downstairs in the first floor apartment, wouldn't appreciate being woken up by twenty pounds of assorted bric-a-brac slamming into his ceiling.

Detective-Sergeant Michael Celluci squinted up at her from the couch and set the half-empty bag of taco chips to one side. "Rough night?" he growled.

Yawning, she shrugged out of her jacket, tossing it over the back of the recliner. "Not really. Why?"

"Those bags under your eyes look more like a set of matched luggage." He swung his legs to the floor and stretched. "Thirty-two just doesn't bounce back the way thirty-one used to. You need more sleep."

"Which I had every intention of getting," she crossed the room and jabbed a finger at the television control panel, "until I came home to find *you* in my living room. And you haven't answered my question."

"What question?" He smiled charmingly, but eight years on the force with him, the last four intimately involved—*Now* that's *a tidy label for a complicated situation,* she mused—had made her pretty much immune to classical good looks used to effect.

"I'm too tired for this shit, Celluci. Cut to the chase."

"All right, I came by to see what you remembered about Howard Balland."

She shrugged. "Small-time hood, always looking for the big score but would probably miss said big score if it bit him on the butt. I thought he left town."

Celluci spread his hands. "He's back, in a manner of speaking. A couple of kids found his body earlier tonight behind a bookstore down on Queen Street West."

"And you've come to me to see if I remember anything that'll help you nail his killer?"

"You've got it."

"Mike, I was in fraud for only three short months

before I transferred to homicide and that was a good chunk of time ago.''

"So you don't remember anything?''

"I didn't say that . . .''

"Ah.'' The single syllable held a disproportionate weight of sarcasm. "You're tired and you'd rather screw around with your little undead friend than help get the bastard who slit the throat of a harmless old con man. I understand.''

Vicki blinked. "What the fuck are you talking about?''

"You *know* what I'm talking about. You've been off playing Vlad the impaler with Henry Fucking Fitzroy!''

Her brows drew down into a deep vee, the expression making it necessary for her to jab her glasses back up onto the bridge of her nose. "I don't believe this. You're jealous!''

They were chest to chest and would've been nose to nose accept for the difference in their heights. Although Vicki was tall at five ten, Celluci was taller still at six four.

"JEALOUS!''

Over the years Vicki had learned enough Italian to get the gist of what followed. The fight had barely begun to heat up when a soft voice slid through a pause in the screaming.

"Excuse me?''

Expressions ludicrously frozen in mid-snarl, they turned to face the wizened concern of Mr. Chin. He clutched a burgundy brocade bathrobe closed with one frail hand and had the other raised as though to snare their attention. When he saw he had it, he smiled into the silence.

"Thank you,'' he told them. "Now, shall we see if we can maintain this situation?'' At their puzzled frowns, he sighed. "Let me make it a little simpler for you. It's 4:22 a.m. Shut up.'' He waited for a moment, nodded, and left the apartment, gently pulling the door closed behind him.

Vicki felt her ears grow hot. She jerked around as a cross between a sneeze and a small explosion sounded from Celluci's direction. "What are you laughing at?"

He shook his head, arms waving as he searched for the words.

"Never mind." She reached up and pushed the curl of dark brown hair back off his face, her own mouth twisting up in a rueful grin. "I guess it was pretty funny at that. Although I'm going to spend the rest of the day with this vaguely unfinished feeling."

Celluci nodded, the thick curl dropping back down into his eyes. "Like not remembering if you've eaten the last bite of doughnut."

"Or drunk the last swallow of coffee."

They shared a smile and Vicki collapsed into the black leather recliner that dominated the small living room. "Okay, what do you need to know about the late Mr. Balland?"

Vicki moved away from the warm cliff of Celluci's back and wondered why she couldn't sleep. Maybe she *should* have told him to go home, but it'd seemed a little pointless making him drive all the way out to his house in Downsview when he was expected back downtown at headquarters in barely six hours. Or less. Maybe. She couldn't see the clock unless she sat up, turned on the light, and found her glasses, but it had to be nearly dawn.

Dawn.

In the center of the city, eighteen short blocks away from her apartment in Chinatown, Henry Fitzroy lay in his sealed room and waited for the day; waited for the rising sun to switch off his life; trusted that the setting sun would switch it on again.

Vicki had spent the day with Henry once, held captive by the threat of sunlight outside the bedroom door. The absence of life had been so complete it had been a little like spending the day with a corpse. Only worse. Because he wasn't. It wasn't an experience she wanted to repeat.

She'd run from him that night, the moment the darkness had granted her safe passage. To this day she wasn't sure if she'd run from his nature or from the trust that had allowed him to be so helpless before her.

She hadn't stayed away for long.

In spite of late nights, or occasionally no nights at all, Henry Fitzroy had become a necessary part of her life. Although the physical attraction still tied her stomach in knots and caught the breath in her throat—even after a year of exposure—what bothered her, almost frightened her, was how much he had invaded the rest of her life.

Henry Fitzroy, vampire, bastard son of Henry VIII, was Mystery. If she spent a lifetime trying, she could never know all he was. And, God help her, she couldn't resist a mystery.

Now Celluci—she rolled onto her side and layered herself around the curve of his body—Celluci was the yin to her yang. She frowned. Or possibly the other way around. He was a shared joke, shared interests, a shared past. He fit into her life like a puzzle piece, interlocking and completing the picture. And now she thought of it, *that* frightened her, too.

She was complete without him.

Wasn't she?

Lord, oh Lord, oh Lord. When did my life start resembling country and western music?

Celluci stirred under the force of her sigh and half roused. "Almost forgot," he murmured. "Your mother called."

The late morning sun had nearly cleared Vicki's bay window when she sat down at the kitchen table and reached for the phone. Returning her mother's call while Celluci was dressing would make it easier to deal with the questions she knew she was going to have to answer. Questions that would no doubt start with, *Why was Michael Celluci in your apartment when you weren't?* and escalate from there to the perpetual favorite, *When will you be coming to visit?*

She sighed, fortified herself with a mouthful of coffee, and wrapped her fingers around the receiver. Before she could lift it out of the cradle, the phone rang. She managed, just barely, to keep the coffee from going out her nose but it took a half a dozen rings to get the choking under control.

"Nelson Investigations."

"Ms. Nelson? It's Mrs. Simmons. I was beginning to think you weren't there."

"Sorry." She hooked a dish towel off the refrigerator door and swiped at the mess. "What can I do for you?"

"The photographs came. Of my husband."

Vicki checked her watch. Nearly noon in Toronto meant nearly eleven in Winnipeg. *Hot damn. Truth in advertising; I've found a courier who can tell time.*

"It *is* my husband, Ms. Nelson. It's him." She sounded close to tears.

"Then I'll take the information to the police this afternoon. They'll pick him up and then they'll get in contact with you."

"But it's the weekend." Her protest was more a whimper than a wail.

"The police work weekends, Mrs. Simmons. Don't worry." Vicki turned up the reassurance in her voice. "And even if they can't actually bring him in until Monday, well, I personally guarantee he's not going anywhere."

"You're sure?"

"I'm sure."

"I need to ask him why, Ms. Nelson; why he did such a horrible thing to us?"

The pain in the other woman's voice tightened Vicki's fingers on the receiver until her knuckles went white. She only just managed to mask her anger with sympathy during the final few moments of the call.

"God-damned, fucking, son of a BITCH!"

Her notepad hit the far wall of the apartment with enough force to shatter the spine and send loose paper fluttering to the floor like a flock of wounded birds.

"Anyone I know?" Celluci asked. As he'd come into the living room barely a meter from the impact point, he supposed he should be thankful she hadn't thrown the coffee mug.

"No." She surged up out of her chair, slamming it back so hard it fell and bounced twice.

"Something to do with your found missing person?" It wasn't that difficult a guess; he knew the bare bones of the case and he'd heard her use the name Simmons during the phone conversation. Also, he knew Vicki and, while she was anything but uncomplicated, her reactions tended to be direct and to the point.

"Lousy bastard!" Her glasses slid to the end of her nose and she jabbed them back up the slope. "Doesn't give a shit about what he put his family through. You should have heard her, Mike. He's destroyed everything she ever believed in. At least when she thought he was dead, she had memories, but now he's fucked those, too. He's hurt her so badly she hasn't even hit anger yet."

"So you're getting angry for her."

"Why not?"

He shrugged. "Why not, indeed." Intimately familiar with Vicki's temper he thought he saw something more than just rage at a woman wronged. Lord knew she'd seen enough of that during her years on the force and had never—all right, seldom—reacted with such intensity. "Your mother, did she ever get angry when your father left?"

Vicki came to a dead stop and stared at him. "What the hell does that have to do with anything?"

"Your father walked out on your mother. And you."

"My father, at least, had the minimal decency not to hide what he was doing."

"And your mother had to support the two of you. Probably never had time to get angry."

Her eyes narrowed as she glared across the apartment at him. "What the fuck are you talking about?"

He recognized the danger signs but couldn't let the opportunity pass. Things had been working toward this for a long time and with her anger for Mrs. Simmons leaving her so emotionally open he knew he might never get a better chance. *What the hell, if it comes to it, I'm armed.* "I'm talking, whether you like it or not, about you and me."

"You're talking bullshit."

"I'm talking about how you're so afraid of commitment that you'll barely admit we're anything more than friends. I understand where it's coming from. I understand that because of the way your father left and because of what happened afterward with your mother that you think you need to put tight little parameters on a relationship . . ."

She snorted. "Did the force just send you to another sensitivity seminar?"

He tightened his grip on his own temper and ignored her. ". . . but all that happened over twenty years ago and, Vicki, it has to stop."

Her lip curled. "Or else?"

"Or else nothing, God damn it. I'm not making threats here."

"This is about Henry, isn't it? You *are* jealous."

No point in forcing her to face the truth if he didn't. "You're god-damned right I'm jealous of Henry! I don't want to share that much of you with *anyone* else. Especially not with someone who . . . who . . ." Mike Celluci didn't have the words to explain how he felt about Henry Fitzroy and even if he had, it was none of Vicki's business. The edge of his hand chopped off the thought. "We're not talking about Henry, we're talking about us."

"There's nothing wrong with *us*." She looked everywhere but at the man standing across the room. "Why can't we just go on the way we have been?"

"Because we're not going anywhere!"

She jerked at each staccato word.

"Vicki, I'm tired of being nothing more than your buddy. You've got to realize that I . . ."

"Shut up!" Her hands had curled into fists.

"Oh, no." He shook his head. "You're going to hear it this time."

"This is *my* apartment. I don't have to hear *anything*."

"Oh, yes you do." He crossed to stand directly in front of her, balancing on the balls of his feet, his hands a careful distance away. As much as he wanted to grab her and shake her, he didn't want to deal with the return violence he knew would follow. A quick game of *Who's more macho?* would add nothing to the situation. "This isn't going to be the last time I say this, Vicki, so you'd better get used to it. I love you. I want a future with you. Why is it so hard for you to accept that?"

"Why can't you just accept me, us, the way I am. We are." The words were forced out through clenched teeth.

He shoved the lock of hair back off his forehead and unsuccessfully tried to calm his breathing. "I've spent five fucking years accepting you and *us*. It's time you met me halfway."

"Get out."

"What?"

"Get out of my apartment! NOW!"

Trembling with the need to hold himself in check, he pushed past her and grabbed his coat off the hook by the door. Jabbing his arms into the sleeves, he turned. His own anger made it impossible for him to read her expression. "Just one more thing, Vicki. I am *not* your fucking father."

The door closed behind him with enough force to shake the building.

A heartbeat later it opened again.

"And don't forget to call your mother!"

The coffee mug exploded into a thousand pieces against the wood.

•

"And did you?"

"Did I what?" Vicki snapped. Giving Henry the gist of the fight had put her in nearly as bad a mood as the fight had. It didn't help that she *knew* she should've kept her mouth shut but when Henry had asked what was bothering her, she couldn't seem to stop a repeat of the whole infuriating conversation from pouring out.

"Did you call your mother?"

"No. I didn't." She turned to face the window, jabbed at her glasses, and glared out at the darkness. "I wasn't exactly in the mood to talk to my mother. I went down to Missing Persons and nailed Mr. Simmons/O'Conner to the wall instead."

"Did that make you feel better?"

"No. Although it might have if they'd let me use real nails."

A facetious comment spoken with complete and utter sincerity. Even from across the room Henry could feel pulsing waves of anger radiating off of her. He wished now that he hadn't asked, that he'd ignored her mood and never been subjected to Detective-Sergeant Michael Celluci's all-too-accurate analysis of Vicki's inability to commit. But now that he'd heard it, he couldn't let it rest. Vicki would continue to think about what Celluci had said, had obviously been thinking of little else since Celluci had slammed out of her apartment, and, now that her nose had been rubbed in it, would in time see it for the truth. At which point she would have to choose.

He wouldn't lose her. If that meant taking the day as well as the night, his love gave him a right equal to Celluci's to assert a claim.

You raised the stakes, mortal, he told the other man silently. *Remember that.*

He stood and crossed the carpet to stand at her side, glorying for a moment in her heartbeat, savoring her heat, her scent, her life.

"He was right," he said at last.

"About what?" The words were forced out through clenched teeth. No need to ask which *he* was meant.

"We can't, any of us, go on the way we have."

"Why not?" The final consonant carried the weight of a potential explosion.

"Because, like Mike Celluci, I want to be the most important person in your life."

She snorted. "And what about what I want?"

He could see the muscles working beneath the velvet surface of her skin, tensing around her eyes and the corners of her mouth and so he chose his next words with care. "I think that's what we're trying to discover."

"And what if I decide I want him?"

Her tone held a bitter, mocking edge. Henry couldn't help but respond.

"Could you give *me* up?"

The power in his voice pulled her around to face him. He heard her swallow hard as she met his gaze, heard her heartbeat quicken, saw her pupils dilate, tasted the change in her scent on the air. Then he released her.

Vicki jerked back, furious at Henry, furious at herself. "Don't ever do that again!" she panted, fighting to get enough air into her lungs. "I give nobody power over my life. Not you. Not him. Nobody!" Barely in control of her movements, she whirled and stomped across the living room. "I am *out* of here." She snatched her coat and bag up off the end of the couch, "And you can just play Prince of fucking Darkness with somebody else."

He hadn't moved from the window. He knew he

could call her back, so he had no need to make the attempt. ''Where are you going?''

''I'm going for a long walk in the sleaziest neighborhood I can find in the hope that some dickweed will try something stupid and I can break his fucking arms! *Don't* follow me!''

Even a security door can be slammed if enough force is applied.

''Vicki? It's your mother. Didn't Mike Celluci give you my message? Well, never mind, dear, I'm sure he has a lot on his mind. While I'm thinking of it though, I *did* wonder why he was in your apartment while you were out. Have you two been getting more serious? Call me when you get a chance. There's something I have to tell you.''

Vicki sighed and rubbed at her temples as the answering machine rewound. It was ten after twelve and she was just not up to a heart-to-heart with her mother, not after the day she'd had. ''Have you two been getting more serious?'' Jesus H. Christ.

First Celluci.

Then Henry.

The powers-that-be had really decided to mess up her life.

''Whatever happened to men who just want to get laid on a regular basis?'' she muttered, flicking off the light and making her way to the bedroom.

The pitcher of draft she'd downed in the gay bar on Church Street—the one place in the city safe from testosterone cases—churned uneasily in her stomach. All she wanted to do was go to sleep. Alone.

She'd call her mother in the morning.

The night had been filled with dreams, or more specifically, dream—the same images occurring over and over. People kept coming into her apartment and she couldn't get them to leave. The new staircase to the third floor bisected her kitchen and a steady stream of real estate agents moved up it, dragging potential tenants. The back of her closet opened into Maple Leaf Gardens and the post-hockey crowds decided to leave through her bedroom. First she tried the voice of reason. Then she yelled. Then she physically picked up the intruders and threw them out the door. But the door never stayed closed and they wouldn't, any of them, leave her alone.

She woke up late with a splitting headache and an aching jaw, her mood not significantly better than when she'd gone to sleep. An antacid and an aspirin might have helped, but as she'd run out of both she settled for a mug of coffee so strong her tongue curled in protest.

"And why did I *know* it would be raining," she growled, squinting out through the blinds at a gray and uninviting world. The sky looked low enough to touch.

The phone rang.

Vicki turned and scowled across the room at it. She didn't have to answer to know it was her mother. She could feel mother vibes from where she stood.

"Not this morning, Mom. I'm just not up to it."

Her head continued ringing long after the bell fell silent.

An hour later, it rang again.

An hour of conscious thought had done nothing to improve Vicki's mood.

"I said *no*, Mom!" She slammed her fist down on the kitchen table. The phone rocked but continued to ring. "I don't want to hear about your problems right now and I sure as shit don't want to tell you about mine!" Her voice rose. "My personal life has suddenly collapsed. I don't know what's going on. Everything is falling apart. I can stand on my own. I can work as part of a team. I've proved that, haven't I? Why isn't that *enough!*"

It became a contest in volume and duration and Vicki had no intention of letting the phone win.

"Odds are good Celluci's about to propose and this

vampire I'm sleeping with—Oh, didn't I tell you about Henry, Mom?—well he wants me as his . . . his . . . I don't *know* what Henry wants. Can you deal with that, Mom? 'Cause I sure as shit can't!''

She could feel herself trembling on the edge of hysteria, but she wouldn't quit until the phone did.

"Celluci thinks I'm angry about the way dear old Dad walked out on you. Henry thinks he's right. How about that, Mom? I'm being fucking double-teamed. You never warned me about something like this, did you, Mom? And we never, ever discuss Daddy!''

The last word echoed around a silent apartment and seemed to take a very long time to fade.

With a trembling finger, Vicki slid her glasses back up her nose. "I'll talk to you tomorrow, Mom. I promise.''

An hour later, the phone rang again.

Vicki turned on the answering machine and went for a walk in the rain.

When she got back, late that evening, there were seven messages waiting. She wiped the tape without listening to any of them.

The phone rang.

Vicki paused, one foot into the shower, sighed, and got back into her robe. Welcome to Monday.

"Coming, Mom." No point putting it off. She'd have to face the music sooner or later and it might as well be sooner.

Today things didn't seem so bad. Yesterday was an embarrassing memory of self-indulgence. Tomorrow, well, she'd deal with tomorrow when it arrived.

She dropped into one of the kitchen chairs and scooped up the receiver. "Hi, Mom. Sorry about yesterday.''

"Is this Victoria Nelson?''

Her ears grew hot. It was an elderly woman's voice, strained and tight and most definitely not her mother.

Let's make a great impression on a potential client there, Vicki. "Uh, yes."

"This is Mrs. Shaw. Mrs. Elsa Shaw. I work with your mother. We met last September . . . ?"

"I remember." Vicki winced. *Mom must really be pissed if she's getting coworkers to call. This is going to cost me at least a visit.*

"I'm afraid I have some bad news for you."

"Bad news?" *Oh, God, don't let her have caught the early train to Toronto. That's all I need right now.*

"Your mother hasn't been feeling well lately, and, well, she came into work this morning, said how she'd been trying to get in touch with you, made the coffee like she always does, came out of Dr. Burke's office and . . . and, well, died."

The world stopped.

"Ms. Nelson?"

"What happened?" Vicki heard herself ask the question, marveled at how calm her voice sounded, wondered why she felt so numb.

"Dr. Burke, the head of the Life Sciences Department—well, you know who Dr. Burke is, of course—said it was her heart. A massive coronary, she said. One minute there, the next . . ." Mrs. Shaw blew her nose. "It happened about twenty minutes ago. If there's anything I can do . . ."

"No. Thank you. Thank you for calling."

If Mrs. Shaw had further sympathy or information to offer, Vicki didn't hear it. She set the receiver gently back in its cradle and stared down at the silent phone.

Her mother was dead.

Two

"Dr. Burke? It's about number seven . . ."

"And?" Receiver tucked under her chin, Dr. Aline Burke scrawled her signature across the bottom of a memo and tossed it into the out basket. Although Marjory Nelson had been dead for only a couple of hours, the paperwork had already begun to get out of hand. With any luck the university would get off its collective butt and get her a temporary secretary before academic trivia completely buried her.

"I think you'll want to see this for yourself."

"For heaven's sake, Catherine, I haven't got the time for you to be obscure." She rolled her eyes. Grad students. "Are we losing it?"

"Yes, Doctor."

"I'll be right over."

"Damn." The surgical glove hit the wastebasket with enough force to rock the container from side to side. "Tissue decomposition again. Just like the others." The second glove followed and Dr. Burke turned to glare at the body of an elderly man lying on the stainless steel table, thoracic cavity open, skull cap resting against one ear. "Didn't even last as long as number six."

"Well, he was old to start with, Doctor. And not in very good physical condition."

Dr. Burke snorted. "I should say not. I suppose I'm moderately surprised it lasted as long as it did." She sighed as the young woman standing by the head of the cadaver looked crushed. "That was *not* a criticism, Catherine. You did your usual excellent job and were certainly in no way responsible for the subject's deplorable habits when alive. That said, retrieve the rest of the mechanicals, salvage as much of the net as you can, be very sure *all* of the bacteria are dead, and begin the usual disposal procedures."

"The medical school . . ."

"Of *course* the medical school. We're hardly going to weight it with rocks and drop it into Lake Ontario—although I have to admit that has a certain simplicity that appeals and would involve a lot less additional work for me. Let me know when it's ready, I should be in my office for the next couple of hours." Hand on the door, she paused. "What's that banging noise?"

Catherine looked up, pale blue eyes wide, fingers continuing to delve into the old man's skull cavity. "Oh, it's number nine. I don't think he likes the box."

"It doesn't *like* anything, Catherine. It's dead."

The younger woman shrugged apologetically, accepting the correction but unwilling to be convinced. "He keeps banging."

"Well, when you finish with number seven, decrease the power again. The last thing we need is accelerated tissue damage due to unauthorized motion."

"Yes, Doctor." She gently slid the brain out onto a plastic tray. The bank of fluorescent lights directly over the table picked up glints of gold threaded throughout the grayish-green mass. "It'll be nice to finally work with a subject we've been able to do preliminary setup on. I mean, the delay while we attempt to tailor the bacteria can't be good for them."

"Probably not," Dr. Burke agreed caustically and, with a last disapproving look in the direction of number nine's isolation box, strode out of the lab.

The pounding continued.

* * *

"Where to, lady?"

Vicki opened her mouth and then closed it again. She didn't actually have the faintest idea.

"Uh, Queen's University. Life Sciences." Her mother would have been moved. Surely someone could tell her where.

"It's a big campus, Queen's is." The cabbie pulled out of the train station parking lot and turned onto Taylor Kidd Boulevard. "You got a street address?"

She knew the address. Her mother had shown her proudly around the new building just after it opened two years ago. "It's on Arch Street."

"Down by the old General Hospital, eh? Well, we'll find it." He smiled genially at her in his rearview mirror. "Fifteen years of driving a cab and I haven't gotten lost yet. Nice day today. Looks like spring finally arrived."

Vicki squinted out the window beside her. The sun was shining. Had the sun been shining in Toronto? She couldn't remember.

"Winter's better for business, mind you. Who wants to walk when the slush is as high as your hubcaps, eh? Still, April's not so bad as long as we get a lot of rain. Let it rain, that's what I say. You going to be in Kingston long?"

"I don't know."

"Visiting relatives?

"Yes." *My Mother. She's dead.*

Something in that single syllable convinced the cabbie his fare wasn't in the mood for conversation and that further questions might be better left unasked. Humming tunelessly, he left her to relative silence.

An attempt had been made to blend the formed concrete of the new Life Sciences Complex in with the older, limestone structures of the university, but it hadn't been entirely successful.

"Progress," the cabbie ventured, as Vicki opened the back door, his tongue loosened by a sizable tip. "Still, the kids need more than a couple of Bunsen

burners and a rack of test tubes to do meaningful research these days, eh? Paper says some grad student
took out a patent on a germ.''

Vicki, who'd handed him a twenty because it was
the first bill she'd pulled out of her wallet, ignored
him.

He shook his head as he watched her stride up the
walk, back rigidly straight, overnight bag carried like
a weapon, and decided against suggesting that she have
a nice day.

''Mrs. Shaw? I'm Vicki Nelson . . .''

The tiny woman behind the desk leapt to her feet
and held out both hands. ''Oh, yes, of course you are.
You poor dear, did you come all the way from Toronto?''

Vicki stepped back but couldn't avoid having her
right hand clutched and wrung. Before she could
speak, Mrs. Shaw rushed on.

''Of course you did. I mean you were in Toronto
when I called and now you're here.'' She laughed, a
little embarrassed, and let go of Vicki's hand. ''I'm
sorry. It's just . . . well, your mother and I were
friends, we'd worked together for almost five years and
when she . . . I mean, when . . . It was just . . . such
a terrible shock.''

Vicki stared down at the tears welling up in the older
woman's eyes and realized to her horror that she didn't
have the faintest idea of what to say. All the words of
comfort she'd spoken over the years to help ease a
thousand different types of grief, all the training, all
the experience—she could find none of it.

''I'm sorry.'' Mrs. Shaw dug into her sleeve and
pulled out a damp and wrinkled tissue. ''It's just every
time I think of it . . . I can't help . . .''

''Which is why I keep telling you, you should go
home.''

Thankfully, Vicki turned to face the speaker, the
calm, measured tone having dropped like a balm over

her abraded nerves. The woman standing just inside
the door to the office was in her mid-forties, short,
solidly built, and wearing an almost practical combi-
nation of gray flannel pants and white, lace-edged
blouse under her open lab coat. Her red-brown hair
had been cut fashionably close, and the heavy frames
of her glasses sat squarely on a nose well dusted with
freckles. Her self-confidence was a tangible presence,
even from across the room, and in spite of everything,
Vicki felt herself responding.

Mrs. Shaw sniffed and replaced the tissue in her
sleeve. "And I keep telling you, Dr. Burke, I'm not
going home to spend the day alone, not when I can
stay here, be surrounded by people, and actually accomplish something. Vicki felt small fingers close
around her arm. "Dr. Burke, this is Marjory's daughter, Victoria."

The department head's grip was warm and dry and
she shook hands with an efficiency of motion that Vicki
appreciated.

"We met briefly a few years ago, Ms. Nelson, just
after your first citation, I believe. I was sorry to hear
about the retinitis. It must have been difficult leaving
a job you cared so deeply about. And now . . ." She
spread her hands. "My condolences about your
mother."

"Thank you." There didn't seem to be much left to
say.

"I had the body taken over to the morgue at the
General. Your mother's personal physician, Dr. Friedman, has an office there. As we didn't know exactly
when you'd be arriving or what the arrangements would
be, that seemed best for all concerned. I did have Mrs.
Shaw call to let you know, but you must have already
left."

The flow of information carried no emotional bag-
gage at all. Vicki found herself drawing strength from
the force of personality that supported it. "If I could
use one of your phones to call Dr. Friedman?"

"Certainly." Dr. Burke nodded toward the desk. "She's already been informed and is waiting for your call. Now, if you'll excuse me." She paused at the door. "Oh, Ms. Nelson? Do let us know when the service is to be held. We'd . . ." Her gesture included Mrs. Shaw. ". . . like to attend."

"Service?"

"It *is* customary under these circumstances to hold a funeral."

Vicki barely noticed the sarcasm, only really heard the last word. *Funeral . . .*

"Well, she doesn't look asleep." There was no mistaking the waxy, gray pallor, the complete lack of self that only death brings. Vicki had recognized it the first time she'd seen it in a police cadet forensic lab and she recognized it now. The dead were not alive. It sounded like a facetious explanation but, as she stared down at the body her mother had worn, she couldn't think of a better one.

Dr. Friedman looked mildly disapproving as she drew the sheet back up over Marjory Nelson's face, but she held her tongue. She could feel the restraints that Vicki had placed around herself but didn't know the younger woman well enough to get past them. "There'll be no need for an autopsy," she said, indicating that the morgue attendant should take the body away. "Your mother has been having heart irregularities for some time and Dr. Burke was practically standing right beside her when it happened. She said it had all the earmarks of a massive coronary."

"A heart attack?" Vicki watched as the door swung shut behind the pallet and refused to shiver in the cold draft that escaped from the morgue. "She was only fifty-six."

The doctor shook her head sadly. "It happens."

"She never told me."

"Perhaps she didn't want to worry you."

Perhaps I wasn't listening. The small viewing room

had suddenly become confining. Vicki headed for the exit.

Dr. Friedman, caught unaware, hurried to catch up. "The coroner is satisfied, but if you're not . . ."

"No autopsy." She'd been to too many to put her mother—what was left of her mother—through that.

"Your mother had a prepaid funeral arranged with Hutchinson's Funeral Parlour, up on Johnson Street, just by Portsmouth Avenue. It would be best if you speak to them as soon as possible. Do you have someone to go with you?"

Vicki's brows drew down. "I don't *need* anyone to go with me," she snarled.

"According to your mother's arrangement, Ms. Nelson, Vicki . . . Ms. Nelson"—the funeral director blanched slightly as his client's expression returned him to last names but managed to continue smoothly—"she wanted to be buried as soon as possible, with no viewing."

"Fine."

"As she also wanted to be embalmed . . . perhaps the day after tomorrow? That would give you time for a notice in the local paper."

"Is the day after tomorrow as soon as possible, then?"

The younger Mr. Hutchinson swallowed. He found it difficult to remain completely calm under such hard-edged examination. "Well, no, we could have everything ready by tomorrow afternoon . . ."

"Do so, then."

It wasn't a tone that could be argued with. It wasn't even a tone that left much room for discussion. "Is two o'clock suitable?"

"Yes."

"About the casket . . ."

"Mr. Hutchinson, I understood that my mother pre-arranged *everything*."

"Yes, she did . . ."

"Then," Vicki stood, slung her bag over her shoulder, "we will do exactly as my mother wanted."

"Ms. Nelson." He stood as well, and pitched his voice as gently as he could. "Without a notice in the paper, you'll have to call people."

Her shoulders hunched slightly and the fingers that reached for the doornob shook. "I know," she said.

And was gone.

The younger Mr. Hutchinson sank back down into his chair and rubbed at his temples. "Recognizing there's nothing you can do to help," he told a potted palm with a sigh, "has got to be the hardest part of this business."

The old neighborhood had gotten smaller. The vast expanse of backyard behind the corner house at Division and Quebec Streets that she'd grown up envying had somehow shrunk to postage stamp size. The convenience store at Division and Pine had become a flower shop and the market across from it—where at twelve she'd argued her way into her first part-time job—was gone. The drugstore still stood at York Street but, where it had once seemed a respectable distance away, Vicki now felt she could reach out and touch it. Down on Quebec Street, not even the stump remained of the huge maple that had shaded the Thompson house and not even the spring sunlight could erase the shabby, unlived in look of the whole area.

Standing in the front parking lot of the sixteen-unit apartment building they'd moved to when her father's departure had lost them the house in Collins Bay, Vicki wondered when it had happened. She'd been back any number of times in the last fourteen years, had been back not so long before and had never noticed such drastic changes.

Maybe because the one thing I came back for never changed. . . .

She couldn't put it off any longer.

The security door had been propped open. *A secu-*

rity door protects nothing unless it's closed and locked. If I told her once I told her . . . I told her . . . The reinforced glass trembled but held as she slammed it shut and stumbled down the half flight of stairs to her mother's apartment.

"Vicki? Ha, I should've known it was you slamming doors."

"The security door has to be kept closed, Mr. Delgado." She couldn't seem to get her key into the lock.

"Ha, you, always a cop. You don't see me bringing my work home." Mr. Delgado came a little farther into the hall and frowned. "You don't look so good, Vicki. You okay? Your mother know you're home?"

"My mother . . ." Her throat closed. She swallowed and forced herself to breathe. So many different ways to say it. So many different gentle euphemisms, all meaning the same thing. "My mother . . . died this morning."

Hearing her own voice say the words, finally made it real.

"Dr. Burke? It's Donald."

Dr. Burke pulled her glasses off and rubbed at one temple with the heel of her hand. "Donald, at the risk of sounding clichéd, I thought I told you not to call me here."

"Yeah, you did, but I just thought you should know that Mr. Hutchinson has gone to get the subject."

"Which Mr. Hutchinson?"

"The younger one."

"And he'll be back?"

"In about an hour. There's no one else here, so he's going to start working on it immediately."

Dr. Burke sighed. "When you say no one else, Donald, do you mean staff or clients?"

"Clients. All the staff are here; the *old* Mr. Hutchinson *and* Christy."

"Very well. You know what to do."

"But . . ."

"I'll see to it that the interruptions occur. All you have to worry about is playing your assigned role. This is vitally important to our research, Donald. It could bring final results and their accompanying rewards practically within our grasp."

She could hear his grin over the phone as he broadly returned the cliché circumstances demanded. "I *won't* let you down, Dr. Burke."

"Of course you won't." She depressed the cutoff with her thumb and contacted the lab. "Catherine, I've just heard from Donald. You've got a little more than an hour."

"Well, I've got number eight on dialysis right now, but he shouldn't take much more than another forty minutes."

"Then you'll have plenty of time. Call me just before you arrive and I'll have Mrs. Shaw begin making inquiries about flowers and the like. The state she's in, she'll probably be able to keep the lines tied up for most of the afternoon. Has number nine quieted?"

"Only after I cut the power again. He's barely showing life signs."

"Catherine, it is *not* alive."

"Yes, Doctor." The pause obviously contained a silent sigh. "It's barely showing wave patterns."

"Better. Did all that banging damage it?"

"I haven't really had time to examine him, but I think you'd better come and take a look at the box."

Dr. Burke felt her eyebrows rise. "The box?"

"I think he dented it."

"Catherine, that's im . . ." She paused and thought about it for a moment, knowing Catherine would wait patiently. With natural inhibitors shut down and no ability to feel pain, enhanced strength might actually be possible. "You can run some tests after you get the new lot of bacteria working."

"Yes, Doctor."

My, my, my . . . Dr. Burke gave the receiver a satisfied pat as it settled into its cradle. It sounded like they could actually have made a breakthrough with number nine. *Now, if we can only keep it from decomposing . . .*

Breakfast dishes were still out on the drying rack and the chair with the quilted cushion sat out a little from the table. The makeup case lay open on the bathroom counter, the washcloth beside it slightly damp. The bed had been made neatly, but a pair of pantyhose with a wide run down one leg lay discarded in the center of the spread.

Vicki sat at the telephone table, her mother's address book open on her lap, and called everyone she thought should know, her voice calm and professional as though she were speaking of someone else's mother. *Mrs. Singh? I'm Constable Nelson, from the Metro Police. It's about your son . . . I'm afraid your husband . . . The driver had no chance to avoid your wife . . . Your daughter, Jennifer, has been . . . The funeral will be at two tomorrow.*

When the funeral home called, Mr. Delgado took her mother's favorite blue suit from the closet and delivered it. When he returned, he forced her to eat a sandwich and kept insisting she'd feel better if she cried. She ate the sandwich without tasting it.

Now, there was no one left to call and Mr. Delgado had been convinced to go home. Vicki sat, one foot dangling over the arm of the old upholstered rocking chair, one foot pushing back and forth against the floor.

Slowly, the room grew dark.

"I'm telling you, Henry, she looked wrecked. Like *Night of the Living Dead.*"

"And she didn't hear you when you called to her?"

Tony shook his head, a long lock of pale brown hair falling into his eyes. "No, she just kept walking, and the guard wouldn't let me go up the stairs after her. Said only ticket holders were allowed and wouldn't

believe me when I said I was her brother. The moth-
erfucking bastard.'' A year under Henry's patronage
hadn't quite erased five years on the street. ''But I
copied down all the places the train was going.'' He
dug a crumpled and dirty piece of paper out of the
front pocket of his skintight jeans and passed it over.
''She was carrying a bag, so I guess when she gets
there she's gonna stay.''

The names of nine towns had been scrawled onto
the blank spaces of a subway transfer. Henry frowned
down at them. Why had Vicki left town without telling
him? He thought they'd moved beyond that. Unless it
had something to do with the fight they'd had on Saturday night. However great the temptation to prove his
power, he knew he shouldn't have coerced her as he
had and he intended to apologize as soon as she cooled
down enough to accept it. ''Her mother lives in Kingston,'' he said at last.

''You think you did something, don't you?''

He looked up, startled. ''What are you talking
about?''

''I like to watch you.'' Tony blushed slightly and
dug his toe into the carpet. ''I watch you all the time
we're together. You've got your Prince-of-Men face,
and your Prince-of-Darkness face, and your sort of
not-there writer face, but when you think about Victory . . . about Vicki . . .'' His blush deepened but
he met Henry's gaze fearlessly. ''Well then it's like
you're not wearing a face, you're just you.''

''All the masks are gone.'' Henry studied the
younger man in turn. A number of the hard edges had
softened over the last year since Vicki and a demon
had brought them together. The bruised and skittish
look had been replaced by the beginnings of a calm
maturity. ''Does that bother you?''

''About you and Victory? Nah. She means a lot to
me, too. I mean, without her, I wouldn't have . . . I
mean, we wouldn't . . . And besides—'' he had to wet
his lips before he could continue—''sometimes, like

when you feed, you look at me like that." Abruptly, he dropped his gaze. "You going after her?"

There really wasn't any question. "I need to know what's wrong."

Tony snorted and tossed his hair back out of his eyes. "Of course you do." His voice returned to his usual cocky tones. "So call her mom."

"Call her mother?"

"Yeah, you know. Like on the telephone?"

Henry spread his hands, willing to allow Tony this moment. "I don't have the number."

"So? Get it out of her apartment."

"I don't have a key."

Tony snorted again. "*You* don't really need one. But," he laced his fingers together and cracked the knuckles, "if you don't want to slip past the lock, there's always our old friend Detective-Sergeant Celluci. I bet he has the number."

Henry's eyes narrowed. "I'll get it from Vicki's apartment."

"I've got Celluci's number right here, I mean if you . . ."

"Tony." He cupped one hand around Tony's jaw and tightened the fingers slightly, the pulse pounding under his grip. "Don't push it."

From the street, he saw the light on, recognized the shape visible between the slats of the blinds, and very nearly decided not to go in. Tony had seen Vicki leave the city in the early morning. Overnight case or not, she could very easily have returned and, if so, she obviously wasn't spending the evening alone. Standing motionless in the shadow of an ancient chestnut, he watched and listened until he was certain that the apartment held only a single life.

That changed things rather considerably.

There were a number of ways he could get what he wanted. He decided on the direct approach. *Out of sheer bloody-mindedness,* honesty forced him to admit.

"Good evening, Detective. Were you waiting for someone?"

Celluci spun around, dropped into a defensive crouch, and glared up at Henry. "Goddamnit!" he snarled. "Don't do that!"

"Do what?" Henry asked dryly, voice and bearing proclaiming that he did not in any way perceive the other man as a threat. He moved away from the door and walked into Vicki's living room.

As if he has every right to. Celluci found himself backing up. *Son of a bitch!* It took a conscious effort, but he dug in his heels and stopped the retreat. *I don't know what game you're playing, spook, but you're not going to win it so easily.* "What the hell are you doing here?"

"I might ask you the same thing."

"*I* have a key."

"*I* don't need one." Henry leaned against the wall and crossed his arms. "My guess is, you've come back to apologize for slamming out of here on Saturday." He read a direct hit in the sudden quickening of Celluci's heartbeat and the angry rush of blood to his face.

"She told you about that." The words were an almost inarticulate growl.

"She tells me about everything." No need to mention the argument that followed.

"You want me to just back off right now, don't you?" Celluci managed to keep a fingernail grip on his temper. "Admit defeat."

Henry straightened. "If I wanted you to back off, mortal, you would."

So if I'm a good eight inches taller than he is, why the hell do I feel like he's looking down at me? "Think pretty highly of yourself, don't you. Look, Fitzroy, I don't care what you are and I don't care what you can do. You should've been dust four hundred years ago. I am *not* letting you have her."

"I think that should be her choice, not yours."

"Well, she's not going to choose you!" Celluci slammed his fist down onto the table. A precariously balanced stack of books trembled at the impact and a small brown address book fell onto the answering machine.

The tape jerked into motion.

"Ms. Nelson? It's Mrs. Shaw again. I'm so sorry to bother you, but your mother's body has been moved over to the General Hospital. We thought you should know in case . . . well, in case . . . I expect you're on your way. Oh, dear . . . It's ten o'clock, April ninth, Monday morning. Please let us know if there's anything we can do to help."

Celluci stared down at the rewinding tape and then up at Henry. "Her mother's body," he repeated.

Henry nodded. "So now we know where she is."

"If this call came in at ten, we can assume she got the original call about nine. She didn't tell you . . ." Celluci broke off and pushed the curl of hair back out of his eyes. "No, of course, she couldn't, you'd be . . . asleep. She didn't leave a message?"

"No. Tony saw her boarding the 10:40 train for Kingston so she must have left the apartment just before that call. She didn't leave a message for you either?"

"No." Celluci sighed and sat back on the edge of the table. "I'm getting just a little tired of this 'I can handle everything myself' attitude of hers."

Henry nodded again. *I thought we'd gone beyond this, she and I.* "You and me both."

"Don't get me wrong, her strength is one of the things I . . ."

The pause was barely perceptible. A mortal might have missed it. Henry didn't. *Well, he's hardly going to tell me he loves her.*

". . . admire about her, but," his expression seemed more weary than admiring, "there's a difference between strength and . . ."

"Fear of intimacy," Henry offered.

Celluci snorted. "Yeah." He reached behind him for the address book. "Well, she's just going to have to put up with a little fucking intimacy because I'm not going to let her stand alone in this." The binding barely managed to survive the force of his search. "Here it is, under M for Mother. Christ, her filing system . . ." Then, suddenly, he remembered who he was talking to. He wasn't, however, prepared for how fast Henry could move—didn't, in fact, see Henry move.

Henry looked down at the address and handed the book back to the detective. "I assume I'll see you in Kingston," he said and headed for the door.

"Hey!"

He turned.

"I thought you couldn't leave your coffin?"

"You watch too many bad movies, Detective."

Celluci bristled. "You've still got to be under cover by dawn. I can see to it that you aren't. One phone call to the OPP and you'll be in a holding cell at sunrise."

"You won't do that, Detective." Henry's voice was mild as he caught Celluci's gaze with his own and let the patina of civilization drop. He played with the mortal's reaction for a moment and then, almost reluctantly, released him. "You won't do it," he continued in the same tone, "for the same reason I don't use the power *I* have on you. *She* wouldn't like it." Smiling urbanely, he inclined his head in a parody of a polite bow. "Good night, Detective."

Celluci stared at the closed door and fought to keep from trembling. Patches of sweat spread out under each arm and his palms, pressed hard against the table, were damp. It wasn't the fear that unnerved him. He'd dealt with fear before, knew he could conquer it. It was the urge to bare his throat that had him so shaken, the knowledge that in another instant he would have placed his life in Henry Fitzroy's hands.

"Goddamnit, Vicki." The hoarse whisper barely shredded the silence. "You are playing with fucking fire. . . ."

"Geez, Cathy, why'd you bring *them?*"

"I thought they could carry the body."

"Oh." Donald stepped back as Catherine helped two shambling figures out of the back of the van. "The program I wrote for them is pretty basic; are you sure they can do something that complicated?"

"Well, number nine can." She patted the broad shoulder almost affectionately. "Number eight may need a little help."

"A little help. Right." Grunting with the effort, he dragged a pair of sandbags out of the van. "Well, if they're so strong, they can carry these."

"Give them both to number nine. I'm not sure about eight's joints."

Although living muscles strained to lift a single bag off the ground, number nine gave no indication that it noticed the weight, even after both bags had been loaded.

"Good idea," Donald panted. "Bringing them along, that is. I'd have killed myself getting those things inside." Fighting for breath, he glanced around the parking lot. The light over by the garage barely illuminated the area and he'd removed the light over the delivery entrance that afternoon. "Let's just make sure nobody sees them, okay. They don't look exactly, well, alive."

"Notices *them?*" Catherine moved number eight around to face the door, then turned and discovered number nine had moved without help. "We better be sure that no one notices *us.*"

"People don't look too closely at funeral homes." Still breathing heavily, Donald slipped his key into the lock. "They're afraid of what they might see." He shot a glance at number nine's gray and desiccated face perched above the collar of a red windbreaker and snickered as he pushed the door open. "Almost makes you wish someone *would* stumble over Mutt and Jeff here, doesn't it?"

"No. Now get going."

Long inured to his colleague's complete lack of a sense of humor, Donald shrugged and disappeared into the building.

Number nine followed.

Catherine gave number eight a little push. "Walk," she commanded. It hesitated, then slowly began to move. Halfway down the long ramp to the embalming room, it stumbled. "No, you don't . . ." Holding it precariously balanced against the wall, she bent and straightened the left leg.

"What took you so long," Donald demanded as the two of them finally arrived.

"Trouble with the patella." She frowned, tucking a strand of nearly white-blond hair back behind her ear. "I don't think we're getting any kind of cell reconstruction."

"Yeah, and it's starting to smell worse, too."

"Oh, no."

"Oh, yes. But hey—" he threw open both halves of the coffin lid— "let's not stand around sniffing dead people all night. We've got work to do."

Number eight's fingers had to be clamped around the corpse's ankles, but number nine took hold of the shoulders with very little prompting.

"I'm telling you, Donald," Catherine caroled as they guided the two bodies back up the ramp, "number nine has interfaced with the net. I'm sure we're getting independent brain activity."

"What does Dr. Burke say?"

"She's more worried about decomposition."

"Understandable. Always a bummer when your experiments rot before you can gather the data. Stop them for a second while I get the door."

The two grad students did the actual loading of the van. Not even Catherine could figure out a series of one-word commands that would allow number eight to carry out the complicated maneuvers necessary. And, as Donald reminded her, both speed and silence were advisable.

"Because," he added, settling number eight into place, "what we're doing *is* illegal."

"Nonsense." Catherine's brow drew down. "It's science."

He shook his head. He'd never met *anyone* who came close to being so single-minded. As far as he'd been able to determine, she had almost as little life outside the lab as their experimental subjects did—and considering that they were essentially dead, that was saying something. Even stranger, she honestly didn't seem to care that what they were doing would result in fame and fortune all around. "Well, in the interest of science, then, let's try to stay out of jail." He gave number nine a push toward the vehicle.

Number nine lowered his head and the reflection of the stars slid off the artificially moist surface of his eyes.

Three

"That is *not* a healthy heart."

Donald peered over the edge of his surgical mask and into the chest cavity. "Not now it isn't," he agreed. "Didn't smoke, didn't drink, and just look at it. Almost makes you want to go out and party."

With a deft stroke of the scalpel, Dr. Burke exposed the tricuspid valve and began to remove the shredded membrane. "I wasn't calling for moral commentary, Donald. Pay attention to what you're doing."

Not noticeably chastened, Donald emptied the hypodermic he held, drew it out of the corner of the eye socket, and picked up a smaller needle. The liquid in the chamber appeared almost opalescent in the glare of the fluorescent lights. "All right, boys," he carefully slid the point through the cornea, "time to go to work. Lift that curve, tote that bail, if you don't repair the iris, then you're in the pail."

"We can do without the poetry, thank you." Tight sutures closed up the incision in the heart. "If you've hydrated both eyes, help Catherine in the abdominal cavity. We've got to get those blood vessels tied off as soon as possible so we can get the nutrient fluid circulating.

"Time is vitally important in work of this nature . . ." The lecture continued as Donald placed soaked cotton swabs over each staring eye and moved around to the side of the table. "Fortunately, the first step in the embalming process toughens the vessels, making them easier to work with at speed and enabling us to . . ."

"Uh, Doctor, this is our tenth cadaver," Donald reminded her, suctioning away the sterile solution they used to force the embalming fluid out of the body. Catherine, who'd been suturing under water, shot him a grateful smile, the corners of her eyes crinkling up above her mask. "I mean, we know all this. And we *did* do six of the previous nine with our own little fingers."

"And you *did* do an excellent job. I only wish my schedule had allowed me to give you more assistance." Dr. Burke was more than willing to give credit where credit was due as, at the moment, it didn't mean anything. She reached behind her for a tiny motor and an electric screwdriver. "That said, it never hurts to be reminded of how important the proper balance of moisture is to healthy tissue."

Donald snickered and in a nearly perfect imitation of the sultry voice in the commercial intoned, "How dead do you think I am?"

Dr. Burke stopped working and turned to stare at him. "I must be more tired than I thought. I actually found that funny."

Catherine shook her head and fished out the end of another artery.

A few moments later, they settled the bag of gel replacing the digestive system into place. Pearly highlights quivered across the thick agar coating.

"We've got bacteria to spare this time," Dr. Burke pointed out as she finished attaching the artificial diaphragm's second motor. "I want those organs saturated."

"Saturated it is," Donald agreed. He accepted the liver culture from Catherine, frowned, and glared over her shoulder. "Stop that!"

"Stop what?" she asked, bending to work on a kidney.

"Not you. Number nine. He's staring at me."

She straightened and checked. "No, he isn't. He's just looking in your direction."

"Well, I don't like it."

"He isn't hurting anything."

"So?"

"Children." Had Dr. Burke's voice been any dryer it would have cracked. "If we could keep our minds on the matter at hand?" She waited, pointedly, until they both began working before she released the rib spreader. "If it bothers you that much, Donald, Catherine can put it in its box."

Donald nodded. "Good idea. Make her put her toys away when she's done playing with them."

Catherine ignored him. "He'd be better left out, Doctor. He needs the stimuli if we want him interfacing with the net."

"Good point," the doctor acknowledged. "Sloppily put, but a good point. Sorry, Donald. It stays out."

Catherine shot him a triumphant look.

"When you finish there, one of you can close while the other starts the pump and begins replacing the sterile solution. I want that circulatory system up and running ASAP. Now, if you think you can manage without my having to act as referee, I'm going to open up the skull."

"He's still looking at me," Donald growled a moment later, his voice barely audible over the whine of the bone saw.

"Hopefully, he's learning from you."

"Yeah?" One latex-covered finger lifted in salute. "Well, learn this."

Across the room, three of the fingers on number nine's right hand curled slowly inward and tucked under the support of the folded thumb. Although the face remained expressionless, a muscle twitched below the leathery surface of the skin.

* * *

Henry guided the BMW smoothly around the curves of the highway off-ramp at considerably more than the posted speed. Two hours and forty-two minutes, Toronto to Kingston—not as fast as it could be done, but considering the perpetual traffic congestion he'd faced leaving the city and the high number of provincial police patrolling the last hundred kilometers, it was a respectable time.

Although he enjoyed high speeds and his reflexes made possible maneuvers that left other drivers gaping, Henry had never understood the North American love affair with the automobile. A car to him was a tool, the BMW a compromise between power and dependability. While mortal drivers blithely risked their lives straining the limits of their machinery, he had no intention of abruptly ending four hundred and fifty years because of metal fatigue or design flaws— but then, unlike mortal drivers, he had nothing to prove.

Vicki's mother's apartment was easy enough to find. Not only did Division Street run directly from the 401, but even from a block away there was no mistaking the man emerging from the late model sedan parked in front of the building. Henry swung into the tiny parking lot and settled the BMW into the adjoining space.

"You made good time," he remarked as he got out of his car and stretched.

"Thanks." The word had left his mouth before Celluci realized he had no reason to feel so absurdly pleased by the observation. "*You* obviously broke a few laws," he snarled. "Or don't you feel our speed limits apply to you?"

"No more than you feel they apply to you," Henry told him with an edged smile. "Or don't the police have to follow the laws they're sworn to uphold?"

"Asshole," Celluci muttered. Nothing dampened righteous anger faster than forced recognition of shaky ethical ground. "And I don't see why you came anyhow. Vicki needs the living around her, not more of the dead.''

"I am no more dead than you are, Detective.''

"Yeah, well, you're not . . . I mean, you're . . .''

"I am Vampire.'' Henry spread his hands. "There, it no longer hangs between us. The word has been said.'' He caught Celluci's gaze and held it but this time used no force to keep the contact. "You might as well acknowledge it, Detective. I won't go away.''

Curiosity overcame better judgment and Celluci found himself asking, "What were you?''

"I was a Prince. A royal bastard.''

The corners of the detective's mouth twitched. "Well, you're a royal bastard, that's for sure.'' He fought his way back to a more equal footing, ignoring the suspicion that a more equal footing was allowed him. "Why isn't anyone ever a fucking peasant?''

"Anyone?'' Henry asked, brows rising.

"You, Shirley MacLaine . . . Never mind.'' He leaned back against his car and sighed. "Look, she doesn't need both of us.''

"So why don't I just go home? I don't think so.''

"What can you give her?''

"Now? In her grief? The same things you can.''

"But I can give them night *and* day. You only have the night.''

"Then why are you so worried about me being here? Surely you have the advantage. Mind you,'' Henry continued, his tone thoughtful, "I left sanctuary for her, risked the sun in order to be at her side. That should count for something.''

"What do you mean, count for something?'' Celluci snorted. "This isn't a contest! Man against . . .'' His eyes narrowed. ". . . romance writer. We're supposed to be here for *her*.''

"Then maybe,'' Henry starting moving toward the building, "we'd better work a little harder at remembering that.''

Goddamned patronizing son of a bitch! Fortunately, longer legs allowed Celluci to catch up without having to run. "So we concentrate on her until this is over."

Henry half turned and looked up at him. "And after?"

"Who the hell knows about after?" *Stop looking at me like that!* "Let's get through this, first."

Listening to the pounding of Celluci's heart, Henry nodded, satisfied.

It took Vicki a moment to realize what the pounding meant.

The door.

Bang. Bang. Bang.

The police at the door. The pattern was unmistakable. She frowned at the dark apartment and stiffly stood up. *How long?* Eyes useless, in spite of the spill of light from the street, she groped her way to the phone desk, then along the wall to the door.

Celluci scowled down at Henry and raised his hand to knock again. "You're certain she's in there?"

"I'm certain. I can feel her life."

"Yeah. Right."

Bang. Bang. Bang.

Her fingers scraped across the light switch and she flicked it on, her eyes watering in the sudden brilliance. Her mother always used hundred watt bulbs.

"I don't care how much more energy it burns, it's more important that you can see when you come home. I can well afford it and the environment can go hang."

Her mother *had* always used 100 watt bulbs.

The lock stuck, halfway around.

"I told her to get this fixed," she growled as she fought to force the tumblers down. "God-damned stupid piece of junk."

Bang. Bang. Bang.

"Keep your fucking pants on!"

Celluci lowered his hand. "She's in there."

The lock finally gave. Vicki took a deep breath, adjusted her glasses, and opened the door.

"What the hell are you doing here?" she asked after a long pause.

"We came to help," Henry told her quietly.

She looked from one to the other, confusion the only emotion she could readily label. "Both of you?"

"Both of us," Celluci agreed.

"I didn't *ask* for your help."

They exchanged identical expressions and Celluci sighed. "We know," he said.

"Vicki?"

All three of them turned.

Mr. Delgado stood just outside his door, weight forward on the balls of his feet, shoulders back, arms loose at his sides, trousers pulled on under a striped pajama top. "Is there a problem?"

Vicki shoved at her glasses. The completely truthful answer would be, *Not yet.* "No," she said. "No problem. These are friends of mine from Toronto."

"What are they doing here?"

"Apparently," her voice grew less vague with every word, "they came to help."

"Oh." His gaze swept over Celluci from head to toe and then began on Henry. For Vicki's sake, Henry kept a grip on his annoyance and let the old man finish. "Well, if there's any trouble," the last two words were a warning, "you let me know."

"I can handle these two, Mr. Delgado."

"I don't doubt it. But you shouldn't have to. Not right now." His chin jutted forward. "You boys understand?"

Celluci's patience showed signs of wear. "We understand, Mr. Delgado."

"Both of you?"

Henry turned a little farther until he faced down the hall. "We both understand."

Mr. Delgado squinted at Henry then almost seemed to come to attention. "Had to ask . . ."

"I know."

"Well, good night."

Henry inclined his head in dismissal. "Good night."

The three of them watched as the door closed and then Vicki stepped back out of the way. "You might as well come in."

". . . did it never occur to either of you that maybe I wanted to handle this myself?" Vicki paced the length of the living room, reached the window, and glared out into the night. The apartment was half a story below ground, not exactly basement, not exactly first floor. The windows looked out over a narrow strip of grass, then the visitor's parking, then the sidewalk, then the road. It wasn't much of a view. Vicki's mother had invested in both blinds and heavy drapes to keep the world from looking back. Vicki hadn't bothered closing either. "That maybe," she continued, her throat tight, "there isn't anything for you to help with?"

"If you want both of us, or either of us, to go back to Toronto, we will," Henry told her quietly.

Celluci shot him a look and his mouth opened, but Henry raised a cautionary hand and he closed it again without speaking.

"I want both of you to go back to Toronto!"

"No, you don't."

Her laugh held the faintest shading of hysteria. "Are you reading my mind, Henry?" She turned to face them. "All right, you win. As long as you're here, you might as well stay." One hand sketched surrender in the air. "You might as well both stay."

"How did you convince Mike to go to sleep?"

"I merely told him that you'd need him rested tomorrow, that I was the logical choice to keep watch over the night.''

''Merely?''

''Well, perhaps I persuaded him a little.''

She sat on the edge of the twin bed in the room she'd grown up in and smoothed nonexistent wrinkles out of the pillow with the fingers of one hand. ''He won't thank you for that in the morning.''

''Perhaps not.'' Henry watched her carefully, not allowing the full extent of his concern to show lest it cause her to bolt. ''But I did explain that it was a little difficult for either of us to give comfort when both of us were there. He seemed to agree.'' He had, in fact, grunted, *''So leave.''* but Henry saw no need to mention that to Vicki.

''All of that while I was in the bathroom?''

''Should it have taken longer?''

''I guess not.''

He'd been prepared for her to be angry at his high-handedness—would have preferred the bright flame of her anger to the gray acceptance he got. He reached out and gently captured the hand that still stroked the pillow. ''You need to sleep, Vicki.''

The skin around her eyes seemed stretched very tight.

''I don't think I can.''

''I do.''

''If you need to feed, I don't think . . .''

Henry shook his head. ''Not tonight. Maybe tomorrow. Now get some sleep.''

''I can't . . .''

''You can.'' His voice deepened slightly and he lifted her chin so that her eyes met his.

They widened as she realized what he was doing and she pushed ineffectually at his fingers.

''Sleep,'' he told her again.

Her inarticulate protest became a long, shuddering sigh, and she collapsed back on the bed.

Frowning thoughtfully, Henry tucked her legs up under the covers and moved her glasses to safety on the bedside table. In the morning, the two of them could trade stories about the unfair advantage he'd taken over mortal minds. Perhaps it would bring them closer together. It was a risk he'd had no choice but to take. But for the moment . . . He reached up and flicked off the light.

"For the moment," he murmured, tucking the blankets around the life that glowed like a beacon in the darkness. "For the moment, I will guard your dreams."

"Henry . . ." She raised herself up on one elbow and groped for her glasses. The room was gray, not black. It couldn't be dawn because she could feel his presence even before she managed to find the deeper shadow by the door.

"I can't stay any longer." He spread his hands in apology. "The sun is very close to the horizon."

"Where are you going?"

She could hear the smile in his voice. "Not far. The walk-in closet in your mother's room will make an adequate sanctuary. It will take very little to block the day."

"I'm going with you." She swung her legs out of the bed and stood, ignoring the lack of light. Her mother had made no real changes in the room since she'd left—she'd have to be more than blind to lose her way.

At the door, Henry's cool fingers wrapped around her arm just above the elbow. She turned, knowing he could see her even though she could barely see the outline of his body.

"Henry." He moved closer as she reached out and laid her palm against his chest. "My mother . . ." The words wouldn't come. She could feel him waiting and finally had to shake her head.

His lips brushed very lightly against her hair.

"You were right," she said instead. "Sleep helped. But . . ." Her fingers twisted in his shirt and she yanked him slightly forward. ". . . don't ever do that again."

His hand covered hers. "No promises," he told her quietly.

Yes, promises, she wanted to insist. *I won't have you messing with my head.* But he messed with her head just by existing and under the circumstances, she wouldn't believe any promises he made. "Get going." She pushed him toward the door. "Even *I* can feel the sun."

Celluci lay stretched out on top of her mother's bed, shoes off but otherwise dressed. She started, seeing him so suddenly appear in the glare of the overhead light and she had to stop herself from shaking him and demanding to know what he was doing there. On her mother's bed. Except her mother wouldn't be sleeping in it any more so what difference did it make?

"He won't wake," Henry told her as she hesitated by the door. "Not until after I'm . . . asleep."

"I wish you hadn't done that."

"Vicki."

The sound of her name pulled her forward until they stood only a whisper apart by the closet door.

He reached up and gently caressed her cheek. "Michael Celluci has the day; I cannot share it with him. Don't ask me to give him the night as well."

Vicki swallowed. His touch drew heated lines across her skin. "Have I ever asked that of you?"

"No." His expression twisted and slid a little into sadness. "You've never asked anything of me."

She wanted to protest that she had, but she knew what he meant. "Not now, Henry."

"You're right." He nodded and withdrew his hand. "Not now."

Fortunately, the closet had plenty of room for a not so tall man to lie safely hidden away from the sun.

"I'll block the door from the inside, so it can't be opened accidentally, and I brought the blackout curtain you hung in my bedroom to wrap around me. I'll be back with you this evening."

With memory's eyes she could see him, rising with the darkness after a day spent . . . lifeless.

"Henry."

He paused, half through the door.

"My mother is dead."

"Yes."

"You'll never die."

The four-hundred-and-fifty-year-old bastard son of Henry the VIII nodded. "I'll never die," he agreed.

"Should I resent you for that?"

"Should I resent you for the day?"

Her brows snapped down and the movement pushed her glasses forward on her nose. "I hate it when you answer a question with a question."

"I know."

His smile held so many things that she couldn't hope to understand them all before the closet door closed between them.

"Vicki, you can't possibly agree with what Fitzroy did!" When she suddenly became engrossed in sponging a bit of dirt off her good shoes, he realized she did, indeed, agree. "Vicki!"

"What?"

"He knocked me out, put me to sleep, violated my free will!"

"He just wanted the same time alone that you're getting now. Guaranteed free of interruption."

"I can't believe you're defending him!"

"I'm not. Exactly. I just understand his reasons."

Celluci snorted and jammed his arms into the sleeves of his suit jacket. A few stitches popped in protest. "And what did the two of you do during that time alone free of interruption?"

"He put me to sleep as well. Then sat and watched over me until dawn."

"That's it?"

Vicki turned to face him, both brows well above the upper edge of her glasses. "That's it. Not that it's any of your damned business."

"That won't wash this time, Vicki." He stepped forward, took the shoe from her hand, and dropped to one knee with it. "Fitzroy made it my business when he pulled that Prince of Darkness shit."

She sighed and let him guide her foot into the plain black pump. "Yeah, I suppose he did. I needed to sleep, Mike." She reached down and brushed the long curl of hair back off his face. "I couldn't have done it without him. He gave me the night to sleep when he could have taken it for himself."

"Very noble of him," Celluci grunted, sliding her other foot into the second shoe. *And it was very noble,* he admitted to himself as he stood. *Noble in the running roughshod I know best so don't bother expressing an opinion sort of a way that went out with the fucking feudal system.* Still, Fitzroy *had* acted in what he considered to be Vicki's best interests. And he honestly didn't think that he *could* have left them alone together—as Fitzroy had no choice but to do come morning. *So I suppose I might have done the same thing under similar circumstances. Which doesn't excuse his royal fucking undead highness one bit.*

What bothered him the most about it was how little Vicki seemed to care, how much she seemed to be operating on cruise control, and how little she seemed to be interacting with the world around her. He recognized the effects of grief and shock—he'd seen them both often enough over the years—but they were somehow harder to deal with because they were applied here and now to Vicki.

He wanted to make it better for her.

He knew he couldn't.

He hated having to accept that.

All right, Fitzroy, you gave her sleep last night, I'll give her support today. Maybe together we can get her through it.

He got her to eat but eventually, when even trying to start an argument failed, he gave up trying to get her to talk.

About noon, Mr. Delgado arrived to ask if Vicki needed a lift to the funeral home. She looked up from where she sat, silently rocking, and shook her head.

"Humph," he snorted, stepping back out into the hall and once again looking Celluci over. "You one of her friends from the police?"

"Detective-Sergeant Michael Celluci."

"Yeah. I thought so. You look like a cop. Louis Delgado." His grip was still strong, his palm hard with a workman's calluses. "What happened to the other guy?"

"He sat up with her all night. He's still sleeping."

"He's not a cop."

"No."

To Celluci's surprise the old man chuckled. "In my day two men fighting over one woman, there would have been blood on the street, let me tell you."

"What makes you think . . ."

"You think maybe I shut my brain off when I retired? I saw the three of you together last night, remember?" His face grew suddenly somber. "Maybe it's a good thing people got more civilized; she doesn't need fighting around her right now. I saw her grow up. Watched her decide to be an adult when she should have been enjoying being a child. Tried to take care of her mother, insisted on taking care of herself." He sighed. "She won't bend, you know. Now that this terrible thing has happened, you and that other fellow, don't you let her break."

"We'll do our best."

"Humph." He snorted again and swiped at his eyes

with a snowy white handkerchief, his opinion of their best obviously not high.

Celluci watched him return to his own apartment, then quietly closed the door. "Mr. Delgado cares about you a great deal," he said, crossing the room to stand by Vicki's side.

She shook her head. "He was very fond of my mother."

She didn't speak again until they were in the car on the way to the funeral home.

"Mike?"

He glanced sideways. She wore her courtroom face. Not even the most diligent of defense attorneys could have found an opinion on it.

"I didn't call her. And when she called me, I didn't answer. And then she died."

"You know there's no connection." He said it as gently as he could. He didn't expect an answer. He didn't get one.

There wasn't anything else to say, so he reached down and covered her left hand with his. After a long moment, her fingers turned and she clutched at him with such force that he had to bite back an exclamation of pain. Only her hand moved. Her fingers were freezing.

"It really is for your own good." Catherine finished fastening the chest strap and lightly touched number nine on the shoulder. "I know you don't like it, but we can't take a chance on you jerking the needles free. That's what happened to number six and we lost her." She smiled down into the isolation box. "You've come so much farther than the rest, even if your kidneys aren't working yet, that we'd hate to lose you, too." Reaching behind his left ear, she jacked the computer hookup into the implanted plug, fingertips checking that the skin hadn't pulled out from under the surgical steel collar clamped tight against scalp and skull.

"Now then . . ." She shook her head over the shallow dents that marred the inner curve of the insulated lid. "You just lie quiet and I'll open this up the moment your dialysis is over."

The box closed with a sigh of airtight seals and the metallic snick of an automatic latch.

Frowning slightly, Catherine adjusted the amount of pure oxygen flowing through the air intake. Although he'd moved past the point where he needed it and he could have managed on just regular filtered air, she wanted him to have every opportunity to succeed. Later, when the muscle diagnostics were running, she'd give him a full body massage with the estrogen cream. His skin wasn't looking good. In the meantime, she flicked the switch that would start the transmission through his net and moved to check on the other two boxes.

Number eight had begun to fail. Not only were the joints becoming less responsive but the extremities had darkened and she suspected the liver had begun to putrefy, a sure sign that the bacteria had started to die.

"Billions of them multiplying all over the world," she said sadly, stroking the top of number eight's box. "Why can't we keep these alive long enough to do some good?"

At the third box, recently vacated by the dissected number seven, she scanned one of a trio of computer monitors. Marjory Nelson's brain wave patterns, recorded over the months just previous to her death, were being transmitted in a continuous loop through the newly installed neural net. They'd never had actual brain wave patterns before. All previous experiments, including numbers eight and nine, had only ever received generic alpha waves recorded from herself and Donald.

"I've got great hopes for you, number ten. There's no reason you . . ." A yawn split the thought in two and Catherine stumbled toward the door, suddenly exhausted. Donald had headed for his bed once the major surgery had been completed and Dr. Burke had left just before dawn. She didn't mind finishing up on her own—she liked having the lab to herself, it gave her a chance to see that all the little extras got done—but if she wasn't mistaken, she was rapidly approaching a day and a half on her feet and she needed to catch a nap. A couple of hours lying down and she should be good as new.

Fingers on the light switch, she paused in the doorway, looked back over the lab, and called softly, "Pleasant dreams."

They weren't dreams, nor were they quite memories but, outside the influence of the net, images stirred. A young woman's face in close proximity, pale hair, pale eyes. Her voice was soothing in a world where too many lights were too bright and too many sounds only noise. Her smile was . . .

Her smile was . . .

Organic impulses moved turgidly along tattered neural pathways searching for the connection that would complete the thought.

Her smile was . . .

Kind.

Number nine stirred under the restraints.

Her smile was kind.

"Ms. Nelson?"

Vicki turned toward the voice, trying very hard not to scowl. Relatives and friends of her mother's were milling about the reception room, all expecting her to be showing their definition of grief. If it hadn't been for Celluci's bulk at her back, she might have bolted—if it hadn't been for his quick grip around her wrist she'd have definitely belted the cousin who, having driven in from Gananoque, remarked that earlier or later would have been a better time and he certainly hoped there'd be refreshments afterward.

She didn't know the heavyset man who'd called her name.

He held out a beefy hand. "Ms. Nelson, I'm Reverend Crosbie. The Anglican minister who usually works with Hutchinson's is a bit under the weather today, so they asked me to fill in." His voice was a rough burr that rose and fell with an east coast cadence.

A double chin almost hid the clerical collar but, given the firmness of his handshake, Vicki doubted that all of the bulk was fat. "My mother wasn't a churchgoer," she said.

"That's between her and God, Ms. Nelson." His tone managed to be both matter-of-fact and sympathetic at the same time. "She wanted an Anglican service read to set her soul at peace and I'm here to do it for her. But," bushy white brows drew slightly in, "as I didn't know your mother, I've no intention of speaking as if I did. Are you going to be doing your own eulogy?"

Was she going to get up in front of all these people and tell them about her mother? Was she going tell them how her mother had given up the life a young woman was entitled to in order to support them both? Tell them how her mother had tried to stop her from getting her first job because she thought childhood should last a little longer? Tell them about her mother, a visible beacon of pride, watching as she graduated from high school, then university, then the police college? Tell them how after her promotion her mother had peppered the phrase, "My daughter, the detective," into every conversation? Tell them how, when she first got the diagnosis about her eyes, her mother had taken a train to Toronto and refused to hear the lies about being all right and not needing her there? Tell them about the nagging and the worrying and the way she always called during a shower? Tell them how her mother had needed to talk to her and she hadn't answered the phone?

Tell them her mother was dead?

"No." Vicki felt Celluci's hand close over her shoulder and realized her voice had been less than clear. She coughed and scanned the room in a near panic. "There. The short woman in the khaki trench coat." To point would expose the trembling. "That's Dr. Burke. Mother worked for her for the last five years. Maybe she'll say something."

Bright blue eyes focused just behind her for a second. Whatever Reverend Crosbie saw on Celluci's face seemed to reassure him because he nodded and said quietly, "I'll talk to Dr. Burke, then." His warm hand engulfed hers again. "Maybe you and I'll have a chance to talk later, eh?"

"Maybe."

Celluci's grip on her shoulder tightened as the minister walked away. "You all right?"

"Sure. I'm fine." But she didn't expect him to believe her, so she supposed it wasn't exactly a lie.

"Vicki?"

This was a voice she recognized and she turned almost eagerly to meet it. "Aunt Esther." The tall, sparse woman opened her arms and Vicki allowed herself to be folded into them. Esther Thomas had been her mother's closest friend. They'd grown up together, gone to school together, had been bride and bridesmaid, bridesmaid and bride. Esther had been teaching school in Ottawa for as long as Vicki could remember, but living in different cities hadn't dimmed the friendship.

Esther's cheeks were wet when they pulled apart. "I thought I wasn't going to make it." She sniffed and dug for a tissue. "I'm driving Richard's six-cylinder tank, but they're doing construction on highway fifteen. Can you believe it? It's only April. They're still likely to get snow. Damn, I . . . Thank you. You're Mike Celluci, aren't you? We met once, about three years ago, just after Christmas when you drove to Kingston to pick Vicki up."

"I remember."

"Vicki . . ." She blew her nose and started again. "Vicki, I have a favor to ask you. I'd . . . I'd like to see her one last time."

Vicki stepped back, trod on Celluci's foot, and didn't notice. "See her?"

"Yes. To say good-bye." Tears welled and ran and she swiped at them without making much impact. "I don't think I'll be able to believe Marjory's actually dead unless I see her."

"But . . ."

"I know it's a closed coffin, but I thought you and I might be able to slip in now. Before things start."

Vicki had never understood the need to look at the dead. A corpse was a corpse and over the years she'd seen enough of them to know that they were all fundamentally alike. She didn't want to remember her mother the way she'd been, stretched out on the table in the morgue, and she certainly didn't want to remember her prepared like a manikin to go into the earth. But it was obviously something Esther needed.

"I'll have a word with Mr. Hutchinson," she heard herself saying.

A few moments later, the three of them were making their way down the center aisle of the chapel, shoes making no sound on the thick red carpet.

"We did prepare for this eventuality," Mr. Hutchinson said as they approached the coffin. "Very often when the casket is closed, friends and relatives still want to say one last good-bye to the deceased. I'm sure you'll find your mother much as you remember her, Ms. Nelson."

Vicki closed her teeth on her reply.

"The service is due to start momentarily," he said as he released the latch and began to raise the upper half of the lid, "so I'm afraid you'll have to . . . have to . . ."

Her fingers dug deep into satin cushioning as Vicki's hands closed over the padded edge of the coffin. In the center of the quilted pillow lay the upper end of a large sandbag. A quick glance toward the foot of the casket determined that a second sandbag made up the rest of the necessary weight.

She straightened and in a voice that ripped civilization off the words asked, ''What have you done with my mother?''

Four

"This would probably go a lot easier if you'd get Ms. Nelson to go home." Detective Fergusson of the Kingston Police lowered his voice a little further. "It's not like we don't appreciate your input, Sergeant, but Ms. Nelson, she hasn't been a cop for a couple of years. She really shouldn't be here. Besides, you know, she's a woman. They get emotional at times like these."

"Get a lot of body snatching, do you?" Celluci asked dryly.

"No!" The detective's indignant gaze jerked up to meet Celluci's. "Never had one before. Ever."

"Ah. Then which times like these were you referring to?"

"Well, you know. Her mother dying. The body being lifted. This whole funeral home thing. I hate 'em. Too damn quiet. Anyway, this'll probably turn out to be some stupid prank by some of those university medical school geeks. I could tell you stories about that lot. The last thing we need scrambling things up is a hysterical woman—and she certainly has a right to be hysterical under the circumstances, don't get me wrong."

"Does Ms. Nelson look hysterical to you, Detective?"

Fergusson swept a heavy hand back over his thinning hair and glanced across the room where his partner had just finished taking statements. A few months before, he'd been given the opportunity to handle one of the new high-tech assault rifles recently issued to the special weapons and tactics boys. Ex-Detective

Nelson reminded him a whole lot of that rifle. "Well, no. Not precisely hysterical."

While he wasn't exactly warming to the man, Celluci wasn't entirely unsympathetic. "Look at it this way. She was one of the best police officers I ever served with—probably ever will serve with. If she stays, think of her as an added resource you can tap into and recognize that because of her background she will in no way disrupt your handling of the case. If she goes," he clapped the older man lightly on the shoulder, "you're telling her. Because I'm not."

"Like that, eh?"

"Like that. It'd be convenient that you're already in a funeral home. Trust me. Things will probably go a lot easier if she stays."

Fergusson sighed, then shrugged. "I guess she'll feel better if she thinks she's doing something. But if she goes off, you get her out of here."

"Believe me, *she* is my first concern." Watching Vicki cross the chapel toward him, Celluci was struck by how completely under control she appeared. Every muscle moved with a rigid precision, and the intensity of suppressed emotion that moved with her made her frighteningly remote. He recognized the expression; she'd worn it in the past when a case touched her deeply, when the body became more than just another statistic, when it became personal. Superiors and psychologists warned cops about that kind of involvement, afraid it would lead to burnout or vigilantism, but everyone fell victim to it sooner or later. It was the feeling that kept an investigation going long after logic said give it up, the feeling that fueled the long and seemingly pointless hours of drudge work that actually led to charges being laid. When "Victory" Nelson wore that expression, people got out of her way.

At this point, under these circumstances, it was the last expression Celluci wanted to see. Grief, anger, even hysterics—". . . and she certainly has a right to be hysterical under the circumstances—" would be preferable to the way she'd closed in on herself. This wasn't, couldn't be, just another case.

"Hey." He reached out and touched her arm. The muscles under the sleeve of her navy blue suit jacket felt like stone. "You okay?"

"I'm fine."

Yeah. Right. It was, however, the expected response.

"Now then." The elder Mr. Hutchinson sat forward, placing his forearms precisely on the charcoal gray blotter that protected his desk and linking his fingers. "I assure you all that you will have our complete cooperation in clearing up this unfortunate affair. Never in all the years that Hutchinson's Funeral Parlour has served the needs of the people of Kingston has such a horrible thing occurred. Ms. Nelson, please believe you have our complete sympathy and that we will do everything in our power to rectify this situation."

Vicki limited herself to a single tight nod of acknowledgment, well aware that if she opened her mouth she wouldn't be able to close it again. She wanted to rip this case away from the Kingston police, to ask the questions, to build out of all the minute details the identity of the scum who dared to violate her mother's body. And once identified . . .

She knew Celluci was watching her, knew he feared she'd start demanding answers, running roughshod over the local forces. She had no intention of doing anything so blatantly stupid. Two years without a badge had taught her the value of subtlety. Working with Henry had taught her that justice was often easier to find outside the law.

"All right, Mr. Hutchinson." Detective Fergusson checked his notes and shifted his bulk into a more comfortable position in the chair. "We already spoke to your driver and to your nephew, the other Mr.

Hutchinson, so let's just take it from when the body arrived.''

"Ms. Nelson, you'll likely find this distressing . . .''

"Ms. Nelson spent four years as a homicide detective in Toronto, Mr. Hutchinson.'' Although he might have his own doubts about her being there, Fergusson wasn't about to have an outsider pass judgment on an ex-member of the club. "If you say something that distresses her, she'll deal with it. Now then, the body arrived . . .''

"Yes, well, after she arrived, the deceased was taken down to our preparation room. Although there was to be no viewing, her arrangement with us made it quite clear that she was to be embalmed.''

"Isn't that unusual? Embalming without viewing?''

Mr. Hutchinson smiled, the deep wrinkles across his face falling into gentle brackets. "No, not really. A number of people decide that while they don't wish to be stared at after death, neither do they wish to, well, not look their best. And many realize, as happened in this instance, that friends and relatives will want one last look regardless.''

"I see. So the body was embalmed?''

"Yes, my nephew took care of most of that. He did the disinfecting, massaged the tissue to bring pooled blood out of the extremities, set the features, drained the body and injected the embalming fluid, perforated the internal organs with the trocar . . .''

Fergusson cleared his throat. "There's, uh, no need to be quite so detailed.''

"Oh, I am sorry.'' The elder Mr. Hutchinson flushed slightly. "I thought you wanted to hear everything.''

"Yes. But . . .''

"Mr. Hutchinson.'' Vicki leaned forward. "That last word you used, trocar, what is it?''

"Well, Ms. Nelson, it's a long steel tube, hollow, you know, and quite pointed, very sharp. We use it to draw out the body fluids and inject a very, very astringent preserving fluid into the cavity.''

''Your nephew didn't mention it.''

''Well,'' the old man smiled self-consciously, ''he was probably being a little more concise. I tend to ramble on a bit if I'm not discouraged.''

''He said,'' she caught his gaze with hers and held it, ''that he'd just placed the incision sealant into the jugular vein when he was called upstairs.''

Mr. Hutchinson shook his head. ''No. That's not possible. When I came down to finish—as the young woman in the office was most insistent she speak with David—the trocar button had already been placed in the abdomen, sealing off the entry wound.''

The silent sound of conclusions being drawn filled the small office.

''I think,'' Detective Fergusson said slowly, ''we'd better speak with David again.''

David Hutchinson repeated what he'd said previously.

The elder Mr. Hutchinson looked confused. ''But if you didn't aspirate the body cavity, and I certainly didn't, who did?''

The younger Mr. Hutchinson spread his hands. ''Chen?''

''Nonsense. He's only here on observation. He wouldn't know how.''

''That would be Tom Chen?''

Both of the Mr. Hutchinsons nodded.

''Before you're accepted into a program to become a funeral director,'' the younger explained, ''you have to spend four weeks observing at a funeral home. This isn't a job everyone can do. Anyway, Tom has been with us for the last two and a half weeks. He was in the room while I prepared the body. He helped a little. Asked a couple of questions . . .''

''And was in the room when I came down to finish. He certainly seemed to indicate that you'd done the aspirating, David.''

"Well, I hadn't."

"Are you sure?"

"Yes!" The word cracked the quiet reserve both men had been trained to wear and they turned identical expressions of distress on the police office sitting across the desk.

"And Tom Chen is where?"

"Unfortunately, not here. He did work through the weekend," the elder Mr. Hutchinson explained, regaining control. "So when he asked for the day off, I saw no harm in giving it to him."

"Hmmm. Jamie . . ."

Fergusson's partner nodded and quietly left the room.

"Where is he going?"

"He's going to see if we can have a talk with Mr. Chen. But for now," Fergusson leaned back and tapped lightly on his notebook with his pen, "let's just forget who did the aspirating, eh? Tell me what happened next."

"Well, that was about it. We dressed the body, applied light cosmetics, just in case, placed the body in the casket and, well, left it there. Overnight. This morning, we brought the casket upstairs to the chapel."

"Without checking the contents?"

"Nothing's ever happened to the *contents* before," the younger Mr. Hutchinson declared defensively.

"It must've happened during the night." The elder Mr. Hutchinson shook a weary head. "After the casket comes upstairs, there's no possible way anyone could remove the body without being seen."

"No sign of a forced entry," Fergusson mused aloud. "Who has keys?"

"Well, we do, of course. And Christy Aloman, who does all our paperwork and has been with the company for years. And, of course, there's a spare set here, in my drawer. That's strange." He opened a second drawer and a third. "Oh, here they are."

"Not where you usually keep them?"

"No. You don't think that someone took them and made copies, do you, Detective?"

Detective Fergusson glanced back over his shoulder at the corner where Vicki and Celluci sat and lifted an eloquent brow. Then he sighed. "I try not to think, Mr. Hutchinson. It's usually too depressing."

"All right." Celluci turned onto Division Street, one hand palming the wheel, the other grabbing air for emphasis. "Why would Tom Chen steal the body?"

"How the hell should I know?" Vicki snarled. "When we find him, I'll ask him."

"You don't know he had anything to do with it."

"No? We're talking fake address and total disappearance the morning after the crime—that sure as shit sounds incriminating to me."

"Granted."

"Not to mention the did-we-or-didn't-we shuffle that went on in the embalming room. That girl who insisted on talking to the younger Mr. Hutchinson was probably a planned distraction."

"Detective Fergusson and his partner are looking into it."

Vicki turned to face him as they pulled into the parking lot at the apartment building. "So?"

"So let them do their job, Vicki." Celluci parked and reached over the back of the seat for the bag of take-out chicken. "Fergusson's promised to keep you completely informed."

"Good." She got out of the car and strode toward the building, the heels of her pumps making emphatic statements in the gravel. "It'll make *my* job easier."

"And your job is?" He had to ask. He didn't need to, but he had to.

"Finding Tom Chen."

Celluci took three long strides to catch up and then one more to cut in front and pull open the door to the apartment building. "Vicki, you do realize that Tom

Chen—the name, the person, the body snatcher—is probably as fake as his address. How the hell are you going to find him?''

"When I find him . . ." Her voice made the finding a fact not a possibility, and Celluci strongly suspected she hadn't heard a word he'd said. ". . . I find my mother's body."

"Of all the lousy luck."

Catherine frowned as she unbuckled number nine's restraints and stepped back so he could climb out of his box. "I suppose it is unfortunate," she said doubtfully, "but it doesn't actually have anything to do with us."

"Yeah, right." Donald snorted. "Earth to Cathy: try to remember that we're the ones who walked off with the body they're looking for. Try to remember that body snatching is a crime." His voice rose. "Try to remember that you'll get bugger all amount of research done if they throw your ass in jail!" He jumped back as number nine suddenly lurched toward him. "Hey! Back off!"

"Stop shouting! He doesn't like it." Catherine reached for an undead arm. It took another two steps for the pressure of her fingers to register, but when it did, number nine obediently stopped. "It's okay," she said softly. "It's okay."

"It is *not* okay!" Donald threw both hands up into the air and whirled to face Dr. Burke. "Tell her, Doctor. Tell her it's not okay!"

Dr. Burke looked up from the alpha wave pattern undulating across the monitor. "Donald," she sighed, "I think you're overreacting."

His eyes bulged. "Overreacting! Try to remember that *I'm* the one they can identify!"

"No, you're not." While not exactly soothing, Dr. Burke's tone was so matter-of-fact that it had the same effect. "They can identify Tom Chen, not Donald Li. But as Tom Chen doesn't exist and there's nothing to tie him to Donald Li, I think we can assume you're safe.''

"But they know what I look like.'' His protest had died to a near whine.

"Yes, the others at the funeral home could pick you out of a lineup, but you have my personal guarantee it will never go that far. What kind of a description can they give the police? A young Oriental male, about five-six; short dark hair; dark eyes; clean-shaven . . .'' Dr. Burke sighed again. "Donald, there are hundreds of students just at this university that fit that description, let alone those in the rest of the city.''

Donald glowered. "You saying we all look alike?''

"Just as alike as young Occidental males about five-eight; short brown hair; light eyes; clean-shaven, of which there are also hundreds at this university. I'm saying the police will never find you.'' She bent over the electrocardiograph. "Just stay close for a few days and everything will be fine.''

"Stay close. Right.'' He paced the length of the room and back, unwrapping a miniature chocolate bar he'd taken from his jacket pocket. "I was a grade A idiot to let you talk me into this. I knew this was going to be trouble, right from the start.''

"You knew,'' Dr. Burke corrected, straightening, "this was going to make us all a great deal of money, right from the start. That the applications for the work we're doing are infinite and the implications are staggering. That we might be talking Nobel Prize . . .''

"They don't give the Nobel Prize to body snatchers,'' Donald pointed out.

Dr. Burke smiled. "They do when they've conquered death,'' she said. "Do you know what people would be willing to do for the information we're discovering?''

"Well, I know what I've done for it.'' Donald watched as across the lab Catherine guided number nine to a chair. Mere weeks ago, the ex-vagrant had been lying unclaimed on a slab. *And now, if death hasn't been reversed, well, it's certainly been given a kick in the teeth.* "Look, why wait any longer? With the tricks we've got Cathy's bacteria to do already, not to mention old number nine's apparent brain-computer interface, we could easily cop the prize now."

"We've been through this, Donald. If we publish before we finish, we'll never be permitted to finish."

"Government," Catherine interjected, "has no business regulating science."

Donald looked from the doctor's stern features to his fellow grad student's obstinate stare. "Hey! I'm on your side, remember? I want my share of the profits not to mention a shot at a Nobel Prize. I just don't want my butt getting tossed behind bars where some lowlife built like a gorilla will no doubt bend me over and ram . . ."

"You've made your point, Donald, but I honestly doubt that the police are going to put that much effort into finding young Mr. Chen. All too soon, there'll be indignities performed on living bodies that will need their attention."

"Yeah? Well what about that Vicki Nelson, the daughter? I hear she's hot shit."

Dr. Burke's brows drew down. "While I find this sudden affection of yours for scatological references distasteful, you have a point. Not only was Ms. Nelson previously a police detective, but she's now a private investigator, and not, by all reports, the sort of person to give up easily. Luckily, there's exactly the same lack of information for her as there is for the police and while it might take her longer to grow discouraged, she still won't find anything because we've been very careful to leave nothing for her to find. Haven't we?"

"Well, yeah."

"So stop worrying. It was unfortunate that they decided to open the casket, but it's hardly the disaster you're making it out to be. Don't you have a tutorial this afternoon?"

"I thought you wanted me to stay close?"

"I want you to behave exactly as you normally do."

He grinned, unable to worry about anything for long. "That is to say, badly?"

Dr. Burke shook her head and half-smiled. "Go."

He went.

"*Is* he in any danger, Dr. Burke?"

"Didn't I just say he wasn't?"

"Yes, but . . ."

"Catherine, I have never lied to Donald. Lies are the easiest way to lose the loyalty of your associates."

Apparently unconvinced, Catherine gnawed on her lower lip.

Dr. Burke sighed. "Didn't I promise you," she said gently, "back when you first approached me, that I'd take care of everything? That I'd see to it you could work without interference? And haven't I kept my promise?"

Catherine released her lip and nodded.

"So you needn't worry about anything but your work. Besides, Donald's dedication to science isn't as strong as ours." She patted the isolation box that held the remains of Marjory Nelson. "Now then, if you could set up the muscle sequences, I'd best get back to my office. With Mrs. Shaw home having hysterics, God only knows what's going on up there."

Alone in the lab, Catherine crossed slowly to the keyboard and sat, staring thoughtfully at the monitor for a few moments. *Donald's dedication to science isn't as strong as ours.* She'd always known that. What she was just beginning to realize was that perhaps Dr. Burke's dedication to science wasn't as strong as it might be either. While there'd always been a lot of talk about the purity of research, this was the first she'd heard of infinite applications and profit sharing.

Behind lids that had lost the flexibility to completely open or completely close, filmy eyes tracked her every movement.

Number nine sat quietly, content for the moment to be out of the box.

And with her.

"So, how is she?"

Celluci stepped out of the apartment and pulled the door partially closed behind him. "Coping."

"Humph. Coping. This evil thing has happened and all you can say is she's coping." Mr. Delgado shook his head. "Has she cried?"

"Not while I've been with her, no." It took an effort, but Celluci managed not to resent the old man's concern.

"Not other times either, I bet. Crying is for the weak; she isn't weak, so she doesn't cry." He thumped a gnarled fist against his chest. "I cried like a baby—like a baby, I tell you—when my Rosa died."

Celluci nodded slowly in agreement. "I cried when my father died."

"Celluci? Italian?"

"Canadian."

"Don't be a smart ass. We, my Rosa and young Frank and me, we came from Portugal just after the second World War. I was a welder."

"My father's family came just before the war. He was a plumber."

"There." Mr. Delgado threw up both hands. "And if the two of us can cry, you'd think she could manage a tear or two without lose of machismo."

Vicki's voice drifted into the hall. "Mr. Chen? Perhaps you can help me, I'm looking for a young man, early twenties, named Tom Chen . . ."

Mr. Delgado's shoulders sagged. "But no. No tears. She holds the hurt inside. You listen to what I'm saying to you, Officer Celluci. When that hurt finally comes out, it's going to rip her to pieces."

"I'll be there for her." He tried not to sound defensive—Vicki's inability to deal with this wasn't his fault—but he didn't entirely succeed.

"What about the other guy? Will he be there, too?"

"I don't know."

"Humph. None of my business? Well, maybe not." The old man sighed. "It's hard when there's nothing to do to help."

Celluci echoed the sigh. "I know."

Back inside the apartment, he leaned against the closed door and watched Vicki hurl the Kingston phone book across the room. "No luck?"

"So he doesn't have a listed number, or a family in town." She jabbed at the bridge of her glasses. "He's probably a student. Lives in residence. I'll find him."

"Vicki . . ." He took a deep breath and exhaled slowly. "You're looking for a fake name. Anyone with the brains to pull this off also had the brains to work under an alias." That he had to keep telling her this was a frightening indication of how deeply she'd been affected both by the death and the loss of the body. It was a conclusion any first-year police cadet would come to and should never have had to be pointed out to "Victory" Nelson. "Tom Chen is . . ."

"All we've got!" A muscle jumped in her jaw as she spat the words at him. "It's a name. It's something."

It's nothing. But he didn't say it because behind the challenge he could hear her desperate need for something to hold onto. *I suppose I should be happy she's clutching at this instead of at Fitzroy.* What would it hurt to go along with her? At least it would keep him close and in time she might decide to hold onto him. "All right, if he lives in residence, where's he keeping . . ." Not *your mother.* There had to be something better to call it. ". . . the body?"

"How the hell should I know? First thing tomorrow, I get my hands on the university registration lists."

"How?" Celluci crossed the room and dropped onto the couch. "You don't *have* a warrant and you can't *get* a warrant. Why don't you let the local police take care of it? Detective Fergusson seems to be positive it's med students so I'm sure he'll check the university."

"So? I don't care what Detective Fergusson checks. I don't care if the whole fucking police force is on the case." She stood and stomped into the tiny kitchen. "I'm going to find this son of a bitch and when I do I'll . . ."

"You'll what?" He surged up off the couch and charged into the kitchen after her, forgetting for the moment that Tom Chen was a name and nothing more. "Why do you want to find this guy before the police do? So you can indulge in a little more participatory justice?" Grabbing her shoulder, he spun her to face him, both of them ignoring the coffee that arced up out of the mug in her hand. "I closed my eyes last fall because there wasn't a way to bring Mark Williams to trial without causing more damage than he was worth. But that isn't the case here! Let the law deal with this, Vicki!"

"The law?"

"Yeah, you remember, what you used to be sworn to uphold."

"Don't bullshit me, Celluci. You know just how much manpower the law is going to be able to allot to this. I'm *going* to find him!"

"All right. And then?"

She closed her eyes for a second and when she opened them again they were shadowed, unreadable. "When I find him, he's going to wish he'd never laid a finger on my mother's body."

The calm, emotionless tone danced knives up Celluci's spine. He knew she was speaking out of pain. He knew she meant every word. "This is Fitzroy's influence," he growled. "*He* taught you to take the law into your own hands."

"Don't blame this on Henry." The tone became a warning. "I take responsibility for my own actions."

"I know." Celluci sighed, suddenly very, very tired. "But Henry Fitzroy . . ."

"Doesn't know what you're talking about." The quiet voice from the doorway pulled them both around. Henry looked from Vicki to Celluci then settled himself on a kitchen chair. "Why don't you tell me what went wrong?"

Henry stared at Celluci in some astonishment. "Why on earth do you think I would know the reason the body is missing?"

"Well, you're . . . what you are." It might have been said, but Celluci still wasn't going to say it. Not right out. "It's the sort of thing you should know about, isn't it?"

"No. It isn't." He turned to Vicki. "Vicki, I'm so sorry, but I have no idea why anyone in this day and age would be body snatching."

She shrugged. She really didn't care why, all she wanted to know was who.

"Unless it wasn't body snatching." Celluci frowned, turning over a new and not very pleasant idea.

Henry's eyes narrowed. "What do you mean?"

"Suppose Marjory's body wasn't taken." He paused, working at the thought. "Suppose she got up and walked out of there."

Vicki's coffee mug hit the floor and shattered.

"You're crazy!" Henry snapped.

"Am I?" Celluci slammed both palms down on the table and leaned forward. "A year ago, some asshole tried to sacrifice Vicki to a demon. I *saw* that demon, Fitzroy. Last summer, I met a family of werewolves. In the fall, we saved the world from the mummy's curse. Now I may be a little slow, but lately I've come to believe that there's a fuck of a lot going on in this world that most people don't know shit about. *You* exist; you tell me why Marjory *couldn't* have got up and walked out of there!"

"Henry?"

Henry shook his head and caught one of Vicki's

hands up in his. "They embalmed her, Vicki. There's nothing that could survive that."

"Maybe they didn't." Her fingers turned until she clutched at him. "They were confused about the rest. Maybe they didn't."

"No, Vicki, they did." Celluci touched her gently on the arm, wondering why he couldn't learn to keep his big mouth shut. He'd forgotten about the embalming. "I'm sorry. I should've thought it through. He's right."

"No." There was a chance. She couldn't let it go. "Henry, could you tell?"

"Yes, but . . ."

"Then go. Check. Just in case."

"Vicki, I assure you that your mother did not rise . . ."

"Henry. Please."

He looked at Celluci, who gave the smallest of shrugs. *Your choice,* the motion said. *I'm sorry I started this.* Henry nodded at the detective, apology accepted, and pulled his hand free of Vicki's as he stood. She'd asked for his help. He'd give it. It was a small enough thing to do to bring her at least a little peace of mind. "Is the casket still at the funeral home?"

"Yes." She began to rise as well, but he shook his head.

"No, Vicki. The last thing you need right now is to be picked up by the police while breaking and entering. If they're watching the place, I can avoid them in ways you can't."

Vicki shoved at her glasses and dropped back in her chair, acknowledging his point but not happy about it.

"If I thought you suggested this merely to remove me," Henry said quietly to Celluci at the door as he pocketed the directions, "I would be less than pleased."

"But you don't think it," Celluci replied, just as quietly. "Why not?"

Henry looked up into the taller man's eyes and

smiled slightly. "Because I know an honorable man when I meet one."

An honorable man. Celluci shot the bolt behind his rival and let his head drop against the molding. *Goddamnit, I wish he'd stop doing that.*

If the embalming had been done, the blood drawn out and replaced by a chemical solution designed to disinfect and preserve, to discourage life rather than sustain it—and from both Vicki's and Celluci's reports, the younger funeral director was certain it had—then there was no way that Marjory Nelson had risen to hunt the night. Nor did the manner of her death suggest the change.

Henry parked the BMW and stared into the darkness for a moment, one hundred percent certain that he would find nothing at the funeral home that the police had not already found. *But I'm not going for information, I'm going for Vicki.* Leaving her to spend the night alone with Michael Celluci.

He shook his head and got out of the car. Whether or not Celluci would take advantage of the time was irrelevant—Vicki had shut everything out of her life except the need to find the person or persons who had taken her mother's body and the need to be comforted had been buried with the grief she hadn't quite admitted. Because he loved her, he wouldn't lie to her. He'd go to the funeral home, discover what he already knew, and let her delete one possible explanation beyond the shadow of a doubt.

But first, he had to feed.

Vicki hadn't had the energy to spare and while he'd been tempted to prove his power to Celluci, that was a temptation he'd long since learned to resist. Besides, feeding required an intimacy he was not yet willing to allow between them and feeding from Celluci would take subtleties they hadn't time for.

Head turned into the wind, he searched the night air. Half a block behind him, a dog erupted in a frenzied protest. Henry ignored it; he had no interest in the territory it claimed. There. His nostrils flared as he caught a scent, held it, and began to track it to its source.

The open window was on the second floor. Henry gained it easily, becoming for that instant just another shadow moving against the wall of the house, flickering too fast for mortal eyes to register what they saw. The screen was no barrier.

He moved so quietly that the two young men on the bed, skin slicked with sweat, breathing in identical tormented rhythms, had no idea he was there until he allowed it. The blond saw him first and managed an inarticulate exclamation before he was caught in the Hunter's snare. Warned, the other whirled, one heavily muscled arm flung up.

Henry let the wrist slap against his palm, then he closed his fingers and smiled. Held in the depths of hazel eyes, the young man swallowed and began to tremble.

The bed sank under the weight of a third body.

He became an extension of their passion which quickly grew and intensified and finally ignited, racing up nerve endings until mere mortals became lost in the burning glory of it.

He left the way he came. In the morning, they'd find the catch on the screen had been broken and have no idea of when it had happened. Their only memory of his participation would keep them trying, night after night, to recreate what he had given them. He wished them joy in the attempt.

The casket had not been moved from the chapel. Henry stared down at it in distaste. He could no more understand why they'd covered the wood with blue-gray cloth than he could the need to enshrine empty flesh in expensive, beautiful cabinets, sealed against rot and protected from putrefaction. In his day, it was the ceremony of interment that had been important, the mourning, the declarations of grief, the long and complicated farewell. Massive monuments to the dead were placed so people could appreciate them, not buried for the pleasure of the worms. *What was wrong,* he wondered, stepping closer, *with a plain wooden box? He'd* been buried in a plain wooden box.

The sandbags had been taken away, but the imprint still showed in the satin pillow. Henry shook his head and leaned forward. There was no comfort for the dead and he couldn't see how denying that comforted the living.

Suddenly, he hesitated. The last time he'd bent over a coffin that should not have been empty he'd ended up nearly losing his soul. But the ancient Egyptian wizard who called himself Anwar Tawfik had never been dead and Marjory Nelson assuredly had. He was being foolish.

There was a hint of Vicki's mother about the interior. He'd spent the day surrounded by her scent and he easily recognized the trace that still clung to the fabric under the patina of odor laid on by the day's investigation. Straightening, he was certain that whatever else she'd done in her life, or her death, Marjory Nelson had not risen as one of his kind.

But there *was* something.

Over the centuries, he'd breathed in the scent of death in all its many variations, but this death, this faint suggestion that clung to the inside of nose and mouth, this death he didn't know.

Five

"Dr. Burke, look at this! We're definitely picking up independent brain wave patterns."

"Are you certain we're not just getting echos of what we've been feeding in?"

"Quite certain." Catherine tapped the printout with one gnawed nail. "Look at this spike here. And here."

Donald leaned over the doctor's shoulder and squinted down at the wide ribbon of paper. "Electronic belching," he declared, straightening. "And after thirty hours of this-is-your-life, I'm not surprised."

"You may be right, Donald." Dr. Burke lightly touched each peak, a smile threatening the corners of her mouth. "On the other hand, we might actually have something here. Catherine, I think we should open the isolation box."

Both grad students jerked around to stare at their adviser.

"But it's too soon," Catherine protested. "We've been giving the bacteria a minimum of seventy-two hours . . ."

"And it hasn't been entirely successful," Dr. Burke broke in. "Now has it? We lost the first seven, number eight is beginning to putrefy, and according to this morning's samples, even number nine hasn't begun any cellular regeneration in muscle tissue. The near disaster with number five proved that we can't continue isolation much past seventy-two hours, so let's see what happens when we cut it short."

Catherine ran her hand over the curved surface of the box. "I don't know . . ."

"Besides," the doctor continued, "if these spikes do indicate independent brain wave activity, then further time in what is essentially a sensory deprivation chamber will very likely . . ."

"Squash them flat."

The two women turned.

"Inelegant, Donald, but essentially correct."

Pale eyes scanned the array of hookups: monitors and digital readouts and one lone dial. "Well, except for the continuous alpha wave input, she isn't actually doing anything in there," Catherine admitted thoughtfully.

Dr. Burke sighed and decided, for the moment, to let Catherine's terminology stand. "My point exactly. Donald, if you would do the honors. Catherine, keep an eye on things and if there are any changes at all, sing out."

The seal sighed open, the hint of formaldehyde on the escaping oxygen-rich air surely an illusion, and the heavy lid rose silently on its counterweights. The body of Marjory Nelson lay naked and exposed on what had been a sterile pad, huge purple scars stapled shut. Hair, already becoming brittle, fell away from the clips that held the top of the skull in place. A faint trace of burial cosmetics painted an artificial blush across cheekbones death-mask prominent.

At her station by the monitors, Catherine frowned. "I'm not sure. It could be a loose connection. Dr. Burke, could you please check the jack."

Pulling on a pair of surgical gloves, Dr. Burke bent over and reached to roll the head a little to the left.

Gray-blue eyes snapped open.

"Holy shit!" Donald danced backward, crashed into number nine's box, and clutched at it for support.

Dr. Burke froze, one hand almost cradling the line of jaw.

One second. Two seconds. Three seconds. An eternity.

As suddenly as they opened, the eyes closed.

Her view of the body blocked by equipment, Catherine ignored Donald's outburst—in her opinion they came too often to mean anything—and sighed. "Just a wiggle. Probably something in the wire."

"In the wire!" The stethoscope around Donald's neck swung in a manic arc. "We didn't get a wiggle, partner, we got recognition."

"What?" Catherine shot to her feet and stared from Donald to Dr. Burke. "What happened?"

"We opened the lid, she opened her eyes, and bam!" Donald punched at the air. "Just for an instant, she knew who was standing over her. I'm telling you, Cathy, she recognized Dr. Burke!"

"Nonsense." Dr. Burke calmly checked the implant before straightening. "It was an involuntary reaction to the light. Nothing more." The peeled gloves slammed into the garbage. "Switch off the oxygen supplement—we've only got three full tanks left and I'm not sure when we can get more from the departmental supplies—and run a complete check on the mechanicals. Draw the usual samples."

"And the alpha waves?"

"Keep recording." A little pale under the glare of the fluorescents, Dr. Burke paused at the door. "But at the first sign of any agitation, cut the power. I have things to catch up on, so I'll see you both later."

Catherine's puzzled gaze traveled from the lab door to Donald.

"Sure as shit looked like recognition to me," he repeated, wiping his palms on his pants. "I think the good doctor's spooked and I don't blame her. Spooked me, too, and I barely knew the woman."

Catherine chewed her lip. "Well, it didn't register electronically."

He shrugged. "Then maybe we've got activity going on outside the net."

On cue, number nine began banging on the inside of his box.

Donald jumped and swore, but Catherine looked suddenly stricken.

"Oh, no! I promised him he wouldn't have to spend more time in there than absolutely necessary to maintain the integrity of the experiment."

Watching her hurry across the lab, Donald fished a candy from his pocket and methodically unwrapped it. *Now that's a person who doesn't get out enough.*

Usually, Dr. Burke considered the sound of her footsteps, leather soles slapping against tile, nothing more than background noise, acknowledged then forgotten. Today, the sound chased her through the empty halls of the old Life Sciences building, across the connecting walkway, and up into the sanctuary of her office. Even tucked into the comforting depths of her old wooden chair, she thought she could still hear the echoing trail she'd left. After a moment, she realized she was listening to the rapid pounding of her heart.

You're being ridiculous, she told herself firmly, palms flat on the desk. *Take a deep breath and stop overreacting.*

Marjory Nelson's heart condition, not to mention her accessibility, had made her the perfect candidate for the next phase of the experiment. Brain waves had been recorded, tissue samples has been taken, bacteria had been specifically tailored to her DNA—all in preparation for her death. Or rather for the attempted reversal of it. Marjory, knowing nothing of what they'd been doing, submitted to the tests she'd been told might help, and died right on schedule.

Right on schedule. A second deep breath followed the first. *It was fast and painless when it otherwise might not have been.* Not to mention that her presence at the collapse had ensured they wouldn't have to worry about the tissue destruction inherent in an autopsy.

Squaring her shoulders, Dr. Burke pulled the morning's mail across the desk. They were reversing death. Catherine might have created the bacteria, but without her involvement this application would still be years, if not decades, in the future. She had made possible the logical progression of Catherine's experiments and she would reap the rewards.

If recognition *had* flashed just for that instant in Marjory's eyes, then they trembled on the brink of success long before empirical data suggested they should.

If recognition had occurred then . . .

Then what?

Marjory Nelson is dead and I'm truly sorry about that. She was an essential member of my staff and I'll miss her. With a deft movement, Dr. Burke slid the letter opener the length of the envelope. *The body in the lab is experimental unit number ten. Nothing more.*

"I already spoke to the police about this, Ms. Nelson." Nervously, Christy Aloman shuffled the papers on her desk. "I don't know if I should be speaking to you."

"Did the police tell you not to speak to anyone else?"

"No, but . . ."

"You have to admit, if anyone has a right to know, it's me." Vicki felt the pencil dig deep into the callus on her second finger and forced her hand to relax.

"Yes, but . . ."

"My mother's body was stolen from these premises."

"I know, but . . ."

"I should think you'd want to do what you could to help."

"I do. Truly I do." She made the mistake of looking at Vicki's face and found she couldn't look away. Gray-blue eyes were like chiseled bits of frozen stone and she felt as she had when, so many winters ago, she'd responded to childish dares and touched the metal gatepost with her tongue—foolish and trapped.

"Then tell me everything you can remember about Tom Chen. How he looked. What he wore. How he acted. What he said. What you overheard."

"Everything?" It was complete surrender and they both knew it.

"Everything."

"I don't suppose you ever wore anything like this when you were alive." Catherine pulled the Queen's University sweatpants up over number nine's hips. Grayish skin glistened with the most recent application of estrogen cream. "I mean all things considered, you were in pretty good shape, but you didn't look like a jock. Sit."

Number nine obediently sat.

"Raise your arms. Higher."

A bit of agar oozed out between incision staples over the sternum as number nine's arms lifted into the air.

Catherine ignored it and tugged a matching sweatshirt down over the arms and head. "There you go. A pair of shoes and you're fit for polite company."

"Cathy, I hate to say this, but you're looney tunes." Donald pushed away from the microscope and rubbed his eyes. "You're talking to an animatronic corpse. It doesn't understand you."

"I think he does." She slid one bony foot into a running shoe, pressing the velcro closed. "And if maybe he doesn't understand all of it now, he'll never learn to understand if we don't talk to him."

"I know. I know. Necessary stimulus. But we're not getting anything back—brain wave wise—that we haven't put in. Granted," he held up a hand to cut off her protest, "we're getting some evidence of interfacing with gross motor skills. You don't need to give every muscle fiber a separate instruction and that's fucking amazing, but face it," he tapped his head, "there's nothing upstairs. The tenant is gone."

Catherine snorted and patted number nine reassur-

ingly on the shoulder. "Great bedside manner. I can
see why you got kicked out of med school."

"I didn't get kicked out." Donald set another slide
under the microscope lens. "I made a lateral move
into graduate studies in organic chemistry."

"Not an entirely voluntary move from what I heard.
I heard Dr. Burke had to save your ass."

"Catherine!" Miming shock and horror, Donald
spread both hands wide. "I didn't know you knew
such words." He shook his head and grinned. "You've
spent too much time with single-celled orgasms . . ."

"Organisms!"

". . . you need to get a life."

Catherine moved to number eight's box and adjusted
the power. "Somebody has to stay here and take care
of them."

Donald sighed. "Better you than me."

Touch.
Her touch.
As electronic impulses continued to move out from
the net, more and more words were returning. Hold.
Want. Have. Number nine didn't know what to do with
those words, not yet.

Wait.

"Is she asleep?"

"Yes." Henry sank down onto the sofa and rested
his arms across his knees, the scattering of red-gold
hair below his rolled-up sleeves glittering in the lamplight.

"Did you have to . . . convince her?"

"Very nearly, but no. I merely helped her to calm
and exhaustion did the rest."

Celluci snorted. "Helped her to calm?" he growled.
"Is that a euphemism for something I don't want to
know about?"

Henry ignored the question. "It's late. What are you
doing up?"

Lifting his feet up onto the coffee table and stretching long legs, Celluci grunted, "Couldn't sleep."

"Do you want to?"

It was asked innocently enough. *No. Not innocently. Nothing Fitzroy did came under the heading of innocent.* Neutrally enough. "No." Celluci tried to keep his response equally neutral. "I just thought that if you had any idea of what we're supposed to do next, well, I'd like to hear it."

Henry shrugged and threw a quick glance back over his shoulder toward the bedroom where Vicki's heart beat slow and steady, finally free of the angry pounding it had no doubt taken all day. "I honestly have no idea." He turned to look through the shadows at the other man. "Don't you have a job to go back to?"

"Compassionate leave," Celluci told him shortly, eyes half closed. "Shouldn't you be out, oh, I don't know, stalking the night or something?"

"Shouldn't you be out detecting?"

"Detecting what? It hardly makes sense to stake out the scene of the crime and you can bet that asshole Chen, or whatever his real name is, has vanished. All the profiles in the world won't help us identify a perp we can't find."

Henry reached down and fanned the papers on the coffee table by Celluci's feet. Vicki had spent the evening compiling the day's data and when he'd risen, just before eight, she'd presented her results.

"I spoke to everyone who might have had contact with him—except one of three bus drivers, and I'll speak to him tomorrow. Clothes and hairstyles may change, but tiny habits are harder to break. He smiles a lot. Even when he's alone and there's nothing apparent to smile about. He drinks Coke Classic exclusively. He usually has some kind of candy in his pocket. He most often sits in the seat in front of the rear door next to the window. He'd get on the Johnson Street bus at Brock and Montreal with a ticket, not a transfer. That probably means he lives downtown."

Henry had been impressed; and equally concerned. "Victory" Nelson appeared to have no room in her investigation for grieving. A steady emotional diet of rage, especially at this time, couldn't be healthy. He scanned the pages of notes and shook his head. "She's got everything here but a picture."

Reluctantly, Celluci agreed. Years of training seemed to have gained a foothold in Vicki's emotional response and she was now searching for the person instead of just blindly clutching at the name. "Detective Fergusson says he'll try to free up the police artist tomorrow."

"Why do I get the feeling that Detective Fergusson doesn't think that's necessary?"

"It's not that. It's resources. Or specifically *lack* of resources. As he pointed out, and this is a quote, 'Yeah, it's a terrible thing, but we can't hardly keep up with indignities done to the living.' " Celluci's lips thinned as he remembered various "indignities" he'd witnessed done to the living that had gone unpunished due to lack of manpower, or departmental budget cuts, or just plain bad management. He didn't, by any means, approve of Vicki's recent conversion to vigilantism, but, by God, he understood it. The satisfaction of *knowing* that Anwar Tawfik was dust and this time would stay dust, of *knowing* Mark Williams had paid for the innocents he'd slaughtered, of *knowing* that Norman Birdwell would loose no further horrors on the city, all of that weighed heavily against law in the scales Justice held.

He peered blearily at Henry Fitzroy from under heavy lids. How many others had there been? Hundreds? Thousands? While he'd been busting his butt and walking his feet flat, had Fitzroy and others like him been spending the night methodically squashing the cockroaches of humanity? Celluci snorted silently. If they were, they were doing a piss poor job.

Vampires. Werewolves. Demons. Mummies. Only for Vicki would he even consider accepting such a skewed view of reality. Maybe he should've listened to his family, married a nice Italian girl, and settled down. Much as Henry had done earlier, he shot a glance over his shoulder toward the bedrooms. *No. A nice girl, Italian or otherwise, couldn't hope to compete.* Vicki was a comrade, and a friend, and, as asinine as it sounded, the woman he loved. He'd stand by her now when she needed him, regardless of who, or what, stood by her other side.

He didn't want to have anything to do with Henry Fitzroy. He didn't want to respect him. He sure as shit didn't want to like him. He appeared to have no choice regarding the first point, had months ago lost the second, and strongly suspected, in spite of everything, that he was losing the third. *Jesus. Buddies with a bloodsucker.* Responses had to be filtered through the memory of power he'd been shown in Vicki's living room. *Safer to play with a pit bull.*

Henry felt the weight of Celluci's gaze and tried to remember the last occasion on which he'd spent this much time alone with a mortal he hadn't been feeding from. Or hadn't intended to feed from. The situation was, to say the least, unusual.

In all his long life, Henry had seldom felt so frustrated. "We can't resolve this," he said aloud, "until the body is found and interred, and her grieving is over."

Celluci didn't bother pretending to misunderstand what *this* referred to, although he was tempted. "So find the body," he suggested, a yawn threatening to dislocate his jaw.

Henry arched a brow. "So easy to say," he murmured.

"Yeah? What about that funny smell Vicki says you ran into last night?"

"I am not a bloodhound, Detective. Besides, I traced it as far as it went—to the parking lot."

"What did it smell like?"

"Death."

"Not surprising. You were in a body parlor." He yawned again.

"Funeral homes go to a great deal of effort *not* to smell like death. This was something different."

"Oh, lord, not again," Celluci groaned, dragging a hand up through his hair. "What is it this time? The creature from the Rideau Canal? The Loch Ness fucking monster? The Swamp Thing? Godzilla? Megatron? Gondor? Rodan?"

"Who?"

"Didn't you ever watch Saturday afternoon monster movies?" He shook his head at Henry's expression. "No, I guess you didn't, did you? Every weekend thousands of kids were glued to their sets for badly dubbed, black and white, Japanese rubber monsters stomping on Tokyo. Not to mention *Jesse James Meets Frankenstein's Daughter, Abbott and Costello Meet the Mummy, The Curse of the Werewolf.*"

A car door, slamming in the parking lot, suddenly sounded unnaturally loud.

"Jesus H. Christ." Celluci's eyes were fully open. Still tired, he no longer had any desire to sleep. He sat up and swung his feet to the floor. "A motive. You don't think . . ."

"That Tom Chen was playing Igor to someone else's Dr. Frankenstein?" Henry smiled. "I think, as I said before, that you watch too many bad movies, Detective."

"Oh, yeah? Well, you know what I think? I think . . ."

Bam. Bam. Bam.

They faced the door, then they faced each other.

"The police," Celluci said, and stood.

"No." Henry blocked his way. He could feel the lives, hear the singing blood, smell the excitement. "Not police although I suspect they'd like us to think so."

Bam. Bam. Bam.

"A threat?"

"I don't know." He crossed the room. When he

stopped, Celluci moved up to stand behind his left shoulder. It had been a very long time since he'd had a shield man. He opened the door.

The flash went off almost before he could react. A mortal would have recoiled—Henry's hand whipped out and covered the lens of the camera before the shutter had completely fallen. He snarled as the brilliant light drove spikes of pain into sensitive eyes and closed his fingers. Plastic and glass and metal became only plastic and glass and metal.

"Hey!"

The photographer's companion ignored both the sound of a camera disintegrating and the accompanying squawk of protest. Sometimes they got a great candid shot when the door opened, sometimes they didn't. She wasn't going to worry about it. "Good evening. Is Victoria Nelson at home?" Elbows primed, her notebook held like a battering ram, she attempted to push forward. Most people, she found, were just too polite to stop her.

The slight young man never budged; it felt like she'd hit a not very tall brick wall. Time for plan B. And if that didn't work, she'd go right through the alphabet if she had to. "We were so sorry to hear about what happened to her mother's bo . . ." Her train of thought derailed somewhere in the depths of hazel eyes.

Henry decided not to be subtle. He wasn't in the mood and they wouldn't understand. "Go away. Stay away."

Darkness colored the words and became threat enough.

Not until they were safely in the car, cocooned behind steel and locked doors, did the photographer, cradling the ruins of his camera in his lap, finally find his voice. "What are we going to do?" he asked, primal memories of the Hunt trembling in his tone.

"We're going to do . . ." With an icy hand and shaking fingers, she jammed the car into gear, stomped on the gas, and sprayed gravel over half the parking lot. ". . . exactly what he said."

Together they'd been threatened a hundred times. Maybe a thousand. Once, they'd even been attacked by an ex-NHL defenseman swinging a hockey stick with enraged abandon. They'd always gotten the story. Or a version of the story at least. This time, something in heart and soul, in blood and bone recognized the danger and overruled conscious thought.

Inside Marjory Nelson's apartment, Celluci glared enviously at the back of Henry's red-gold head. If he hated anything, it was the press. The statements they insisted on were the bane of his existence. "I wish I could do that," he muttered.

Henry wisely kept from voicing the obvious and made sure all masks were back in place before turning. This was not the time for Michael Celluci to see him as a threat.

Celluci rubbed at the side of his nose and sighed. "There'll probably be others."

"I'll deal with them."

"And if they come in the daytime?"

"You deal with them." Henry's smile curved predator sharp. "You're not on duty, Detective. You can be as rude as . . ." Just how rude Celluci could be got lost in a sudden change of expression and a heartbeat later he was racing for the bedroom.

To mortal eyes, one moment he was there, the next gone. Celluci turned in time to see Vicki's bedroom door thrown open, swore, and pounded across the living room. He hadn't heard anything. What the hell had Fitzroy heard?

How could she have forgotten?

She dug frantically at the tiles in the kitchen. As they ripped free, she flung them behind her, ignoring the fingernail that ripped free with them, ignoring the blood from her hands that began to mark its own pattern on the floor. Almost there. Almost.

The area she cleared stretched six feet long by three feet wide, the edges ragged. Finally only the plywood subfloor remained. Rot marked the gray-brown wood and tendrils of pallid fungus grew between the narrow boards. Fighting for breath, she slammed her fists against this last barrier.

The wood cracked, splintered, and gave enough for her to force a grip on the first piece. She threw her weight against it and it lifted with a moist, sucking sound, exposing a line of gray-blonde curls and perhaps a bit of shoulder.

How could she have forgotten where she'd left her mother?

Begging for forgiveness, she clawed at the remaining boards. . . .

"Vicki! Vicki, wake up, it's only a dream."

She couldn't stop the first cry, but she grabbed at the second and wrestled it back where it came from. Her conscious mind clung to the reassurances murmured over and over against her hair. Her subconscious waited for the next board to be removed. Her hands clung of their own volition, fingers digging deep into the shoulder and arm curved protectively around her.

"It's all right, Vicki. It's all right. I'm here. It was only a dream. I'm here. I've got you . . ." The words, Henry knew, were less important than the tone and as he spoke he drew the cadence around the fierce pounding of her heart and convinced it to calm.

"Henry?"

"I'm here."

She fought the terror for control of her breathing and won at last. A long breath in. A longer breath out. And then again.

Henry almost heard the barriers snap back into place as she pushed away, chin rising defiantly.

"I'm okay." *It was only a dream. You're acting like a child.* "Really, I'm okay." The darkness shifted things, moved furniture that hadn't been moved in fifteen years. *Where the hell is the bedside table?* "Turn on the light," she commanded, struggling to keep new panic from touching her voice. "I need my glasses."

A cool touch against her hand and her fingers closed gratefully around the heavy plastic frames. A second touch helped her settle them on her nose just as the room flooded with light. Squinting against the glare, she turned to face the switch and Michael Celluci's worried frown.

"Jesus. Both of you."

"I'm afraid so." Henry shifted his weight on the edge of the bed and asked, without much hope of success, "Do you want to talk about it?"

Her lip curled. "Not likely." Talking about it would mean thinking about it. Thinking about what she'd have found, what she'd have seen, if she'd managed to tear up just one more piece of floor. . . .

"Celluci? Fergusson. Med school's got three Chens. One of them's even a Tom Chen—Thomas Albert Chen. And guess what, the kid's got an airtight alibi not only for that night but for the whole two and a half weeks our boy was at the body parlour. Rough luck, eh?"

Celluci, receiver pinned between shoulder and ear, washed down a forkful of scrambled eggs with a mouthful of bitter coffee. He hadn't thought Fergusson a subtle enough man for sarcasm. Obviously, he'd been wrong. "Yeah, rough. You take his picture around to Hutchinson's just in case?"

"Give it up, Celluci, and stop wasting my fucking time. You and I both know that we're not looking for any Tom Chen." Fergusson sighed at Celluci's noncommittal grunt, the sound eloquently saying *give me a break.* "Tell Ms. ex-Detective Nelson that I'm sorry about her mother, but I know what the fuck I'm doing. I'll get back to you if we get any *real* information in."

Celluci managed to hang up and shovel another pile

of eggs into his mouth before he succumbed to Vicki's glare and repeated the conversation. *She* might have dropped off, reassured by Fitzroy's supernatural protection but *he'd* spent a restless night stretched out in the next room, straining to hear any sound that might make its way through the wall, wondering why he'd so easily surrendered the field. *You've got the day,* he reminded himself, reaching for another piece of toast. Which was really no answer at all. *Goddamn Fitzroy anyway.* Hopefully, massive quantities of food would make up for lost sleep.

Vicki pushed her plate away. She knew she had to eat, but there was a limit to how much she could choke past the knots. "I want you to check that alibi."

Oh, God, not again. He'd really thought that she'd shaken her obsession that Tom Chen could be the actual name of their suspect. The profiling she'd done had been good solid police work and he'd taken it—*prematurely as it turns out*—as an indication that she was beginning to function. Hiding concern she wouldn't appreciate, he reached across the table and covered one of her hands with his. There was no point in restating the obvious when she refused to hear him, so he tried a different angle. "Vicki, Detective Fergusson *knows* his job."

"Either you check it or I do." Pulling her hand free, she regarded him levelly. "I won't let this go. You can't make me. You might as well help; it'll be over sooner."

Her eyes were too bright and he could see the tension twisting her shoulders and causing her fingers to tremble slightly. "Look, Vicki . . ."

"I don't need a babysitter, Mike. Not you. Not him."

"All right." He sighed. She'd asked for his help. While it wasn't exactly the kind of help he wanted to give, it was something. "I'll check the alibi and I'll run a picture over to Hutchinson's. I don't think you should be alone, but you're an adult and you're right, this will go faster with both of us working on it.''

"All three of us."

"Fine." Too much to expect she'd want Fitzroy to butt out, "What'll you be doing?"

She set her empty coffee mug down on the table with a sharp crack. "Tom Chen wanted my mother's body specifically. In the time he was at that funeral home, he passed up two other women of roughly equal age and condition. I'll be finding out why." As she stood, she knocked her knife to the floor. It bounced once, then slid across the kitchen floor, across tiles still whole, still covering . . .

How could she have forgotten where she'd left her mother?

The eggs became a solid lump the size of her fist, shoved up tight against her ribs. Eyes up, she stepped over the knife. Another two steps took her off the tiles.

Gray-blonde curls and perhaps a bit of shoulder.

Just one more board. . . .

"Raise right leg." As Donald spoke, he fed the stored brain wave pattern corresponding to the command directly into the net.

In the open isolation box, the right leg trembled and slowly lifted about four inches off the padding.

"Hey, Cathy, we've got a fast learner here. Remember how ol' number nine's leg flew up? Like he was trying to kick the ceiling?"

'I remember how Dr. Burke was worried he might have damaged his hip joint," Catherine replied, continuing to adjust the IV drip that nourished the rapidly deteriorating number eight. "And at least we didn't have to manipulate his leg for the first hundred times like we had to on all the others."

"Hey, chill out. I wasn't saying anything against super-corpse. I was only pointing out that number ten seems to have quantitative control."

"Well, we are using *her* brain wave patterns."

"Well, number nine used *my* brain wave patterns for gross motor control." He echoed her supercilious tone. "So *he* should've had the advantage."

"I'm amazed he learned how to walk."

"Ow." Donald dramatically clutched at his heart. "I am cut to the quick." Rolling his eyes at her non-responsive back, he tapped another two computer keys. "And it's painful going through life with a cut quick, let me tell you. Lower right leg."

Surrendering to gravity, the right leg dropped.

"Raise left leg. I've got a feeling that number ten's going to be the baby that makes our fortune."

Catherine frowned as she moved to check on number nine. There's been too much talk of "making fortunes" lately. The discovery of new knowledge should be an end in itself; the consideration of monetary gains clouded research. Granted number ten represented a giant step forward as far as experimental data was concerned, but she was by no means as far as they could go.

There was something she had to do.
The need began to force definition onto oblivion.

"Frankly, Vicki, I'm amazed your mother didn't tell you all this." Adjusting her glasses, Dr. Friedman peered down at Marjory Nelson's file. "After all, we had a diagnosis about seven months ago."

Vicki's expression didn't change, although a muscle twitched in her jaw. "Did she know how bad it was?" *She* could refer to anyone's mother, not that the illusion of distance helped. "Did she know that her heart could give out at any time?"

"Oh, yes. In fact, we'd agreed to try corrective surgery but, well . . ." The doctor shrugged ruefully. "You know how these things keep getting put off, what with hospitals having to trim beds."

"Are you saying budget cutbacks killed her?" The words came out like ground glass.

Dr. Friedman shook her head and tried to keep her tone soothing. "No. A heart defect killed your mother. She'd probably had it all her life until, finally, an aging muscle couldn't compensate any longer."

"Was it a usual condition?"

"It wasn't a *usual* condition . . ."

Vicki cut her off with a knife-edged gesture. "Was it unusual enough that her body may have been stolen in order to study it?"

"No, I'm sorry, but it wasn't."

"I'd like to see the file."

Brow furrowed, Dr. Friedman studied the plain brown folder without really seeing it. Technically, the file was confidential, but Marjory Nelson was dead and beyond caring. Her daughter, however, was alive, and if the contents of the file could help to bring healing out of dangerously strong denial, then confidentiality be damned. And it wasn't as if the file contained anything she hadn't already divulged during the last hour's interrogation—details had been lifted out of her memory with a surgical precision both frightening and impressive. Reaching a decision she pushed the folder across the desk and asked, "If there's anything else I can do?"

"Thank you, Doctor." Vicki slid the file into her purse and stood. "I'll let you know."

As that hadn't been exactly what she had in mind, she tried again. "Have you spoken to anyone about your loss?"

"My loss?" Vicki smiled tightly. "I'm speaking to everyone about it." She nodded, more a dismissal than a farewell, and left the office.

Loss, Dr. Friedman decided, as the door swung shut, had been an unfortunate choice of words.

She almost had it. Almost managed to grab onto memory. There was something she *had* to do. Needed to do.

* * *

"Cathy. She made a noise."

"What kind of a noise? Tissue stretching? Joints cracking, what?"

"A vocal noise."

Catherine sighed. "Donald . . ."

"No. Really." He backed away, still holding the sweatshirt he'd been about to pull over electronically raised arms. "It was a kind of moan."

"Nonsense." Catherine took the shirt out of his hands and gently tugged it down into place. "It was probably just escaping air. You're too rough."

"Yeah, and I know the difference between a belch and a moan." Cheeks pale, he crossed to his desk and dropped into the chair, fingers shredding the wrapper off a mint. "I'm going to start running today's biopsies. *You* can finish dressing Ken and Barbie."

"Your mother was a pretty everyday sort of person." Mrs. Shaw smiled sadly over the edge of her coffee mug. "You were probably the most exotic thing in her life."

Vicki let the sympathy wash past her—waves over a rock—and pushed at her glasses. "You're certain she wasn't involved in any unusual activities over the last few months?"

"Oh, I'm certain. She would've told me about it if she had been. We talked about everything, your mother and I."

"You knew about the heart condition."

"Of course. Oh." Flustered, the older woman cast about for a way to erase her last words. "Uh, more coffee?"

"No. Thank you." Vicki set what had been her mother's cup down on what had been her mother's desk, then reached over and gently laid her academy graduation portrait facedown.

"An investigation must not become personal." The voice of a cadet instructor echoed in her head. *"Emo-*

tions camouflage fact and you can charge right past the one bit of evidence you need to break the case.''

"Actually, if anything, well, unusual was going on with your mother, Dr. Burke might know." Mrs. Shaw set her own mug down and leaned forward helpfully. "When she found out about the heart condition, she convinced your mother to have a whole lot of tests done."

"What kind of tests?"

"I don't know. I don't think your mother . . ."

Stop saying that! Your mother! Your mother! She had a name.

". . . knew."

"Is Dr. Burke available?"

"Not this afternoon, I'm afraid. She's in a departmental meeting right now, but I'm sure she'll be able to make time for you tomorrow morning."

"Thank you." Moving carefully, Vicki stood. "I'll be back." Lips twisted in a humorless smile. She felt more like Charlie Brown than Arnold Schwarzenegger.

"Goddamn, look at the time. It's almost 8:30 in the p.m. No wonder I'm so hungry."

Catherine carefully set the petri dish in the incubation chamber. "Hungry? I don't see why, you've been eating sugar all day."

"Cathy. Cathy. Cathy. And you a scientist. Sugar stimulates hunger, it doesn't satisfy it."

Pale brows drew in. "I don't think that's exactly right."

Donald shrugged into his jacket. "Who cares. Let's go for pizza."

"I still have work to do."

"*I* still have work to do. But I doubt I'll be capable of working to my full potential if all I can think of is my stomach. And," he crossed the room and punched her on the shoulder, brows waggling, "I'm sure I heard your tum demanding attention mere moments ago."

"Well . . ."

"Doesn't your research deserve to have your full attention?"

She drew herself up indignantly. "Without question."

"Distracted by hunger, who knows what damage you could do. Come on." He picked up her coat. "I hate to eat alone."

Recognizing truth in the last statement at least, Catherine allowed herself to be herded to the door. "What about them?"

"Them?" For a moment, he had no idea of who she was referring to, then he sighed. "We'll bring them back a pepperoni special, pop it in a blender, and feed it to them through the IV, okay?"

"That's not what I meant. They're just sitting there, out of the boxes. Shouldn't we . . ."

"Leave them. We're coming right back." He pulled her over the threshold. "You're the one who said they needed the stimulation."

"Yes. I did."

With Catherine safely in the hall, Donald reached back and flicked off the overhead lights. "Don't do anything I wouldn't do," he caroled into the room, and pulled the door closed.

One by one, the distractions ceased. First the voices. Then the responses she couldn't control or understand. Finally, the painful brightness. It grew easier to hold on to thought. To memory.

There was something she had to do.

Raise your right leg.

Raise your left leg.

Walk.

She remembered walking.

Slowly, lurching to compensate for a balance subtly wrong, she crossed the room.

Door.

Closed.

Open.

It took both hands, fingers interlaced, to turn the handle—not the way memory said it should work, but memory lay in shredded pieces.

There was something she had to do.

Needed to do.

Number nine watched. Watched the walking. Watched the leaving.

This new one was not like the other. The other had no . . .

No . . .

The other was empty.

This new one was not empty. This new one was like him.

Him.

He.

Two new words.

He thought they might be important words.

He stood and walked, as he'd been taught, toward the door.

Six

"This isn't the eighteenth century, Fitzroy. Medical schools stopped hiring grave diggers some time ago."

Henry tugged at the lapels of his black leather trench coat, settling it forward on his shoulders. "You have a better idea, Detective?"

Celluci scowled. He didn't, and they both knew it.

"Historical precedents aside," Henry continued, "Detective Fergusson seems certain that there were medical students involved; an opinion based, no doubt, on local precedents."

"Detective Fergusson blames Queen's students for everything from traffic jams to the weather," Celluci pointed out acerbically. "And I thought your opinion of Detective Fergusson wasn't high."

"I've never even met the man."

"You said . . ."

"Enough," Vicki interrupted from her place on the couch, the tap, tap, tap of her pencil end against the coffee table a staccato background to her words. "Logically, all the storage facilities in the city should be searched. Also logically, for historical reasons, if nothing else, the medical school is the place to start."

"Those who refuse to learn from history," Henry agreed quietly, "are doomed to repeat it."

"Spare me the wisdom of the ages," Celluci muttered. "These places don't do public tours at midnight, you know; how are you planning on getting in?"

"It's hardly midnight."

"At twenty to nine, it's hardly open house either."

"It's April, the end of term, there'll be students around, and even if there aren't, it isn't easy to deny me access."

"Don't tell me. You turn into mist?" He raised a weary hand at Henry's expression. "I know; I watch too many bad movies. Never mind, I meant it when I said don't tell me. The less I know about your talents for B&E the better."

"You have the photograph?" Vicki asked. Tap. Tap. Tap. "You'll be able to make an identification?"

"Yes." Henry doubted Marjory Nelson still looked much like her picture, but it was a place to start.

Tap. Tap. Tap. "I should go with you."

"No." He crossed the room and dropped to one knee by her side. "I'll be able to move faster on my own."

"Yes, but . . ." Tap. Tap.

Henry covered her hand with his, stopping the pencil from rising to fall again. Her skin felt heated and he could feel the tension sizzling just under the surface. "I'll be able to move faster," he repeated, "on my own. And the faster I move, the sooner you'll have the information."

She nodded. "You're right."

He waited a moment, but when she said nothing further, he stood, reluctantly releasing her hand.

Tap. Tap. Tap.

Very lightly, he brushed his fingertips across her hair then turned.

Celluci met him at the door. Together, they glanced back at the couch. Vicki had removed the shades from both end-table lamps and, in the harsh light, the area around her mouth and eyes looked both bruised and painfully tight.

"Don't leave her alone," Henry murmured, and left before the detective could decide on a reply.

The sound of the pencil tapping followed him out of the building.

* * *

The door almost stopped her; the latching mechanism was almost beyond her abilities. The line of stitches just above the hairline gaped as her brows drew in and she forced her fingers to push and pull and prod until finally the door swung open.

There was something she had to do. Perhaps it was on the other side of the door.

Most of the overhead lights were off and she shuffled along from shadow to shadow. She was going somewhere. The halls began to look familiar.

She passed through another doorway and then into a room so well known that, for an instant, chaos parted and she knew.

I am . . .

Then the maelstrom swept most of it up again and she was left with only scattered fragments. For a single beat of her mechanically enhanced heart, she was aware of what she'd lost. Her wail of protest throbbed against the walls, but even before the last echo died, she'd forgotten she'd ever made it.

She crossed the room to a pair of desks, pulled one of the chairs out, and sat. It felt right. No, not quite right. Frowning, she carefully moved the *World's Greatest Mother* coffee mug from the center of the blotter over to the far right side. It always sat on the right side.

Something was still wrong. After a moment of almost thought, she scrabbled at a silvery frame lying facedown, finally managing to grab hold and lift it. With trembling fingers, she gently touched the face of the uniformed young woman whose photograph filled the frame. Then she stood.

There was something she had to do.

She shouldn't be here.

She had to go home.

He didn't know where the other one was, so he walked, following the path of least resistance, until he bumped up against a tiny square of reinforced glass that showed him the stars.

Outside.

He remembered outside.

Face pressed to the glass, eyes on the stars, he pushed at the barrier, sneakers pedaling against the tile floor. More by luck than design, his hands clutched at the waist-high metal bar. Another push, and the fire door swung open.

The alarm drove the stars from his head. He moved away from the hurting as fast as he was able, onto the dark and quiet pathways that ran between and behind the university buildings. He would find her. Find the kind one. She would make it better.

"Now, then, don't you feel better?"

"I suppose so."

"You suppose so?" Donald sighed and shook his head. "The best pizza in Kingston, not to mention my congenial company, and you'd probably rather have stayed in the lab, munching on a stale sandwich, if you'd remembered to eat at all, exchanging wisecracks with the dead stooges."

"Did you leave the door open?"

"Did I what?" He peered down the dimly lit hall at the door angled out into the corridor. "You sure that's ours?"

"Of course, I'm sure."

"Well, I closed it when we left *and* I heard the lock catch."

Catherine broke into a run. "If something's happened to them, I'll never forgive myself."

Donald followed considerably more slowly, half inclined to bolt. Although Security kept an eye on entrances and exits, they didn't bother to patrol the interior. The old Life Sciences building was a rabbit warren of halls and passageways and strangely subdivided rooms and, had the university budget extended to demolition, it would have long ago been turned into a much more useful three-story parking garage. While Donald had occasionally wondered if they were the *only* clandestine lab operating, he'd never been worried about discovery.

Except that he knew he'd closed the door.

And Dr. Burke, who carried the only other set of keys, would never leave it open.

So it appeared they'd been discovered.

The question is, he mused, bouncing on the balls of his feet, uncertain whether he should go forward or back, *have we advanced far enough that the end will justify the means in the eyes of the authorities?* Numbers one through nine, after all, had been bodies donated for research purposes. Unfortunately, he didn't think that even Dr. Burke could talk her way around body number ten, not without the final payoff of death overcome, and they were a while away from that.

Right. He had no intention of going to jail. Not for science. Not for anything. *I'm out of here.*

"Donald! They're gone!"

He froze, half-turned. "What do you mean they're gone?"

"Gone! Not here! They left!"

"Cathy, get a grip! Dead people don't just get up and walk away."

Her glare, anger and exasperation equally mixed, burned through the shadows between them. "You taught them to walk, you idiot!"

"Oh, lord, we're fucked." He ran for the lab. "You sure somebody didn't break in and steal them?"

"Who? If someone found them, they'd still be here waiting for an explanation."

"Or off calling the cops." He waved aside her protest and pushed past her. A quick glance at the monitors showed number eight remained in its isolation box, refrigeration units humming at full capacity in an attempt to prevent further decomposition. The chairs where they'd left numbers nine and ten were empty. The other two boxes were empty. He checked under the tables, in the closet, in the storeroom, around and below every bit of machinery in the lab.

If no one had found them, and logic pointed to that conclusion, then they had to have left on their own.

"It's impossible." Donald sagged against the door-frame. "They don't *have* abstract thought processes."

"They saw us leave." Catherine grabbed his arm and dragged him back out into the hall. "It was imitation if nothing more." She shoved him to the left. "You go that way!"

"Go where that way?"

"We have to search the building."

"Then call out the Mounties," he snapped, rubbing at his forehead with trembling fingers, "because it'll take you and me alone years to search this place."

"But we have to find them!"

He couldn't argue with that.

Voices.

Number nine moved toward the sound, drawn by almost familiar cadences.

Was it her?

"Cathy!" Donald pounded the length of the hall and rocked to a panting stop beside the other grad student. "Thank God I found you. We've got bigger trouble than we thought. I went over to talk to the guys at the security desk in the new building, just to see if they might have heard something. Well, they did. They heard the fire alarm. Someone went out the fire door at the back."

"Outside?" Pale skin blanched paler. "Unsupervised?"

"At least one of them. Where's your van?"

"In the lot behind the building." She turned and raced toward the exit. "We've got to find them before someone else does!"

Hand pressed tight against the stitch in his side,

Donald followed. ''Brilliant deduction, Sherlock,'' he gasped.

The voices were closer. He stopped at the border between soft ground and hard, head turning from side to side.

''I'm telling you, Jenny, sweetheart, no one ever comes back here. It's perfectly safe.''

''Why can't we park by the tower, like everyone else?''

''*Because* everyone else parks there and I have a moral objection to cops shining flashlights in my face at delicate moments.''

''At least let's close the windows.''

''It's a beautiful night, let's celebrate spring. Besides, steamy windows are a sure sign that something naughty is going down if anyone happens to pass. And speaking of going down . . .''

''Pat! Wait, I'll put the seat back. Be careful . . . oh . . .''

His soles scuffed as he lurched forward, aiming for the deeper shadows where two buildings joined. He didn't understand the new noises, but he followed them to a metal bulk he recognized as *car*.

He didn't know what car meant. Was it hurting her?

Bending carefully, he peered inside.

Pale hair.

Her face but not her face.

Her voice but not her voice.

Confused, he reached out and touched the curve of her cheek.

Her eyes snapped open, widened, then she screamed.

It hurt.

He began to back away.

Another face rose out of the darkness.

Hands grabbed for him.

His wrist caught, he clutched at air. He only wanted to get away. Then his fingers closed on something soft and kept closing until the screaming stopped. The second face lolled limp above his grip. Her face, not her face, gazed up at him. Then she screamed again.

He turned and ran.

He remembered running.

Run until it stopped hurting.

Soft ground under his feet.

He slammed hard against a solid darkness and pulled himself along it until he reached a way through. There were lights up ahead. She—the real she, the kind one— was where there were lights.

"There! Coming around that building!"

"Are you sure?"

"For chrissakes, Cathy, how many dead people are walking around this city tonight? Get over there!"

The van hadn't quite stopped when Donald threw himself out onto the road. He stumbled, picked himself up, and raced toward the shambling figure just emerging from the shadows.

He ignored the sound of screaming rising from behind the building. Catching sight of number nine's face under the streetlights, he figured he could pretty much guess what had caused it. Some of the sutures holding the scalp in place had torn and a grayish-yellow curve of skull was exposed above a flapping triangle of skin.

Dr. Burke's going to have my balls on a plate! He skidded to a stop, took a deep, steadying breath, and, as calmly as he was able, said, "Follow."

Follow.

He knew that word.

"Donald, I can hear screaming. And a car horn."

"Look, don't worry about it. Number nine's in, so just drive."

"Well, we should check to see if he's all right. They might have hurt him.

"Not *now,* Cathy. He's safe for the moment, but number ten isn't. We've got to find her. It."

Catherine glanced back over her shoulder at number nine lying strapped in place, nodded reluctantly, and pulled out into the street. "You're right. First we find number ten. Where to?"

Donald sank back against the passenger seat, sighed, and spread his hands. "How the hell should I know?"

Marjory Nelson had not been in the university's medical morgue; not in whole nor in part. Motionless beside the trunk of an ancient maple, ridding himself of the scent of preserved death, Henry considered how best to spend the remainder of the night. The city's two large hospitals were close. If he checked both their morgues before dawn, and he saw no reason why he shouldn't be able to, it would leave him available to . . . to . . . to what?

Over the last year, he'd learned that private investigators spent most of their time pulling together bits of apparently unconnected information into something they hoped would resemble a coherent whole—a little like first doing a scavenger hunt for jigsaw puzzle pieces and then constructing it with no idea of the final picture. They were more likely to spend time in libraries than in car chases and results were about equally dependent on training, talent, and luck. Not to mention an obstinate determination to get to the bottom of things that bordered on obsession.

Obsession. Vicki's obsession with finding her mother's body blocked the grief she should be feeling, blocked getting on with the rest of her life. Henry leaned back against the tree and wondered how long he was going to let it continue. He knew he could break through it, but at what cost. Could he do it without breaking her? Without losing her? Without leaving Detective-Sergeant Michael Celluci to pick up the pieces?

Suddenly he smiled, the moon-white crescent of his

teeth flashing in the darkness. *You measure your life in centuries,* he chided himself. *Give her some time to work through this. It's only been a couple of days.* Too much of the twentieth century's preoccupation with getting through unpleasantness as quickly and as tidily as possible had rubbed off on his thinking. Granted, repressing emotions was unhealthy but . . . *two days hardly deserves to be called an obsession.* It was, he realized, the presence of Michael Celluci that had made it seem so much longer. *He can do no more for her than you can. Trust in her strength, her common sense, and the knowledge that as much as she is able, she loves you.*

Both, added a small voice.

Shut up, he told it savagely.

Straightening, he stepped away from the tree, and froze, the hair rising on the back of his neck. A second later, the screaming started.

The sound echoed around the close-packed buildings, making it difficult for him to locate its source. After chasing down a number of false leads, he arrived at the small secluded parking lot just as the campus police screeched to a stop, their headlights illuminating a terrified teenage girl backing away from a rust-edged car and the body of an equally young man sprawled half out of it onto the pavement. The boy had obviously been dead when the car door was opened—only the dead fall with such boneless disregard for the landing.

Eyes narrowed against the intrusive glare, Henry slid into a patch of deep shadow. While it wouldn't be unusual for a passerby to be drawn by the screams, anonymity when possible ensured a greater degree of survival for his kind. With less noise than the wind made brushing up against the limestone walls, he began to move away. The girl was safe and although he would have intervened had he been in time, he had no interest in the myriad ways that mortals killed mortals.

"Like the guy looked like he was dead! Like all

rotten and dead! I am *not* hysterical! Like I've seen movies, you know!'' The last word trailed off into a rising wail.

The guy looked like he was dead.

And a corpse gone missing.

Henry stopped and turned back. There was probably no connection. He moved silently forward, around the edge of a building, and almost choked. The scent of the death he'd touched at the funeral home lay so thick on the grass that he had to back away. Skirting the edges, and *that* was closer than he wanted to go, he traced it to a pothole shattered access road and lost it again.

At the sound of approaching sirens, he pulled the night around him once more and made his way back to the parking lot. He would watch and listen until the drama played itself out. The girl could very well be hysterical, terror painting a yet more terrifying face on murder. The police would surely think so. Henry didn't.

If Henry comes up empty at the morgue, I'll have him start riding the buses. A young Asian male sitting just in front of the back door eating candy shouldn't be too hard to spot. Celluci can do the day shift. Vicki circled the Brock Street transfer point on her bus map. It wasn't much of a lead, but it was the only one they had and she knew it was one the police would have neither time nor manpower to follow. If Tom Chen— or whatever his name was—was still in Kingston, and till riding the buses, they'd find him eventually.

Eventually. She sat back on the couch and rubbed her eyes under her glasses. *That is,* if *he's still in Kingston, and* if *he's still riding the buses.*

And if he wasn't?

What if he'd thrown her mother's body into a car and driven away? He might not only have left the area but the country as well. The Ivy Lea Bridge over The Thousand Islands to the States wasn't far and with the amount of traffic that crossed daily, the odds of his car being searched by Customs were negligible. He could be anywhere.

But he knew her mother. There was no other reason for him to pass over the other bodies that had come through the funeral home and then run off with hers. Specifically hers. So the odds were good he had his base in the area.

That took care of who and where. Or, at least, that assembled as much information as they had.

Vicki dug her fingers into the back of her neck, trying to ease the knots of tension that tied her shoulders into solid blocks, then bent over the coffee table again, ignoring the knowledge that she'd be more comfortable in the kitchen. Stacking her notes on Tom Chen neatly to one side, she spread the contents of Dr. Friedman's file over the table. *Who* and *where* and *when* and even *how;* she had notes on all of these, a sheet of paper for each with the heading written in black marker at the top of the page. Only *why* remained blank. Why steal a body? Why steal her mother's body?

Why didn't she tell me she was so sick?
Why didn't I answer the phone?
Why didn't I call her?
Why wasn't I there when she needed me?

The pencil snapped between her fingers and the sound drove Vicki back against the sofa cushions, heart pounding. Those questions weren't part of the investigation. Those questions were for later, for *after* she'd got her mother back. Left hand pressed against the bridge of her glasses, Vicki fought for control. Her mother needed her to be strong.

All at once, the lingering smell of her mother's perfume, cosmetics, and bath soap coated nose and throat with a patina of the past. Her right fist dug into her stomach, denying the sudden nausea. The ambient noise of the apartment moved to the foreground. The refrigerator motor gained the volume of a helicopter taking off and a dripping tap in the bathroom echoed against the porcelain. An occasional car sped by on the street outside and something moved in the gravel parking lot.

Gradually, the other sounds faded back into the distance, but the footsteps dragging across the loose stones continued. Vicki frowned, grateful for the distraction.

It could be Celluci returning from the fish and chip store across the street, his footsteps hesitant because . . . well, because both he and Henry had been hesitant around her since they'd arrived. It wasn't that she didn't appreciate their help, because she did, but she wished they'd get it through their mutually thick heads that she could take care of herself.

Something brushed against the living room window.

Vicki straightened. The large ground level windows of the basement apartment had always been a tempting target for neighborhood kids and over the years had been decorated with soap, paint, eggs, lipstick, and, once, with Smurf stickers. Standing, she walked over and flicked on the floor lamp with its three, hundred watt bulbs. With luck, enough of the brilliant white light illuminating the living room would spill out into the night and she'd actually be able to see the little vandals before they ran.

She paused at the window, one hand holding the edge of the curtain, the other the cords of the venetian blind that ran behind. This close, she could hear that something was definitely rubbing against the other side of the glass. With one smooth, practiced motion, she threw the curtain aside and yanked the length of the blind up against its top support.

Pressed up against the glass, fingers splayed, mouth silently working, was her mother. Two pairs of eyes, an identical shade of gray, widened in simultaneous recognition.

Then the world slid sideways for a second.

My mother is dead.

* * *

Fragmented memory fought to become whole. Desperately, she grabbed at the pieces.

This is my . . .

This is my . . .

She couldn't find it, couldn't hold it.

A teenager, legs pumping, a ribbon breaking across her chest. A tall, young woman standing proudly in a blue uniform. A tiny pink mouth opening in what was surely the first yawn in creation. A child, suddenly grown serious, small arms reaching out to hold her while she cried. A voice saying, "Don't worry, Mother."

Mother.

This is my daughter. My child.

She knew now what it was she had to do.

The window was empty. No one moved in the parking lot as far as the spill of light and Vicki's vision went.

My mother is dead.

Around the corner, out of sight on the gravel path that lead to the entrance of the building, the same faltering footsteps sounded.

Vicki whirled and ran for the apartment door.

She'd turned the lock behind Celluci, a habit ingrained after years spent in a larger, more violent city. Now, as trembling fingers twisted the mechanism, the lock jammed.

"GODDAMNED FUCKING SON OF A BITCH!"

She couldn't hear the footsteps any longer. Couldn't hear anything but the blood roaring in her ears.

She'll be on the step now . . . The metal pushed bruises into her hands. . . . *opening the outer door . . .* Had the security door been locked when Celluci left? Vicki couldn't remember. *If she can't get in, she'll go away.* The whole door shuddered as she slammed the lock with her fists. *Don't go away!* Through fingers white with strain, she felt something give.

Don't go away again. . . .
The hall was empty.
The security door open.
Over the scream of denial that slammed echoes up against the sides of her skull though no sound passed teeth ground tight together, Vicki heard a car door slam. Then tires retreating across gravel.

Adrenaline catapulted her up the half flight of stairs and flung her out into the night.

"That was close, Cathy, too close. She was inside the building!"

"Is she all right?"

"What do you mean, is she all right? Don't you mean, did anyone see you?

"No." Catherine shook her head, the flying ends of hair gleaming ivory under the passing street lights. "The repairs we did aren't designed for so much activity. If any of those motors have burned out . . ."

Donald finished strapping the weakly struggling body in and made his way to the front of the van. "Well, everything seems to be working," he sighed, settling into his seat. "But it sure didn't want to come with me."

"Of course not, you interrupted the pattern."

"What pattern?"

"The body was responding to leaving the Life Sciences building by retracing a path followed for years."

"Yeah? I thought it was going home."

"Her home is with us now."

Donald shot an anxious glance over his shoulder into the back of the van. Number nine lay passively by, but number ten continued to push against the restraints. It had followed on his command, but he'd be willing to bet his chances for a Nobel Prize that it hadn't wanted to.

"Lie still," he snapped, and was only mildly relieved when it followed the programming.

* * *

Mike Celluci stepped out of the tiny fish and chip shop, inhaling the smell of french fries and greasy halibut overlaid on a warm spring night. Just at that particular moment, things didn't look so bad. While finding Marjory Nelson's body as soon as possible would be best for all concerned, Vicki was an intelligent adult, well acquainted with the harsh reality that some cases never got solved. Eventually, she'd accept that her mother was gone, accept that her mother was dead, and they could return to solving the problem all of this had interrupted.

He'd be there to comfort her, she'd realize Fitzroy had nothing to offer, and the two of them would settle down. Maybe even have a kid. *No.* The vision of Vicki in a maternal role, brought revision. *Maybe not a kid.*

He paused at the curb while a panel van pulled out of the apartment building's driveway, turning south toward the center of the city. A moment later, the food lay forgotten in the gutter as he sprinted forward to catch hold of the wild-eyed figure charging out onto the road.

"Vicki! What is it? What's happened?"

She twisted in his grip, straining to follow the van. "My mother . . ." Then the taillights disappeared and she sagged against him. "Mike, my mother . . ."

Gently, he turned her around, barely suppressing an exclamation of shock at her expression. She looked as though someone had ripped her heart out. "Vicki, what about your mother?"

She swallowed. "My mother was at the living room window. Looking in at me. The lock stuck, and when I got outside she was gone. She went away in that van. It's the only place she could have gone. Mike, we have to go after that van."

Cold fingers danced down Celluci's spine. Crazy words tucked in between shallow gasps for breath, but she sounded like she believed them. Moving slowly, he steered her back toward the apartment. "Vicki." His voice emerged tight and strained, her name barely recognizable, so he started again. "Vicki, your mother is dead."

She yanked herself free of his hands. "I know that!" she snarled. "Do you think I don't know that? So was the woman at the window!"

"Look, I only left her alone for a few minutes." Even as he spoke, Celluci heard the words echoed by a thousand voices who'd returned to find disaster had visited during those *few minutes* they were gone. "How was I supposed to know she was so close to cracking? She's never cracked before." He leaned his forearm against the wall and his face against the cushion of his arm. After that single outburst, Vicki had begun to shake, but she wouldn't let him touch her. She just sat in her mother's rocking chair and rocked and stared at the window. Years of training, of dealing with similar situations, seemed suddenly useless. If Mr. Delgado hadn't shown up, hadn't cajoled her into swallowing those sleeping pills—"And how can you be strong tomorrow if you don't sleep tonight, eh?"— he didn't know what he would have done; shaken her probably, yelled certainly, definitely not done any good.

Henry rose from his crouch by the window. There was no mistaking the odor that clung to the outside of the glass. "She didn't crack," he said quietly. "At least not the way you think."

"What are you talking about?" Celluci didn't bother to turn his head. "She's having hallucinations, for chrissakes."

"No. I'm afraid she isn't. And it seems I owe you an apology, Detective."

Celluci snorted but the certainty in Henry's voice made him straighten. "Apology? What for?"

"For accusing you of watching too many bad movies."

"I don't need another mystery tonight, Fitzroy. What the hell are you talking about?"

"I'm talking about," Henry stepped away from the window, his expression unreadable, "the return of Dr. Frankenstein."

"Don't bullshit me, Fitzroy. I'm not in the . . . Jesus H. Christ, you're not kidding, are you?"

He shook his head. "No. I'm not kidding."

Impossible not to believe him. *Werewolves, mummies, vampires; I should've expected this.* "Mother of God. What are we going to tell Vicki?"

Hazel eyes met brown, for once without a power struggle between them. "I haven't the faintest idea."

Seven

"I think we should tell her."

Arms crossed over his chest, Henry leaned against the wall near the windows. "Tell her that we think someone has turned her mother into Frankenstein's monster?"

"Yeah. Tell her exactly that." Celluci rubbed at his temples with the heels of his hands. It had been a very long night and he wasn't looking forward to morning. "Do you remember that little *incident* last fall?"

Henry's brows rose. There could be little doubt what the detective was referring to, although he'd hardly describe the destruction of an ancient Egyptian wizard as an *incident*. "If you're speaking of Anwar Tawfik, I remember."

"Well, I was thinking of something Vicki said, after it was all over, about there being a dark god out there who knows us and that if we give in to hopelessness and despair it'll be on us like a politician at a free bar." He sighed, a long, shuddering exhalation, and was almost too tired to breathe in again. "If it hasn't noticed her yet, it'll be on her soon. She's on the edge."

"Vicki?"

"You didn't see her."

Henry had difficulty believing Vicki would ever give in to anything, least of all to hopelessness and despair, but he recognized that under the present circumstances even the strongest character might succumb. "And you think that if we tell her what we suspect? . . ."

"She'll be furious and there's nothing that wipes out hopelessness and despair faster than righteous anger."

Henry thought about it, arms crossed, shoulder blades pressed against the wall. Tawfik's dark god continued to exist because the emotions it fed on were part of the human condition, but the three of them—he, Celluci, and Vicki—knew its name. If it wanted acolytes, and what god didn't, it would have to go to one of them. If Celluci was right about Vicki—and Henry had to admit that the years the mortal had known her should make him a fair judge—giving her anger as a protection would be the best thing they could do. There was also one other factor that shouldn't be ignored. "She'd never forgive us if we didn't tell her."

Celluci nodded, lips pursed. "There is that."

Silence reigned for a moment as they considered the result of having Vicki's fury directed at them. Neither figured their odds of survival would be particularly high, at least not as far as maintaining a continuing relationship went. Henry spoke first. "So, we'll tell her."

"Tell her what?" Vicki stood in the entrance to the living room, clothing creased, eyes shadowed, cheek imprinted with a fold from the pillowcase. Stepping forward carefully, she swayed and grabbed for the back of a chair, bracing herself against its support. She felt distant from her own body, an effect of the sleeping pills she'd barely managed to fight off. "Tell her that she's out of her mind? That she couldn't have seen her dead mother at the window?" Her voice rode crazy highs and lows; she couldn't seem to keep it steady.

"Actually, Vicki, we believe you." Henry's tone left no room for doubt.

Taken by surprise, Vicki blinked then tried to focus a scowl on Celluci. "You *both* believe me?"

"Yes." He met her scowl with one of his own. "We *both* believe you."

* * *

Celluci flinched as the Royal Dalton figurine hit the far wall of the living room and smashed into a thousand expensive bone china shards. Henry moved a little farther away from the blast radius.

"Goddamn, fucking, shit-eating bastards!" The rage that turned her vision red and roared in her ears, stuck in Vicki's throat, blocking the stream of profanity. She scooped up another ornament and heaved it as hard as she could across the room. As it shattered, she found her voice again. "How DARE they!"

Breathing heavily, she collapsed back onto the couch, teeth clenched against waves of nausea, her body's reaction to the news. "How can someone do that to another human being?"

"Science . . ." Celluci began, but Vicki cut him off—which was probably for the best as he wasn't entirely certain what he was going to say.

"This isn't science, Mike. This is my *mother*."

"Not your mother, Vicki," Henry told her softly. "Just your mother's body."

"Just my mother's body?" Vicki shoved at her glasses with her fist so they wouldn't see her fingers tremble. "I might not have been the world's best daughter, but I know my own mother, and I'm telling you that was my *mother* at the window. Not just her fucking body!"

Celluci sat down beside her on the couch and caught up one of her hands in both of his. He considered and discarded four or five comforting platitudes that didn't really seem to have any relevance and wisely decided to keep his mouth shut.

Vicki tried halfheartedly to pull her hand away, but when his fingers only tightened in response, she let it lie, saving her strength to throw into the anger. "I *saw* her. She was dead. I *know* dead. Then I saw her again at the window. And she was . . ." Again, a wave of nausea rose and crested and sullenly retreated. "She was *not dead*."

"But not alive." As the words themselves denied

consolation, Henry offered them as they were, un-adorned by emotion.

Once again, her mother's face rose up out of the darkness, eyes wide, mouth working silently. Celluci's grip became a warm anchor and Vicki used it to drag herself out of the memory. "No." She swallowed and a muscle jumped in her jaw. "Not alive. But up, and walking." For a moment, the thought that there'd been only a pane of glass between them, made it impossible to go on. *I want to scream and cry until all of this goes away and I don't have to deal with it. I want it to be last Saturday. I want to have answered the phone. I want to have talked to her, to have told her I love her, to have said good-bye.* Her whole body ached with the effort of maintaining control but of all the maelstrom barely held in check by will, she could only release the anger. "Someone did that to her. Someone at that university has committed the ultimate violation, the ultimate rape."

Celluci flinched. "At the university? Why at the university?"

"You said it yourself, science. It's hardly going to be someone at the fucking grocery store." She knuck-led her glasses again, then bent forward and swept her notes off the coffee table, the force of the blow scat-tering them as far as the apartment door. Her voice, in contrast, had gained rigid control. "This changes everything. We can find her now."

Reluctantly, Celluci released her hand; she'd ac-cepted all the comfort she was going to. He watched in silence as she pulled a blank sheet of paper toward her, wanting to shake her but not entirely certain why.

"All right. We know the body is still in the city, so we know where to look for the lowlife, sons of bitches who've done this to her." The pencil point snapped off against the paper, and she fought against the urge to drive it right through the table. "She's in the city. They're in the city."

"Vicki." Henry crossed the room to kneel by her

side. "Are you sure you should be doing this now?"
When she raised her head to look at him, the hair on
his arms lifted with the tension in the air.

"What am I supposed to do? Go to sleep?"

He could hear her heart pounding, hear the effects of
the adrenaline pumping through her system. "No . . ."

"I need to do this, Henry. I need to put things together. Build some sort of a structure out of this. I
need to do it now." The alternative was implicit in her
tone. *Or it will eat away at me until there's nothing of
me left.*

The hand that settled on his, just for an instant, was
so hot it nearly burned. Because he could do nothing
else, Henry nodded and moved to the rocker by the
door, from which he could watch her face. For the
moment, he would let her deal with her horror and her
anger in her own way.

He found it interesting that Celluci looked no happier about it than he felt. *We want to ride to her rescue
and instead we find ourselves* allowed *to help. Not
exactly a comfortable position for a knight errant to
be in.* But then, Vicki wasn't exactly a comfortable
woman to love.

"All right, shifting the emphasis from finding my
mother's body to finding the people who did this to
her, what are we looking for?" With a new pencil,
she etched "What?" across the top piece of paper.
"Someone who can raise the dead. Discounting the
Second Coming, as I doubt it was as simple as *pick
up your bed and walk,* we turn to science." She wrote
"A scientist" under the heading, then shuffled out a
fresh page and wrote "Where?"

Celluci leaned forward, old patterns winning out
over his concern. "All signs point to the university.
One, it's where you find scientists. Two, who can afford a private lab these days, especially containing the
equipment they'd have needed to . . ."

"Three," Vicki interrupted. The last thing she

wanted to deal with right now were the details of what had actually been done.

"Not the last thing," said a little voice in the back of her head.

"Three," she said again, slamming it over the certain knowledge that somehow, if she'd just answered the phone, all of this could have been prevented. "We've already determined it had to be someone who knew she was going to die. She worked at the university. Her friends were at the university. She had tests done at the university. Four, the campus is less than ten blocks south on Division Street. We're close." Her laugh held more hysteria than humor. "Even a dead woman could walk it."

"And five," Henry added softly, while Vicki fought to bridle her reactions again and Celluci's arm hovered helpless behind her back, certain that she'd refuse sympathy, unable not to offer it. "There is another, and it was *on* the campus tonight."

Vicki's chin came up, Henry's reminder that it wasn't strictly personal helping her to regain a little distance. Celluci's arm dropped back to his side. She wrote down his words verbatim, took another sheet, wrote "Why?" and had to fight for distance again. "At least we know what they wanted the body for. But why *my* mother? What was so special about her?"

"They knew she was going to die." Celluci couldn't find a way to finish the thought that wouldn't rub salt in emotions already raw and bleeding, so he drew in a fortifying breath and said instead, "Vicki, why don't you let me deal with this?"

"While I do what? Pour ashes on my head? Fuck you, Celluci. They knew she was going to die and they needed a fresh body. There. It's been said. Now let's go on."

His own nerves rubbed raw, Celluci shot a glance across the room at someone who might understand. *I didn't want to hurt her!*

I know. Henry's gaze flicked to Celluci's left and

back, adding as clearly as if he'd spoken aloud, *And she knows.*

"There wasn't an autopsy done." Vicki's pencil began to move again. "I expect that if you're going to get the body up and around, that's important. With a diagnosis of death in six months from heart failure, there'd be no need to do an autopsy when my mother had her heart attack. I wonder." She looked up and frowned. "Did they wait around for this other guy to die as well? We can check personnel, find out who else died recently, see if there's a connection to my mother, and trace it back."

With one hand she fanned the three sheets of paper. The other bounced the eraser end of the pencil on the tabletop. "Okay. That's what, where, why . . ." The pencil stilled. "I don't think we need to worry about *how.*"

A body stretched out on a slab, its grotesque shadow thrown upon a rough, rock wall. In the background, strange equipment. In the corners, darkness, broken by the faint gray tracery of a spider's web. Up above, a Gothic dome open to the night. Thunder cracks and lightning arcs down from the heavens. And Death is pushed aside.

"Vicki?"

"What!" She whirled on Celluci, eyes wide.

"Nothing." Now that he had her attention, he wasn't sure what to do with it. "You just looked a little . . ." *haunted.* He closed his teeth on the last word.

"Tired." Henry stepped smoothly into the pause. "Don't you think you should get some sleep?"

"No. We're not done. I'm not going to sleep until we're done." She knew she sounded a bit frantic, but she'd gone past the point where she cared. "So, what do we have for *who.* A scientist, or a group of scientists, at the university, who knew my mother was going to die, who has the knowledge to raise the dead and the arrogance to use that knowledge."

"Most criminals are arrogant." Celluci sagged back against the sofa cushions. "It's what makes them criminals. They think society's laws don't apply to them."

Vicki shoved at her glasses. "Very profound, Detective, but this is hardly like ripping off a corner store for beer money. We need a motive."

"If you had the ability to raise the dead, wouldn't that be motive enough?" Henry asked, his eyes suddenly very dark. "They're doing this because they *can* do it. They probably don't even see it as a crime—this godlike ability puts them above such petty concerns."

"Well," Celluci snorted, "you should know."

"Yes."

The single syllable lifted the hair on the back of Celluci's neck and he realized, belatedly, that no one understood the abuse of power quite so well as those who shared the potential.

Vicki ignored them both, shuffling her notes into a tidy pile, her movements jerky. "So we're looking at the university for an arrogant scientist with a medical background who knew my mother was about to die. That'll be like finding the needle in the proverbial haystack."

Celluci fought his attention free of Henry Fitzroy and back to the matter at hand. "What about your mother's boss?"

"Dr. Burke? I don't think so. My mother said she was the most gifted administrator she'd ever worked for, and that doesn't leave a lot of time to put into raising the dead."

"So? If she signed the death certificate she must be a medical doctor, whatever else she is. She knew your mother was going to die and, as department head, she's sure as shit in a position to acquire equipment for a secret lab." He shoved both hands up through his hair and tried to force his tired brain to function for just a while longer. "She's a place to start."

"I have an appointment to see her in the morning.

I'll see what I can find out.'' Her tone made it clear
she didn't expect to discover much.

"*We'll* see what *we* can find out."

"No, Mike." She shook her head, and wished she
hadn't as the room spun. "I want you to tie up a few
loose ends with Mr. Chen."

"Vicki, Tom Chen is a dead end."

She swiveled around to face him, bracing herself
against the back of the couch. "He still may be the
only end we've got. I don't need you with me, Mike."

"You shouldn't be doing this alone."

"I'm not. Unless you want to go home."

He looked across the room at Henry. Who was no
help. "Of *course* I'm not going home," he snarled.
Surrender might be his only option, but nothing said
he had to do it graciously. "So what do we do now?"

To his surprise, it was Henry who answered. "We
sleep. I have no choice. It's very nearly dawn. I can
feel the sun. You, Detective, have been up all night.
And, Vicki, I can smell the drugs in your system—you
need to sleep to clear the clouding from your mind."

"No, I . . ."

Henry cut her off with the lifting of an imperious
brow. "A few hours will make no difference to your
mother and a great deal to you." Crossing the room,
he extended a hand. "I can make you forget for a time,
if you like."

"I don't want to forget, thank you." But she took
his hand and pulled herself to her feet, a piece of broken china shattering further under the sole of her shoe.
His fingers were as cool as Celluci's had been warm.
An anchor of a different sort. "And, in spite of what
both of you think, I'm fully aware that self-abuse will
contribute nothing at all toward finding the shit eaters
who did this. I will sleep. I will eat. And then . . ."
Anger and exhaustion, equally applied, destroyed the
rest of the thought before she had it barely formed.
She gripped Henry's arm and stared intently into his

face. "I won't be able to wait for you. Sunset's just too damned far away."

He touched her cheek with his free hand and repeated, "Too damned far away. I couldn't have said it better, myself. But be careful while I'm not with you." His gaze lifted over her shoulder to meet Celluci's. "*Both* of you be careful."

Donald secured the slide, stared down at the spread of purple stain for a moment, sighed, and turned. "Cathy, I don't like what we're getting into here."

"Trouble with number eight?" Catherine glanced up from her dissection, brow furrowed, hands buried under one of number eight's decomposing organs.

"Number eight's past the point where it can give us any trouble," Donald snorted. "I'm more concerned with the dynamic duo over there."

Puzzled, Catherine peered over her mask at the two working isolation boxes. "I'm sure all the damage they took last night was superficial. You stitched number nine's lacerations closed. We both checked for mechanical overload. I adjusted their nutrient levels to compensate for the strain on the bacterial restructuring . . ."

"That's not what I meant." He ripped the paper off a candy, balled it up, and threw it in the general direction of a waste basket. "Don't you think those two have gone just a tad outside the parameters of the experiment?"

"Of course not." Catherine set a kidney down on a sterilized tray. "We're going to need tissue samples from the others for comparison."

"Yeah, yeah, I know. I'll break out the biopsy needle in a minute, but first we're going to have a chat about last night's little walkabout. *It* had nothing to do with Organ Regeneration through Tailored Bacteria or even Reanimation of the Human Body by Tailored Bacteria and Servomotors."

"What are you talking about? If last night wasn't

animation I don't know what is; you want them any
more animated, you'll have to call in Disney.''

"Was that a joke?" Donald demanded. "Because if
it was, it wasn't very funny. She," he pointed at Marjory Nelson's box, "wasn't supposed to go home and
he . . . well, he wasn't supposed to go anywhere.''

Catherine shrugged, her hands once again buried to
the wrist. "Obviously, feeding her own brain wave
patterns through the neural net stimulated buried
memories. Considering that when she was alive she
walked home from the Life Sciences building every
night for years, it was only logical that she follow that
programming. We should've anticipated it happening
and taken precautions.'' Her voice dropped into a fair
approximation of Dr. Burke's lecturing cadence. "The
more impulses are sent along a given memory trace,
the easier it becomes for later impulses to follow the
same circuit. *And* considering the pains we've taken to
teach number nine to follow us, I should think you'd
be pleased that he followed her. After all, you're the
one who said he wasn't learning anything.''

"Yeah, well, I'm also the one who says he doesn't
like this.'' He bit down hard on the candy in his mouth
and it crunched between his teeth. "I mean, suppose
we're not just re-creating physical responses.''

Catherine laid the second kidney beside the first. "I
don't know what you're talking about.''

"I'm talking about souls, Cathy!" His tone grew a
little shrill. "What if, because of what we've done,
Marjory Nelson has come back to her body?''

"Don't be ridiculous. We're not bringing back an
old life, we're creating new ones, like—putting new
wine in old skins.''

"You're not supposed to do that,'' Donald pointed
out acerbically. "The old wine taints the new.'' He
swiveled around on his stool and bent over the microscope. He could see there was no point in discussing
this; souls had no place in Cathy's world. And maybe
she was right. She was the certified genius, after all,

and it was her experiment. He was just in it for curiosity's sake—and for the final payoff, of course.

Still, he mused, the edge of his lower lip caught between his teeth, uncomfortably conscious of the questions that lay in the isolation boxes behind him, *I'd be happier if I knew we were remaking* Frankenstein *instead of* Night of the Living Dead. A moment's reflection reminded him that Frankenstein had not exactly had a happy ending. *Or a happy middle, for that matter.*

He could hear voices. Her voice and *his* voice. He couldn't hear what they were saying, but he could hear the tone.

They were arguing.

He remember arguing. How it ended in hitting. And pain.

He often argued with her.

Number nine didn't . . .

. . . didn't . . .

. . . didn't like that.

"Good morning, Dr. Burke. The coffee's ready."

"Good." Dr. Burke dropped her briefcase at the door to the inner office and circled back to the coffeepot. "You are a lifesaver, Mrs. Shaw."

"It's probably not as good as when Marjory made it," Mrs. Shaw sighed. "She always had such a way with coffee."

Her back to the room, Dr. Burke rolled her eyes and wondered how long the melodrama of office grieving would continue. Two days of every report, every memo, every little thing delivered with a eulogy was about as much as she could take. She lifted her mug off its hook and dropped three heaping spoonfuls of sugar into the bottom of it. If the university would just come through with the promised temporary—or better still, a permanent replacement for Marjory Nelson's position—she'd tell Mrs. Shaw to take a few days off.

Unfortunately, Dr. Burke topped up her mug and glared down into the dark liquid, *the wheels of academia grind geologically slow.*

Behind her, Mrs. Shaw turned on the radio. The Village People were just finishing up the last bars of "YMCA."

Dr. Burke turned and transferred her glare to the radio. "If they're doing another '70s retrospective, we're changing stations. I lived through disco once, I shouldn't have to do it again."

"This is CKVS FM, it's nine o'clock, and now the news. Police still have no leads in the vicious murder last night of a QECVI student on the Queen's University campus. The only witness to the crime is under observation at Kingston General Hospital and has not yet been able to give police an accurate description of the murderer. While the young woman was not physically hurt in the incident, doctors say she is suffering from shock. Both police and medical personnel report that until she was sedated she continued to scream, 'He looked dead. The guy looked dead.' Anyone with information concerning this tragic incident is asked to contact Detective Fergusson at Police Headquarters.

"Elsewhere in the city . . ."

"Isn't it awful." Mrs. Shaw dabbed at her eyes with the back of her hand. "That poor young man, cut down in his prime."

The guy looked dead. Dr. Burke's fingers tightened around the handle of her mug. *The girl obviously has an overactive imagination. This has nothing to do with . . .*

"The other stations had a much more complete report. She said that he lurched when he walked, that his skin was gray and cold, and that his expression never changed even while he was strangling her boyfriend. Terrifying. Just terrifying."

It was impossible. "Did she say what he was wearing."

"Some kind of athletic clothing. A tracksuit I think. Dr. Burke? Where are you going?"

Where was she going? She stared down at her coffee, then set the mug firmly down on the filing cabinet, the fingers of her other hand already taking a white-knuckled grip on the door handle. Thank God no one around the office *expected* her to smile. "I just remembered, I had a grad student running a program last night and I promised I'd check it this morning. Don't know why I bothered, he keeps getting it wrong."

Mrs. Shaw smiled and shook her head. "You bothered because you always hope they'll get it right. Oh, my." The smile disappeared. "Marjory's daughter will be coming by this morning."

Marjory Nelson's daughter, the ex-detective, the private investigator, was the last person she wanted to talk to right now. "Give her my apologies and . . . No. If she comes while I'm gone, ask her to wait. I'll be back as soon as I can." Better to know the direction Ms. Nelson was heading in the search for her mother's body. Information was knowledge; ignorance, a potential for disaster.

"There was a young man killed on campus last night. Do either of you know anything about it?"

Donald spun around so fast he nearly threw himself off the stool. "Dr. Burke! You startled me!"

She took another step into the lab, a muscle jumping in her jaw and her eyes narrow behind her glasses. "Just answer the question."

"The question?" He frowned, heart still racing, and sorted the words out of the fear. *There was a young man killed last night.* "Oh, fuck." In his memory, number nine staggered out into the light while screams sounded behind a building. "What, what makes you think we'd know anything?"

"Don't bullshit me, Donald." Dr. Burke used the voice that could command attention from the back row of a seven hundred and fifty seat lecture hall. Donald tried not to cringe. "There was a witness. Her description drew a pretty accurate picture of number nine, and what I want to know—" her palm slapped down on the table, the crack of flesh against metal echoing like a gunshot—"is what the hell was going on down here."

"He didn't do it on purpose." Catherine rose gracefully from behind number nine's isolation box and stood, both hands resting lightly on the curved lid.

"I was wondering where you were." Dr. Burke turned, nostrils flaring, the younger woman's calm acting as a further goad. Her gesture toward the box had a cutting edge. "As it has no purpose, being dead, it needs no defense. The two of you, however, have no such excuse. So let's *begin* with an explanation of why the experiments were taken from the lab."

"Uh, they weren't." Donald cleared his throat as she directed her basilisk gaze back at him but continued. He had no intention of being blamed for something that wasn't his fault. "They left on their own."

"They left on their own?" Her quiet repetition was less than reassuring. "They just decided to get up and go out on an evening constitutional, did they?" A sudden rise in volume slapped her words against the walls. "What kind of an idiot do you take me for!"

"He's right." Catherine raised her chin. "We locked the door behind us. When we came back, the door was unlocked, from the inside, and they were gone. We found number nine wandering on campus." Her fingers stroked the box comfortingly. "We found number ten just outside the apartment building she lived in when she was Marjory Nelson."

"She went home," Donald added.

Catherine sighed. "She merely followed old programming."

"You didn't see her face, Cathy."

"I didn't need to. I *know* the parameters of the experiment."

"Well, maybe they've changed!"

"Shut up, both of you." *Gray eyes suddenly snapped open, widening with an instant of recognition.* Dr. Burke closed her own eyes for a moment and when she opened them again, muttered. "Maybe this has gone too far."

Catherine frowned. "What has?"

"All of this."

"But, Dr. Burke, you don't understand. If number nine killed that boy, he acted on his own. It wasn't anything we programmed in. It means he *can* learn. He *is* learning."

"It means he—it—killed someone, Catherine. That boy is dead."

"Well, yes, and that's too bad, but nothing we can do will bring him back." She paused, weighing possibilities, frowned, and shook her head. "No. It's too late." Her eyes refocused. "But we *can* explore and develop this new data. Don't you understand? Number nine must be thinking. His brain is functional again!"

"Cathy!" Donald jumped down off his stool and came over to her, incredulity written across his face. "Don't *you* understand? Some guy is *dead*. This bit of your experiment," he whacked number nine's box, "is a killer and the other is, is . . ." He couldn't find the words. No, that wasn't exactly true. He knew the words. He just couldn't say them. Because if he said them, he might have to believe them. "Dr. Burke, you're right. This has gone too far. We've got to close down and get out of here before the police track number nine back to his lair!"

"Donald, be quiet. You're hysterical. The police do not now believe, nor are they likely to, that a dead man is out roaming around committing homicide."

"But . . ."

Dr. Burke silenced him with a look, her own crisis of conscience pushed aside in the light of new information. She hadn't actually considered the incident from the perspective of experimental results. This could indicate a giant step forward. "If number nine is thinking, Catherine, I *don't* like what it's thinking about.''

Two spots of color appeared on Catherine's cheeks. ''Well, yes, but he's thinking. Isn't that the important thing?''

''Perhaps,'' the older woman allowed. ''If it is actually thought and not merely reaction to stimuli. We may have to devise a new series of tests.''

Donald swallowed and tried again. ''But, Dr. Burke, that kid is dead!''

''Your point?''

''We have to do something!''

''What? Give ourselves up?'' She caught his gaze with hers and, after a moment, half smiled. ''I didn't think so. Terminate the experiment? That wouldn't bring him back to life.'' She squared her shoulders. ''That said, I am very annoyed about your carelessness. You will make certain it doesn't happen again. Remove them from their boxes only when absolutely necessary. Never leave them alone and unconfined. Have you run an EEG on number nine since it happened?''

Catherine's color deepened. ''No, Doctor.''

''Why not?''

''Number eight died in the night, and we had to begin . . .''

''Number eight has been dead for some time, Catherine, and isn't going anywhere. Run the EEG now. If there's a brain wave pattern in there, I want it recorded.''

''Yes, Doctor.''

''And for heaven's sake, keep them under control. I will not have my career destroyed by premature discovery. If anything like this happens again, I will not hesitate to pull the plug. Do you understand?''

''Yes, Doctor.''

''Donald?''

He nodded toward the second box. ''What about her? What if . . . what if . . .''

What if we've trapped Marjory Nelson's soul? She read the words off his face. Heard them whispered in the silence. And refused to share his fear. "We're here to answer *what ifs,* Donald; that's what scientists do. And now," Dr. Burke glanced at her watch. "I have an appointment with Marjory Nelson's daughter." She paused at the door and turned to face the lab again. "Remember. Anything else goes wrong and we're cutting our losses."

As her footsteps faded down the corridor, Donald drew a long and shaky breath. Things were getting just a little too deep for him. Maybe it was time he started thinking about cutting his own losses. "Can you believe that, Cathy? Some guy gets offed and she's *annoyed.*"

Catherine ignored him, her full attention on the muffled pounding coming from the box in front of her. She didn't like the way things were going. Surely Dr. Burke realized the importance of number nine acquiring independence and how vital it was to protect the integrity of the experiment. What did careers have to do with that? No, she didn't like the way things were going at all. But all she said was, "He doesn't like being confined."

Daughter.

The word filtered through the hum of machinery and the sound-deadening properties of the box itself. She used it to pick an end of thread from the tangled mass of memory.

She had a daughter.

There was something she had to do. •

Eight

Unable to remain still, Vicki paced the outer office, uncomfortably conscious of Mrs. Shaw's damp and sympathetic gaze following her every move. She didn't need sympathy, she needed information.

All right, so she hadn't reacted particularly well to being presented with a box of her mother's personal effects, but that was no reason for Mrs. Shaw to assume anything. If the last notation in the date book hadn't been, *Call Vicki,* she would've been fine.

"Would you like a cup of coffee, dear?"

"No. Thank you." Actually, she'd love a cup of coffee, but she couldn't face using her mother's mug. "Will Dr. Burke be long?"

"I don't think so. She just had to check on one of her grad students."

"Students? What does she teach?"

"Oh, she doesn't actually teach, she just takes a few of the grad students under her wing and helps them along."

"Medical students?"

"I'm not sure." Mrs. Shaw reached for a fresh tissue and dabbed at her eyes. "Your mother would know. She was Dr. Burke's *personal* secretary."

My mother isn't here. Vicki tried not to let the thought show on her face, given that the accompanying emotion was annoyance not grief.

"Your mother really respected Dr. Burke," Mrs. Shaw continued with a wistful glance across the room at the empty desk.

"She sounds like a person worth respecting," Vicki broke in before a flood of teary memories began. "She's got, what, two degrees?"

"Three. An MD, a doctorate in organic chemistry, and an MBA. Your mother always said hiring her to run this department was the smartest thing the university ever did. Most academics are not particularly good administrators and most administrators are completely insensitive to the needs of academia. Your mother called Dr. Burke a bridge between two worlds."

Why the hell does it have to keep coming back to my mother? Vicki wondered, as Mrs. Shaw fielded three phone calls in quick succession.

"Yes, Professor Irving, I'll see that she gets the message as soon as she comes in." Mrs. Shaw dropped the receiver back into the cradle and sighed. "That's how it goes all day. They *all* want a piece of her."

"I guess she doesn't have much time for lab work."

"Lab work? She barely has time to grab a bite to eat before someone needs her again." Patting the pile of memos, already impressive before the addition of the latest three, Mrs. Shaw's voice grew sharp. "They've got her running from meeting to meeting, solving this problem, solving that problem, burying her under forms and surveys and reports, annual this and semiannual that and biweekly the other . . ."

"And God only knows how I'm going to dig myself out without your mother's help."

Mrs. Shaw colored and Vicki turned to face the door.

"Sorry to keep you waiting, Ms. Nelson." Dr. Burke crossed the room and held out a hand for her memos. "But as you've already heard, I'm quite busy."

"No problem at all, Doctor." Something about that sturdy figure in the starched white lab coat had a calming effect, and Vicki followed her gesture into the inner office feeling more under control than she had in days. She suddenly remembered her mother describing her new boss—just after Dr. Burke had taken over the department—as being so completely self-assured that the urge to question anything became lost in her vicinity. Vicki'd laughed at the time, but now she thought she could see what her mother had meant. She'd felt a bit of the effect herself, earlier in the week. It had been Dr. Burke who'd grounded her and sent her to the hospital morgue and Dr. Burke she'd turned to for a eulogy.

Before they'd discovered a eulogy would be unnecessary.

As Vicki settled into one of the almost comfortable wood and leather chairs, Dr. Burke moved around behind the desk and sat down, dropping the dozen or so pink squares of paper into a tidy pile. "I'm not usually in quite this much demand," she explained, shooting an annoyed glare at the pile. "But it's end of term and bureaucratic nonsense that could have been taken care of months ago has to be dealt with immediately."

"You can't delegate?"

"Science and Administration speak two different languages, Ms. Nelson. If I delegate, I end up having to translate. Frankly, it's much easier just to do it myself."

Vicki recognized the tone; she'd used it herself once or twice. "I imagine you'd rather be, oh, fiddling about with test tubes or something?"

"Not at all." Dr. Burke smiled, and there was no mistaking the sincerity behind her words. "I very much enjoy running other people's lives, seeing that each cog in a very complicated machine continues to run in its appointed place." It might have been more accurate to say, *in the place I appoint,* but Dr. Burke had no intention of allowing that much insight into her character. *Now that we have established I enjoy my job, shall we get on with the investigation, Ms. Nelson?* "Mrs. Shaw tells me you want to ask about the tests I ran on your mother."

"That's right." An early call to Dr. Friedman had

determined that her mother's doctor had known about
the tests, so they probably had nothing to do with . . .
with the end result. But they were a place to start.
Vicki pulled a pad of paper and a pen from the depths
of her shoulder bag. "I assume they had to do with
her heart condition?"

"Yes. Although I haven't practiced medicine for
some time, I am a medical doctor and your mother,
understandably upset, wanted a second opinion."

"And you told her?"

"That she had perhaps six months to live without
corrective surgery. Pretty much exactly what her own
doctor told her."

"Why didn't she go in for the surgery?"

"It's not that easy," Dr. Burke said, leaning back
in her chair and lacing her fingers across her stomach.
"There are always waiting lists for major surgery, especially transplants, which is what your mother would
have needed, and with budget cuts . . ."

Vicki's pen gouged through the paper and her voice
emerged through clenched teeth. "So Dr. Friedman
said." *My mother could've died from god-damned
fucking budget cuts.* "I'd like to see copies."

"Of the tests? I didn't keep any. I gave copies to
your mother, who, I assume, gave them to her doctor,
but I saw no point in keeping a set myself." Dr. Burke
frowned. "I did what I could for her. Do you doubt
my diagnosis, Ms. Nelson?"

"No. Of course not." *So you were there for her
and I wasn't. That's not the issue now.* "Who else
knew about the tests?"

"Why?"

The question came as no surprise, and Vicki realized it came primarily in response to her aggressive
tone. She'd have asked it herself if someone slammed
a question at her with that amount of force. *Brilliant
interrogation technique, Nelson. Forgotten everything
you ever learned?* Maybe she should've brought Celluci. Maybe she wasn't thinking clearly. *No. I don't*

need him holding my hand. I've worked through anger before. She'd been one of the best; top of her class; the fair-haired girl of the Metro Police. She took a deep breath and fought for some semblance of professionalism. "My mother's body is missing, Dr. Burke. I intend to find it and any information you might be able to give me can only help."

Dr. Burke leaned forward, both hands flat on the desk. "You think that the body was taken by someone who knew she was going to die?"

Celluci'd always said she was a lousy liar. Vicki looked Dr. Burke in the eye and decided not to even make the attempt. "Yes. That's exactly what I think."

Dr. Burke held her gaze for a moment, then sat back again. "Besides myself and Dr. Friedman, I can only be certain of Mrs. Shaw, although it's likely Dr. Friedman's nurse knew. I didn't tell anyone, Mrs. Shaw might have, and your mother could have mentioned it to friends, of course."

"She never mentioned it to me," Vicki snarled and then pressed her lips tightly shut, afraid of what else might slip out. She hadn't intended to say that.

"Given that we were using university equipment," Dr. Burke continued, graciously ignoring the outburst, "I can't guarantee that no one else knew about the testing, you understand."

"Yes." A single word seemed safe enough. Pity she had to use more; every syllable carried more heat than the last and there didn't seem to be anything she could do about it. "I need to speak with those members of your department my mother came into frequent contact with."

"That would be all of them," Dr. Burke told her dryly. "But surely you don't believe that someone in my department is responsible?"

"They do seem to be the first people I should check, don't they?"

Answering a question with a question. Nice try, Ms. Nelson, but I have no intention of surrendering con-

trol. "I'd certainly be interested in your reasons for thinking so."

As her reasons for thinking so were based solely on a midnight visit she had no intention of mentioning, Vicki found herself momentarily at a loss. "The members of your department are scientists."

"And why would a scientist take your mother's body?" Dr. Burke kept her expression outwardly neutral while inwardly she kicked Donald's careless butt. She knew Catherine couldn't be counted on to consider the more mundane aspects of the situation, but she'd expected better of him. It was obvious that last night's side trip had been observed. Nothing else but the knowledge that a dead woman was up and walking around could logically account for the sudden obstinate certainty that someone at the university had to be responsible. "It could just as easily," she continued, "have been taken by a spurned lover. Have you looked into that possibility?"

"She had no lover," Vicki ground out, "spurned or otherwise."

Behind a mask of polite apology, Dr. Burke enjoyed the reaction. Of course she didn't. Mothers never do. Aloud she said, "That brings us back to my scientists, then. Shall I have Mrs. Shaw make some phone calls for you, set up appointments?" It was a large university and there were ways to make it larger still.

"If you would. Thank you." Well aware that Dr. Burke's assistance could cut through the time-consuming tangle of academic red tape, Vicki had been about to ask. That Dr. Burke remained on the list of potential suspects devalued that assistance not at all. The manner of the assistance, could, in fact, be used as further evidence. "I need to talk to the faculty in the school of medicine." She'd start with the obvious. Later, if necessary, she'd widen the circle. If necessary, she'd tear the bloody university apart, limestone block by limestone block.

"I'll do what I can. If I might make a suggestion,

your mother was quite friendly with a Dr. Devlin, a cellular biologist." *And talking with that old Irish reprobate should keep you busy sorting fact from fancy for days.* "In fact, he comfortably covers both our theories as I believe he was very fond of her."

"*Both* our theories?"

"The scientist and the spurned lover."

Just for a moment, Vicki wondered if her mother *had* gotten involved with someone who'd refused to surrender to death; wondered if a twisted love had tried to force a return of life and created the travesty of her mother she'd seen at the window. *No. Impossible. Henry said there was another one. And besides, she'd have told me if she'd met someone new.*

The way she told you about her heart condition? asked a small voice.

Dr. Burke watched the emotional storm playing out across her visitor's face and decided the experiment was in no immediate danger. Although last night's unfortunate lapse in security had brought Ms. Nelson closer to the truth, when it came right down to it, close didn't count. *And now I've given her something new to think about. Dr. Devlin should be in for an interesting interview.* When that played out, another wild goose could always be found.

In the meantime, it was obvious to even the most casual observer—which she most certainly was not—that Marjory Nelson's daughter rode a precarious balance between rigid control and a complete breakdown. An emotional teeter-totter that could only get in the way of an objective investigation and a situation easy to exploit.

"It's amazing," she murmured, almost as though she were speaking to herself, "how much you resemble your mother."

Vicki started. "Me?"

"You're taller, of course, and your mother wore no glasses, but the line of your jaw is identical and your mouth moves very much the way hers did."

Did . . . Her mother's face rose up in memory, a sheet of glass between them, eyes wide, mouth silently working.

"In fact, you have many of the same mannerisms."

Vicki desperately tried to banish the horror her mother had become and replace it with an earlier memory. The sheet lifted, the gray and waxy pallor of death, the chemical smell of the hospital morgue . . . In the memory before that, a phone rang on, unanswered.

"Ms. Nelson? Are you all right?"

"Fine." The word was a warning.

Dr. Burke stood, satisfaction covered with polite regret. "If you have no further questions, I'm afraid I have a list as long as my arm of meetings to attend. I'll have Mrs. Shaw set up those appointments for you."

Vicki shoved her notes into her bag and stood as well, jabbing at her glasses. "Thank you," she said, forcing her mouth to form the conversational phrases. "And thank you for your time this morning." Throwing the bag up onto her shoulder, she headed quickly toward the door. She neither knew nor cared if she'd covered all she'd intended to. She wanted out of that office. Of that building. She wanted to be somewhere where no one knew her mother. Where no one could see reflections of the dead in her face.

"Ms. Nelson? We miss your mother around here." Intended to be a parting dig at damaged defenses, Dr. Burke found to her surprise that she meant what she was saying and instead of twisting the knife, finished simply with, "The office seems empty without her."

Halfway out the door, Vicki turned and acknowledged the observation with a single nod. She couldn't trust herself to speak and wished, just for that instant, that she'd listened to Celluci and not come here alone.

Dr. Burke spread her hands and her voice picked up the cadence of a benediction. "I guarantee, she didn't suffer at the end."

* * *

"No. I'm sorry, Detective, but none of these photographs are of the Tom Chen that we employed."

Celluci pulled the shot of Tom Chen, medical student, out of the pile. "You're sure about this one?"

"Quite. Our Mr. Chen had slightly longer hair, more prominent cheekbones, and a completely different eyebrow line. We reshape a lot of faces in this business, Detective," the younger Mr. Hutchinson continued in response to Celluci's silent question. "We become used to observing dominant characteristics."

"Yeah, I suppose you do." Celluci slid the grainy black and white photographs back into the large manila envelope. Tom Chen, or whatever his name actually was, was not now attending medical school at Queen's, nor had he graduated from the program over the last three years.

Detective Fergusson had been more than willing to call the registrar's office on campus and suggest they release the pictures.

"No problem," the Kingston police officer had declared with complete insincerity. "I'm more than willing to humor ex-Detective Nelson and her wild corpse chase." The distinctive sound of hot coffee being slurped from a cardboard cup echoed over the line. "You catch the news this morning? Half the fucking force goes out with some kind of spring flu and some asshole starts strangling young lovers. We got a hysterical witness—who's seen Michael Jackson's 'Thriller' video one too many times, if you ask me—and no suspects. And I don't need to tell *you* that the fresher the corpse, the higher the priority. If a phone call will keep your girlfriend happy and off my back while I deal with this new situation, it's worth the two minutes it'll take."

Celluci'd been tempted to tell him that the two were connected in one final attempt at enlisting law and order against whatever it was that Vicki and Fitzroy were dispensing but at the last minute decided he'd better not. *Your murderer is a reanimated corpse, Detective. How do I know? A vampire told me.* Kingston had a large psychiatric facility and he had no intention of ending up in it.

Meanwhile, the search for Igor moved no further ahead.

"All right, Mr. Hutchinson." Time to try another angle. "You said that all funeral directors have to serve a four-week observation period at a funeral home before they're accepted into a training program."

The younger Mr. Hutchinson leaned back in his chair. "That's correct."

"Well, where do these observers come from?"

"From the applicants to the program at Humber College in Toronto."

"So this young man, whoever he was, had to have applied to that program?"

"Oh, yes, *and* gone through an interview. The Health Sciences people try very hard to weed out unsuitable candidates before they're placed for observation."

Celluci frowned. "So, it was just chance that Ig . . . Tom Chen, for lack of a better name, ended up here?"

"No, not at all. He asked to come here. Said he'd been impressed by the way we handled the funeral of his aunt some years before and wanted to work with us." Mr. Hutchinson sighed. "All fabricated, I presume, but at the time we were flattered and agreed to take him on. He was a very pleasant fellow and everyone liked him."

"Yeah, well everyone makes a bad call now and then." Celluci finished scrawling a note to call Humber College, shoved his notebook in his pocket and stood, glad to be leaving. Funeral homes, with their carpets and flowers and tastefully arranged furniture gave him the creeps. "I wouldn't worry about it. I don't suppose you get much opportunity to practice character assessment."

Mr. Hutchinson rose as well, his expression stony.

"Our services are for the benefit of the living, Detective," he snapped. "And I assure you, we are quite as capable of character assessment as, say, the police department. Good day."

As he had nothing more to ask, Celluci accepted the dismissal. Once outside, he snorted and headed for the nearest bus stop—with the suspect's transit habits still their only concrete clue, he'd left his car at the apartment building. "Quite as capable of character assessment as the police department," he repeated, digging for change. "Just a little sensitive there, aren't we?" Still, he supposed that funeral directors were as sick of stereotypes as, well, police officers, so the comment hadn't been entirely undeserved.

Swinging up onto the Johnson Street bus, he glanced back at the seat just in front of the rear door, hoping for a young, Oriental male, eating candy. The seat was empty.

"Of course it is," he muttered, sitting in it himself. "Or it would be too easy."

"Violent Crimes. Detective-Sergeant Graham."

"Why the hell aren't you out working? Jesus, I can't take my eyes off you for a second."

"Hello, Mike. I miss you, too."

Celluci grinned and braced the phone against his shoulder. "Listen, Dave, I need you to do me a favor."

On the other end of the line, his partner sighed with enough force to rattle the wires between Toronto and Kingston. "Of course you do. Whey else would you call?"

"I want you to call Humber College and talk to someone in Health Sciences about a Tom Chen who applied recently to their funeral director's program."

"Humber . . . Health Sciences . . . Tom Chen . . . Okay. What do you want to know?"

"Everything they know."

"About this Chen?"

"No, about life in general." Celluci rolled his eyes at his reflection in the etched mirror over the couch. "The name's an alias, but that shouldn't make any difference to your inquiries. And I need the info ASAP."

The wires rattled again. "Of course you do. How's she holding up?"

"Vicki?"

"No, her mother, asshole."

"About as well as can be expected, all things considered."

"Yeah. Well . . ." There was a pause while things were considered. "So, you going to be at Vicki's mother's place for the next couple of days?"

Celluci looked around the apartment. "Far as I know. You got the number?"

"Yeah. I'll call collect."

"Cheap Scots bastard," Celluci muttered and hung up, smiling. Dave Graham was a good cop and a loyal friend. Except in their dedication to their work, they were nothing alike, and their partnership was both successful and uncomplicated.

"Uncomplicated; I could use a little of that right now." Celluci headed for the kitchen and the coffee maker. "Vicki's dead mother is paying house calls. Some joker who's equally dead is murdering teenagers. And there's a vampire in the closet."

He froze, a step half taken.

"A completely helpless vampire in the closet."

Even with the door braced from the inside, it would still be so easy to remove his rival. To have Vicki to himself. To let in just enough sunlight . . .

He finished the step and picked up the coffeepot. Fitzroy was too smart, had lived too long, to be in that closet if he thought he was in any danger. Celluci shook his head at the subtlety of trust and lifted a mug of coffee in salute.

"Sleep well, you son of a bitch."

* * *

Rubbing at her temples with both hands, Vicki exhaled noisily. Adrenaline had run out some time before and she was mind-numbingly tired. The physical exhaustion she could cope with—had coped with many times in the past—but emotionally she felt as though she'd spent the day being flayed and then salted.

Dr. Burke had begun it, with her sudden sympathy, and then Dr. Devlin had finished the job. He had been more than fond of her mother and, still devastated by her death, had, in typical Irish fashion, poured out his grief. Vicki, unable to stop him, had sat dry-eyed while the middle-aged professor railed against the cruelties of fate, told of how universally Marjory Nelson had been liked and respected, and went on in detail about how proud Marjory Nelson had been of her daughter. Vicki knew how to stop him— *"Sometimes,"* the cadet instructor had told them, *"you want to give the person you're questioning their head. Let them talk about whatever they want, we'll teach you how to separate the gold from the dross. But sometimes, you have to cut it short and take control—"* she just couldn't do it.

She didn't want to hear what a wonderful person her mother had been, how much they'd all depended on her, how much they missed her, but not listening felt like a betrayal. And she'd done enough of that already.

The box of personal effects she'd taken from the office sat accusingly at the end of the coffee table. She hadn't been able to do more with it than get it back to the apartment and even that hadn't been easy. It had weighed a lot more than it looked like it should.

All at once, she became aware that Celluci had just asked her a question and she had no idea what it had been. "Sorry," she said, shoving her glasses back into place with enough force to drive the plastic bridge into her forehead.

He exchanged a look with Henry and although she didn't catch the content, she didn't like the possibilities. Separately, she could barely handle them. At this point a united front, on any issue, would be beyond her.

"I asked," he repeated levelly, "about Dr. Burke's grad students. You told us she had some. Any chance they could be doing the work under her supervision?"

"I doubt it. According to Mrs. Shaw, when I went back for that appointment list, one's into bacteria, a couple have something to do with computers, and one—and I'm paraphrasing here—is a fuck-up who can't make up his mind. I'll . . ." Celluci opened his mouth but she corrected herself before he could speak, "we'll check them out further tomorrow."

Henry sat forward in his chair, his expression one she'd begun to recognize as his hunting face. "So you *do* suspect Dr. Burke?"

"I don't know what I think about Dr. Burke." Looking back on the interview, all Vicki could hear was the doctor's voice saying quietly, *"It's amazing how much you resemble your mother."* Which was an irrelevant observation at the best of times and doubly so now; her mother was dead. "She's got the necessary arrogance, that's for damned sure, and the intelligence and the background, but all anyone can talk about is what a brilliant administrator she is." She shrugged and wished she hadn't; her shoulders felt as though they were balancing lead weights. "Still, until we know she *didn't* do it, she stays on the list. I think, though, we can safely ignore Dr. Devlin."

"Why?"

"Because he could never have kept the research secret. If he were doing *this*," she made the innocuous pronoun sound like a curse, "he wouldn't be able to keep from telling the world. Besides, I gather he's a devout Irish Catholic and until recently, they weren't even keen on autopsies."

"He's also a scientist," Celluci pointed out. "And he could be acting."

"All the world's a stage," Henry added quietly, "and we but players on it."

Celluci rolled his eyes. "What the hell is that supposed to mean."

"That if you do talk to the person responsible, they're going to lie."

"That's why you build a body of evidence, Fitzroy. To catch the liars. We know more tonight than we did last night and we'll know more tomorrow than we do now. Eventually the truth will out. Nothing stays hidden forever."

We haven't got forever. Henry wanted to say. *Every moment that passes eats into her. How long before there's nothing left but a cause?* "We need a smoking gun," he said instead.

Celluci snorted in disbelief. The phrase sounded ridiculous coming from Henry's mouth. "You *have* been reading the literature."

Henry ignored him. "I'm going to track the other one; the male who killed the teenager. There were too many police around to do it last night. If I find him, I'll find your mother's body as well."

"And then?" Vicki demanded. "What do we do then?"

"We give them to Detective Fergusson. Lead him to the laboratory. Let him deal with the . . ."

"Wait a minute," Celluci interrupted. "You're actually suggesting we let the police handle this?"

"Why not? We have no one to protect this time, except me, and unlike ancient Egyptian gods of darkness or demons summoned up out of hell, mad scientists should fall within the capabilities of the law."

Celluci closed his mouth. Wasn't that *his* argument?

"Henry, you can't go to the police," Vicki began.

Henry smiled and cut her off. "I won't. I'll deliver the information to you. You'll deliver it to the police. Detective Fergusson will be so happy to have his murderer, I think he'll let you be a bit vague as to where and how you found it."

Vicki's lips almost curved. "You know, most guys just give a girl flowers or candy."

"Most guys," Henry agreed.

The air in the apartment seemed suddenly charged and Celluci felt the hair on his arms rise. Fitzroy's eyes had darkened and even from across the room he thought he could see Vicki's reflection gazing out of their depths. The sudden flash of understanding snapped the pencil he held. Neither of them noticed.

Vampire.

How often do vampires have to feed?

Had Fitzroy fed at all since they'd come to Kingston?

Yeah, well you're not feeding in front of me, boyo. And you're not sending me off to never-never land again while you . . . while you . . .

While you offer her a comfort she won't take from me.

Another look at Henry's face and he knew the offer wouldn't be made at his expense. Somewhere, somewhen, they'd gone beyond that.

"I've got to get out of here." His voice brusk but determined, Celluci stood. *I can't believe I'm doing this.* "I need a nice long walk to clear my head. Help me think." Half a dozen long-legged strides took him to the door. He yanked his jacket off the coat stand and charged out into the hall before they had a chance to try and stop him. *'Cause I sure as shit can't offer this more than once.*

Safely outside, door closed behind him, he sagged against the wall and closed his eyes for a second, amazed at what he'd just done. *Yes, ladies and gentlemen, see a man act like a fool completely of his own free will.*

But he had the day.

Was it fair to deny Fitzroy the night?

And anyway, he shoved both hands up through his hair. *It should be Vicki's choice. Not a choice forced on her by my presence.*

If you love something, let it go. . . .

"Jesus H. Christ. What kind of idiot takes advice from a fucking T-shirt?"

Vicki stared across the room at the apartment door and then turned to stare at Henry. "Did he just? . . ."

"Leave?" Henry nodded, more than a little amazed himself. "Yes."

She couldn't get her brain around it. "Why?"

"I believe he is removing himself as an obstacle between us."

"Between us? You mean so we can? . . ."

"Yes."

"Why that arrogant shit!" Her brows snapped down, but she was so tired the exclamation had little force. "Didn't he think I might have something to say about that?"

Henry spread his hands, the fine red-gold hairs glinting in the lamplight. "No one's stopping you from saying it, Vicki."

She glared at him for a moment longer, then sighed. "All right. Valid point. But I think you two are getting along too god-damned well."

"Wouldn't it make things easier for you if Detective-Sergeant Celluci and I got along?"

"That depends." She sank back against the sofa cushions and added dryly, "On how *well* you get along."

"Vicki!" Her name dripped with exaggerated shock. "Surely you don't think . . ."

It took her a moment to catch the implication and when she did, she couldn't stop herself from giggling. It had to be the exhaustion; she never giggled. "You wish. Michael Celluci is straight enough to draw lines with."

Henry's smile changed slightly and his eyes darkened, enough of the hunter showing to make his desire plain. "Then I shall have to find someone else."

Vicki swallowed, if only to move her heart down out of her throat. He was making no attempt to catch her gaze, to draw her into his power. If she said no, and she could taste the word on her tongue, he would hunt elsewhere. *But he needs me.* Even from across the room, she could feel his Hunger. It wouldn't be a betrayal. There was nothing more she could do for her mother tonight. More important, his needs covered hers and behind their camouflage, she could, if only for the duration, let go.

He needs me. Repeated, it drew attention from the more dangerous, *I need him.*

"Vicki?"

His voice stroked heat into her skin. "Yes."

Celluci watched Henry cross the parking lot, and worked at unclenching his teeth. There was nothing in the way the other man—*vampire-slash-romance writer*, Celluci savagely corrected the thought—moved to give any indication of what had gone on in the apartment. *Well, he doesn't brag. I'll give the little fucker that.*

"Detective."

"Fitzroy."

"Be quiet when you go into the apartment. She's asleep."

"How is she?"

"Some of the knots have loosened. I wish I could say they'll still be that way in the morning."

"You shouldn't have left her alone." *I left her alone and look what happened.* They both heard the corollary. They both ignored it.

"I'm listening to her heartbeat, Detective. I can be at her side in seconds. And this is as far as I'll go until you're ready to take over."

Celluci snorted and wished he could think of something to say.

Henry lifted his face and breathed deeply of the night. "It's going to rain. I'd best not linger."

"Yeah." Hands shoved into his jacket pockets, Celluci pushed himself up off his car. All right, so he hadn't walked far. He hadn't said he was going to. He wanted to believe that Fitzroy had left her no choice but he knew better; he wouldn't have left if that had been even a possibility.

"Michael."

Pulled around by his name, he tried not to let any of what he was feeling show on his face. It wasn't hard. He didn't *know* exactly what he was feeling.

"Thank you."

Celluci started to ask, *For what?,* but he bit it back. Something in Henry's tone—he'd call it honesty if forced to put a name to it—denied a facetious response. Instead, he nodded, once, and asked, "What would you have done if she'd said no?" Even before the last word left his mouth, he wondered why he was asking.

Henry's gesture seemed to move past the overlapping yellow-white of the streetlights. "We're in the middle of a small city, Detective. I'd have managed."

"You'd have gone to a stranger?"

Red-gold brows, darkened by shadow, rose. "Well, I wouldn't have had time to make friends."

Sure, take the cheap shot. "Don't you know there's a fucking epidemic on?"

"It's a disease of the blood, Detective. I *know* when someone is infected and am therefore able to avoid it."

Celluci tossed the curl of hair back off his forehead. "Lucky you," he grunted. "I still don't think that you should . . . I mean . . ." He kicked at the gravel and swore when a rock propelled by his foot clanged off the undercarriage of his car. Why the hell was he worrying about Fitzroy anyway? The son of a bitch had lasted centuries, he could take care of himself. *Trusting him is one thing. And I'm not sure I do. I am certainly not beginning to like him. Uh-uh. No way. Forget it.* "Look, even if you can sense it, you shouldn't be . . ." *Be what? Jesus, normal vocabulary is not up to this.* ". . . doing it with strangers," he finished in a hurry.

Henry's lips curled up into a speculative smile. "That could be difficult," he said softly, "if we stay here for very long. Even if she were willing, I can't feed off Vicki every time the Hunger rises."

The night air suddenly got hard to breathe. Celluci yanked at his collar.

"And after all," Henry continued, the corners of his eyes crinkling with amusement, "there's only one other person in this city who I can't consider a stranger."

It took Celluci the same moment it had taken Vicki. "You wish," he snarled, whirled on one heel, and stomped toward the apartment building.

Smile broadening, Henry watched him go, listening to the angry pounding of Celluci's heart as he charged around the corner and out of sight. It had been less than kind to tease the mortal when he'd been honestly concerned but the opportunity had been impossible to resist.

"And if I wished," he reminded the night when he had it to himself again. "I would."

Nine

The night held countless different kinds of darkness, from the wine-dark sky arching over the Mediterranean, to the desert cut into sharp relief by edged moonlight, to cities that broke it into secret pieces with a kaleidoscope of bright lights. Henry knew them all. He was never certain whether the night had more faces than the day or if he'd merely had more time to find them—four hundred and fifty years rather overshadowed barely seventeen. Were those faces each, in its own way, truly beautiful, or was he finding beauty in inevitability?

Walking south along Division Street, toward the university, he drank in yet another night. The return of a sun he would never see had warmed the earth and the scent of new growth nearly overwhelmed asphalt and concrete and several thousand moving bits of flesh and blood. Infant leaves, still soft and fragile, danced tentatively on the wind, the whispers of their movement a counterpoint to the hum of electrical wires and the growl of automobiles and the never-ending sounds of humanity. He knew if he took the time to look in the shadowed places of the city, he would find others pulled back to the hunt by the rising temperatures; some on four legs, most on two.

He crossed Princess Street, eyes hooded against the blaze of light bracketing the intersection. A young woman waiting for the opposing green studied him as he passed and he acknowledged her interest with a slow smile. The heat of her reaction followed him for several paces. When it came right down to it, cities, and their people, were very much the same the world over.

And thank God for that, he conceded with a silent salute to the heavens. *It makes* my *night so much easier.*

Division Street spilled him out onto the actual campus and he slid into the shadow of a recessed doorway as a police car drove by. Twenty-four hours after a murder, they were likely to ask a number of questions he didn't want to answer. Questions like, *where are you headed* and *why.* Over the centuries, he'd found that the easiest way to deal with the police was not to deal with them at all.

By the time he reached the tiny hidden parking lot where the murder had actually occurred, he'd avoided that same cruiser twice more. The Kingston constabulary were taking their media-delivered promise of increased patrols very seriously.

Senses extended, Henry ducked under the yellow police tape and slowly crossed the asphalt. At the blurry chalk lines that isolated the victim's final resting place, he crouched and laid his fingers lightly on the pavement. The boy's death lingered; the scent of his terror, the imprint of his body, the instant of change when flesh became meat. Layered over it, layered over the whole area, was the other death; the scent of putrefaction, of chemicals, of machines, of death gone very, very wrong.

Straightening, trying not to gag, Henry's hand traced the sign of the cross. Abomination. The word lodged in his brain and he couldn't shake it loose. He supposed it was as good a word as any to describe the creature whose trail he had to follow. Abomination. Perversion. Evil. Not of itself perhaps, but evil in the creation of it.

When he tracked the creature to its sanctuary, if he found Marjory Nelson beside it, he would take steps to ensure that Vicki never saw what had been made of

her mother. The one quick glimpse she'd already had
was all that anyone should be required to live with.

"Geez, Cathy, don't you ever go home?"

Catherine looked up from the monitor and frowned.
"What do you mean?"

"You know, *home.*" Donald sighed. "Home with a
bed, and a television, and a refrigerator full of con-
diments and half a container of moldy cottage
cheese." He shook his head and laced his voice with
exaggerated concern. "I'm not getting through to you
here, am I?"

It was Catherine's turn to sigh. "I know what home
is, Donald."

"Can't prove it by me. You're always *here.*"

Catherine's gaze swept the lab and her expression
smoothed into contentment. "This is where my work
is," she said simply.

"This is where your life is," Donald snapped.
"Don't you even go home to sleep?"

"Actually," pale cheeks darkened, "I have a bit of
a place set up down in the subbasement."

"What? Here? In this building?"

"Well, sometimes the experiments can't be left or
they have to be checked three or four times in the night
and my apartment is way out on Montreal Street by
the old train station and, well, it just seemed more
practical to use one of the empty rooms here." The
explanation spilled out in a rush of words. She
watched, lower lip caught between her teeth, as Donald propped a buttock on the corner of a stainless steel
table, pulled a candy from his pocket, unwrapped it,
and popped it in his mouth.

"I'll be damned," he said at last, grinning broadly.
"You never struck me as the squatting type."

"It's not squatting!" she protested hotly. "It's . . ."

"Caretaking." When she continued to scowl, he
tried again. "Behaving in a responsible manner toward your experiments?"

"Yes. That's it exactly."

Donald nodded, his grin returned. "Squatting." She could rationalize any way she liked, but that's still what it was, not that he disapproved. In fact, he considered it an amazing show of initiative from someone he considered too tied to her test tubes. "Why the subbasement?"

She glared at him for a moment before she answered. "There aren't any windows to seal off." They both glanced at the plywood covered west wall. "And I'm less likely to be disturbed."

"Disturbed?" His brows jumped for his hairline. "What are you doing down there besides sleeping?"

"Well . . ." Catherine rubbed the top edge of the monitor with the ball of her thumb, her eyes on the screen.

"Come on, Cathy, you can tell me."

"You won't mention it to Dr. Burke?"

He traced an X across his chest. "Cross my heart and hope to die."

"I've got a small lab set up down there."

Rolling his eyes, Donald pulled out another candy. "Why am I not surprised? You've got yourself a secret hideout, a perfect opportunity for debauchery, and what do you do in it? You work." He dropped off the table and walked across the room to a clutter of microscopes and chemicals and a small centrifuge. "You work all the time, Cathy. That's *not* normal. I can't remember even being in this lab without you being here, too."

"Like you said, I have a sense of responsibility to my work."

"Like I said, you're looney tunes."

Her chin rose. "It's late. What are *you* doing here?"

Instead of answering, he began to wander around the room, fidgeting with the laser array, peering at a readout, finally drumming his fingers down the length of one of the isolation boxes. "Hey! Hang on!" He jerked a thumb at the shadowed cubbyhole between the isolation box and the wall. "What's he doing out? Dr. Burke said . . ."

"To remove them from their boxes only when absolutely necessary. To never leave them alone and unconfined. He isn't alone, I'm here with him. And I think that it's absolutely necessary for him to be out of his box as much as possible. He's *got* to have the stimulus He's *thinking*, Donald."

"Yeah, right." But for all the bravado in his voice, Donald couldn't meet number nine's gaze. "So why don't you let them both out and they can play rummy or something. Look, Cathy," he came around the bank of monitors and threw himself down on the other chair at the computer station, legs straddling the back, arms folded across the top, "can we talk?"

She swiveled her own chair around to face him, her expression confused. "We *are* talking."

"No, I mean *talk*." Staring down at his hands, he picked at a hangnail beside his left thumb. "Talk about what we're really doing here. I've got to tell you, Cathy, I'm getting kind of concerned. This has gone way beyond the stuff Dr. Burke said we were going to be doing. I mean we're definitely doing more than just developing a repair and maintenance system."

"Is this about what happened last night?"

"Sort of, but . . ."

"It won't happen again. I'm going to be very careful to never leave them alone. We were so lucky they didn't damage themselves out walking around unsupervised."

Donald's gaze snapped up to meet hers. "Geez, Cathy, some guy died last night and all you can worry about is the effect of a little mileage on the Bobbsey Twins?"

"I'm sorry that happened," she told him earnestly, "but worrying about it won't bring him back. Number nine made an amazing breakthrough last night and that's what we should be concentrating on."

"What if he was just reacting?"

She smiled. "Then it wasn't a programmed reaction and he had to have learned it on his own."

"Yeah? From where?" Donald twisted around and stared at number nine sitting impassively against the wall. "Those are my brain wave patterns bouncing around in there and I certainly never strangled anyone."

"That's a very good point." Catherine considered it for a moment, brow furrowed. "Perhaps we should bring a psychologist in?"

"Sure. Great." Donald faced her again, arms waving. Behind him, number nine tracked his movement. "Put him into therapy. The answer of the decade. Time for a reality break here, Cathy. This guy was dead and I don't think he is anymore. It's time to ask ourselves—what have we created?"

"Life?"

"Full points. Now then," his gestures grew broader as his voice rose, "what does that actually *mean?* Besides getting up and walking around and all that scientific bullshit about interfacing with the net, and ignoring for the moment whether it's an old life or a new one. It means we've got a person here. Just like you or me. Except," he flung a hand back in number nine's direction without turning, "he's rotting on his feet."

On his feet.

It was almost the command. Slowly, number nine stood.

He liked to hear her talk. Liked to listen to her voice. He didn't like the other one. The other one was loud.

Moving carefully, a hand braced against the container he recognized as his, he walked forward quietly.

"So what you're saying is that we have a live man in a dead body?"

"Yes! And what are we going to do about it?"

Catherine regarded him calmly. "The bacteria are keeping the body functional."

"Yeah, but only for a limited time. He's alive and he's decomposing, and doesn't that bother you just a little bit! I mean, ethical considerations about grave robbing aside, that's one hell of a thing to do to somebody!"

"Of course it bothers me." She brushed her hair back off her forehead and noted how well number nine was controlling his movements. Any residual lurching probably resulted from mechanical failure in the knees and hips. "What I really think we need are fresher bodies. I have high hopes for number ten."

"Fresher bodies!" Donald almost shrieked the words. "Are you crazy?"

"I've come to believe that the sooner the bacteria are applied the better they do." Her fingers danced over the keyboard. A moment later she offered him the printout. "I've graphed the time factor against the life of the bacteria and the amount of repair they were able to do. I think you'll find my conclusions to be unquestionable. The fresher the body, the longer it will last, the greater the chance of complete success."

Donald looked from the papers to Catherine and his eyes widened with a sudden realization. He didn't know why he hadn't seen it before. Maybe the money and recognition Dr. Burke kept talking about had interfered. Maybe the whole godlike concept of raising the dead had clouded his judgment. Maybe he just hadn't wanted to see.

When he looked number nine in the eyes, he saw a person and that was pretty terrifying. When he put Catherine under the same scrutiny, he didn't recognize what he saw and that was more terrifying still. Heart pounding, he stood and began to back away. "You *are* crazy."

His shoulder blades slammed up against number nine. He whirled and screamed.

* * *

The sound hurt.
But he had learned how to make it stop.

Donald clawed at the hand wrapped around his throat, fingernails digging into dead flesh.

Catherine frowned. It looked very much as though number nine had merely responded to Donald's scream. The sound appeared to hurt him, so he stopped it. Without further data, the obvious conclusion was that the young man last night had also screamed. Still, number nine *was* applying last night's lesson to a new situation and *that* was encouraging.

The wet noises were better. Quiet would be better still.
He tightened his grip.

Release! Release! The command had been implanted. Number nine would have to obey. The word roared inside Donald's skull, but he couldn't force it out. His vision went red. Then purple. Then black.

Number nine looked down at what he held, then up at her. Slowly, he straightened his arm, offering the body.
She also looked down. Then up. Then she nodded, and he knew he had done the right thing.

"Put him on the table." As number nine moved to obey, Catherine saved the program she'd been working on and loaded Donald's brain wave patterns into the system. She'd needed a fresher body to test her hypothesis and now she had one. The perfect one. Even the bacteria had already been tailored.
Except the bacteria were in her other lab down in the subbasement because Dr. Burke had told her to stop wasting valuable experimental time on something that wouldn't be used.

She could put the net in now and then go for the
bacteria or she could go for the bacteria and leave
Donald where he was or . . .

Moving quickly—whatever she did, time was of the
essence—she opened the isolation box that had held
number eight. If she put him in here, she could at least
keep him cold while she ran downstairs. Decision
made, she touched number nine lightly on the arm.

''Put him in here.''

Number nine knew the box.
The head went so.
The feet went so.
The arms lay straight at the sides.

''Good.'' Catherine smiled her approval, lowered
the lid, then switched on the refrigeration unit. She
didn't bother latching the box. She wouldn't be gone
long. Pushing him gently, she guided number nine up
against the wall and out of the way. ''Stay here. Don't
follow.''

Her rubber soled shoes made no sound against the
tile as she sprinted for the door.

Stay here. Don't follow.
He wanted to be with her, but he did as she said.

Henry glared at the fire door. Obviously, he couldn't
go into the building the same way the creature had
come out. Although he might be able to work his way
around the lack of an external handle, he could do
nothing about the alarm. From the outside, he couldn't
even destroy it. Somewhere, there had to be another
way in.

Plywood covered the first floor windows between
the wire grilles and the glass and a quick tour of the
entrances showed them to have been similarly barri-
caded and wired besides. Frustrated and back by the
fire door, Henry shoved his fingers behind the lower

edge of a grille and gave an experimental tug. *If the direct approach is necessary . . .*

The bolts pulled out of the concrete and the side bars began to bend, metal screaming.

Bad idea. He froze, listening for reaction. In the distance, he heard leather soles slap against concrete and felt two lives, coming closer. Stepping away from the building, he became part of the night and waited.

". . . so he said, 'Chicago? In four? You've got to be out of your mind. I'll bet you twenty bucks they don't even make it out of the quarterfinals.' So I took the bet and in a couple of days, I'll take the twenty."

"Ah, man, how can you think of hockey at a time like this?"

"A time like what?"

"Baseball season, man. Opening day was the sixth. You got no business thinking about hockey, talking about hockey, playin' hockey, after baseball season starts."

"But hockey season isn't over."

"Maybe not, but it should be. Shit, this keeps up they'll be giving out ol' Stanley's cup in June."

They wore the uniform of university Security; two men bracketing forty, both with flashlights, both with billies in their belts. One of them carried his weight forward on his feet, daring the world to try something. The other balanced an impressive gut with enormous shoulders and arms. They passed inches from the shadow where Henry stood and never knew they were observed.

"This the door?"

"Yeah." The steel rattled under a slap from a beefy hand. "Some asshole genius student probably cutting through from the new Life Sciences building."

"Cutting through? In the dark?"

"What dark? They keep one in four lights on in there just in case."

"Just in case what?"

"Beats the hell out of me, but the place still has power."

"What a friggin' waste of money."

"No shit. Maybe if they turned off the lights and saved the dough they could afford to tear this ratbox down and build that parking garage."

"A parking garage? Now, man *that's* a building we could use around here."

From the Parthenon to the parking garage; how much further can civilization deteriorate? Henry wondered as the patrol moved on. Hands shoved into his pockets, he turned toward the new Life Sciences building, a brightly lit contrast to the dark and boarded structure it had replaced. *So the buildings are connected. The creature went into the old and Dr. Burke works in the new—along with a couple of hundred other people. Just exactly the sort of not quite information that Vicki and Celluci have been collecting all day.*

Let's see if the night can find some answers for them.

The guard at the front entrance noticed only the brief touch of a breeze that ruffled her newspaper but missed the movement that had made it. Once inside, Henry headed silently for the lower levels at the north end of the building. As the connection had not been visible, it had to be underground.

In the basement, he crossed a scent he knew. Or rather, the perversion of a scent he knew. He'd spent the last three days in the dark of Marjory Nelson's closet surrounded by her clothes and the stored bits and pieces of her life. The scent of her death, robbed of its peace and twisted back into a grotesque existence, clung to the tiles and paint much the way it had clung to the apartment window.

It led him to the passage, through it, up a flight of stairs, down a hall, up another flight of stairs, across an empty lecture hall with scars in the floor where the seats had been. Finally, it led him to a corridor, so thick with the stench of abomination, he could no longer separate individual paths.

Halfway down the corridor, a razor's edge of light showed under a door.

He could hear the low hum of electronic equipment, he could hear motors, and he could hear a heartbeat. He couldn't sense a life.

When he tried to step forward, his legs refused to obey.

Henry Fitzroy, Duke of Richmond and Somerset, bastard son of Henry VIII, had been raised to believe in the physical resurrection of the body. When the Day of Judgment came and the Lord called the faithful to Him, they would come not only in spirit, but also in flesh. He had gone to chapel nearly every day of his seventeen years, and this belief had been at the core of his religious upbringing. Even when his royal father had split from Rome, the resurrection of the body had remained.

Four and a half centuries had changed his views on religion but he had never been able to fully rid himself of his early training. He had been raised a sixteenth-century Catholic and, in some ways, a sixteenth-century Catholic he remained.

He couldn't go into that room.

And if you're not going to do it, who is? A bit of wood trim splintered beneath his fingers. *Michael Celluci? Will you give him that much? Give him the opportunity to ride to the rescue while you cower in superstitious terror? Vicki, then? What of the vow you made to keep this from her?*

He managed a step, a small one, toward the door. Had his nature allowed him to sweat, his hand would have left a damp signature on the wall. As it was, his fingertips imprinted the plaster.

Legend named his kind undead but, in spite of how it had appeared to the medical establishment of his time, he had changed, not died. In that room, the dead were up and walking. Robbed of their chance for eternal life. Removed from the grace of God. . . .

I will not be ruled by my past at Vicki's expense.

The door was unlocked.

The room it bisected was enormous, stretching half the length of the hall. Henry raised a hand to shield sensitive eyes from the brilliant white glare of the fluorescents, noting as he did how the windows had been carefully blocked to prevent any of that light from escaping and marking the room as in use. He recognized almost none of the equipment that filled much of the available space. Fictional precedent aside, the working of the perversion obviously involved more than a scalpel and a lightning rod.

Perhaps I'd recognize it if I wrote science fiction instead of romance, he mused, moving silently forward accompanied by the demons of his childhood.

The stench of abomination had become so pervasive it coated the inside of his nose and mouth and lungs and spread like a layer of scum across his skin. He could only hope he could eventually be rid of it, that he wouldn't be forced to carry it throughout eternity like an invisible mark of Cain.

There were brass tanks lined up below the windows, shelves of chemicals, two computers, and a door leading to a small and mostly empty storeroom. The door leading out the other side of the storeroom was locked.

Finally, unable to avoid it any longer, Henry turned toward the slow and steady beat that he'd been all too aware of since he'd entered the room.

The creature stood behind a row of metal boxes, eight feet long and four feet wide. Too large to be coffins, they reminded Henry of the outer sarcophagus that had kept an ancient Egyptian wizard imprisoned, undying, for three centuries. Most of the electrical noise that Henry could hear came from the boxes. The mechanical noise came from the creature.

Cautiously, Henry slid along the wall, never in its direct line of sight. When he drew even with the creature, he paused and forced himself to acknowledge what he saw.

Unkempt dark hair fell back from a long line of face

where green-gray skin wore the look of fine-grained leather and a black-threaded seam stitched a flap of forehead down. A nose that had obviously been broken more than once folded back on itself above purple-gray lips no longer able to close over the ivory curve of teeth. Even taking the desiccation of death into account, the muscles were wiry and the bones prominent through the navy blue tracksuit. It had been a man. A man who had not been very old when he died.

The narrow chest rose and fell, but it gave no indication it was aware.

Sweet Jesu! Henry took a step forward. And then another. Then he turned to face it.

Its eyes were open.

Number nine waited. She would be back soon.

He saw the strange one enter the room and he watched the strange one come closer.

The strange one looked at him.

He looked back.

Snarling, Henry broke contact and jerked away.

It was alive.

The body was dead.

But *it* was alive.

Whoever has done this thing should be damned for all eternity and beyond!

Trembling with anger and other emotions less easily defined, Henry dropped his hands to the lid of the box in front of him. Marjory Nelson, Vicki's mother, had to be in one of these. He no longer knew what he would do when he found her.

We give them to Detective Fergusson. So easy to decide in the abstract.

And what will Detective Fergusson do?

He opened the box.

The smell of recent death, free of any taint, rose with the lid and for an instant Henry hoped—but the body in the box had never belonged to Marjory Nelson. A young Oriental male wearing a band of purple finger marks around his throat, eyes bulging, tongue protruding, lay stretched out in the padded plastic hollow. He'd been dead for such a short time that the flush of blood caused by strangulation had not yet left his face.

Marjory Nelson suddenly became of lesser importance. She had already been lost and he could do no more for her than find her. This boy he could save.

Moving quickly, he closed the staring eyes then slid his arms behind knees and shoulders and lifted the chilled body free. The weight meant nothing but the load was awkward and he had to shuffle sideways until he cleared the row of boxes and could turn.

"What do you think you're doing?"

Drowning in the stink of abomination, Henry hadn't scented her approach nor, with ears tuned only to a heart that should be making no noise, had he heard her. In no mood to be subtle, he raised his head to meet her eyes, to order her away, and found behind a surface veneer of normalcy nothing he could touch. Her thoughts spiraled endlessly; starting nowhere, going nowhere.

Pale eyes narrowed. Pale cheeks flushed. "Stop him," she said.

Hands clamped onto Henry's shoulders and yanked him back. Across the top of his head, he could feel death breathing. *This is not life!* his senses screamed. His skin crawled in revulsion. He lost his grip on the boy, felt himself lifted and slammed down onto a surface that gave beneath the force of the blow. He twisted and looked up in time to see the lid coming down.

"NO!"

"He's not back yet."

Celluci jerked away, head snapping up painfully, muscles suddenly tense. "Wha . . . ?"

"He's not back yet," Vicki repeated from the center

of the living room, arms wrapped tightly around herself. "And it's nearly dawn."

"Who's not back? Fitzroy?" Shoving his fist in front of a jaw-cracking yawn, Celluci glanced down at his watch. "6:12. When's the sun due up?"

"6:17," Vicki told him. "He's got five minutes." She kept her face and voice expressionless, reporting the facts, just the facts, because if she gave the screaming panic clawing at her from inside any chance to get free she was horribly afraid she'd never be able to control it again.

Celluci recognized the defense. There wasn't a cop on the planet who hadn't used police training to cover a personal terror at least once. The ones who cared too much used it frequently. Occasionally, it started to use them. Joints protesting, he heaved himself up out of the armchair he'd fallen asleep in, muttering, "How the hell do you know when the sun comes up?"

All at once, a terrifying possibility hit him. Had Fitzroy been . . . been . . . his mind shied away from the whole concept of sucking blood, of feeding. Had Fitzroy been *with* her long enough that she was becoming like him? Wasn't that how it worked? He shot an anxious glance at the mirror over the couch and was relieved to see her reflection still in it. Then he remembered that it had reflected Fitzroy just as clearly. "You're not turning into a . . . a . . . one of them, are you?" he snarled.

Vicki pushed at her glasses with the back of one hand. "What the hell are you talking about?"

"How do you know that sunrise is at 6:17?" He wanted to cross the room and shake the answer from her and barely managed to hold himself back.

"I read it in the paper last night." Her brows drew in, confused by the unexpected attack. "What is your *problem*, Mike?"

She read it in the paper last night. "Sorry, I, uh . . ." The surge of relief was so intense it left him feeling weak and a little dizzy. He spread his hands in apology and sighed. "I thought you were becoming like him," he said quietly, "and I was afraid I was going to lose you."

Drawing her lower lip between her teeth, Vicki stared at him for a long moment, although in the dim dawn light she could barely make out individual features. With no resources left to throw at denial, she could sense his caring, his fear, his love—and knew he put no conditions on it, no conditions on her. To her surprise, rather than diminishing her sense of self, it added to it and made her feel stronger. Even the panic over Henry calmed a little. Her eyes grew damp.

I am not *going to cry.*

Shoving the words past the lump in her throat, she said, "It doesn't work like that."

"Good." He heard, if not acceptance, at least acknowledgment in her tone and was content for the time to leave it at that.

The room grew perceptibly lighter.

Vicki turned toward the windows, arms wrapped tightly around herself once more. "Open the curtains."

They both heard the silent corollary. *You open them because I can't. Because I'm afraid of what I might see.*

"Who was your slave last year," Celluci grumbled to cover it.

It was going to be a beautiful day. Several dozen birds were noisily welcoming the dawn and the air had the kind of clarity that only occurred in the morning in spring.

His watch said 6:22. "How long can he last in the sun?"

"I don't know."

"I'm going to check outside. Just in case he almost made it home."

No twisted, blackened body crawled toward the door. No pile of ash spread man-shaped in the parking lot. When Celluci came back inside, he found Vicki standing where he'd left her, staring at the window.

"He isn't dead."

"Vicki, you have no way of knowing that."

"So?" Her teeth were clenched so hard her temples began to throb. "He *isn't* dead."

"All right." Celluci crossed the room to her side and gently turned her to face him. "I don't want to believe it either." It was true, he didn't. He didn't understand half the responses Fitzroy evoked in him, but he didn't want him gone. "So we won't believe it together."

Together. Face twisted into a scowl to stop the threat of tears, Vicki nodded. Together sounded a whole lot better than alone.

He could feel the dawn. Even through the terror and the frenzy and the panic, he could feel the morning approach. For a moment he fought harder, slamming his whole body up against the lid of his prison, then he collapsed back against the padding and lay still.

The familiar touch of the sun trembling on the edge of the horizon brought sanity with it. For too long he had known only the all pervasive stench of abomination and the pain he inflicted upon himself to get free. Now he knew who he was again.

Just in time to lose himself to the day.

Working on her own, it took Catherine until after seven to finish preparing Donald's body and hook it up in number nine's box. She'd intended to use number eight's, but the intruder locked inside had forced her to change her plans. It wouldn't hurt number nine to stay out for a while. It might even be good for him.

She yawned and stretched, suddenly exhausted. It had been a long and eventful night and she was in desperate need of a couple of hours sleep. The constant pounding from number eight's box had been very irritating and more than a little distracting during certain delicate procedures. She very nearly turned the refrigeration unit back on just to see if that would cool him down.

How unfortunate that, when the pounding finally stopped, she'd been nearly finished and able to appreciate the quiet for only a short time.

Ten

Vicki woke first and lay staring blindly at the ceiling, uncertain where she was. The room felt unfamiliar, the dimensions wrong, the patterns of shadow that made up the world without her glasses not patterns she recognized. It wasn't her bedroom, nor, in spite of the man still asleep beside her, was it Celluci's.

Then she remembered.

Just past dawn, the two of them had lain down on her mother's bed. Her dead mother's bed. Two of them—where there should've been three.

All three of us in my dead mother's bed? The edge on the sarcasm very nearly drew blood. *Get a grip, Nelson.*

She slid out from under Celluci's arm without waking him and groped on the bedside table for her glasses, the daylight seeping around the edges of the blinds providing barely enough illumination for her to function. Her nose almost touching the surface of the clock radio, she scowled at the glowing red numbers. Ten minutes after nine. Two hours' sleep. Add that to the time Henry had granted her and she'd certainly functioned on less.

Pulling her robe closer around her, she stood. She couldn't go back to sleep now anyway. She couldn't face the dreams—Henry burning and screaming her name while he burned, her mother's rotting body a living barrier between them. If she wanted to save Henry, she had to go past her mother. And she couldn't. Feelings of fear and failure combined, lingered.

My subconscious is anything but subtle.

Bare feet moving soundlessly over the soft nap of the carpet—it was still nearly new; Vicki could remember how pleased her mother had been to have replaced a worn area rug with thick wall-to-wall plush—she made her way to the walk-in closet where Henry had been spending his days. After a moment's groping to find the switch, she flicked on the closet light and closed the door silently behind her.

It was, as Henry had said, just barely large enough for a not-so-very-tall man. Or a not-so-very-tall vampire. A pad of bright blue compressed foam, the sort commonly used for camping, lay along one wall under the rack of woman's clothes. On it, a neatly folded length of heavy blackout curtain rested beside a leather overnight bag. Another piece of curtain had been tacked to one side of the door which itself had been fitted out with a heavy steel bolt.

Henry must've put it up. Vicki touched the metal slide and shook her head. She hadn't heard hammering but, given Henry's strength, hammering might not have been necessary. *We'd better remember to take it down or it'll confuse the hell out of the next tenant.*

The next tenant. It was the first time she'd considered the apartment as anything but her mother's. *Only reasonable, I suppose.* She let her head fall back against the wall and closed her eyes. *My mother's dead.*

The scent of her mother's cologne, of her mother, permeated the small enclosure, and with her eyes shut it almost seemed that her mother was still there. Another time, the illusion might have been comforting—or infuriating. Vicki was honest enough to admit the possibility of either reaction. At the moment, though, she ignored it. Her mother wasn't the reason she was here.

Opening her eyes, she dropped to her knees beside the pallet and lifted the makeshift shroud to her face, breathing in the faint trace of Henry trapped in the heavy fabric.

He wasn't dead. She refused to believe it. He was too real to be dead.

He *wasn't* dead.

"What are you doing?"

"I'm not entirely certain." With knuckles white around the folds, she set the piece of curtain down and turned to face Celluci, standing outlined in the doorway. He'd opened the blinds in the bedroom and the morning sun behind him threw his face into shadow. Vicki couldn't see his expression, but his tone had been almost gentle. She didn't have a clue to what he was thinking.

He held out his hand and she put hers into it, allowing him to pull her to her feet. His palm was warm and callused. Henry's would have been cool and smooth. With her free hand resting on a crumpled expanse of shirtfront, she had the sudden and completely irrational desire to take that one extra step into the circle of Celluci's arms and to rest her head—not to mention the whole mess she found herself in—if only for a moment, on the broad expanse of his shoulders.

This is no time to be getting soft, Vicki, she told herself sternly, fighting the iron bands tightening around her ribs. *You've got far too fucking much to do.*

Celluci, who'd read both the desire and the internal response off Vicki's face, smiled wryly and moved out of her way. He recognized the growing strain that painted purple half-circles under her eyes and pinched the corners of her mouth and knew that some of it needed to be bled off before it blew her apart. But he didn't know what to do. Although their fights had often been therapeutic, this situation went a little beyond the relief that could come from screaming at one another over trivial disagreements. While he could think of a few nontrivial disagreements available for argument, he had no intention of hurting her by bringing them up. All he could do was continue to wait and hope he was the one in the right place to pick up the pieces.

Of course, if Fitzroy's actually bought it . . . It was a dishonorable thought, but he couldn't stop it from taking up residence.

"So." He watched her cross to the open bedroom door and wondered how long he'd have been content with the status quo had Fitzroy *not* come into their lives. "What do we do now?"

Vicki turned and stared at him in some surprise. "We do exactly what we *have* been doing." She jabbed her glasses up onto the bridge of her nose. "When we find the people who have my mother's body, we'll find Henry."

"Maybe he just went to ground, got caught out too late and had to take what shelter he could."

"He wouldn't do that to me if he could help it."

"He'd call?" Celluci couldn't prevent the mocking tone.

Vicki's chin went up. "Yeah. He'd call." *He wouldn't leave me to think he was dead if he could help it. You don't do that to someone you say you love.* "We find my mother. We find Henry." *He couldn't call if he was dead. He isn't dead.* "Do you understand?"

Actually, he did. After nine years, he'd gotten proficient at reading her subtext. And if his understanding was all she'd take˙ . . . Celluci spread his hands, the gesture both conciliatory and an indication that he had no wish to continue the discussion.

Some of the stiffness went out of Vicki's stance. "You make coffee," she told him, "while I shower."

Celluci rolled his eyes. "What do I look like? Live-in help?"

"No." Vicki felt her lower lip tremble and sternly stilled it. "You look like someone I can count on. No matter what." Then, before the lump in her throat did any more damage, she wheeled on one bare heel and strode out of the room.

His own throat tight, Celluci pushed the curl of hair back off his face. "Just when you're ready to give up on her," he muttered. Shaking his head, he went to make the coffee.

Running her fingers through her wet hair, Vicki wandered into the living room and dropped onto the couch. She could hear Celluci mumbling to himself in the kitchen and, remembering what had happened on other occasions, decided it might be safer not to bother him when he was cooking. Without quite knowing how it happened, she found herself lifting the box of her mother's personal effects and setting it in front of her on the coffee table.

I suppose no day's so bad that you can't make it worse.

There was surprisingly little in it: a sweater kept hanging over the back of the office chair, just in case; two lipsticks, one pale pink, the other a surprisingly brilliant red; half a bottle of aspirin; the coffee mug; the datebook with its final futile message; her academy graduation portrait; and a pile of loose papers.

Vicki picked up the photograph and stared into the face of the smiling young woman. She looked so young. So confident. "I looked like I thought I knew everything."

"You still think you know everything." Celluci handed her a mug of coffee and plucked the picture out of her grasp. "Good God. It's a baby cop."

"If I ignore you, will you go back into the kitchen?"

He thought about it for a second. "No."

"Great." Pulling her bathrobe securely closed, Vicki lifted out the loose paper. *Why on earth did Mrs. Shaw think I'd want a bunch of Mother's notes?* Then she saw how each page began.

Dear Vicki: You're probably wondering why a letter instead of a phone call, but I've got something important to tell you and I thought I might get through it

easier this way, without interruptions. I haven't written a letter for a while so I hope you'll forgive . . .

Dear Vicki: Did I tell you the results of my last
checkup? Well, I probably didn't want to bore you with
details, but . . .

Dear Vicki: First of all, I love you very much
and . . .

Dear Vicki: When your father left, I promised you
that I'd always be there for you. I wish I . . .

Dear Vicki: There are some things that are easier to
say on paper, so I hope you'll forgive me this small
distance I have to put between us. Dr. Friedman tells
me that I've got a problem with my heart and I may
not have long to live. Please don't fly off the handle
and start demanding I see another doctor. I have.

Yes, I'm afraid. Any sensible person would be. But
mostly I was afraid that something would happen before I found the courage to tell you.

I don't want to just disappear out of your life like
your father did. I want us to have a chance to say good-
bye. When you get this letter, call me. We'll make
arrangements for you to come home for a few days
and we'll sit down and really talk.

I love you.

The last and most complete letter was dated from
the Friday before Marjory Nelson died.

Vicki fought tears and with shaking hands laid the
letters back in the box.

"Vicki?"

She shook her head, unable to push her voice past
an almost equal mix of grief and anger. Even if the
letter had been mailed, they still wouldn't have had
time to say good-bye. *Jesus Christ, Mom, why didn't
you have Dr. Friedman call me?*

Celluci leaned forward and scanned the top page. "Vicki, I . . ."

"Don't." Her teeth were clenched so tightly it felt as though there was an iron band wrapped around her temples. One more sympathetic word—one more word of any kind—would destroy the fingernail grip she had on her control. Moving blindly, she stood and hurried toward the bedroom. "I've got to get dressed. We've got to look for Henry."

At 10:20, Catherine lifted the lid of the isolation box and smiled in at the woman who had once been Marjory Nelson. "I know; it's pretty boring in there, isn't it?" She pulled on a pair of surgical gloves and deftly unhooked the jack and laid it, gold prongs gleaming, to one side. "Just give me half a sec and we'll see what we can do about getting you out of there." Nutrient tubes were tugged gently from catheters and tucked away in specific compartments in the sides of the box. "You've got amazingly good skin tone, all things considered, but I think that working a little estrogen cream into the epidermis might be in order. We don't want things to tear while you're up and moving around."

Catherine hummed tunelessly to herself as she worked, stopping twice to make notes on muscle resilience and joint flexibility. So far, number ten proved her theory. None of the others, not even number nine, had responded to the bacteria quite so well. She couldn't wait to see how Donald—number eleven—turned out.

Had she seen the girl before? Why couldn't she remember?

The girl was not the right girl, although she didn't understand why not.

Hooking her fingers over the side of the box, she pulled herself up into a sitting position.

There was something she had to do.

* * *

Catherine shook her head. Initiative was all very well but at the moment a prone, immobile body would be of more use.

"Lie down," she said sternly.

Lie down.

The command traveled deeply rutted pathways and the body obeyed.

But she didn't want to lie down.

At least she didn't think she did.

"You're trying to frown, that's wonderful!" Catherine clapped gloved hands together. "Even partial control of the zygomaticus minor is a definite advance. I've got to take some measurements."

Number nine watched closely as she moved about the other one like him. He remembered another word.

Need.

When she needed him, he'd be there.

Just for an instant, he thought he remembered music.

With number ten measured, moisturized, dressed, and sitting at the side of the room, Catherine finally turned her attention to the intruder. She'd heard no sounds at all from what had been number nine's box since she'd returned to the lab and she rather hoped he hadn't died. With no brain wave patterns and no bacteria tailored, it would be a waste of a perfectly good body, especially as, if he'd suffocated or had a heart attack, there wouldn't even be any trauma to repair.

"Of course, if he *has* died, we could use Donald's brain wave patterns and the generic bacteria," she mused as she lifted the lid. "After all, it worked on number nine and he wasn't exactly fresh. It'd be nice to have a little backup data for a change."

She frowned down into the isolation box. The intruder lay, one pale hand curled against his chest, the other palm up at his side. His eyes were closed and long lashes, slightly darker than the strawberry blond hair, brushed against the curve of pale cheeks. He didn't look dead. Exactly. But he didn't look alive. Exactly.

Head to one side, she pushed his collar back and pressed two fingers into the pulse point at his throat. His flesh responded with more resilience than she'd expected, far more than a corpse would have but, at the same time, it seemed his body temperature had dropped too low to sustain life. She checked to make sure that the refrigeration unit had, indeed, been shut off. It had.

"How very strange," she murmured. Then things got stranger still for just as she was about to believe his heart had stopped, for whatever reason, a single pulse throbbed under her fingertips. Frown deepening, she waited, eyes on her watch as the seconds flashed by. Just over eight seconds later, the intruder's heart beat again. And then eight seconds after that, again.

"About seven beats a minute." Catherine drummed the fingers of both hands on the side of the isolation box. "The alternation of systole and diastole occurs at an average rate of about seventy times per minute in a normal human being at rest. What we have here is a heart beating at one tenth the normal rate."

Brows knit, she carefully lifted an eyelid between thumb and forefinger. The eye had not rolled back. The pupil, rather than being protected under the ridge of brow bone, remained centered, collapsed to pin-prick dimensions. There was no reaction of any kind to light. Nor, for that matter, to any other kind of stimuli by any other part of the body—and Catherine tried them all.

Accompanied by low level respiration, the heart continued to beat between seven and eight times a minute, undetectable had she not been specifically searching for it. These were the only signs of life.

She'd heard of Indian fakirs putting themselves into trances so deep they appeared to be in comas or dead and she supposed this was a North American variation on that ability; that when her intruder had found himself trapped, he'd lowered his metabolism to conserve resources. Catherine had no idea what he'd been hoping to accomplish as he seemed, at the moment, totally unable to defend himself, but she had to admit that, minor point aside, it was a pretty neat trick.

Finally, she had number nine help her remove his leather trench coat and, rolling up his shirtsleeve, she pulled two vials of blood. She'd intended to take three but, with the intruder's blood pressure so low, two used up all the time she was willing to allow. Closing the box, she headed for one of the tables at the other end of the lab. Running the blood work might give her some answers to this trance thing but, even if it didn't, she could always use the information later should the intruder happen to die.

"Look, Detective Fergusson, I'm aware that my mother died of natural causes before the crime was committed and I realize that this makes her a very low priority but . . ."

"Ms. Nelson." Detective Fergusson's voice hovered between exasperation and annoyance. "I'm sorry you're upset, but I've got a murdered teenager on my hands. I'd like to find the asshole who offed him before I've got another body bag to deal with."

"And you're the only detective on the force?" Vicki's fingernails beat a staccato rhythm against the pay phone's plastic casing.

"No, but I am the one assigned to the case. I'm sorry if that means I can't give your mother the attention you think she deserves . . ."

"The cases," she snarled, fingers curling into a fist, "are connected."

Behind her, leaning on the open door of the phone booth, Celluci rolled his eyes. Even without hearing the other end of the conversation, he had some sympathy for Fergusson's position. Although she could be surgically delicate with a witness, Vicki tended to practice hammer and chisel diplomacy on the rest of the world.

"Connected?" The exasperation vanished. "In what way?"

Vicki opened her mouth then closed it again with an audible snap. *My mother has been turned into a monster. Your boy was killed by a similar monster. We find my mother, I guarantee we find your perp. How do I know all this? I can't tell you. And he's missing anyway.*

Shit.

She shoved at her glasses. "Look, call it a hunch, okay?"

"A hunch?"

Realizing that she'd have had much the same reaction had their positions been reversed, her tone grew sharply defensive. "What's the matter? You've never had a hunch?"

Anticipating disaster should the current conversation continue, Celluci used a shoulder to lever Vicki back from the phone, then dragged the receiver from her grip. Scowling, she allowed his interference with ill grace and the certain knowledge that antagonizing the Kingston Police was a bad idea.

"Detective Fergusson? Detective-Sergeant Celluci. We've determined that one of Dr. Burke's grad students, a Donald Li, at least superficially fits the description of Tom Chen. We'd appreciate it if you could call the registrar's office and have them release a copy of his student photo so we can check his identity with the funeral parlor."

Detective Fergusson sighed. "I called the registrar's office yesterday."

"And they released the photos of the medical students. But Li isn't studying medicine and they won't release his picture without another call from you."

"Why do you think Li's involved?"

"Because he works for Dr. Burke, as did Marjory Nelson."

"So. What make you think Dr. Burke's involved?"

"Because she appears to have the scientific qualifications to raise the dead as well as access to the necessary equipment."

"Give me a break, Sergeant." Incredulity fought with anger for control of Fergusson's voice. "How did you come up with raising the fucking dead?"

Good question, Celluci admitted, ignoring a glare from Vicki so intense that he could almost feel its impact. Making a quick decision—given that the police were already involved—he pulled out as much of the truth as he thought Fergusson could swallow. "Ms. Nelson thought she saw her mother outside the apartment window, two nights ago."

"Her dead mother?"

"That's right."

"Walking around?"

"Yes."

"Next thing you're going to tell me," Fergusson growled, "is that her dead mother offed my teenie bopper."

"No, but . . ."

"No buts, Sergeant." His voice clipped off the words. "And I've listened to as much of this crap as I'm going to. Go back to Toronto. Get a life. Both of you."

Celluci got the receiver away from his ear just barely fast enough to save his hearing from the force of Fergusson's disconnection. He hung up the phone with an equal emphasis. "I knew I shouldn't have let you talk to him."

Behind her lenses, Vicki's eyes narrowed. "And *you* did so much better? What the hell made you tell him about my mother? About Dr. Burke?"

Celluci pushed his way out of the phone booth. She stepped back, giving him *just* enough room to get by.

"This is science, Vicki, not one of the weird supernatural situations your undead buddy has pulled us into over the last year. I thought he could handle it. I thought he should know."

"You didn't think we should discuss it first?"

"You brought it up. 'The cases are connected.' Jesus H. Christ, Vicki, you knew you couldn't support a statement like that."

"I didn't notice you supporting *your* statements with much, Celluci." With an effort, she unclenched her teeth. "I assume he's *not* going to make the call?"

Celluci's scowl answered the question. And then some.

"All right." She hoisted her bag off the sidewalk and threw it onto her shoulder. "I guess we do it the hard way."

"You're a lot more philosophical about this than I expected you'd be."

"Mike, my recently dead mother has been turned into some kind of grade B movie monster, my—*what word to use?*—friend who also happens to be a vampire is missing, in the daylight, and possibly captured. When I sleep, I have nightmares. When I eat, the food turns to rock and just sits there." She turned to face him and her expression closed around his heart and squeezed. "I find it difficult to give a shit that local police don't see things exactly my way."

"You've still got me." It was the best he could offer.

Her lower lip began to tremble and she caught it savagely between her teeth. Unable to trust her voice, she reached up and pushed the long curl of dark brown hair back off his forehead then turned and strode away from the Administration buildings, heels hitting pavement with such force that they should have imprinted crescent moons into the concrete.

Celluci watched her for a moment. "You're welcome," he said quietly, his own voice not entirely steady. With a dozen long strides, he caught up and fell into step by her side.

* * *

"All right, Catherine, I'm here." Dr. Burke pushed the lab door shut behind her and walked purposefully across the room. "What is it you've found that's so important I had to see it immediately?"

Catherine came out from behind the computer console and offered a page of printout. "It's not that it's important, precisely, it's more that I don't understand what I've found. If you could just take a look at the results of this blood work."

Dr. Burke frowned down at the piece of paper. "Formed elements sixty percent of whole blood—that's high. Plasma proteins, twelve percent—high as well. Organic nutrients . . ." She looked up. "Catherine, what *is* this?"

Catherine shook her head. "Read the rest."

Although inclined to demand an immediate explanation, respect for the grad student's abilities—manipulating the younger woman's genius had, after all, been a main component of the plan from the beginning—dropped Dr. Burke's gaze back down to the printout. "Ten million red blood cells per cubic millimeter of blood? That's twice human norm." Her brows drew in as she continued. "If this data on the hemoglobin is correct . . ."

"It is."

"Then just what *is* this?" Dr. Burke punctuated her questions by shoving the paper back into Catherine's hands. "A replacement for the nutrient solution?"

"No, although . . ." Her eyes glazed and two spots of color began to come up on pale cheeks.

Dr. Burke recognized the signs, but she didn't have the time to allow genius to percolate. She'd had to reschedule an end of term meeting to come here and she had no intention of falling farther behind. "Think about it later. I'm waiting."

"Yes. Well . . ." Catherine took a deep breath and smoothed down the front of her lab coat. She hadn't even begun to consider the experimental applications yet. The ability to leap so far ahead, she mused, was what made Dr. Burke such a brilliant scientist. "We had an intruder in the lab last night."

"A what!"

Catherine blinked at both volume and tone. "An intruder. But don't worry, number nine took care of him."

"Number nine took care of him?" Dr. Burke suddenly saw her world becoming infinitely more complicated. She shot a disgusted glance across the room to where both number nine and Marj . . . and number ten sat motionless by the wall. "The way he, it, took care of that boy?"

"Oh, no! He captured the intruder, and with only the most basic of instructions. There really can be no more doubt that he's reasoning independently, although I haven't had time this morning to run a new EEG."

"Catherine, that's fascinating I'm sure, but the intruder? What did you do with him?"

"I locked him into number nine's isolation box."

"Is he still in there?"

"Yes. He made a horrible racket at first, very distracting while I was working—especially since I had to do the whole job alone—but he quieted around sunrise."

"Quieted." Dr. Burke rubbed at her temples where an incipient headache had begun to pound. Thank God, Catherine had been mucking about in the lab long after the rest of the world had gone to sleep. Had there been no one around to stop him, they would have all very likely been in a great deal of trouble. On the other hand, *Catherine* stopping an intruder was a mixed blessing, her grip on the world's standard operating procedures not being particularly strong. "He didn't die, did he? I mean you *did* check on him?" *And if he's alive, what the hell are we going to do with him?*

"Of course I did. His metabolic rate is extremely

low, but he's alive.'' She held the printout higher. ''This is a partial analysis of his blood.''

''That's impossible,'' Dr. Burke snapped. With a captured intruder to deal with, she didn't have time for the grad student's delusions.

Catherine merely shook her head. ''No, it isn't.''

''No one has blood like that. You had to have done something wrong.''

''I didn't.''

''Then the sample was contaminated.''

''It wasn't.''

Unable to break past Catherine's calm certainty, Dr. Burke snatched the printout back and glared down at it, scanning the data she'd already read, looking more closely at the rest. ''What's this? This isn't blood work.''

''I also did a cheek swab.''

''Your intruder has thromboplastins present in his saliva? That's ridiculous.''

''He's not my intruder,'' Catherine protested. ''And if you don't trust my results, run the tests yourself. Besides, if you'll notice, they don't exactly register as thromboplastins although there is a ninety-eight point seven percent similarity.''

''No one has that kind of clotting initiators in their sa . . .'' Ten million red blood cells per cubic millimeter of blood . . . thromboplastins present in his saliva . . . he quieted around sunrise . . . his metabolic rate is extremely low . . . quieted around sunrise . . . around sunrise. . . . ''No, that's impossible.''

Eyes narrowed, Catherine squared her shoulders. She couldn't understand how Dr. Burke continued to deny the experimental results. Science didn't lie. ''Obviously, it *isn't* impossible.''

Dr. Burke ignored her. Heart pounding, she turned toward the row of isolation boxes. ''I think,'' she said slowly, ''I'd better have a look at your intruder.''

''He isn't *my* intruder,'' Catherine muttered again as she followed the other woman across the room.

Palms resting on the curve of number nine's isolation box—apparently no longer only number nine's—Dr. Burke told herself she was letting fantasy get the best of both common sense and education. *He can't be what evidence suggests he is. Such creatures exist in myth and legend. They aren't walking around in the twentieth century.* But if the test results were accurate . . . *There's probably a perfectly normal, scientific explanation for all this,* she told herself firmly, and opened the lid.

"Good Lord, he's paler than you are. I didn't think that was possible." She hadn't expected him to look so young. Much as Catherine had done earlier, she pushed her fingers up against the pulse point at the base of the ivory column of throat. Thirty seconds passed while she stood silently, eyes on her watch, then she wet her lips and said, "Not quite eight beats a minute."

"I got the same," Catherine nodded, pleased to have her figure corroborated.

She reached to check his pupils but instead, her hand moving almost of its own volition, she peeled up a lip barely tinted with color.

Catherine's brow furrowed. "What are you looking for?"

Her heart beat so loudly she nearly missed the question. "Fangs," she said softly, realizing she was being one hundred sorts of an old fool. "Fangs."

Bending forward, Catherine peered down at the exposed line of white. "Although the canines are somewhat prominent, I wouldn't go so far as to . . ."

"Son of a bitch! They're sharp!"

Together, the two women watched the drop of blood roll from the puncture in Dr. Burke's finger. It splashed crimson against the barrier of the teeth, seeped into sculpted crevices, drained into the mouth beneath. So slowly that they would have missed the movement had they not been staring so hard, the young man swallowed.

In the long moment that followed, Dr. Burke reviewed a thousand rational reasons why this creature could not be what it had to be. Finally, she said, "Catherine, do you realize what we have here?"

"Incipient percutaneous infection. Better sterilize the puncture."

"No, no, no. Do know what he *is*?"

"No, Doctor." Catherine rocked back on her heels and shoved her hands deep into the pockets of her lab coat. "I realized I didn't know what he was when I saw the results of the blood work. That's why I called you."

"This," Dr. Burke's voice rose with an excitement she didn't bother to suppress, "is a vampire!" She whirled to face Catherine, who looked politely interested. "Good lord, girl, don't you find that amazing? That this is a *vampire?* And *we* have him?"

"I guess."

"You guess?" Dr. Burke stared at the grad student in disbelief. "We have a vampire break into the lab and you *guess* it's amazing?"

Catherine shrugged.

"Catherine! Pull your head out of your test tubes and consider what this means. Up until this moment, vampires were creatures of myth and legend. We can now prove that they exist!"

"I thought vampires disintegrated in daylight."

"He hasn't been in daylight, has he?" An expansive gesture indicated the wall of boarded up windows. "The scientific community will go crazy over this!"

"If he *is* a vampire. So far we can only prove he has a hyperefficient bloodtype, clotting agents in his saliva, and sharp teeth."

"And doesn't that say vampire to you?"

"Well, it doesn't prove it. Sunrise may have caused his metabolic rate to drop, but we can't actually prove that either." She frowned. "I suppose we could push him up against an open window and see what happens."

"No!" Dr. Burke took a deep breath and leaned back against number eight's isolation box, allowing the soft vibration of the machinery to soothe her jangled nerves. "This is a vampire. I'm as certain of it as I've ever been of anything in my life. You saw how he reacted to my blood."

"That was pretty strange."

"Strange? It was incredible." With her left hand supporting the vampire's hip—he was heavier than she expected—she slid her right hand into his pants pocket and pulled out a slim, black leather wallet. "Now then, let's find out who you are."

"Would a vampire carry identification?"

"Why not? This is the twentieth century. Everyone carries identification of some kind. Here we are; Henry Fitzroy. I suppose they can't all be named Vladimir." Lips pursed and eyes gleaming, Dr. Burke turned over a gold patterned credit card. "Don't leave the crypt without it, as Donald would probably say. Speaking of Donald . . ." She paused and frowned. "Where is he, anyway?"

"Well, you see . . ." Catherine laid a gentle hand on number eight's isolation box. "He . . ."

"Has that damned tutorial this morning, doesn't he? And I expect he was long gone before our visitor showed up. It's his loss, you'll have to fill him in later. Now then, ownership, insurance, ah, driver's license. Apparently the myth that vampires show no photographic image is also false."

"I just can't believe we have vampires in Kingston."

"We don't. He's from Toronto." Gathering up the contents of the wallet, Dr. Burke tossed them onto a pile of clothes draped over a nearby chair. "We'll have to do something about his car . . . no, we don't. He'll just disappear. Become another tragic statistic. He's already living a lie; who's going to look for him?" She patted the back of one pale hand, fingers lightly stroking the scattering of red-gold hair. "Of all the laboratories in all the world, you had to stumble into mine.''

"But, Dr. Burke, what are we going to do with him?''

"Study him, Catherine. Study him.''

Head cocked to one side, Catherine examined the doctor. The last time she'd seen the older woman this excited had been the day number four had made the initial breakthrough with the neural net. Her eyes had held the same brilliant mix of greed and self-satisfaction then that they did now and, now that she thought about it, Catherine hadn't liked the expression that day either. "Dr. Burke, vampires are outside my experimental parameters."

Eleven

Vicki lifted her face into the wind blowing in off Lake Ontario and remembered how this slab of stone jutting into the water had once been both refuge and inspiration. All through her teens, whenever life got too complicated and she couldn't see her way clear, she'd come to the park, clamber out on the rock, and the world would simplify down to the lake and the wind. The city at her back would disappear and life would be back in perspective. Winter or summer, good weather or bad—it hadn't mattered.

The lake still crashed rhythmically against the rock below her feet, and the wind still picked up the spray and threw it at her but, even together, they were no longer strong enough to uncomplicate the world. Tightening her arm on the bulk of her shoulder bag, she blocked out the pounding of the waves and listened for the crackle of paper; heard her mother's words read from the letter in her mother's voice.

I don't want to just disappear out of your life like your father did. I want us to have a chance to say good-bye.

She swiped at the water on her cheeks before turning and climbing back up the bank to where Celluci waited, more or less patiently, by the car.

The detour had given her nothing but damp sneakers and the certain knowledge that the only way out of the situation she found herself in was going to be the hard way.

So we concentrate on finding my mother.

We find her, we find Henry.
And then we'll . . .
. . . we'll . . .

She shoved viciously at her glasses, jamming the
plastic bridge up into her forehead, ignoring the drops
of water that spotted the lenses—refusing to acknowledge drops that were salt water not fresh and were on
the inside of the lenses. *Let's just concentrate on finding them.* Then *we'll worry about what we do next.*

"Good morning, Mrs. Shaw. Is Dr. Burke in?"

"No, dear, I'm sorry, but you just missed her."

Vicki, who had been watching and waiting until she
saw Dr. Burke hurry from the office, manufactured a
frown.

"Is there anything I can do to help?"

She shifted the expression to hopeful. "I need to
talk to Donald Li about my mother and I'm finding it
impossible to track him down around the campus. I
was wondering if Dr. Burke could give me his home
address."

Mrs. Shaw smiled up at her and pulled an overflow-
ing rolodex forward. "You don't need to bother Dr.
Burke about that, I've got Donald's address right
here."

"Uh, Mrs. Shaw . . ." The young woman tempo-
rarily assigned to the office shot an uneasy glance from
Vicki to her coworker. "Should you be giving that
out? I mean that's private information and . . ."

"Don't worry about it, Ms. Grenier," Mrs. Shaw
instructed firmly, flipping through the cards with practiced fingers, "this is Marjory Nelson's daughter."

"Yes, but . . ."

Vicki leaned forward and caught the temporary's
eye. "I'm sure Donald won't mind," she said quietly.

Ms. Grenier opened her mouth, closed it, and decided she wasn't being paid enough to interfere with
someone who'd just made it quietly clear that any op-

position would be removed from the field on a stretcher if necessary.

Mrs. Shaw copied the address onto the back of a message form and handed it to Vicki. "Here you go, dear. Has there been any news from the police about your mother's body?"

"No." Vicki's fingers crushed the small square of pink paper. "Not yet."

"You'll let me know?"

"Yes." She didn't bother attempting a smile. "Thank you for this." It was probably fortunate that the outer office door had been designed in such a way that it couldn't be slammed.

"First to have her mother die and then to find that the body had been stolen." Mrs. Shaw sighed deeply and shook her head. "The poor girl was devastated."

Ms. Grenier made a silent but eloquent moue and bent back over her keyboard. As far as she was concerned, devastated might describe anything that got in that woman's way but it could hardly be applied to her emotional condition.

Celluci made no comment as Vicki slid into the passenger seat and slammed the car door. Although she'd insisted before going up that she could handle any sympathy expressed by her mother's ex-coworker, something had obviously gotten through. As nothing he could say would help, he merely started the engine and pulled carefully away from the curb.

"Make the next left," Vicki instructed tersely, yanking the seat belt into position then slamming it home. "We're heading for Elliot Street."

Three blocks later, she sighed deeply and said, "Odds are good that was a lot less trouble than breaking into the records office."

"Not to mention less illegal," Celluci pointed out dryly.

He got his reward in the quick flicker of a smile,

there and gone so fast he would've missed it had he not been watching.

"Not to mention," Vicki agreed.

"Catherine." Dr. Burke turned to face the wall, cupping the mouthpiece of the receiver with her free hand. It wouldn't do to be overheard. "I thought I'd give you a quick call between meetings to see how those tests are going."

"Well, his leukocytes are really amazing. I've never seen white blood cells like these."

"Have you looked at any tissue samples?"

"Not yet. I thought you wanted the blood work done first. I've drawn another two vials as well as a sample of lymphatic fluid and, Doctor, his plasma cells are just as unique as the rest."

Dr. Burke ignored a gesturing colleague. They couldn't start the damned meeting without her anyway. "Unique in what way?"

"Well, I'm not an immunologist, but given a little time I may be able to . . ."

A sudden realization threw everything into sharp-edged relief. "Good lord, you might be able to develop a cure for AIDS." That would mean more than just a Nobel prize; an AIDS vaccine would practically net her a sainthood.

Catherine hesitated before replying. "Well, yes, I suppose that might be one result. I was thinking more along the lines of my bacteria and . . ."

"Think big, Catherine. Look, I've got to go now. Concentrate on the plasma cells, I think they're our best bet. Oh, for pity's sake, Rob, I'm coming." She hung up the phone and turned to the worried looking man hovering at her elbow. "What *is* your problem?"

"Uh, the meeting . . ."

"Oh, yes, the meeting. God forbid we shouldn't waste half our life in meetings!" She practically danced her way back across the hall. *I've got a vam-*

pire and he's going to give me the world! An AIDS vaccine would be only the beginning.

As he followed her, Dr. Rob Fortin, associate professor of microbiology, found himself wishing he had an excuse to cut and run. When Aline Burke looked that cheerful, someone's ass was grass.

In the lab, Catherine stared at the phone for a moment, then somberly shook her head. "It's not like I don't have other things to do," she muttered.

Turning slightly, she shot a reassuring smile at number nine and number ten. She'd been shuffling them in and out of the one remaining isolation box all day as their physical needs had dictated but hadn't really been able to spend any quality time with them. "I'm not ignoring you," she said earnestly. "I'll just finish up this analysis for Dr. Burke and then we can get back to important things."

Donald, she could guiltlessly ignore for another twelve hours or so, but it wasn't fair to the others that all her time be taken up by Mr. Henry Fitzroy, vampire.

After all, he wasn't going anywhere.

The key had hardly entered the lock when the door to the next apartment opened and Mr. Delgado came out into the hall.

"Vicki, I thought it was you." He took a step toward her, the lines around his eyes deepening into worried grooves. "The police haven't found anything?"

"The police aren't exactly looking," Vicki told him tersely.

"Not looking? But . . ."

"The murder at the university has tied up their manpower," Celluci interjected. "They're doing what they can."

Mr. Delgado snorted. "Of course you'd say that, Mister Detective-Sergeant." He gestured at Vicki.

"But she shouldn't have to be doing this. She shouldn't have to go out looking."

Vicki's fingers whitened around the key. "It's my responsibility, Mr. Delgado."

He spread his hands. "Why?"

"Because she's my mother."

"No." He shook his head. "She *was* your mother. But your mother isn't anymore. Your mother is dead. Finding her body won't bring your mother back to you."

Celluci watched a muscle jump in Vicki's jaw and waited for the explosion. To his surprise, it didn't come.

"You don't understand," she said through clenched teeth and moved swiftly into the apartment.

Celluci remained in the hallway a moment longer.

"I'm right. I watched her grow up." Mr. Delgado sighed, the deep, weary exhalation of an old man who'd seen more death than he cared to remember. "She thinks it's her fault her mother died and if she can just find the body it'll make amends."

"Is that such a bad thing?"

"Yes. Because it *isn't* her fault Majory died," Mr. Delgado pointed out, turned on his heel, and left Celluci standing alone in the hall.

He found Vicki sitting on the couch, staring down at her notes, all the lights in the apartment on even though it was barely mid-afternoon and the living room was far from dark.

"He doesn't know about Henry," she said without looking up.

"I know," Celluci agreed.

"And just because I've reacted to my mother's body being stolen by attempting to find it again, well, that doesn't mean I'm repressing anything. People grieve in different ways. Damn it, if *you* were in my situation, you'd be out looking for *your* mother's body."

"Granted."

"My mother's dead, Mike. I know that."

So you keep saying. But he closed his teeth on the words.

"And my mother isn't the fucking point anymore. We've got to find Henry before they turn him into . . . Christ!" She ripped off her glasses and rubbed at her eyes. "You think Donald Li's made a run for it?" she asked, somehow forcing the question to sound no different than it had on a hundred other occasions looking for a hundred other young men.

"I think that if a university student spends the night away from home it usually means he's gotten lucky." Celluci watched her closely but matched his tone to hers.

"On the other hand, if he *was* Tom Chen, he's probably aware we're looking for him and he's gone to ground. Maybe we *should* stake out his apartment."

"The little old lady on the first floor promised she'd call the moment he came home. My guess is she doesn't miss much."

"My guess is she doesn't miss anything." Her glasses back in place, Vicki scowled down at the pile of papers on the coffee table then jumped to her feet. "Mike, I can't just sit here. I'm going back to the university. I'm going keep poking around. Maybe I'll turn something up."

"What?"

"I don't know!" She charged toward the door and he had no choice but to get out of her way or be run down.

"Vicki? Before you go, can I ask you something?" She stopped but didn't turn.

"*Do* you think you're responsible for your mother's death?"

He read the answer in the lines of her back, the sudden tension clearly visible even through shirt, sweater, and windbreaker.

"Vicki, it wasn't your fault when your father left and that didn't make your mother's life your responsibility."

He almost didn't recognize her voice when she answered. "When you love someone, they *become* your responsibility."

"Jesus H. Christ, Vicki! People aren't like puppies or kittens. Love isn't supposed to be that kind of a burden." He grabbed her shoulder and spun her around. Then wished he hadn't when he saw the look on her face. It was almost worse when that expression smoothed into one that told him nothing at all.

"If you are completely finished, Dr. Freud, you can get your god-damned hands off of me." A twist of her upper body, a step back, and she was free. "Now, are you going to help or are you going to sit around here all day with your psychoanalysis up your ass?"

She whirled, flung open the door, and stomped out into the hall before he had time to answer.

Well, Mr. Delgado. Celluci dragged both hands up through his hair and tried very hard not to grind the crowns off his teeth. *When you're right, you're really right. Still, she asked for my help. Again. I suppose that's progress of sorts.* Closing and locking the apartment behind him, he hurried to catch up. *Mind you, I'd feel better about that if it wasn't so obvious that she now feels responsible for Mr. Henry fucking Fitzroy.*

Dr. Burke acknowledged Mrs. Shaw's greeting but continued into her office without pausing. She couldn't decide what she hated more, bureaucracy itself or the sycophants that fawned around it. *Why,* she wondered, *does it have to be so difficult to end a term? Just send the students home and hose down the blackboards.*

The last thing that she needed, after not one but three meetings in which she valiantly attempted to impose logic onto rules and regulations, was to see Marjory Nelson's daughter wandering the halls of the Life Sciences building, peering through windows into labs and lecture halls and generally making a nuisance of herself. Watching the younger woman's progress from the anonymity of a shadowed recess, she'd very nearly called Security and had her escorted out. The presence of the Toronto police officer—whom she'd been introduced to briefly at the truncated funeral—changed her mind. Arbitrary actions were just the sort of thing that tended to make the police suspicious.

Besides, the chances of Vicki Nelson stumbling onto the lab, and her mother's body, were slim. First, she'd have to find the access passage into the old building. Then, she'd have to negotiate through the rabbit warren of halls that crossed and recrossed the hundred-year-old structure—halls that had occasionally, in the past, defeated freshmen armed with maps—to find the one room in use.

No, Vicki Nelson had no chance of finding her mother's body, but that didn't mean Dr. Burke liked seeing her hanging around.

Why the hell doesn't she just go home? She dropped into her chair and fanned the pile of messages on her desk. *Without her prodding, the police would've back-burnered this before they'd even begun.*

If only the coffin hadn't been opened; no one would have been the wiser.

If only Donald hadn't allowed Marjory Nelson to walk out of the lab and home.

If only the sight of the mother reanimated hadn't convinced the daughter that the answer lay at the university.

Vicki Nelson was an intelligent woman; even allowing for maternal prejudices, the facts spoke for themselves. Eventually, in her search for her mother, she'd stumble onto something that would jeopardize Dr. Burke's position. Dr. Burke had no intention of allowing that to happen.

Slowly, the Director of Life Sciences smiled. The incredible circumstance that had dropped a vampire into her hands had also given her an easy answer to the problem. "If Ms. Nelson wants to find her mother so badly," she murmured, tapping out the number for the lab, "maybe she should."

Catherine answered the phone on the third ring with a terse, "What is it, Doctor? I'm busy."

"How are the tests going?"

"Well, you want rather a lot done and . . ."

"Isn't Donald helping?"

"No, he . . ."

"Has he even been in today?"

"Well, no, he . . ."

"I don't want to hear his excuses, Catherine, I'll deal with him myself later." This wasn't the first time Donald had taken an unscheduled holiday, but it *was* time she put her foot down about it. "Have you run into anything this afternoon that might prevent us developing an AIDS vaccine?"

"Well, actually, I've observed that certain nonphagocytic leukocytes have a number of specialized functions on a cellular level that might possibly be developed into just that." She paused for a moment, then continued. "We'd have to practically drain Mr. Fitzroy to acquire a serum, though, and his pressure's already awfully low. I keep having to take new samples because even a minute amount of ultraviolet light destroys the cell structure."

"For pity's sake, Catherine, don't let any ultraviolet light fall on him. We can always replenish his blood . . ." The thought brought an interesting evisceral response that could possibly be explored later when they had more time. ". . . but if he loses cellular integrity, even your bacteria won't be able to rebuild him."

"I am aware of that, Doctor. I'm being very careful."

"Good. Now, then, since Mr. Fitzroy so fortuitously fell into our hands, I've altered our plans somewhat. Here's what we're going to do: run one final analysis on numbers nine and ten—*no point in wasting data that might be useful later*—then terminate them, strip them of all hardware, do the usual biopsies, and process both of them out through the medical morgue.

We'll work up the standard paperwork on number nine, but someone's sure to recognize Marjory Nelson. I'll see to it that she can't be traced back to us, everyone will claim ignorance, there'll be a six days' wonder, and then we'll be safely able to continue with no threat of discovery.''

She could hear breathing so she knew Catherine was still on the line, but moments passed and there was no response. ''Catherine?''

''Terminate numbers nine and ten?''

''That's right. We don't need them anymore.'' She felt a triumphant smile spread across her face and made no effort to stop it. ''We have captured a creature who in and of himself can unlock the Nobel door.''

Catherine ignored the triumph. ''But that'll kill them!''

''Don't be ridiculous, they're already dead.''

''But, Dr. Burke . . .''

Dr. Burke sighed and moved her glasses up on her head so she could rub at her temples. ''No buts, Catherine. They're becoming a liability. I was willing to overlook that when they were our best chance for success, but with Mr. Fitzroy under our control we have an unlimited potential to make scientific history.'' She softened her voice. Once again Catherine would have to be manipulated onto the most productive path. ''If you can fuse the elements of Henry Fitzroy's blood into your bacteria, it will make everything we've done so far redundant. We're moving onto a new level of scientific discovery here.''

''Yes, but . . .''

''Science moves forward, Catherine. You can't let yourself be trapped in the past. An opportunity like this doesn't come along every day.'' *Now, that was an understatement*, she mused as the triumphant smile returned. ''You begin the termination. I'll be down as soon as I can. Sunset is at 7:47, see that Mr. Fitzroy is locked up tightly a good half an hour before then.''

Sounding numb, Catherine murmured, "Yes, Dr. Burke," into the phone and hung up.

Shaking her head, Dr. Burke replaced the receiver. In a few days Catherine would be so immersed in new discoveries that she'd forget numbers nine and ten even existed as anything but collections of experimental data. *Which, of course,* she reminded herself acerbically, *is all they are.*

Catherine stared at the phone for a moment, turning Dr. Burke's words over and over in her head. Science had to keep going forward. It couldn't remain stuck in the past.

Science had to keep going forward.

She truly believed that.

The quest for knowledge, in and of itself, is of primary importance. Those were her own words, spoken to the doctor during her search for the funds and lab space necessary to develop her bacteria to their full potential. Dr. Burke had agreed and they'd taken the quest together.

Terminate numbers nine and ten.

She couldn't do it.

Dr. Burke was wrong. They were alive.

She wouldn't do it.

Taking a deep breath and smoothing the front of her lab coat, she turned. Sitting where she'd left them against the far wall, they were both watching her; almost as if they knew. They trusted her. She wasn't going to let them down.

Unfortunately, bundling them into the back of her van and disappearing into the sunset wasn't an option. In order to keep them functional, she needed the lab. Dr. Burke, therefore, had to be made to change her mind.

. . . with Mr. Fitzroy under our control we have an unlimited potential to make scientific history.

Suppose Mr. Fitzroy was no longer under her control?

Brow furrowed in thought, Catherine crossed the room to the isolation box that held the quiescent vampire. Essentially, it was operating as nothing more than a containment unit with none of its specialized functions working. It wasn't even plugged in. Theoretically, it was mobile. In actuality, its weight made it difficult to move.

Catherine placed both hands against one end and shoved as hard as she could. Nothing. Bracing her feet against the wall, she shoved again, straining until her vision went red.

The isolation box jerked forward six inches and stopped when she did.

It had taken all three of them, her and Donald and Dr. Burke to move the empty boxes in. Catherine bowed her head over her folded arms, breath misting the cool metal, and admitted she couldn't move it out, not on her own.

Number nine stood and walked carefully forward, supporting himself once on the back of a chair as his left leg nearly folded beneath him. He had no way of knowing that inside the knee, tendons and ligaments were finally surrendering to rot.

He saw she was sad.

That was enough.

He stopped beside her and laid his hand on her shoulder.

Catherine turned at the touch and looked up. "If we hide the vampire," she said, "we'll have time to convince Dr. Burke that she's wrong."

There were many words number nine didn't understand, so he merely placed his palms where hers had been, and pushed.

The isolation box rumbled forward.

"Stop."

Number nine stopped pushing. The box moved a few inches farther, then ground to a halt under its own weight.

"Yes! We can do this together!" Catherine threw her arms around number nine in an impulsive hug, ignoring the way tissue compacted under her touch, ignoring the smell that had begun to rise.

Number nine struggled to recognize what he felt.

It was . . .

It was . . .

Then her arms were gone and it was lost.

Stepping back, Catherine glanced around the lab. "We can hide the vampire and the other isolation box as well. That way, Dr. Burke won't be able to hold you hostage for his return. The dialysis machine is portable and an IV drip can replace the nutrient pump for a few days. We'll take one of the computers with us just in case Dr. Burke takes too long to come to her senses. You shouldn't suffer from lack of input just because she's being stubborn."

Then she paused. "Oh, no. Donald." Reaching out, she patted the box that enclosed the body of the other grad student. "I can't unplug you, Donald, it's too soon. I'm sorry, but we'll have to leave you here." She sighed deeply. "I only hope that Dr. Burke will allow you to finish developing. She's just not thinking straight, Donald. I've had this feeling lately that all she wants is fame and money, that she doesn't care about the experiments. I care. I know you'll understand."

Checking her watch, she hurried back across the room to the computer terminal, copied the day's work onto a disk, and then scrubbed it from the main memory. "Just in case," she murmured, slipping the copy into her lab coat pocket. "I can't leave her a way out."

On her way back to where number nine waited patiently, she picked up the vampire's trench coat and the shirt she'd had to remove as well. She didn't have time to dress him again, but she spread them neatly over the body before closing the lid and latching it.

"This is going to take all of us. Number ten, come here."

Released from the compulsion to stay, she rose to her feet. "Come here" was not an implanted command so, although she knew what it meant, she moved toward the door.

She had something she had to do.

"Stop." Catherine shook her head and circled around number ten until she could look her in the face. "There's something the matter, isn't there? I wish you could tell me what it was, maybe I could help. But you *can't* tell me and, right now, we've all got problems."

Taking hold of one gray-green wrist, Catherine led Marjory Nelson's body over to stand beside the front end of the box, wrapped dark-tipped fingers around a metal handle, and said, "Hold."

The fingers tightened.

With number nine pushing and number ten obeying rapid orders to push or pull, the massive piece of equipment, and the body it contained, rumbled across the lab and out into the hall.

. . . you could tell me what it was . . .
. . . you could tell me . . .
She remembered *talking*.

If vampires exist . . . Dr. Burke scribbled a question mark in the margin of an application for summer research funds that had been handed in at absolutely the last minute. *. . . and they very obviously do, then just think of what else might be out there. Demons. Werewolves. The Creature from the Black Lagoon.* Even though her cheeks were beginning to ache, she couldn't control the spreading grin. Hadn't been able to control it all afternoon. *Henry Fitzroy's blood will enable me to collect every accolade the scientific community possesses on a silver platter. In fact, they'll have to create new awards, just for me.*

They would have to take precautions, of course. The legendary vampire had been accredited with a number of abilities that could be a threat. While many of them could be discounted out of hand—as he hadn't been able to get out of the isolation box before sunrise, the actual vampire appeared incapable of becoming mist— he *was* very strong; the dents he'd added to number nine's pattern on the inside of the lid testified to that. *So it's probably best that he spend his nights locked in that box.*

He'd have to be fed, of course, if only to replace the fluids Catherine removed during the day. Fortunately, there were a number of small tubes available that blood could be passed through.

And as for the granting of eternal life. Dr. Burke drummed her fingertips on the desk. Henry Fitzroy's identification seemed to indicate that he lived a reasonably normal life, even considering that the day was unquestionably denied him, and nothing but legend indicated that he'd lived any longer than the twenty-four years his driver's license allowed him. She'd have to discuss his history with him later—not that it mattered much. What point in living forever if forever had to be lived in hiding? *Skulking about in the dark. Helpless in the day. Not, I think, for me.*

After years of being anonymously responsible for keeping the infrastructure of science running, she wanted recognition. She'd spent long enough tucked away out of sight, tilting with bureaucracy while others garnered the glory.

One lifetime, properly appreciated, would be long enough. Conquering death had always been merely a means to an end and she had no more intention of becoming a blood-drinking creature of the night than she did of allowing her body to be used to create one of those shambling monstrosities she'd told Catherine to destroy.

Although, perhaps when Catherine has all the bugs worked out . . .

Resisting the temptation to begin composing her acceptance speech for Stockholm, Dr. Burke forced herself to concentrate on the grant application. When she'd dealt with this last bit of unavoidable paperwork, she'd be free to spend a few hours in the lab. She was actually looking forward to the unavoidable conversation with their captured vampire.

Half an hour later, a tentative knock at the office door brought her up out of a projected balance sheet that proved at least one of the department's professors had taken a course in economics—and not paid much attention.

"Come in."

Mrs. Shaw leaned into the room. "I just wanted to let you know that I'm leaving now, Doctor."

"Is it as late as all that?"

The older woman smiled. "It's later. But Ms. Grenier and I pretty much cleared the backlog."

Dr. Burke nodded approvingly. "Good. Thank you for all the hard work." Appreciation made the best motivator regardless of where it was applied. "There'll be another stack out there tomorrow," she added, indicating the pile of folders on the corner of her desk.

"You can count on me, Doctor. Good night. Oh." The door, in the process of closing, opened again and Mrs. Shaw reappeared. "Marjory's daughter was around this morning. She wanted Donald Li's home address. I hope you don't mind."

"A little late now if I did, isn't it?" Somehow, she managed to keep the question light. "Did Ms. Nelson tell you *why* she wanted Donald's address?"

"She wanted to talk to him about her mother." Mrs. Shaw began to look worried at the expression on her employer's face. "I know it's against policy, but she *is* Marjory's daughter."

"*Was* Marjory's daughter," Dr. Burke pointed out dryly. "Never mind, Mrs. Shaw." There was no point in getting annoyed so long after the fact. "If Donald doesn't want to talk to her, I'm sure he can take care of it himself."

"Thank you, Doctor. Good night."

Dr. Burke waited a moment, to be certain that this time the door would stay closed, then pulled the phone across the desk and tapped in Donald's number. After four rings, his answering machine came on with a trumpet fanfare and the message that ". . . autographed pictures are available for twenty dollars plus a self-addressed, stamped envelope. For personal dedications, add five dollars. Those actually wishing conversation with Mr. Li can leave a message after the tone and he'll get back to you the moment he has a break in his too, too busy schedule."

"This is Dr. Burke. If you're there, Donald, pick up."

Apparently, he wasn't there. After leaving instructions that she be called at his earliest opportunity, Dr. Burke hung up and shoved the phone away.

"He's probably spent the day avoiding that woman. At least he didn't lead her to the lab."

The lab . . .

A memory nibbled at the edge of conscious thought. Something to do with the lab. She leaned back in her chair and frowned up at the ceiling tiles. Something not quite right that the incredible discovery of the vampire had distracted her from. Something so normal . . .

. . . *leaned back against number eight's box, allowing the soft vibration of machinery to soothe her jangled nerves.*

Number eight no longer existed. The vampire was in number nine's box but both number nine and number ten had been sitting passively against the wall.

Who was in number eight's box?

Then a second memory surfaced.

Gathering up the contents of the wallet, she tossed them onto a pile of clothes draped over a nearby chair.

It suddenly got very hard to breathe.

"Oh, lord, no . . ."

They could hear the phone ringing from the hall. As could be expected under the circumstances, the key jammed.

Four rings. Five.

"God*damn*it!" Her mood not exactly sunny, Vicki backed up and slammed the bottom of her foot against the door just below the lock. The entire structure shuddered under the impact. When she grabbed the key again, it turned.

"Nothing like the Luke Skywalker method," Celluci muttered, racing for the phone.

Nine rings. Ten.

"Yes? Hello?"

"Good timing, Mike. I was just about to hang up."

Celluci mouthed "Dave Graham" at Vicki, jammed the receiver between ear and shoulder, and readied a pen. "What've you got for me?"

"I had to call in a couple of favors—you owe me for this, partner—but Humber College finally came through. Your boy was recommended to the course by a Dr. Dabir Rashid, Faculty of Medicine, Queen's University. And as a bonus, they threw in the information that he requested young Mr. Chen serve his four-week observation period at Hutchinson's."

"No mention of a Dr. Aline Burke?"

"Nary a word. How's Vicki?"

Good question. "Damned if I know."

"Like that, is it? You gotta remember that death affects different people different ways. I know when my uncle died, my aunt seemed almost relieved, handled the funeral like it was a family reunion. Two weeks later, blam. Completely fell apart. And my wife's cousin, he . . ."

"Dave."

"Yeah?"

"Later."

"Oh. Right. Listen, Cantree says to take as much time as you need for this. He said we'll manage to muddle through somehow without you."

"Nice of him."

"He's a saint. Let me know how it shakes down."

"You got it, buddy." He turned from hanging up the phone to find Vicki glaring at him. "Our Tom Chen got his recommendation from a Dr. Dabir Rashid, Faculty of Medicine, Queen's University. I don't suppose that could be an alias for Dr. Burke?"

"No. I met Dr. Rashid briefly yesterday." Vicki stomped across the room and threw herself down onto the couch. "He's a year older than God and isn't sure if he's coming or going. I assume he has tenure."

Celluci dropped a hip onto the telephone table and shrugged. "Easy to confuse, then, if you wanted him to do you a favor you didn't want traced."

"Exactly." Vicki spit the word out. "He probably thought he was recommending the Tom Chen who's actually studying medicine." She jabbed at her glasses. "From what I saw, if he even remembers giving it, he'll never remember who asked him to do it."

"Then we'll have to stimulate his memory."

Vicki snorted. "The shock would probably kill him."

"You never know. The recommendation included a request that Chen serve his four-week observation period at Hutchinson's—the more details, more chance one of them stuck."

"Yeah. Maybe." Snatching up a green brocade cushion, she threw it against the far wall. "Jesus, Mike; why isn't it ever easy?"

Another good question. "I don't know, Vicki, maybe . . ."

His voice trailed off as he watched all the color suddenly drain out of her face. "Vicki? What's wrong?"

"It's a four-week observation period." Her hands

were shaking so violently she couldn't lace the fingers together, so she curled them into fists and pressed the fists hard against her thighs. "My mother was given six months to live." She had to force the words out through a throat closed tight. "They couldn't keep placing people in that funeral home." Why hadn't she seen it before? "My mother had to die during those four weeks." She turned her head and met Celluci's gaze square on. "Do you know what that means?"

He knew.

"My mother was murdered, Mike." Her voice became steel and ice. "And who was with my mother seconds before she died?"

He reached behind him and scooped up the phone. "I think we've got something Detective Fergusson will listen to now . . ."

"No." Vicki got slowly to her feet, her movements jerky and barely under control. "First, we've got to rescue Henry. Once he's safe, she's history. But not until."

She wasn't going to fail Henry the way she'd failed her mother.

Twelve

As the day surrendered its power to hold him, Henry fought the panic that accompanied awareness—the steel coffin still enclosed him, wrapped him in the stink of death perverted and the acrid odor of his own terror. He couldn't prevent the first two blows that slammed up into the impervious arc of padded metal, but he managed to stop the third and the fourth. With full consciousness came greater control. He remembered the futile struggles of the night before and knew that mere physical strength would not be enough to free him.

His head swam with images—the young man, strangled, newly dead; the older man, long dead, not dead, not alive; the young woman, pale hair, pale skin, empty eyes. He swallowed, tasted the residue of blood, and was nearly lost as the Hunger rose.

It was too strong to force back. Henry barely managed to hold the line between the Hunger and self.

He had fed the night before. The Hunger should be his to command. Then he realized his struggles had tangled his arms in the heavy folds of his leather trench coat. Someone had removed both it and his shirt and not bothered to replace them. Bare to the waist, he found the marks of a dozen needles.

And I no more want to be strapped to a table for the rest of my life than to have my head removed and my mouth stuffed with garlic.

He'd made that observation, somewhat facetiously, just over a year ago. It seemed much less facetious now. Over the course of the day someone had obviously been conducting experiments. He was helpless during the oblivion of the day. He was captive in the night.

The panic won and a crimson tide of Hunger roared free with it.

Consciousness returned a second time that night, bringing pain and an exhaustion so complete he could barely straighten twisted limbs. His body, weakened by blood loss, had obviously set a limit on hysteria.

Can't say . . . as I blame it. Even thinking hurt. Screaming had ripped his throat raw. Bruising, bone-deep on knees and elbows, protested movement. Two of the fingers on his left hand were broken and the skin over the knuckles, split. With what seemed like the last of his strength, he realigned the fractures then lay panting, trying not to taste the abomination in the air.

They've taken so much blood, I have to assume they know what I am.

The Hunger filled his prison with throbbing crimson need, bound for the moment by his weakness. Eventually, the weakness would be devoured and the Hunger would rule.

In all his seventeen years, Henry had never been in a darkness so complete and, in spite of Christina's remembered reassurances, he began to panic. The panic grew when he tried to lift the lid off the crypt and found he couldn't move. Not stone above him but rough wood embracing him so closely that the rise and fall of his chest brushed against the boards.

He had no idea how long he lay, paralyzed by terror, frenzied need clawing at his gut, but his sanity hung by a . . .

"No." He could manage no more than a whispered protest, not quite enough to banish the memory. The terror of that first awakening, trapped in a common grave, nearly destroyed by the Hunger, would reach out to claim him now if he let it. "Remember the rest, if you must remember at all."

. . . he heard a shovel blade bite into the dirt above him, the noise a hundred thousand times louder than it could possibly have been."

"Henry!"

The Hunger surged out toward the voice, carrying him with it.

"Henry!"

His name. It was his name she called. He clutched at it like a lifeline, the Hunger a surrounding maelstrom.

"Henry, answer me!"

Although the Hunger tried to drown him out, he formed a single word. "Christina . . ."

Then, the nails shrieking protest, the coffin lid flew back. Pale hands, strong hands, gentle hands held him in his frenzy. Rough homespun ripped away from alabaster skin and a wound in a breast reopened so he could feed again on the blood that had changed him, safe behind a silken curtain of ebony hair.

He couldn't free himself.

Four hundred and fifty years ago, a woman's love had saved him.

He couldn't surrender to despair.

But it had taken Christina three days . . .

Vicki, come quickly. Please. I can't survive that again.

The halls had always been empty when she walked them, empty, echoing, and dimly lit. *And they are no different tonight,* Aline Burke told herself firmly, placing one foot purposefully before the other. *They are still empty. I am making the only sounds. Shadows are merely absences of light.*

But air currents moved where she'd never felt air

currents before and the whole building exuded an aura of expectant doom.

Which is not only overly melodramatic, it's ridiculous. She dried moist palms against her pants and kept her eyes firmly focused on the next band of illumination. She would not give in to fear; she never had and she wasn't about to begin now.

Who was in number eight's isolation box?

There could be any number of very good reasons why Donald hadn't been around all day; Vicki Nelson's investigation was only the most obvious. Donald, charming, brilliant, and undisciplined, had never had any trouble in coming up with reasons to take a day off.

Who was in number eight's isolation box?

Memory continued to replay the fall of Henry Fitzroy's wallet onto the pile of clothes.

Who was in number eight's isolation box?

There was only one way to find out.

Rounding a corner, she could see the outline of the lab door. No light escaped, but then they'd gone to a great deal of trouble to ensure that none did.

They're probably both in there. Arguing about something trivial. Or he's watching her work, letting those damned candy wrappers fall on my floor.

She put her hand on the metal doorknob, the stainless steel cold under her fingers. Stainless steel. Like the isolation boxes.

Her heart began to pound. The metal warmed under her grip. Fifteen seconds passed. Twenty. Forty-five. A full minute. She couldn't turn the knob. It was as if the link between brain and hand had been severed. She knew what she had to do, but her body refused to respond.

Lips compressed into a thin line, she jerked her arm back to her side. This kind of betrayal could not be allowed. She drew in a calming breath, exhaled, and then in one continuous motion grabbed the knob,

turned it, pushed the door open, and stepped into the
room.

The lights were off. She could see a number of red
and green power indicators at the far end of the room
but nothing else. Stretching out her left arm, she
groped along the wall, the sound of her breathing
moving outward to meet the hum of working equipment. The light switches were just to the right of the
door. Turning her back was out of the question.

Her fingers touched a steel plate, recoiled, then continued on until finally they hooked behind a protruding
bit of plastic.

A heartbeat later, Dr. Burke blinked in the sudden
blue-white glare of the fluorescents.

At the far end of the room, number eight's isolation
box—number eight's no longer—hummed in unat-
tended solitude. The other two boxes were gone and
with them the portable dialysis machine and one of the
computers. A quick scan showed smaller pieces of
equipment were missing as well and apprehension
turned to anger as Dr. Burke stomped the length of the
room to the remaining computer.

"That vindictive little bitch!"

The message on the screen was succinct and to the
point.

*I've hidden Mr. Fitzroy. You can have him back when
you agree that numbers nine and ten can continue to
their natural conclusions. I have the only copy of today's data. I'll be in touch. – Catherine.*

Obviously, she'd not only hidden the vampire but
numbers nine and ten as well.

"Damn her! She must've started the second I hung
up the phone." This would ruin everything! If Catherine couldn't be brought round and quickly, the whole
plan would be as dead as . . .

. . . as dead as . . .

She raised her head and bands of pressure settled
around her temples. The distorted reflection of a small,

warped figure in white stared back from the curved side of the only remaining box.

Why hadn't Catherine hidden this box as well?

Because it couldn't be unplugged.

Why couldn't it be unplugged?

Because the bacteria still worked on the body it contained.

Who was in number eight's isolation box?

The clothes remained on a chair on the other side of the lab, a pale brown windbreaker draped over the back.

Lots of people wear jackets like that in Kingston in April.

She made the largest circle around the box she could without admitting to herself that she was avoiding it. Desperately holding on to the anger, using it as a weapon against the rising fear, she reached out and lifted the jacket off the chair. It could still belong to anyone. Ignoring the damp smudges her fingers printed on the fabric, she reached into one of the front pockets and drew out two wrapped candies and a half-eaten chocolate bar, package neatly resealed with a bit of tape.

There's nothing that says Donald couldn't have left his jacket in the lab.

But she was losing the fight and she knew it.

Henry Fitzroy's identification lay where she'd tossed it. Draping the jacket over one arm, she watched her free hand reach out and scoop the wallet and its contents up off a neatly folded pile of clothes. A jacket might be accidentally left behind but not jeans and a shirt, socks and underwear. These were Donald's clothes, no question of that, and beneath the chair, heels and toes precisely in line, were the black high-top basketball sneakers he'd been so absurdly proud of.

"But Donald, you don't play basketball."

Donald continued to vigorously pump the bright orange ball set into the tongues of his new shoes. "What does that have to do with anything?'' he asked, grinning broadly. ''We're talking the cutting edge of footwear here. We're talking high tech. We're talking image.''

Dr. Burke sighed and shook her head. ''The perception of athletics without the sweat?'' she offered.

The grin grew broader. ''The point exactly.''

Still holding the jacket and the vampire's wallet, Dr. Burke slowly turned to face the isolation box. Numbers one through nine had been pulled from the medical school morgue already very dead. Marjory Nelson was dying. But Donald, Donald had been very alive.

She took a step forward, feeling so removed from reality that she had to concentrate on placing her foot down on the floor. Walking no longer seemed to be a voluntary movement. She could see Donald, dark eyes sparkling, completely unrepentant, as he sat in her office and listened to the reasons why he should not only be thrown out of medical school but brought up on charges. When she'd asked him why he'd done it, he'd actually looked thoughtful for a moment before answering. *''I wanted to see what would happen.''* She'd gotten him off. The particulars were buried when the professor who'd uncovered the incident had moved out west the next semester.

She took another step. She could see Donald frowning over the neural net, clever fingers running along the gold strands, bottom lips caught between his teeth as he struggled with the design.

Another step. She could see Donald lifting a confused Catherine's hand aloft for a high-five when number four finally responded to their combined genius.

Another. She could see Donald joining her in a private toast to fame and fortune, barely touching the single malt to his lips for he never drank.

Another. She could see Donald agreeing that Marjory Nelson was the inevitable next step.

Her knee touched the box, the vibration burrowing into the bone. She flinched back, then froze.

Staring down at her reflection, she saw it become a progression of gray faces, contorted, robbed of rest, bodies disfigured by gaping incisions hastily tacked together with knotted railway lines of black silk. What would she see when she lifted the lid? How far had Catherine gone?

Forcing a deep breath past the constriction in her throat, she let Henry Fitzroy's wallet drop from her right hand to floor. It wasn't really important anymore. Anymore. Anymore . . .

She reached out, unable to stop the trembling but refusing to give in, and wrapped her empty hand around the latch. Her fingers were so cold, the metal felt warm beneath them.

"Knowledge is strength," she whispered.

The latch clicked open.

From inside the box came a sigh of oxygen rich air as the seal broke, then, following it, a noise that had nothing to do with electronics or machinery.

Dr. Burke froze. The muscles in her arm, already given the command to lift, spasmed and shook.

A moan.

"Donald?"

Vowels began to form. A tortured shaping. Still recognizable.

There was nothing even remotely human in the sound.

Sweat dribbled in icy tracks down her sides. Fingers fought to close the latch. Whatever was in there, wasn't getting out.

"Doc . . . tor . . ."

She jerked back; panting, whimpering. Then she turned and ran.

Terror that couldn't be banished by intellect, or rationalizations, or strength of purpose ran beside her through the empty halls. The echoes mocked her. The shadows bulged with horror.

"What if she's not there?"

"She's not at home," Vicki replied through set teeth—they'd found Dr. Burke's address in the brown leather book beside her mother's phone. "She has to be somewhere."

"Not necessarily at the office."

Vicki turned to face him, even though the darkness left her blind. "You have a better idea?"

She heard him sigh. "No. But if she isn't there, what then?"

"Then we rip her office apart. We look for anything that might tell us where Henry is."

"And if we don't . . ."

"Shut up, Celluci." She spat the words in his direction. "We'll find him."

He drew in breath to speak again, then let it out silently.

Vicki twisted back around in the passenger seat, her grip on the dashboard painfully tight. *We'll find him.* All she could see through the windshield was the glare of the headlights, nothing of what they illuminated, not even the surface of the road. The lights of other cars appeared suspended, red and yellow eyes on invisible beasts. She felt the car turn, then slow, then finally stop. Silence fell, then darkness.

"I parked around beside the building," Celluci said. "A little less obvious if we have to slip past Security."

"Good idea."

For a moment, neither of them moved, then Vicki turned toward her door just as Celluci opened his. The interior light came on and for a heartbeat she saw herself reflected in the car window.

Pressed up against the glass, fingers splayed, mouth silently working, was her mother.

"Mike!"

He was at her side in an instant, the door mercifully closing as he slid across the front seat. She backed into the circle of his arms, squeezed her eyes so tightly shut they hurt, and tried to stop shaking.

"Vicki, what is it? What's wrong?" He'd never

heard his name called in such a way before and he hoped like hell he'd never hear it called that way again. The pain in Vicki's voice not only gouged pieces out of his soul, it clutched at him in a way *she* wasn't able to. She had her back pressed so hard against his chest he could barely breathe, but her fingers were folded into fists and her arms wrapped tightly around herself.

"Mike, my mother is dead."

He rested his cheek against the top of her head. "I know."

"Yeah, but she's also up and walking around." A hint of hysteria crept into her tone. "So, it just occurred to me, when we find her, what are we supposed to do. I mean, how do we bury her?"

"Jesus H. Christ." The whispered profanity came out sounding more like a prayer.

"I mean," she had to gulp air between every couple of words, "am I going to have to kill her again?"

"Vicki!" He held her closer. It was all he could think of to do. "Goddamnit! You didn't kill her the first time! As much as it seems cruel to say it, her dying had *nothing* to do with you."

He could feel her fighting for control.

"Maybe not the first time," she said.

The Hunger clawed and fought to be free and it took almost all the strength he had left to contain it. Released, it would quickly drive his abused body back into unconsciousness, probably breaking more bones as it fought to feed. Henry had no intention of allowing that to happen. He *had* to remain aware in case his captors should actually be stupid enough to open the box between dusk and dawn.

With so little left to fuel fear, he was able to view his imprisonment almost dispassionately. Almost. Memories of being trapped in darkness flickered mothlike against the outside edges of his control but worse even than that were images of the experiments that would begin when sunrise made him vulnerable once more.

Henry had seen the Inquisition, the slave trade, and the concentration camps of World War II and knew full well the atrocities people were able to commit. He'd seen his own father condemn men and women to the pyre for no better reason than temper. *And these particular people,* he thought, *have already proven themselves less than ethically bound.* There had been three containers. He was in one of them. Vicki's mother was, no doubt, in one of the other two.

Turning his head slightly so that the flow of fresh air through the grille—through the unbreakable grille—passed over his mouth and nose, he concentrated on breathing. It wasn't much of a distraction, but it was one of the few he had.

A minor comfort that I don't have to worry about suffoca . . .

The stench of abomination suddenly engulfed him. He jerked back against the far side of his prison, shoulder blades pressed hard into the plastic, laboring heart pounding in his ears. The creature was right outside the box; it had to be.

Cupping his injured hand against his chest, Henry fought for calm. This might be his only chance for freedom; he couldn't allow blind panic to take it from him.

Something dragged across the top of the box, something large and soft. Henry had a sudden vision of an old Hammer film, where Dracula brought his pair of hungry brides a child to feed on.

Oh, lord, not that.

Given an opportunity to feed, he wouldn't be able to stop the Hunger. The child would die. He'd killed many times over the centuries; sometimes because he had to, sometimes only because he could. But never an innocent. Never a child.

The dragging stopped.

When the lid opens . . . Henry made himself as

ready as he was able. But the lid remained closed and a moment later, muscles trembling, he sagged back against the padded bottom.

"If I call her in the morning, she'll have had time to think it over and she'll realize that I'm serious."

Although he could still smell nothing but abomination, Henry recognized the voice. It belonged to the pale young woman with the empty eyes.

"She's a reasonable person and I'm sure that as a scientist she'll come to see my position."

The young woman was crazy. Henry, who had touched her mind, had no doubt about that. But she was also on the outside of the box, capable of releasing him, and crazy or not, she was, at this moment, the only game in town. Ignoring the pain, he squirmed around until his mouth pressed up against the dented surface of the air vents and pitched his voice to carry, keeping his tone as matter-of-fact as he could.

"Excuse me? Would you mind opening the lid?"

For a very little while, he thought normalcy might have worked where an attempt at coercion or charm would've found no reaction. He caught a trace of her scent threaded through the stink of perverted death—not, he thanked God, enough to pull the Hunger out of his control—he heard her hands at the latch, then he heard her reply.

"Yes, I would mind actually, because I didn't have time today to take any tissue samples."

"If all you want are tissue samples, let me out and I'll stay around so you can take them." Henry swallowed, his throat working around the fear. *Just let me out!*

"Well, actually, I'm not very good at biopsies on living subjects. I think I'll wait until tomorrow."

Not very good at biopsies on living subjects? What the hell was she talking about? "But I'll still be alive!"

"Not exactly." She sounded as though she were pointing out something so obvious that she couldn't understand why he even brought it up.

He heard her move away. "Wait!"

"What is it now? I have a lot on my mind tonight."

"Look, do you know what I am?" All things considered, she *had* to know.

"Yes. You're a vampire."

"Do you know what that means?"

"Yes. You have fascinating leukocytes."

"What?" He couldn't stop himself from asking.

"Leukocytes. White blood cells. And your hemoglobin has amazing potential as well."

Much more of this and I'll be as crazy as she is. "If you know what I am, you know what I can give you." His voice reverberated inside the box; ageless, powerful. "Let me out and I can give you eternal life. You'll never grow old. You'll never die."

"No, thank you. I'm working on something else at the moment."

And he heard her move away.

"Wait!" He forced himself to lie quiet and listen, but all he could hear was the pounding of his own heart and Henry Fitzroy, bastard son of Henry the VIII, four-hundred-and-fifty-year-old vampire, became suddenly just Henry Fitzroy.

"DON'T LEAVE ME ALONE!"

"You know," Catherine said, pulling the heavy steel door closed behind her. "I hadn't realized he'd be so noisy. Good thing we put him in here." She slid a lock through the eye of the security bar and snapped it shut. "Dr. Burke will never be able to hear him."

Number nine stared at the door. The "Warning: High Voltage" meant nothing to him, but he remembered being locked in the box. In the same box. He hadn't liked it.

Slowly, the two fingers on his right hand that were still working, closed around the security bar.

Already halfway across the room, Catherine turned at the noise as the lock jumped but held. "What is it? What's wrong?"

Without releasing the bar, he carefully turned to face her. He hadn't liked being locked in the box.

"You think I should have let him out?" She came back to his side, shaking her head. "You don't understand. If I can isolate the factors that result in his continuous cell regeneration, I can integrate them into a bacterium that will actually repair you." Taking hold of his wrist, she very gently pulled his hand from the door and smiled up at him. "You can stay with me forever."

He understood the smile.

He understood forever.

That was enough.

His walk had degenerated into a lurch and a shuffle as he followed her from the room.

He remembered joy.

The level in the bottle of single malt whiskey had dropped rather considerably over the last . . . Dr. Burke peered at her watch but couldn't quite make out the time. Not that it mattered. Not really. Not any more.

"Nothing can stop me from garnering the glory." Bracing her elbow, she poured a little more whiskey into her mug. "I said that. Nothing can stop me." She took a long drink and sat back, cradling the mug against her stomach.

"Doc . . . tor . . ."

She couldn't hear him. He was locked in a stainless steel box in another building.

"Doc . . . tor . . ."

She took another drink to drown out the sound.

"Are you all right?"

Vicki slid into the outer office and started across the room. Why was he asking her now? She'd managed to regain control before they left the car. "I'm fine."

"Would you tell me if you weren't?"

Unable to see, she slammed her knee into the side

of a desk and bit back a curse. Obviously, her memory of the office layout was less than perfect. "Fuck off, Celluci."

Aware she could no more see him than she could see anything else, he rolled his eyes. She certainly sounded a lot better.

Dr. Burke heard the impact of flesh against furniture even through the covering noise of the whiskey. Her heart stopped. She *had* latched the isolation box. It *couldn't* have climbed out and followed her.

Could it?

Then she heard the voices and her heart started beating again.

"How nice." The alcohol she'd consumed, while not yet enough to insulate her from the memory of what she'd left in the lab, was enough to make her feel removed from the rest of the world. "I've got company."

Bending carefully down from her chair so as not to put more stress on an already overloaded sense of balance, she lifted Donald's jacket from the carpet and laid it on the desk in front of her.

"Please come in, Ms. Nelson. I can't abide a person who lurks."

Celluci pivoted to face the door. "Sounds like we've found the doctor." Through the light grip around Vicki's biceps he felt her shudder, but her voice remained steady.

"So let's not keep her waiting."

Together they moved into the inner office.

The street lamp, outside the window and five stories down, provided enough illumination for Celluci to see the doctor sitting at her desk. He couldn't make out her expression, but he could smell the booze. Twisting around, he stretched back a long arm and flicked on the overhead light.

In the sudden glare, no one moved, no one said

anything, until Vicki stepped forward, watering eyes squinted almost shut, and said with no trace of humor, "Dr. Frankenstein, I presume."

Dr. Burke snorted with laughter. "Good God, wit under stress. We could use a little more of that around here. Grad students are generally a boring, academically intensive bunch." One hand closed tightly around a fold of the jacket on her desk, the other lifted the mug to her mouth. "Generally," she repeated after a moment.

"You're drunk," Vicki snarled.

"A-plus for perception. C-minus for manners. As obvious as it obviously is, that's not the sort of thing you're supposed to point out."

Vicki charged the desk, barely stopping herself from going over it with a white-knuckled grip on the edge. "Enough bullshit! What have you done with Henry Fitzroy?"

Dr. Burke looked momentarily surprised. "Oh, good lord, is *that* what this is about? I should have realized he was too good to be an accident. I should have realized he was with you. You strike me as just the sort of person who'd keep company with vampires. Detective-Sergeant!" She swung her head around to face Celluci who'd come up on her right side. "Do you know that your buddy here aids and abets the bloodsucking undead?" She set the empty mug carefully on the desk and reached for the bottle. Celluci was faster. Shrugging philosophically, Dr. Burke sat back in her chair. "So, what brought you to the conclusion that your Mr. Fitzroy was with me?"

"Realizing that you killed my mother." Behind her glasses, Vicki's eyes blazed. Although she remained motionless, every line of her body screamed rage.

"And what makes you say that?" The question could have concerned a thesis footnote for all the emotion Dr. Burke showed.

Vicki glared at her. Her voice trembled with the effort it took to keep from shrieking accusations. "My

mother's death had to occur during the four weeks
Donald was at the funeral home. Preferably near the
end of those four weeks when the Hutchinsons had
come to trust him."

"Donald was very charming," Dr. Burke agreed,
her left hand continuing to work in the jacket.

"That kind of timing can't be left to chance," Vicki
continued, a muscle jumping in her jaw. "You were
with her just before she died! You killed her!"

"You forget that Mrs. Shaw was with her *when* she
died. But, never mind." Dr. Burke held up her hand.
"Why don't I just tell you what happened. I gave your
mother vitamin shots every morning. You must have
read that in Dr. Friedman's records?"

Vicki nodded, gaze locked on the other woman's
face.

"These shots, they couldn't actually do anything to
help, but they made your mother feel like she *was*
doing something, so she felt better, was under less
stress, and the last thing she needed in her condition
was stress." She frowned and shrugged. "You'll have
to bear with me if I'm less than usually coherent. As
you pointed out earlier, I'm drunk. Anyway, I had a
lovely talk with Dr. Friedman about stress. That last
morning your mother didn't get a vitamin shot; she
got 10ccs of pure adrenaline. Her heart slammed into
action and the strain was too much for it."

"An autopsy would find that much adrenaline,"
Celluci pointed out quietly. "And there's be little difficulty in tracing it back to you."

Dr. Burke snorted. "Why the hell would anyone do
an autopsy? Everyone was waiting for Marjory to die."
She shot a smug look at Vicki. "Well, everyone but
you."

"Shut up."

"She kept saying she was going to tell you. I guess
she never got around to it."

"SHUT UP!"

Dr. Burke watched half the items from the top of

her desk crash to the floor and turned to Celluci. "What are the chances of me getting that bottle back if I told you I needed it for medical reasons."

Celluci smiled unpleasantly. "Shut up," he said.

"You two have a decidedly limited vocabulary." Dr. Burke shook her head. "Don't you even want to know why I did it?"

"Oh, yes," Vicki snarled. "I'd love to know why you did it. My mother thought you were her *friend!*"

"It's a good thing I'm not a melancholy drunk, or you'd have me in tears. Your mother was dying, no way out. I saw to it she died for a reason. No, don't bother." Again Dr. Burke raised her hand. "I know what you're going to ask. If she was dying anyway, why not wait and have her leave you her body in her will or something. Well, it doesn't work that way. We had tissue cultures, brain wave patterns, everything to go to the next experimental step and this was our only way to get the body."

"So she was just a body to you?"

Dr. Burke leaned forward. "Well, she was after she died, yes."

"She didn't *die*. You killed her."

"I expedited the inevitable. You're just angry because you seem to be the only person she didn't confide in."

"Vicki! No!" Celluci threw himself forward and managed to prevent Vicki's hands from going around the doctor's throat. He pushed her back and held her until blind rage faded enough for reason to return, then released her. When he was certain she had herself under control, he turned to Dr. Burke and said with quiet passion. "The next time you make a crack like that, I won't stop her and you'll get exactly what you deserve."

"What I deserve?" The smile was humorless, the tone bitter. "Detective-Sergeant, you have no idea."

Celluci frowned. His gaze dropped down to the jacket, then slowly lifted back to Dr. Burke's face.

"You said, Donald *was* charming. Why *was?* Why past tense? What's happened to Donald?"

Dr. Burke picked up the bottle from where Celluci had dropped it in order to restrain Vicki's charge and refilled her mug. "I expect that Catherine killed him."

"Catherine's your second graduate student? . . ."

"Go to the head of the glass." She took a long swallow and sighed in relief; the world had been threatening to return. "Perhaps I'd better start at the beginning."

"No." Vicki slapped both palms down on the desk. "First, we get Henry back."

Dr. Burke met Vicki's gaze and sighed again. "You need to save him because you couldn't save your mother." Her voice held so much sympathy that Vicki lost her reaction in it. "I think you'd better know about Catherine."

Celluci swiveled his attention from one woman to the other but held his tongue. It was Vicki's call.

"All right," she said at last, straightening. "Tell us what's going on."

Dr. Burke took another drink, then visibly slipped into lecture mode. "I am a good scientist but not a great one. I just don't possess the ability to devise original concepts that greatness requires. I *am* a great administrator. Probably the best in the world. Which means diddley squat. I make a reasonable amount of money, but do you have any idea what a couple of biological patents with military applications could net you? Or something that the pharmaceutical companies could really sink their teeth into? Of course you don't. This is where Catherine comes in.

"She's a genius. Did I mention that? Well, she is. As an undergraduate she'd patented the prototype of a bacterium that should, with further development, be able to rebuild damaged cells. When I became her adviser, it soon became obvious that she was, like many geniuses, extremely unstable. About to suggest that she seek professional help, I realized that this was my chance. Her research was the only thing that she related to and I was her only touchstone with reality. The whole situation begged to be exploited.

"Pretty soon I realized we weren't just heading toward monetary rewards but that there was a distinct possibility of a Nobel prize. Once we actually managed to defeat death, of course. Sounds insane, doesn't it?" She took another drink. "Let's not rule it out; it might be a valid defense. Anyway, Catherine came up with some pretty amazing possibilities and we began working out experimental parameters."

"Don't you guys usually work with rats," Celluci growled.

"Usually," Dr. Burke agreed. "Are you familiar with the theory of synchronicity? Just as Catherine finished working out the theory, someone in Brazil published a paper involving roughly the same ideas. There was only one way to guarantee we'd win the race. We went directly to experimentation on human cadavers. I set up a lab and rerouted the freshest bodies from the medical morgue—you'll excuse me if I don't go into the tedious bureaucratic details of how that was accomplished with no one the wiser, but if you'll remember I did say I was a great administrator. . . ." Confused, she stared down into the mug. "Where was I?"

"Human cadavers," Vicki snarled.

"Oh, yes. That was when I realized we needed someone else. Donald had gotten himself in a little trouble at medical school and I'd smoothed things over for him. Mostly because I liked him. Also a genius, he was charming and pretty much completely unethical." With exaggerated care, she smoothed out the wrinkles she'd folded into the jacket. "After a while, we began to have some success. We'd been using nonspecific bacteria and brain wave patterns, but if we wanted to move on we had to get our hands on a body we'd been able to type before death. That turned out to be Marjory Nelson. When I was certain she was going to die anyway, under the cover of tests on her condition, we took tissue samples and recorded her brain wave patterns.''

''Then you brought her back to life.''

Gray eyes opened with a flash of recognition. ''More or less. We brought back the mechanics of life, that was all.'' That *was* all. ''Organic robots, if you like. Trouble was, the bacteria are very short-lived and we had a problem with rot. Which, in case you were wondering, was why I wanted your mother partially embalmed.'' She finished the whiskey remaining in the mug, then lifted it to Vicki in a mocking salute. ''If you'd just left that casket closed, no one would have been the wiser.''

''You seem to be forgetting that you murdered my mother!''

Dr. Burke shrugged, refusing to argue the point any further. ''So now you know the whole story, or at least the edited for television version. There'll be a test in the morning. Any questions?''

''Yeah, ignoring for the moment a teenage boy whose death you're also directly responsible for, I've got two.'' Vicki shoved at her glasses. ''Why are you telling us all this?''

''Well, there are theories that say confession is a human compulsion, but mostly because our little experiment has now moved completely out of my control. Catherine slipped into the abyss and I have no intention of following her.'' Although just for a moment, with her hand on the latch of the casket, she'd come close. How far, she'd wondered, *would* they be able to go with a really fresh corpse? And then Donald had told her. But that was personal and no one's business but hers. ''And because Donald's dead.''

''So's that kid and so's my mother!''

''The kid was an accident. Your mother was dying. Donald had everything to live for.'' For an instant her face crumpled then it smoothed again. ''What's more,'' she continued, pouring the final dregs from the bottle, ''I liked Donald.''

''You *liked* my mother!''

Dr. Burke looked placidly across the desk at Vicki. ''You said you had two questions. What's the second?''

How could this creature sit there so calmly and admit to such horror? Caught up in an emotional maelstrom, Vicki was unable to speak. Realizing that the next time she broke, Celluci wouldn't be able to stop her, she spread her hands and stepped back from the desk.

He recognized the signs and moved forward.

''Where,'' he asked, ''is Henry Fitzroy?''

''With Catherine.''

He took a deep breath and ran both hands up through his hair. ''All right. Where is Catherine?''

Dr. Burke shrugged. ''I haven't the faintest idea.''

Thirteen

"All right. Let's see if I understand what you're saying." Vicki drew in a deep breath and exhaled slowly. Screaming and throwing things would contribute nothing to the situation. "Your graduate student, Catherine, who is crazy, has murdered your other graduate student, Donald. When you went back to the lab, late this afternoon, you discovered she'd hidden Henry and you don't know where she is—they are."

Dr. Burke nodded. "Essentially."

So much for good intentions. "WHAT THE FUCK DO YOU MEAN, ESSENTIALLY?"

Alcohol-induced remoteness cracked as Vicki grabbed the lapels of Dr. Burke's lab coat and nearly dragged her over the desk. "If you could loosen your grip," she gasped, "I might find it easier . . . to answer your question."

Vicki merely snarled inarticulately.

"Detec . . . tive!"

Celluci shifted his gaze to a point about six inches over the doctor's head, expression aggressively neutral.

Collar cutting into her windpipe, Dr. Burke realized further hesitation would only make things worse. "She's in the old Life Sciences building. Your vampiric friend is locked in a big metal box. Trying to maneuver that out the door and into her van would've attracted a bit of attention. *Where* in the building . . ." Considering her position, the shrug was credible. ". . . I have no idea."

Vicki didn't so much release her hold as shove the older woman back into the chair. "Your lab is in there? In the old building?"

"Yes." Rubbing the back of her neck where the fabric had dug in, Dr. Burke snapped, "And so is your mother. Somewhere." She shot a superior look up over the edge of her glasses. "Your dead mother. Walking around."

My dead mother. Walking around. Anger couldn't stand under the weight of that pronouncement.

"Vicki?"

She fought free of the image of her mother flattened against the window and met Celluci's worried gaze.

"We have a confession. We can call in Detective Fergusson now. You don't have to have anything more to do with this."

"Nice try, Mike." She swallowed, trying to wet a throat gone dry. "But you're forgetting about Henry."

"Mustn't forget Henry." Above the hand still rubbing at her throat, Dr. Burke almost grinned. "I'd love to hear you explain *him* to the local police. Until you find Henry, you've got to keep this quiet. And after? What about after?" She shook her head at their expressions and sighed, placing both hands flat on her desk. "Never mind, I'll tell you. There won't *be* an after. Until Catherine contacts me, you haven't a chance of finding your friend. There's a million stupid, useless cubbyholes in that building and she could've stuck him in any of them. You're just going to have to sit here with me and wait for her phone call."

"And then?"

"Then I play along, she tells me where she's stashed him, you get him out, call the police, and she pays for Donald."

Vicki's eyes narrowed. "And *you'll* pay for my mother."

"Ms. Nelson, if it makes you happy, I'll even pay for dinner."

''What if she doesn't call?'' Celluci demanded, cutting off Vicki's response.

''She said she would.''

''You said she's crazy.''

''There is that.''

''Mike, I can't wait.'' Vicki took four steps toward the door, turned on one heel, and took three steps back. ''I can't base everything on what a crazy woman may or may not do. I'm going to find him. *She* . . .'' A toss of her head indicated the doctor. ''. . . can take us to the lab. We'll work a search pattern from there.''

''Not on your life.'' *She* wasn't going near the lab. Bad enough she could still hear him calling her in spite of half a bottle of Scotch. ''You'll have to drag me. Which might alert Security. There'll be a brouhaha. Your Henry Fitzroy ends up confiscated by the government. You want to go to the lab, you can find it on your own.''

Vicki leaned forward, laying her hands on the desk, fingertips not quite touching the doctor's, her posture more of a threat than her earlier actions had been. ''Then you'll give us very precise directions.''

''Or you'll what? Try to pay attention, Ms. Nelson—you can't do *anything* until you rescue your friend.''

''I can beat your fucking face in.''

''And what will that accomplish? If you beat the directions out of me, I can guarantee they won't be accurate. Try to be realistic, Ms. Nelson, if you can. You and your flat-footed friend here can go and try to find Mr. Fitzroy, but you'll have to leave me out of it.'' Not even in words would she trace the path to the lab again. ''But just to show there's no hard feelings, I'll let you in on a nonsecret. There's a way into the old building from the north end of the underground parking lot. Security's supposed to have video cameras down there, but they ran out of money. Don't say I never gave you anything. Happy trails.''

Celluci took hold of Vicki's shoulder and pulled her gently but inexorably away from the desk. "And what will you be doing while we're searching?"

"The same thing I was doing when you showed up." Dr. Burke bent and opened the bottom drawer of her desk, pulling out an unopened bottle of Scotch. "Attempting to drink myself into a stupor. Thank God, I always keep a spare." It took three tries before the paper seal tore. "I assure you, I'm not going anywhere."

"Why not, when at the very least you'll be facing a murder charge?" Vicki asked, shaking free of Celluci's hold.

"You're still on about your mother, aren't you?" The doctor sighed and stared for a moment into the pale depths of the amber liquid before continuing. "I lost interest in the game when Donald died." The bottle became a silver casket. She shuddered and raised her head, looking past Vicki's glasses, meeting her eyes. "Essentially—and I beg your pardon, Ms. Nelson, if the word offends you, but it's the only one that fits—essentially, I just don't care any more."

And she didn't. Even through her own grief and rage and confusion, Vicki could see that. "Come on." Pulling her bag up onto her shoulder, she jerked her head toward the door. "She's not going anywhere right now."

"You believe her?"

Vicki took another look into Dr. Burke's eyes and recognized what she saw there. "Yeah. I believe her." She paused at the door. "One more thing; you may not care now but don't think you'll be able to use your knowledge of Henry as a bargaining chip later . . ."

"Later," Dr. Burke interrupted, both hands around the bottle to keep from spilling any of the Scotch as she refilled her mug, "without an actual creature to run tests on, I can scream vampire until I'm blue in the face and no one will believe a word I say. Grave robbing does not help to maintain credibility in the scientific community."

"Not to mention murdering one of your grad students," Celluci pointed out dryly.

Dr. Burke snorted and raised the mug in a sarcastic salute. "You'd be surprised."

"Jesus H. Christ." Celluci slammed the flat of his hand against the wall in frustration. "This place is like a maze; hallways that don't go anywhere, classrooms that lead to hidden offices, labs that suddenly appear . . ."

Vicki played the powerful beam of her flashlight down the hall. With the one in four emergency lighting on in the old building, she could see well enough to keep from crashing into things but not well enough to identify the things she wasn't crashing into. Only the area starkly illuminated by her flashlight held any definition. It was like she was moving through the slides of a bizarre vacation, stepping into a scene just as it was replaced by the next. Her nerves were stretched so tightly she could almost hear them twang with every movement.

Her dead mother was walking around in this building.

Every time she moved her circle of sight she wondered, *Will this be the time I see her?* And when all that showed was another empty room or bit of hall, she wondered, *Is she standing in the darkness beside me?* Under her jacket and sweater, her shirt clung to her sides, and she had to keep switching the flashlight from hand to hand to dry her palms.

"This isn't going to work." Her arm dropped to her side and the hall slid into darkness except for the puddle of illumination now spilling over her feet. "The layout of this place defeats any kind of a systematic search. "We've got to use our heads."

"Granted," Celluci agreed. He tucked himself up against her left shoulder; close enough, he judged, for her to see his face. "But we've got a crazy woman who's run off with a vampire. That doesn't exactly lend itself to logical analysis."

"It has to." Adjusting her glasses, more for the comfort of a familiar action than from necessity, she gave half her mind over to searching the scant information they had for clues. The other half of her mind filtered the noises of an old building at night, listening for the approach of shuffling footsteps. Suddenly, she turned to squint up at Celluci. "Dr. Burke said Henry was in a large metal box."

"So?"

"And she implied it was heavy."

"Again, so?"

Vicki almost smiled. "Look at the floor, Celluci."

Together, they bowed their heads and stared at the pale, institutional gray tile, dulled by the passage of thousands of feet. A number of nicks and impressions dimpled the surface with shadow and darker still were a half-dozen signatures of black rubber heels.

"If the box is as massive as Dr. Burke implied," Vicki said, raising her head and looking Celluci in the eyes, "one way or another it'll have left its mark. Rubber wheels will scuff. Metal wheels will imprint."

Celluci nodded slowly. "So we look for the tracks she left moving the box. It's still a big building. . . ."

"Yeah, but we know damn well she didn't take it up and down the stairs." Vicki raised her arm and shone the flashlight down the hall. "The power's on, so the elevators must be working. We check just outside them on every floor for the marks and then backtrack from there."

An appreciative grin spread over Celluci's face. "You know, that's practically brilliant."

Vicki snorted. "Thanks. You needn't sound so surprised."

For no reason other than that they had to start somewhere, they began working their way down from the eighth, and highest, floor. On three, they found what they were looking for—pressed not only into the tile but into the metal lip leading onto the elevator, were the marks of two pairs of wheels about four feet apart. Silently, they stepped ut into the hall and let the door wheeze closed behind them.

No one appeared to investigate the noise.

Unwilling to risk the flashlight and a premature discovery, Vicki grabbed Celluci's shoulder and allowed him to lead her down the hall. To her surprise, moving in what was to her total darkness was less stressful than the peep show the flashlight had offered. Although she still listened for approaching footsteps, the accompanying tension had lessened. *Or maybe,* she conceded, her grip tightening slightly, *it's just that now I have an anchor.*

When they reached the first intersection, even she could see the way they had to go.

The harsh white of the fluorescent lights spilled out through the open door and across the corridor.

Vicki felt Celluci's shoulder rise as he reached beneath his jacket and she heard the unmistakable sound of metal sliding free of leather. Up until this moment, she hadn't realized he'd brought his gun. Considering the amount of trouble he could get into for using it, she couldn't believe he'd actually drawn it.

"Isn't that just a tad *American,*" she whispered, lips nearly touching his ear.

He drew her back around the corner and bent his head to hers. "What Dr. Burke neglected to mention," he said in a voice pitched to carry to her alone, "was that there's something else wandering around in here besides a mad scientist and your uh . . ."

"Mother," Vicki interjected flatly. "It's okay." Her feelings were irrelevant to the situation. *And I'll just keep telling myself that.*

"Yeah, well, something else killed that kid and we're not taking any more chances than we have to."

"Mike, if it's already dead, what good will shooting it do?"

His voice was grim as he answered. "If it died once, it can die again."

"So what am I supposed to use, strong language?"

"You can wait here."

"Fuck you." And under the bravado, fear. *Not alone. Not in the dark. Not here.*

They made their way to the open door. Vicki released her hold on Celluci's shoulder at the edge of the light. "Give it a five count." His breath lapped warm against the side of her face, then he darted across the opening.

The next five seconds were among the longest Vicki had ever spent as she closed her eyes, leaned her head back against the wall, and wondered if she'd have the courage to look. On five, she swallowed hard, opened her eyes, and peered around and into the room, conscious of Celluci across the doorway mirroring her movements.

Even with lids slitted against the glare, it took a moment for her eyes to stop watering enough for her to focus. It *was* a lab. It had obviously been in use recently. It had just as obviously been abandoned. Eight years with the police had taught her to recognize the telltale mess left behind when suspects had cut and run.

Cautiously, they moved away from the door, slowly turned, and simultaneously spotted the isolation box, humming in mechanical loneliness at the far end of the room.

Vicki took two quick steps toward it, then stopped and forced her brain to function. "If this is the original lab, we know Catherine moved Henry away . . ."

"So Henry's not in that box."

"Maybe it's empty."

"Maybe."

But neither of them believed it.

"We have to know for sure." Somehow, without her being aware of it, Vicki's feet had moved her to within an arm's length of the box. All she had to do was reach out and lift the lid.

. . . and lift the lid. Oh, Momma, I'm sorry. I can't. She despised herself for being a coward, but she couldn't stop the sudden cold sweat nor the weakness in her knees that threatened to drop her flat on her face.

"It's all right." It wasn't *all right,* but those were the words to say, so Celluci said them as he came around her and put one hand on the latch. This, at least, he could do for her. "You don't have to stay."

"Yes. Yes, I do." She could be a passive observer, if only that.

Celluci searched her face, swore privately that someone would pay for the pain that kept forcing its way out through the cracks in the masks she wore, and lifted the lid.

The release of tension was so great that Vicki swayed and would have fallen had Celluci not stepped back and grabbed her. She allowed herself a moment leaning on the strength of his arm, then shook herself free. From the beginning, she'd declared she was going to find her mother. *Why am I so relieved that we didn't?*

Thick purple incisions, tacked closed with coarse black thread, marked the naked body of the young Oriental male in an ugly "y" pattern. A collar of purple and green bruises circled the slender column of the throat. Plastic tubes ran into both elbows and the inner thigh. Across the forehead, partially covered by a thick fall of ebony hair, another incision appeared to have been stapled closed.

Over the years, both Vicki and Celluci had seen more corpses than they cared to remember. The young man in the box was dead.

"Mike, his chest . . . it's . . ."

"I know."

Two steps forward and she was close enough to reach over the side and gently touch her fingertips to the skin over the diaphragm. It was cold. And it rose and fell to the prompting of something that vibrated beneath it.

"Jesus . . . There's a motor." She withdrew her hand and scrubbed the fingers against her jacket. Raising her head, she caught Celluci making the sign of the cross. "Dr. Burke never mentioned this."

"No. Not quite." He shifted his gun to his right hand and slipped it back into the shoulder holster. It didn't look like he'd be needing it right away. "But something tells me we've finally found Donald Li."

The young man's eyes snapped open.

Vicki couldn't have moved had she wanted to. Nor could she look away when the dark eyes tracked from her to Celluci and back again.

A muscle shifted behind the purple bruises on the throat.

Gray-blue lips parted.

"Kill . . . me . . ."

"Holy Mary, Mother of God, he's alive."

In the box, the dark eyes slid slowly back to Celluci. "No . . ."

"No? What the hell do you mean no?"

"He means he's not alive, Mike." Vicki could hear a part of herself screaming. She ignored it. "He's like my mother." *Hands splayed against the glass. Mouth moving soundlessly.* "He's dead. But he's trapped in there."

"Kill . . . me . . . please . . ."

Her fingers digging into the bend of Celluci's elbow, Vicki backed away, pulling him with her. She stopped when the high rim of stainless steel replaced Donald Li's face with her own. "We have to do something."

Celluci continued to stare in the direction of the box. "Do what?" he demanded harshly.

Vicki fought the urge to turn and run, thankful Celluci seemed frozen to the spot because she didn't have
the strength to stop them both. "What he asks. We
have to kill him."

"If he's alive, killing him is murder. If he's
dead . . ."

"He's dead, Mike. He says himself he'd dead. Can
you walk away and leave him like that?"

She felt the shudder run down the length of his body
and barely heard his answer.

"Vicki, we're out of our depth here." This was the
stuff of nightmares. Not demons or werewolves or
mummies or a four-hundred-and-fifty-year-old romance writer—this. He'd thought that thirteen years of
police work had equipped him to deal with anything
and that the events of the last year had covered everything else. He'd been wrong. "I can't . . ."

"We have to."

"Why?" Weighed down by horror, his voice hardly
rose above a whisper.

"Because we found him. Because we're all he has."

*There's a whole world out there. Let someone else
deal with it.* But when he turned and looked down into
Vicki's face, he couldn't say it. He recognized the look
of someone very nearly at the end of her resources,
someone who'd been hit too hard and too often, but
he also recognized the determined set to her jaw. *She*
couldn't walk away leaving Donald Li trapped in his
prison of dead meat. He couldn't walk away and leave
her. Although he had to force his mouth to form the
words, he asked, "How do we do it?"

Speaking slowly—if she lost control even a little
she'd lose it all—Vicki laid out what they knew.
"He's dead. We know it. He says so. But his . . ."
Twentieth-century attitudes added difficulty to expressing what was so terrifyingly clear. ". . . his
soul is trapped. Why? The only difference between
this corpse and any other . . ." *Except my mother's.*
She felt herself begin to slide toward the edge. *No!*

Don't think of that now. ". . . is that someone has given it an artificial resemblance to life. That has to be why he's trapped."

"So we unhook his life support?"

"Yeah. I guess."

"Vicki. One of us has to be *sure*."

She lifted her head and met his gaze.

After a moment, he nodded. "Let's do it."

It didn't take long for them to unhook the tubes and hoses, training and practice shoehorning distance in between what had to been done and feelings about doing it. Neither of them touched the body any more than was absolutely necessary. When they'd finished, although Donald Li said nothing, they saw him still staring up out of dead eyes and knew it hadn't been enough.

"We should've known. The others are up and walking around."

Then Vicki found the input jack hidden under a thick fringe of hair and traced the cable back to the computer. She squinted at Catherine's message on the screen and tried to keep her hands from shaking just long enough to work the keyboard.

"It seems to be loading programming into . . ." There was only one place it could be loading programming. "Okay. Odds are good that if programming can be loaded, it can also be erased." Wiping her palms on her thighs, she dropped into the chair.

"You sure you know what you're doing?" Celluci asked, grateful for an excuse to walk away from the horror in the box. "This setup's more complicated than the gear you've got at home."

"How complicated can it be?" Vicki muttered, making a note of the destination file. "It all comes down to ones and zeros. Besides," she added grimly, hitting the reset button, "how could I possibly make it any worse?"

She scanned the main menu. "Mike, what does initialize mean to you?"

"Something to do with starting up?"

"That's what I thought." Under the list of things that could be initialized was the destination code the program had been downloading into.

"Well?"

"I just told it to reinitialize Donald's brain."

"And?"

"And that should wipe it clean."

"Are you sure?"

"No, but I wiped my hard drive that way once." Shoving the chair back from the desk, Vicki stood and pushed at her glasses. "Hopefully, it'll release him."

"And if it doesn't?"

She shook her head. "I don't know." If it didn't work, they'd have to leave him there and hope that as the body slowly decayed so would whatever held him to it. *To know you're dead. To watch your body rot. To have that be your only hope.* . . . She clamped down hard on the hysteria she could feel rising. *Later,* she told it. *Later, when Henry's safe and my mother's . . . my mother is . . .*"

Celluci's voice cut through the thought. "No change."

"Give it a minute." One step at a time, she managed to return to the box and to Celluci's side. If he hadn't gone back before her, she didn't think she could've made it. With her arm pressed up against the warm resilience of his, she looked down at Donald Li's face.

Dark eyes caught her gaze and held it. Wrung dry, Vicki didn't even attempt to pull away. Suddenly, she realized that as all encompassing as her terror and revulsion might be it was *nothing* next to the terror that shrieked from behind the eyes of Donald Li.

She had nothing to be afraid of in comparison.

As the fear faded, anger rose to take its place.

What sort of a person could do this to another human being?

All at once, the dead man's eyes widened and just

for an instant his expression changed to one of incredulous joy.

Then his face held no expression at all.

Vicki released a breath she didn't remember holding. "You see that?"

"Yeah."

"Any doubts that we did the right thing?"

"Not one."

Together they reached up and pulled the lid closed.

Alone in the dark, Henry wondered how much of the night he had left. Surely he'd endured a dozen hours or more since sunset. *Why can't I feel the dawn?* With the Hunger clawing for freedom and steel wrapped about him like a shroud, he yearned for oblivion even as he dreaded it.

He'd run through all the moments of Vicki he had. *Unfair that a year slips through memory so fast.* While some of what they'd shared had added to the Hunger, most had helped to force it back. Vicki had given him her life, not just her body and blood. Had forged friendship out of circumstance. Had helped him when he needed it. Had come to him for help. Had trusted him. Been trusted in return.

Passion. Friendship. Need. Trust.

Together, love. Considered in that light, he supposed it wasn't actually necessary for Vicki to *say* she loved him. *Although it would have been good to hear. . . .*

He tried to remember how many times he had heard the words. A hundred voices cried out; women's voices, men's voices—he quieted them all, searching the past for the glint of gold among the dross. A thousand nights slipped by, a hundred thousand, and out of all the shared passion and friendship and need there were only four, three women and a man, with whom there had also been trust enough for love.

"Ginevra. Gustav. Sidonie. Beth." He murmured

their names into the darkness. So many others he'd let go of, forgotten, but those he still held. "Only four in all those years. . . . "

Two had been taken from him by violence, one by accident, one by time.

He could feel the melancholy gathering into a tangible presence, threatening to crush him under its weight.

"Vicki." A fifth name. A living name. "And as they say . . ." Although he knew it would do no good, Henry pressed his uninjured hand up against the lid as hard as exhaustion and pain allowed. ". . . where there's life, there's hope."

Muscles strained, the darkness developed a reddish hue, then the arm collapsed down across his chest and he was nearly deafened by the sound of his heart slamming up against his ribs. He had no idea what he'd been trying to prove.

One last effort for the sake of love? He shifted slightly, changing his position as much as he could, the plastic padding beneath him tugging at the bare skin of his back. *At least this time I won't be the one left behind to mourn.*

Melancholy turned to despair and closed icy fingers around him.

It would be so easy to surrender.

I am Henry Fitzroy, Duke of Richmond, the son of a king.

I am Vampire.

He was too tired. It just wasn't enough anymore.

Vicki wouldn't quit.

Vicki won't quit. Not until she finds you. Find strength in that. Trust her.

She will come.

Christina had come. She had birthed him from the darkness, nourished him, guarded him, taught him, and finally let him go.

"*Listen to what your instincts tell you, Henry. Our nature says we hunt alone. This is your terri-*

*tory, I give it to you, and I will not stay to fight you
for it.''*

"Then stay and share it with me!"

She only smiled, a little sadly.

He paced the length of the room and back to throw
himself down on his knees at her feet. Even a short
time before, he would have finished the motion by
burying his head in her lap but now, in spite of the
position, he was unable to close the distance.

Her smile grew sadder still. "The bond of your creation is nearly broken. If I stay," she added softly,
"one of us will very soon drive the other away and
that will wipe out even the memory of what we
shared."

The voice of the Hunter growing louder in his head
told him she spoke the truth. "Then why," he cried,
"did you change me, knowing this would happen?
Knowing we would have so little time together?"

Ebony brows drew down as she considered it. "I
think," she said slowly, "I think I forgot for a while."

His voice rose, echoing off the damp, stone walls of
the abandoned tower. "You forgot?"

"Yes. Perhaps that is why we are able to continue
as a race."

He bowed his head, eyes squeezed shut, but his nature no longer allowed tears. "It hurts. As though you
cut my heart out and take it with you."

"Yes." Her skirts whispered as she stood and he
felt her fingers touch his hair in gentle benediction.
"Perhaps that is why we are so few."

He never saw her again.

"And that," he told the darkness as despair's grip
tightened, "is not helping." Surely there were pleas-
anter times to use as weapons against the knowledge
that he was trapped, and alone. . . .

"No. There have been prisons and prisoners before," he snarled. "I can survive it."

You can survive the nights, despair whispered,
but what of the days? So much blood has been

taken. How much more will they take? How much more can you lose and still have a night to return to? What else will they do that you will be unable to prevent?

Lips drawn back from his teeth, Henry tried to twist away from the voice. It surrounded him, sounded within him, echoed against the metal that enclosed him. "Vicki . . ."

She doesn't know where you are. What if she doesn't find you in time? What if she doesn't *come?*

"NO!"

He released his hold on the Hunger and let the Beast take him as it clawed its way free.

It was all he had left to fight with.

"As long as these are working, we have no guarantee that she's going to leave Henry in one place." Vicki squinted in the brightly lit interior of the elevator and switched off her flashlight. "She can keep rolling him around this building with us two steps behind like some kind of bad Marx Brothers movie."

"So we jam them?" Celluci asked, stepping over the threshold and matching his companion's don't-fuck-with-me tone. That either of them was still functioning at all, he considered to be some sort of miracle. *Let's hear it for the human animal's ability to cope.*

Vicki shook her head and hit the button for the sub-basement with enough force to nearly crack the plastic cover. "Not good enough. The elevators are in opposite ends of the building. She can unjam them as fast as we can jam them. We're going to shut them off."

"How?"

"By shutting off the power supply to the building."

"I repeat, how?"

Vicki turned to stare at him through narrowed eyes. "How the hell should I know? Do I look like an electrician? We'll find the electrical room and pull the plug.''

"Metaphorically speaking."

"Don't give me any of your fucking attitude, Celluci.''

"My attitude? Nelson, you've got one hell of a nerve.''

"Nerve!''

"You want attitude?''

Their voice overlapped, the sound slamming up against the confining walls and crashing back. Words got tangled in the noise and were stripped of meaning. Toe to toe, they stood and screamed invective at each other.

The elevator reached the subbasement. Stopped. The door opened.

". . . patronizing asshole!''

The echoes changed. The words shot into the darkness and didn't come back.

They realized it together and together fell silent.

Vicki was trembling so violently, she wasn't sure she could stand. Her legs felt like cooked pasta and there was a metal band wrapped so tightly around her throat that breathing hurt and swallowing was impossible. Her glasses had slid so far down her nose they were almost useless. She peered over them, through the tunnel the disease had pared her vision down to, and tried to focus on the face just inches from her own. Her hand came up to push them back into place but instead continued moving until it brushed the curl of hair off Celluci's forehead. She heard him sigh.

Slowly, he raised his arm and, with one finger against the bridge, slid her glasses back into place. "We okay?''

His breath was warm against her cheek. She nodded jerkily and stepped back, out of the range of that comfort.

"What about the tracks?'' he asked.

She switched on her flashlight and walked out into the subbasement, a little amazed her legs would obey even such basic commands. "We look for tracks *after* we immobilize Catherine."

Celluci paused for a moment on the threshold of the elevator, his presence preventing the door from closing. "We turn off the power to the building," he said, "and we'll turn off any other experiments she might be running."

Vicki stopped and half turned to face him. "Yes."

He recognized the raw anger that spit the word out. Recognized it because he felt it himself. It had nothing to do with the contest in vitriol they'd held in the elevator—that had been nothing more than tension given voice—and everything to do with the horror they'd found in the lab. He wanted to find whoever had been responsible, take them by the throat and . . . Words didn't exist for what he wanted to do.

Over the last week, layer after layer of Vicki's control, of her protection, had been stripped away. He was afraid there was nothing left to keep her anger from being acted on.

He was afraid that if they found Henry the way they'd found Donald Li, she'd go right over the edge and he wouldn't be able to stop her.

He was more afraid that he wouldn't even try.

On the second floor, in a utility cupboard that shared a wall with the elevator shaft, Marjory Nelson worked the muscles of her face into the closest she could come to a frown. She heard voices.

Voices.

Voice.

She knew that voice.

She had been told to stay. It was one of the commands enforced by the neural net. One of the commands that had worn a rutted passage into memory.

Stay.

Trembling, she stood . . .

Stay!
. . . shuffled toward the door . . .
STAY!
. . . opened it and lurched out into the hall.
There was something she had to do.

Fourteen

"Radio room. Constable Kushner."

"This the police . . . stashun?"

"Yes, ma'am, it is."

Dr. Burke took a deep breath and, enunciating very carefully, said, "I'd like to speak to De-tective Fergusson, plead . . . please."

"I'll put you through to homicide."

"You do that." Eyes nearly closed, Dr. Burke sagged against the receiver.

"Homicide. Detective Brunswick."

"Right. De-tective Fer-gusson, please."

"Detective Fergusson's not here right now, can I help?"

"Not here?" She pivoted the receiver around on her mouth, just far enough so she could glare blearily at it. "Whadda you mean, not here?"

By the time she remembered that the other half had to stay against her ear, she'd missed the first part of Detective Brunswick's reply. ". . . but can I take a message?"

"A meshage?" Sipping at her Scotch, she took a moment to think about it. "Well, I was gonna . . . confesh. Theories say confeshun is necess . . . ary. But if he's not . . . there, maybe I won't."

Detective Brunswick's voice picked up a distinct, let's-humor-the-crazy-person inflection. "If you give me your name, I can tell him you called."

Heaving herself more-or-less erect in the chair, Dr. Burke declared in ringing tones, "*I* am the Director of . . . Life Sciencesh. He knows who I am. Everyone knows . . . who *I* am.'' Then she hung up.

''So much . . . for tha.'' She pulled Donald's jacket off the desk and onto her lap. ''I really feel . . . awful 'bout thish, Donald. I'm gonna make it up . . . to you. You'll see.'' An idea somehow forced its way through a bottle and a half of single malt. ''You know, if the iso-lation box is running then the re-frigeration is running and you're prob-ly cold.'' With a desperate grip wrapped around the arm of her chair, she managed to get to her feet. ''If you're cold, you're gonna want your jacket.'' Finishing the mouthful of Scotch in the mug nearly knocked her over. She swayed, steadied, and started for the door. ''I'm gonna take you your . . . jacket.''

Somewhere, far behind the layers of insulation provided by the alcohol, a terrified voice shrieked, *''No!''*

Dr. Burke ignored it.

''How many electrical rooms can one lousy building have?'' Breathing heavily, Vicki backed out into the hall, trying to shine her flashlight in all directions at once. Her voice scraped across her teeth in a strained whisper. ''Every time we open a door, I expect to see my mother behind it.''

Celluci reached out and closed one hand over her shoulder, the other catching her wrist and directing the beam of light away from his eyes. The last thing they needed was for both of them to be wandering around blind. ''Let *me* open the doors,'' he suggested quietly, turning her to face him.

''No.'' She shook her head. ''You don't understand. She's *my* mother.''

''Vicki . . .'' Then he sighed because there really wasn't anything he could say that would change things and if the thought of opening a door and finding Marjory Nelson staring at them out of a corpse's eyes had him scared spitless, God only knew what it was doing to Vicki. Donald Li had been bad enough, but Marjory

Nelson was, as Dr. Burke had so kindly reminded them, up and walking. Up and walking and dead. But if Vicki had the guts to face it, he'd face it beside her. Besides, as much as he might wish that Henry Fitzroy had never appeared on the scene, he couldn't abandon him to the kind of living death that Donald had been trapped in. "Let's shut that power off, find Fitzroy, and get out of here."

She nodded, head barely moving, the motion more intent than actuality, and twisted out from under Celluci's hands. The shadows pressed against her, trying to undermine the precarious balance she maintained. *We're going to find Henry. To do that, we're going to confine him to one floor. So we're going to shut the power off. Then we're going to tear this place apart, one floor at a time. We're going to find Henry. I will not fail him. Like I failed my mother.* As long as she clung to that, she could function. Let the shadows push as they would.

The air in the subbasement tasted of damp concrete and rust and disuse and the building itself—creaking, settling, hiding secrets—made more noise than both of them; although the sound of their breathing seemed to linger where they passed. The rooms to the right of the corridor were up against the outside wall and so every one of them had to be checked; the door opened, the light shone in, the potential horror realized. They'd found two small electrical substations with panels labeled "labs three" "labs four" and "lecture one" but hadn't touched the breakers. *"All at once,"* Vicki had growled. *"So we don't warn her."*

One door remained before the corner; one door, one room and they'd finished the north side of the building. Celluci checked his watch as they hurried toward it. *11:17? Is that all?* They still had over half the night. Not so long, he amended as he realized it was probably *all* the time they had.

A square shadow of darker paint at eyelevel, metal dimpling all four corners, indicated a missing sign. A security bar resting loosely over a steel eye suggested that the room had once held something worth guarding.

"This could be it." Jerking the bar free, Vicki hauled the heavy door open. Stiff hinges shrilled a clichéd protest that scraped against the inside of her skull like nails on a blackboard. She gritted her teeth and scythed the flashlight beam across the darkness.

Something moved just beyond the edge of the light. She froze. The circle of illumination froze with her. Just past it, something moved again.

All she had to do was direct the flashlight less than a meter to the left. All she had to do . . .

The single, naked bulb hanging caged from the ceiling cut black silhouettes around a complex arrangement of pipes. About four feet off the ground, a humped brown body and naked tail disappeared down an impossibly narrow crevice.

Vicki remembered how to breathe. "Rat," she said, because she had to say something.

"Or a mouse trying out for the Olympics," Celluci allowed, his hand still covering the light switch. He wet his lips and tried to push his heart down out of his throat. "I'm beginning to think that finding her would be better than the constant fear that we will."

Wiping at her streaming eyes, Vicki battled the knot in her stomach. *You will not puke!* she commanded herself, swallowing bile. After a moment, she lifted her head and muttered, "I'm beginning to think you're right." She jabbed her glasses back into place. "This is obviously the sprinkler room. Not what we're looking for."

Out in the hall, she paused and said, before he could follow, "Leave the light on."

He caught up to her as she was about to check the first room on the west wall. Frowning, he squinted down the length of the corridor, attempting to isolate the sheen of polished metal that had caught his eye. "Vicki, there's a padlock on that door down there."

Vicki turned. The cone of light stretching out from her hand didn't quite stretch far enough. Not only could she not see a lock, she only had Celluci's word for it that there was a door.

"In my experience," he continued, "you lock rooms you don't want people to go into."

"Or get out of," Vicki added. "Come on."

Unlike the entrance to the room they'd just left, this door retained its sign. *Danger. High Voltage. Keep out.*

"Odds are good this is the electrical room." Handing Celluci the flashlight—"Here. Hold this. I'm going to need both hands."—Vicki rummaged her lockpicks out of her purse. "Keep it steady." Dropping to one knee, she flicked open the case and drew out the two largest picks.

Her hands were shaking so violently, she couldn't get either of them into the lock.

Her second attempt was no more successful.

On the third attempt, she dropped one of the probes. It bounced off her knee, chimed against the tile, and came to rest with the hooked end over the toe of Celluci's shoe. Vicki stared down at it. Then she scowled at the remaining pick, so tightly gripped that her fingertips had gone white behind the nails, spun suddenly, and flung it down the hall.

"God*damn*it!"

She couldn't stop her hands from shaking. There was no way she was going to be able to pick that lock. *So much for finding the fucking electrical room.* They were going to turn off the power. Prevent Henry from being moved from floor to floor. They were going to tear the building apart one floor at a time. They were going to find Henry. She had to hold onto that. It was all she had. *Except that it's all falling apart!* She wanted to beat her head against the door and scream with fear and frustration.

As if he'd read her mind, Celluci reached out and cupped her chin, gently drawing her around to face him. "Let me try."

Not trusting herself to speak, she nodded and stood, holding out the remaining picks.

"No. Not quite my style." Passing her back the flashlight, he added, "Wait here."

He disappeared before she could object and for one terrifying moment it seemed that the darkness had devoured him. By the time she'd swung the light around, he'd gone beyond its range. All at once, with a familiar squeal of metal, the far end of the hall leapt, if not into focus, at least into sight.

What the hell is he doing in the sprinkler room?

A moment later, not bothering to close the door behind him, he came back around the corner, both hands holding . . .

. . . a length of pipe?

She moved out of his way as he returned, jammed one end of the pipe down through the loop of the padlock and braced it against the metal covering the door. Taking a deep breath, he threw his weight against the other end.

The pipe bit into the door, metal buckling.

Face darkening, Celluci growled an inarticulate challenge, grateful for a place to finally throw all the terror-produced adrenaline of the night.

The security bar slowly bowed.

"Mike? . . ."

"Not. Now."

Bit by bit the screws dragged free.

"Just. A little. Fur . . ."

The sudden surrender flung him backward as the entire assembly crashed to the floor. He staggered, nearly fell, and leaned panting on the pipe.

Vicki stepped forward and retrieved her fallen lockpick from under the mess. "Obviously, your break-and-enter specialist was a little more direct than mine," she muttered dryly.

Celluci gulped for air. "Obviously."

Caught by the sheer normalcy of the exchange, they stared at one another for a moment, then Vicki's mouth curved into almost a smile as she reached up and pushed the curl of hair back off his forehead. "Well, then," she stretched the words out, feeling some of the desperation go with them, "let's hear it for testosterone."

Celluci snorted, straightened, and let the pipe drop. "Personally, I'm amazed you didn't pull a package of plastique out of that suitcase you carry." Shoving the junked security bar out of the way, he pulled open the door and fumbled around the corner for the light.

They'd definitely found the electrical room.

And something else.

"Vicki . . ."

She struggled for command of her voice. "I see it."

The bloodscent drew him out of the pit where exhaustion had flung him and threw the Hunger loose again.

Someone, something, was banging on the inside of the box.

"Henry?" Vicki called, one foot moving in front of the other through no conscious decision she could remember.

There was no answer—only the continued banging.

She couldn't call for the other. In case there *was* an answer.

"Vicki, let me . . ."

"No. This is something *I* have to do."

"Of course it is," Celluci growled, fighting the paralysis that the sight of the stainless steel box invoked and moving up behind her left shoulder. *Goddamnit, Vicki, why can't you turn and run? So I can turn and run.*

She watched her reflection grow larger as she approached. The closer she got, the more distance her mind insisted on until, not quite touching the box, she stopped, stared into her own eyes, and straightened her glasses feeling as though the whole experience had slid out of reality.

I don't even watch horror movies, she told herself. *What the hell am I doing starring in one?*

She watched her arm come up, her hand cover the latch, her fingers twist slightly sideways. . . .

The lid flew open, slapping her hand aside.

She caught a glimpse of a pale face under red-gold hair. Then, before she could react, something black and heavy swooped down upon her and she stumbled back, blind. Cold and clammy, it wrapped tightly around her head and draped over her shoulders with obscene familiarity. Her throat pumping out shrill sounds of incoherent terror, she tore at it in panicked frenzy.

Finally, as terror began to pick up some of the shading of rage, she wrenched it loose and flung it to the floor. Her glasses, secured over only one ear, began to fall, and the greater fear their loss roused brought her back to sanity as she shoved them back into place.

At her feet lay a pile of black leather.

Henry's trench coat.

All at once, as if recognition had thrown a switch, she became aware of snarling, cursing, and the impact of flesh on flesh. Looping the strap of her bag over her wrist—it was the only weapon she had—she whirled in time to see Celluci get a leg between his body and Henry's and use it to fling the smaller man across the room.

Naked to the waist, Henry's torso gleamed like alabaster, amethyst bruises marking the inside of both arms. He used the momentum of the blow to roll up onto his feet and, snarling, charged again.

Celluci grunted under the impact and slammed his elbow into the side of Henry's head—to no apparent effect.

Once or twice over the last year, Vicki had been given a glimpse of what lay behind the mask of civilization Henry wore. Had—even while cold sweat

beaded her skin and common sense screamed
"Run!"—been aroused by so much deadly power so
lightly held in control.

He had warned her once, *"The beast is much closer
to the surface in my kind."*

The beast was loose.

Celluci had barely registered that the box was open
when he found himself flat on his back and fighting
for his life. He'd hit the floor with Henry Fitzroy's
hands around his throat and had only survived those
first few seconds because one hand, swollen and nearly
useless, had not been able to maintain its grip.

With his left forearm shoved up under Fitzroy's chin
and his right hand trying to rip the crushing fingers
from his windpipe, Celluci had a sudden, unavoidable
epiphany about vampires.

He'd caught a glimpse of the reality last August when
Mark Williams had died, but that had been easy to
bury in the tangled mix of reaction that Henry evoked.
Even through his jealousy, he'd recognized and responded to Fitzroy's personal power. Respect had been
inevitable when stopping Anwar Tawfik had thrown
them together. Other emotions, less easily defined, had
been, for the most part, ignored.

Now, it all distilled down to survival.

He's stronger. Faster. The frenzy of the attack gave
him an opening. Hooking his foot into the top of Fitzroy's pelvis, Celluci heaved the smaller man across the
room. Less than a heartbeat later, the vampire charged
him again.

"Fuck!"

Nails gouged into his cheek. He knew the skin had
been broken by the intensity of Fitzroy's response.
Frantically twisting his head to one side, he heard teeth
snap beside his ear. *I never noticed his fucking teeth
were so god-damned long!*

I'm meat to him.

I'm a dead man.

* * *

This isn't something they did to him. He's after the blood! Emotional response insisted she throw herself into the battle, ripping Henry off Celluci's throat. A more visceral reaction suggested she run for her life. She stomped down hard on both and stood trembling where she was. *Goddamnit, Vicki, think! Remember what he's told you!*

He'd talked about his desire to feed like it was a force separate from the rest of him—a force over which he had to exert a certain amount of conscious control.

All right. He's lost control. He's hungry. It wasn't a difficult deduction; his need was a tangible presence, beating against the walls of the small room. *Those bastards have probably been drawing blood for tests all day. Blood's all Henry has. He has to replace it. He'll rip Mike's throat out to get to it.*

So I give him an easier source. One he doesn't have to fight for.

Dropping to her knees, Vicki upended her purse, searching for her knife.

Mike Celluci was a large man in excellent physical condition, speed and strength enhanced by the certain knowledge that if he lost, he died.

Fortunately for him, Henry Fitzroy had been not only weakened by blood loss but also exhausted and injured by the Hunger's fight to get free.

Which only delayed the inevitable.

Bleeding from half a dozen small wounds, breath burning in his throat, joints popping as Fitzroy's teeth slowly descended in spite of everything, Celluci knew with cold certainty that he was losing. And there wasn't a damned thing he could do about it.

Blood trickling down into her hand, Vicki dove across the room, buried her fingers in Henry's hair and yanked his head up.

* * *

Celluci felt lips peel back against his skin and the lightest kiss of pain. Then the heated contact jerked away and teeth sheared the air in the hollow between jaw and neck.

Vicki straddled both men and yanked again, harder. Howling, Henry reared back onto his knees.

Without the grip on his hair she would have lost her balance, but she managed to bring her arm around, blood soaking her cuff and dripping to the floor, and shove the wound against his face.

She cried out as his teeth cut deeper into flesh and the fingers of his good hand clutched almost to the bone. Then she cried out again as he began to suck, mouth working desperately at her wrist.

Vaguely aware of Celluci scrambling clear, she half slid down Henry's body until she knelt behind him, free hand moving from his hair to his shoulder. Eyes closed, she could feel the blood leave her body for his, feel his urgency catch her up and sweep her along, feel herself begin to be lost in his Hunger. He'd been a passive recipient the last time she'd forced her blood on him. While his need might be no greater now, it was far from passive.

This had a reality that burned, that consumed the memories of all the other times Henry had fed.

Her eyes snapped open as, snarling with frustration, he thrust her wrist aside and whirled to face her. She rocked back. He followed, lips and teeth stained crimson, eyes compelling her to offer her throat, to submit.

She felt her chin begin to rise and forced it back down. "Fuck that!" The hoarse whisper traveled just far enough. "You feed where *I* allow." She brought her left hand up between them, trailing scarlet streamers in the air.

It wasn't enough. The blood came too slowly.

He batted the wound aside, laid his teeth against the

soft flesh of the throat, and breathed in the rich scent of life.

Life . . .

He knew this life.

Then the Hunger roared forward, out of control, and his teeth pierced skin.

A blow struck him hard in the side. He lost his hold, twisted as he fell and landed on his back, staring up at a dark-haired male who dared to take him from his prey.

Another blow. He grabbed at the leg and heaved it away, surging back onto his knees as part of the same motion.

Vicki winced as Celluci hit the wall but kept her eyes locked on Henry. Just for a second, she'd felt the Hunger falter. She *could* reach him. She *had* to reach him. It was the only chance for all three of them.

Right hand clamped tourniquet tight above the wound—from the pain involved she suspected his teeth had torn a hole significantly larger than her initial incision—she again offered her left.

He started to dive at her, checked, and slowly raised his eyes up from the welling blood to her face.

The Hunger bucked and writhed, but he held it tight, pulling strength from the blood he'd already taken. Pulling strength from her blood.

"Henry?"

Henry. Yes. A name to leash the Hunger with. He forced his lips to form a name to help recage it.

"Vicki."

She frowned as he swayed, and shuffled toward him, still on her knees. "Henry, you've got to keep feeding. You haven't taken nearly as much as you need. Besides . . ." She glanced down at her wrist and looked quickly away again. "Besides," she repeated, "we're just wasting it on the floor."

Henry moaned and crumpled.

Vicki caught him, smearing his back with blood. Holding him awkwardly, she dragged her legs out from under, and gathered him onto her lap.

"No . . ." He pushed her wrist away as she laid it against his mouth. The brief taste of her nearly catapulted the Hunger to freedom. The bloodscent alone tore at hastily erected barricades. "I don't trust . . . myself."

She laid her wrist against his mouth again, blood dribbling down over lips clamped shut and staining his cheeks. That he was too weak to stop her merely proved her point. "Oh, for Christ's sake, Henry, stop being a martyr. *I* trust you."

She felt him hesitate, then she felt his lips part. The torn flesh wrapped barbed lines of pain around her arm as he pressed against her and began to suckle. Muscles tensed, but she managed not to pull away and slowly the familiar rhythm pushed the pain to one side, her body responding with something very like post-coital lassitude. Resting her cheek against the top of Henry's head, she sighed.

"Isn't that nice," Celluci grunted, glaring down at the tableau and wiping at the blood on his face. "Love conquers all." Sucking his breath through his teeth, he squatted beside them and peered into what he could see of Vicki's face. "Are you okay?"

Caught in the incessant pull of Henry's need, she didn't bother to raise her head, wouldn't have even bothered to answer except that the concern in his voice demanded a response. "I'm fine." And then, because she belatedly realized Celluci deserved more than that, added, "I *think* I'm fine."

"Great." He shifted position. Somehow, this was more intimate than watching them make love. He barely resisted the urge to grab Henry and violently stuff him back into the isolation box. "How do you know when he's had enough?"

"He'll know. He'll stop."

"Yeah? What if he needs more than you can spare?"

Vicki sighed again, but this time the exhalation had an entirely different sound. "He won't *take* more than I can spare."

Celluci reached up for the open lip of the box and hauled himself to his feet. "You'll excuse me if I don't put a lot of faith in that. A few minutes ago he was ready to kill both of us."

"That was then . . ."

"And this is now? Very deep, Vicki. Very deep bullshit. He stops in fifteen seconds or I'm yanking him off the tit."

"There'll be no need, Detective." The statement, although barely audible, left no room for argument. Henry, having pulled away just enough for speech, molded his mouth back over the wound, pressing the edges of the torn flesh together in order for the coagulant in his saliva to work. He could feel Vicki's life wrapped around his own and, while the last thing he wanted right at this moment was to break free of it, continuing to feed would only endanger them both. She would die from loss of blood and he would die from loss of her. He had taken all he was going to.

This was the second time she had saved him. The first time, she hadn't known the risks and, defeated by the demon, the Hunger had lain in darkness with him beyond the need for control. This time, she knew what she was offering and offered in spite of the Hunger raging free. *I wanted to hear her say I love you. I just heard it.*

And what had he given in return?

"I'm sorry, Vicki." He rested his head against her breast, conserving the little strength he'd regained. "I can stop most of the bleeding, but I can't repair the damage. You're going to need a dressing of some kind."

Vicki glanced down at her wrist and her stomach twisted. "Jesus H. Christ." She swallowed bile. "It looks like it should hurt a lot more than it does.'' Then suddenly, it did. "Oh, damn . . .''

Celluci grabbed Henry's shirt out of the box and dropped to his knees. "I think Jesus H. Christ about sums it up. Fuck, Fitzroy, you're a god-damned animal!''

Henry met the detective's stormy glare with a calm gaze of his own. "Not when I can help it,'' he said quietly.

"Yeah. Well.'' Celluci looked away first, burying his confusion—*He almost kills both of us. He chews a big fucking hole in Vicki. And I feel sorry for* him?— in the wrapping of Vicki's arm. "You're lucky,'' he grunted as he began to bind Henry's shirt around the wound. "It's messy, but I don't think there's any tendon damage. Move your fingers.''

"It hurts.''

"Move them anyway.''

Muttering profanities under her breath, Vicki did as instructed, all three of them anxiously watching the digits perform.

"What did I tell you.'' Relief made Celluci's own fingers tremble as he tied off the thick bandage and held a sleeve up in each hand. "We'll use these as a sling, to immobilize it, but you're going to Emergency as soon as we get out of here.'' Vicki bowed her head as he knotted the cuffs at the back of her neck and he rested his cheek for a moment against her hair, much as she'd done earlier with Henry—who still reclined against the support of her good arm. "I thought . . .'' He'd thought she was going to die when he'd kicked the teeth away from her throat. He'd thought she was suicidal when she'd presented herself again. And when it had actually worked, he'd thought . . . he'd thought . . . He didn't know what he thought anymore. "I thought it was all over,'' he finished lamely and sat back on his heels. *And if she asks me what I meant by* all, *I don't know what to tell her.*

Then his eyes widened, and he snickered.

Henry looked startled and pulled himself up into a shaky but nearly erect sitting position.

Vicki's brows snapped down. "What the hell are you laughing at?" she demanded.

Celluci waved a hand at the two of them and snickered again. "Just for a minute there I was reminded of Michelangelo's Pietà. You know, the statue of the Madonna holding the body of Christ across her lap?"

"And you think me an inappropriate Christ?" Henry asked.

Celluci took a good long look at the other man—at the bruising, at the horror that still lurked around hazel eyes, at the mixture of physical youth and spiritual age, at the nearly visible sense of self now firmly back in place—and shook his head. "Actually," he said, "as Christs go, I've seen worse. But the Madonna . . ." The snicker returned at Vicki's indignant stare. "But the Madonna has definitely been miscast."

Vicki's lips twitched. "You rotten bastard," she began. Then she lost it and howled with laughter.

Which pushed Celluci over the edge.

Henry hesitated, nerves scraped raw and unsure if he should be finding insult when Vicki didn't or blasphemy where none was intended—although honesty forced him to admit that Celluci had a valid point. Unable to withstand the purge of emotion, he joined in.

If some of the laughter had a slightly hysterical tone, they all agreed to ignore it.

"Hey, Fergusson! What are you doing back here, man?"

"Forgot something." Detective Fergusson picked a long narrow paper bag up off his desk and pulled a bottle of bubble bath shaped like a ninja turtle out far enough for the other man to identify it. "My daughter sent me back for it. Informed me on her way to bed that broken promises make blisters."

"How old is she now, four? Five?"

"Five."

Detective Brunswick shook his head. "Five years old and she's already got you asking how high on the way up. Man, when she becomes a teenager, she's going to run you ragged."

Fergusson snorted, cramming bag and bottle into his coat pocket. "By that time maybe her mother'll be slowing down." He leaned over and squinted at the piece of pink message paper topping a stack of reports like a square of icing. "What the hell's this?"

"Just some drunk calling you to confess."

"Confess to what?"

"The sinking of the Lusitania? The shooting of JFK? Repatriating the constitution? I don't know. She didn't want to confess to me."

"Geez, why do *I* always get them?"

Brunswick grinned and snapped his gun. "Because you're such a sweetie."

"Fuck you, too," Fergusson muttered absently, reading the actual message. "Director of Life Sciences? . . ."

"She seemed to think I should know who she was. In fact, she told me that *everyone* knew who she was." He watched the other man's face for a moment and his grin faded. "You don't think there's actually anything in this, do you?"

"I don't know." He crumpled the paper and stuffed it in the pocket with his daughter's bubble bath, his expression resembling that of a hound worrying at a bone. "Maybe." Then he shrugged and sighed. "Maybe not."

"You haven't even begun to convince me that we shouldn't haul ass out of here right now," Celluci growled. "You," he jabbed a finger at Henry, "are operating on half a tank. And you," the finger moved to wave in front of Vicki's nose, "are about three pints short."

"Not that much," Vicki protested, although from the way she felt, she wasn't going to bet on it.

Celluci ignored her. "We *all* look like we've been through the wars. Let's just clear out of here and leave the mopping up to the police."

"Mike . . ."

"Don't *Mike* me. And I want that wrist of yours looked at by a doctor before you get gangrene in it and have to have your fucking hand chopped off."

"The wound won't infect," Henry said with quiet assurance. "And *I* am going to the lab." He stretched out both arms. Although the bruising had faded from purple to green and the broken bones in his hand had begun to knit, the marks of needles were still very evident. "If, as you say, Catherine didn't move me until late afternoon, any samples, any test results, will be there. They have to be destroyed."

"Oh, come on, Fitzroy," Celluci sighed. "No one's going to believe anything these people say after their attempt to play Dr. Frankenstein has been discovered."

"I can't risk that."

Celluci looked from Henry to Vicki and back again, then he savagely shoved both hands up through his hair. "Jesus, there's nothing to choose between you. All right, all right, we'll go."

"I said *I* was going," Henry pointed out. "You don't have to come with me."

"Fuck that," Celluci told him bluntly. "We went through too much to find you. You're not moving out of our sight until we stuff you back in that god-damned closet come morning. Unless? . . ." He raised an eloquent brow.

Henry half smiled. "You're both perfectly safe. Although I still hunger, Vicki's blood was more than enough to return my control."

Celluci's hand rose involuntarily to the place on his throat that Henry's teeth had grazed. Angrily, he turned the motion into an abrupt gesture at the wall of wiring and electrical panels. "We still shutting off the power?"

Vicki nodded and instantly regretted the motion as her head seemed to want to keep on falling. "The reasons for doing it haven't changed. If there're any more of those . . . experiments in this building, I want them shut down." She paused and swallowed, hard. Dr. Burke had said her mother was up and walking around. It wouldn't be so easy to turn her mother off; to see that her mother died a second time. "We should have about forty-five minutes on the emergency lighting—not that it'll make any difference to me. Plenty of time to get to the lab, do what we have to, and get out. Then the police can handle the rest." She caught Celluci's gaze and held it. "I promise."

"Fine." He moved toward the corner of the room where a thick plastic pipe came through the wall and disappeared into a metal box about two feet square. "This is the main feed, so this must be the main disconnect box."

Close behind him, Vicki peered over his shoulder. "How do you know? I thought your father was a plumber?"

"It's a guy thing, you wouldn't under . . . Ow! Damn it, Vicki, that was the last bit of unbruised flesh I had."

"Had," Vicki repeated, flicking on her flashlight. "Just pull the switch."

The switch, about a foot long and rust-pitted down its entire length, refused to surrender so easily. "This thing," Celluci grunted, throwing his weight on it, "hasn't been moved since they wired the building." He managed to force it down to a forty-five-degree angle but could budge it no farther. "I need something to lever it with. The pipe we used on the door . . ."

"May I?" Henry reached past Celluci, wrapped long pale fingers around the switch, and slammed it down in one, fluid motion, snapping it off at the base.

The light in the electrical room went out.

"I thought you hadn't regained all your strength." Celluci squinted in the circle of illumination thrown by Vicki's flashlight.

Henry, who'd stepped back to shield sensitive eyes, shrugged, forgetting for the moment that he couldn't be seen. "I haven't."

"Jesus H. Christ. How strong *are* you?"

Resisting the urge to brag, to further advance himself over a rival who had somehow become much more, Henry settled for a diplomatic, "Not strong enough to get free on my own." Which was, after all, only the truth.

Catherine frowned down into the microscope. There had to be a way to use the regenerative properties of the vampire's cells to extend the limited life of her bacteria. Once found, she could tailor new bacteria for number nine and keep him from decomposing like all the rest. She looked up and shot a smile across the room to where he sat patiently watching her from the edge of the bed.

All at once, the lights went out and the constant hum of her computer was swallowed by the silence that swept in with the darkness.

"It's her!" Catherine gripped the table tightly with both hands until the world steadied. "She's done this. She wants you to die." Knocking over her stool, she stood and stumbled to the door, arms stretched stiffly out before her. A moment's fumbling with the lock and she stepped out into the hall.

At each bend of the corridor, battery-operated emergency lights provided enough illumination for movement.

"This has gone far enough. We have to get to the lab. Come on," she called back over her shoulder. "We'll stop her together."

Number nine could just barely see her outlined in the doorway. He stood and slowly shuffled toward her.

Together.

He wished he could see her better.

Gaze jerking from one shadow to the next, searching out the possibility of Dr. Burke, Catherine never noticed that number nine's eyes now shone in the darkness with the faint phosphorescence of rot.

Fifteen

.

The sudden darkness hurled Dr. Burke up against the wall, heart in her throat, palms prickling with sweat. She could feel the jolt of adrenaline eating away at the alcohol-induced distance and struggled to calm herself. Being sober, in *this* building, was no part of her plan.

"I knew, I knew, I knew I should've brought the resht . . . of the sec . . . ond bottle," she muttered, her voice very nearly lost in the passage of throat and teeth and lips it had to negotiate before it could clear her mouth.

The equally sudden appearance of light from the battery-operated floods at each end of the hall brought a victorious wave of Donald's jacket. "Ha, ha! Let's hear it for modern engin . . . eering! Power goes off, emer . . . gency lights . . . go on. Rah! Damn good thing they did, too," she continued, stumbling forward again. "Never find the damn lab . . . otherwise. Wander around here for . . . days. Maybe even . . . months."

She squinted down the length of the corridor. "Speaking of . . . which. Where the hell am I?" It took a moment's concentrated effort before she recognized the upcoming t-junction. The left wing, after crossing a lecture hall and going down a small flight of stairs, was a dead end, she thought, but the right, with a little luck, would eventually lead her to the back door of the lab. The small wooden door led into the storeroom; they'd never used it, but Dr. Burke had seen to it in the beginning that she carried the key.

"Maybe I knew something like this was . . . going to happen," she confided to a fire extinguisher. "Maybe I was just being . . . prepared for crazy-Cathy to pop her . . . cork."

And were you prepared, asked the voice of reason, *for what happened to Donald?*

Not even a bottle of single malt whiskey could shut the voice up, but it did make it very easy to ignore. So Dr. Burke did.

While Vicki could see the emergency lights as white pinpricks in a black shroud, her companions apparently found them more than sufficient illumination. Given that Henry needed so little light, he could probably see quite clearly, and she knew from experience that Celluci had better than average night vision. God, how she envied them; to be able to move freely without fear of misstep or collision, to be able to see movement in the shadows in time to . . .

To what?

Vicki pushed the question away and concentrated on not outpacing her circle of sight. Although she kept the flashlight beam trained closely on the floor in front of her so as not to blind the two men, she allowed a small part to overlap onto Henry. After everything they'd been through—everything all three of them had been through—she wasn't letting him slip into darkness just because of her lousy eyes.

Henry was safe.

They'd saved him.

Her mother was dead, but Henry was alive and he was safe with them.

That made up for a lot.

Breathing heavily, Celluci's hand tucked into the elbow of her good arm, she followed the little bit of Henry out of a stairwell and squinted up at the red pinprick in the darkness that had to be the exit sign. "You guys sure this is the right floor?"

"I'm sure." Henry's voice was flat and atonal. "The stink of perverted death is strongest here."

"Henry . . ." Shaking free of Celluci's grip, Vicki reached out and poked him gently in the hip with the side of the flashlight. "It's going to be worse in the lab." They'd told him about Donald down in the electrical room. All three of them had needed a moment to recover from the telling. "You can wait in the hall if you think it's going to be too strong."

"It's only a difference of degree," Henry told her abruptly, not turning. He could see the outline of the door at the end of the hall. "I might as well go into the lab because I can't smell anything else even here." Then he reached back and brushed his fingers over the warmth of her hand, softening his tone. "We've all moved past the time for running. Now it's time to face those last few fears and . . ."

"And get the hell out of here," Celluci finished. "Which we won't do if we continue to stand here flapping our lips. Come on." He caught hold of Vicki again and dragged her forward, forcing Henry to move ahead or be run down. If they lost momentum, they'd never get this finished. He hadn't wanted to see anything finished quite so much in a very long time. "It can't possibly be worse than the last visit, for any of us."

Vicki tightened her hand around the barrel of the flashlight, giving thanks the grip was heavy ridged rubber. Her palm was so wet that a slicker surface would've squirted right out of her grasp. *Face our last few fears. Oh, God, I hope not.*

The lab—possibly because it was such a large room, possibly because after a century of renovation the building just generally defied logic—rated an emergency light of its own.

"Well, thank God for small favors," Celluci muttered as they entered. "I didn't much want to be in the dark with *that.*"

Vicki let her light lick over *that,* the stainless steel blazing momentarily then sliding into shadow again. All the horror lay in memory now for the body the isolation box contained was merely dead, and they'd all dealt with death before. *He's really most sincerely dead.* She bit back a giggle and stomped down hard on the thought. It would be frighteningly easy to lose control.

Henry ignored the box and strode quickly down the length of the room to the one remaining computer, trench coat flapping back from his naked torso. With the power off, he had no way to tell if it contained the files concerning him, but he had to assume that if Catherine did the tests in this lab then she entered the data into this machine.

"Fitzroy."

He turned, fingers already wrapped around a fistful of cables.

"You might want to clear this out of here as well." Celluci offered him the wallet he'd picked up off the floor, various pieces of ID stuffed loosely inside. "Let's not give Detective Fergusson a chance to cash in on the obvious."

"Thank you." A quick check, and Henry shoved it all into his coat pocket. "If the police managed to connect me to all of this, I'd have had to disappear." One corner of his mouth twisted in the detective's direction. "Maybe you should have left the wallet on the floor."

Celluci mirrored both expression and tone. "Maybe I should have."

Setting cables and monitor keyboard carefully to one side, Henry lifted the actual computer over his head and threw it into the corner as hard as he could.

Catherine jerked back at the sound of plastic shattering, eyes snapping open impossibly wide. "It's her.

She's wrecking things.'' Her fingers wrapped around number nine's arm, molding imprints into the increasingly malleable flesh. ''We've got to stop her!''

Number nine stopped moving, obedient to the pressure. He would do what she wanted.

From the lab up ahead came the sound of further destruction, small pieces being made smaller still until they were beyond all hope of repair.

''All right.'' Catherine rose on her toes and rested her forehead on number nine's skull just below where the staples held the cap of bone in place. ''This is my plan. I'll distract her, get her to chase me and lose her in the halls. You go in and get Donald. He should be viable outside the box by now. Don't let anything stop you.''

He couldn't feel her breath, warm against his ear and neck—the nerves in the skin had never regenerated—but he could feel her closeness and that was enough. He reached up and awkwardly patted her arm.

''I knew I could count on you!'' She squeezed his hand in return, never feeling the tiny bones shifting out of their moorings, tendons and ligaments beginning to let go. ''Come on!''

While Henry smashed hardware into progressively smaller pieces and Celluci snapped disks, Vicki, flashlight tucked under her chin, flipped through reams and reams of printout.

''Finding anything?'' Celluci asked, reaching for yet another plastic square.

Vicki shook her head. ''Mostly EEG records.''

He craned his neck and peered down at the paper bisected with a black ink trail of spikes and valleys. ''How the hell do you know that?''

She snorted. ''They're labeled.''

''Stop it!''

All three of them jerked around.

''Stop it this instant!''

Vicki's flashlight just barely managed to pick out a

pale circle of face and hair over a paler rectangle of lab coat in the doorway at the far end of the long room.

"Stop it! Stop it! Stop it!" Fury and madness were stridently obvious in her voice.

"Catherine." Leaping the wreckage at his feet, Henry charged forward.

The figure in the doorway disappeared.

"Fitzroy!"

"Henry!"

He ignored them, intent on the hunt. This madwoman had imprisoned him, tortured him, left him alone in the darkness; she was his. Knowing what she was, he would avoid sinking into the emptiness of her eyes. He would take her down. Her blood was not tainted even if her mind was. And she owed him blood.

In spite of his speed, not yet fully returned but still greater than mortal, she was out of sight when he reached the hall. Her scent lay buried under the clinging stench of death perverted, which not only filled the air but covered the inside of his mouth and nose like a noxious film of oil. He *could* hear her life so he sped after it.

But sound became a twisting and uncertain trail, easy to lose track of in the maze of rooms and passageways and, so long used to hunting by sight or scent, Henry found it more difficult than he'd believed possible to close the distance. Her life grew closer, but embarrassingly slowly.

Madness gives strength of limb even while it destroys strength of mind. He couldn't remember who had said that to him, so many years ago, but it appeared that madness gave fleetness of foot as well as strength for Catherine continued to elude him, using the peculiarities of the building to her advantage.

Around a corner and through a lecture hall and out a small door only someone with intimate knowledge of the building would know existed, her heartbeat led him on. The emergency lighting provided patches of too bright light alternating with bands of shadow much easier on his eyes. He was beginning to grow tired, his body protesting the demands he was making on it so soon after the punishment it had endured. Vicki's blood could only do so much.

In the instant before flight, Catherine had recognized the vampire and it hadn't taken her long to realize that she couldn't outrun him. Her knowledge of the building was her only advantage and while it prevented an immediate confrontation, she soon saw it wasn't enough to throw him off her trail.

She had no idea what he would do when he finally caught her, nor did she care. Her only thoughts were for number nine and how she'd been forced to leave him alone and outnumbered in the lab. She had to get back to him.

Rounding a corner, the angle of the emergency light caught her eye and she skidded to a stop. The heavy battery contained in the base had proved too much for the antique plaster and lath expected to hold the screws and the unit had sagged away from the wall. Chest heaving, she jumped for it and hooked her fingertips over a narrow metal lip.

Henry followed Catherine's life around another corner and down a corridor much darker than the rest had been. Her heartbeat grew louder. Then he saw her outlined against the institutional gray of the wall; cowering, cornered.

His lips drew off his teeth and the Hunter closed in on his prey.

She straightened, her body no longer blocking the object cradled in her arms.

Brilliant white light drove spikes of hot metal into night-sensitive eyes. Crying out in pain, Henry fell back, hands raised, an ineffectual barrier now that the damage had been done. He heard her go by, recoiled as her life brushed its shattered edges over him, and could not follow.

* * *

Celluci had taken three quick steps after the running vampire, saw he was fast being left behind and stopped. "God damn him!" He flung the disk he was holding at the wall, as hard as he was able, and found his feelings were not in the least relieved by its shattering. "After all we went through to haul his ass out of danger, that god-damned undead bastard runs off on us!"

Vicki merely shook her head, hand clutched tightly around the barrel of her flashlight. Although the sound of her own heartbeat nearly deafened her, she felt surprisingly calm. "It's not," she said softly, "like he's a tame lion."

Celluci turned on her, both hands driving up through his hair. "And what the hell is *that* supposed to mean?"

"It's a line from a children's book. I used it to describe him last spring, when we met."

"Great, just great. You're taking a literary trip down memory lane and Fitzroy's buggered off." He took another step toward the door, then changed his mind, whirled, and stomped back to her side. "Vicki, that's it. We're out of here." Feelings of betrayal outweighed worry and concern. "If Fitzroy's able to go running off like some kind of bloodsucking avenging angel, he can manage without us around and . . ."

All at once, he realized she wasn't listening to him. Which was, in itself, not particularly unusual but her expression, pointed fixedly down the flashlight beam, was one he'd seen on her face only once before—about an hour and a half before when they'd opened the metal coffin and Donald Li had opened his eyes.

The flesh between his shoulder blades crawling, he spun around.

Standing in the doorway, was a parody of a man.

She had told him to rescue Donald. She had not

mentioned the people standing beyond the box, so number nine ignored them.

He shuffled forward.

Celluci's right hand came up and sketched a quick sign of the cross. "That girl, the witness the night the boy was killed, she said that he was strangled by a dead man."

The creature continued to shuffle forward, the stink of it growing with every step.

A sane man would run. But his feet and legs refused to obey. "This has got to be the thing that killed the boy."

"Odds are good," Vicki agreed, her voice sounding as though she'd forced it through clenched teeth. "So what are you going to do? Arrest it?"

"Oh, very funny." Without taking his eyes off the lurching obscenity, he moved sideways until his shoulder came in contact with hers; the warmth of another life suddenly important. "What do you suppose it wants?"

He felt her shrug. "I'm afraid to guess."

It arrived at the isolation box and reached out for the latch.

"Fuck that!" Barely aware he was moving, Celluci charged forward. After what they'd gone through to save Donald Li—after what Donald Li had gone through—he'd be damned if he'd let the kid be dragged back into the ranks of the undead. *Ranks of the undead . . . Jesus! I sound like the cut line on a made-for-TV movie.* He rocked to a halt at the end of the box and bellowed, "Go on! Get away from there!"

It ignored him.

"God damn you, I said get away!" He didn't remember pulling his gun, but there it was in his hand. "Just back away from the box! Now!"

Finally recognizing some sort of threat, it turned its head and looked right at him.

* * *

Get Donald. Don't let anything stop you.

Number nine stared at the man by the box. The voice had held command, but the words had not been words he had to obey.

Don't let anything stop you.

The words were not enough to stop him. The man could be ignored.

He turned his attention back to the latch, trying to get his fingers to close.

The worst of it wasn't the grave-gray of the skin, lips and fingertips greenish-black, nor was it the line of staples across the forehead or even the obvious signs of the triumph of decay. The worst of it was that there was someone in there—that not only an intelligence but a personality existed within the ruin.

Trembling violently with horror and pity and revulsion in about equal proportion, Celluci braced his gun with his left hand and, whispering a "Hail Mary" through dry lips, pulled the trigger. The first shot missed. The second creased the back of the creature's skull with enough force to spin it around and throw it over the stainless steel curve of the isolation box. He never got the chance to fire a third.

The blow caught him just below the shoulder, knocking him into the trio of oxygen tanks lined up under the window. He lost his grip on the gun, was vaguely aware of it skittering away across the floor, and saw Vicki charging around the end of the box, flashlight raised like a club.

Vicki had watched Celluci advance on the creature with a curious detachment. It was as though, when she'd seen it appear in the doorway and realized both what it was and what it wasn't, an overload switch had been tripped and she could no longer react, only wait. Her mouth had moved in response to comments made, but her mind had been disconnected. After the last few days of constant internal turmoil, charges and countercharges and just general hysteria, the peace and quiet was kind of nice. She kept the flashlight beam trained on the creature as it shuffled along and refused to wonder what it was she waited for.

She thought she understood what motivated Celluci to try and prevent the opening of the box, but she couldn't seem to make it matter. She heard him speak, but the words got tangled and made no sense. When he pulled his gun, the only thing she felt was mild surprise.

Muscles spasmed with the first shot, her brain slamming back and forth between her ears. The crack of the second shot jerked her out of her retreat and shook her awake.

She saw the creature's arm come up and Celluci fly back. She started moving before he hit the floor. Keeping the beam pointed along her path until she got near enough to finish blind, she raised the heavy flashlight like a club and slammed it down. Contact had a strangely muffled feel.

Although she'd come so close that the slightly sweet stink of decomposing flesh wrapped around her, she couldn't actually see the creature she faced. *And thank God for small mercies*. It had been terrifying enough from a distance. Unfortunately, neither could she see the return blow.

With only one arm for balance, she went down hard, more concerned with hanging onto her only means of sight than with breaking her fall. She struck, rolled, and crushed her injured wrist against the floor.

Celluci heard her gasp of pain as he launched himself back at the creature. *What are you doing?* screamed the still rational part of his brain. But even while recognizing that the question had merit, the night had gone on too long for him to listen to it.

With a dull squelch, his shoulder drove into the creature's ribs, forcing it back toward the door. They went down together, grappled, rolled. He lost track of

time, lost track of place, lost track of self until he
found himself staring up at the hall ceiling as his spine
smashed into the tile. He grunted as the heavy muscles
of his back absorbed most, but not all, of the blow.
He tried to kick free. Was lifted. Thrown against a
wall of shelves. Slid down them. Saw a door closing.
And was suddenly alone in darkness.

Number nine had put the last intruder in the box.
She had been pleased with that. So he found a box for
this intruder as well.
Pressing down with both hands, he bent the round
metal thing until it would no longer turn.
Now the intruder would stay in the box.

It was undoubtedly a storage closet—not that it mattered. Celluci flung himself against the door. It didn't
budge. And when, screaming Italian profanity, he finally found the knob, it didn't turn.

Vicki levered herself up onto her knees, head spin-
ning. She assumed the sounds of impact she heard
were Celluci and the creature, but at the moment she
was physically incapable of going to his aid. Curled
around her injured arm, she dry retched, fighting the
waves of dizziness that threatened to knock her flat
again.
*Damn it, Vicki, get it together! Mike needs you! So
you've lost a little blood, big fucking deal. It isn't the
first time. Get UP!*
Panting through locked teeth, she groped for the
flashlight and suddenly realized she wasn't alone.
Her vision consisted of only a very narrow path
along the floor, illuminated by the flashlight and bound
by the disease that had destroyed her sight. Into that
path shuffled a pair of feet wearing new track shoes
with velcro tabs. Beyond horror, Vicki froze, unable
to move, unable to think, unable to look away as the
feet shuffled toward her. When they stopped, she could

also see sweatpants covering the legs from knees to ankles. The creature by the box had been wearing sweatpants, but she could still hear the sounds of fighting. . . .

Finally, she got her fingers closed around the rubber grip and, clutching it like a talisman, she slowly forced herself to straighten.

Her mother looked down at her, much as her mother had looked down at her a thousand times before. Except this time, her mother was dead.

She felt reason slipping away and scrambled desperately for its edges. This was her mother. Her mother loved her. Dead or not, her mother would never harm her.

Then the dead lips parted and a dead mouth formed her name.

Too much.

Henry heard the scream, turned, and ran toward it. Still half blind, his sense of smell useless in corridors saturated with abomination, he raced back along the path of Vicki's terror and came up facing a dead end.

Howling with rage, he doubled back, senses straining for the touch of her life to guide him.

"VICKI!" Celluci threw himself against the door in impotent fury. Again, and again.

And again.

Mouth dry, heart pounding in the too-small cage of her ribs, Vicki slowly backed away. Hands reaching out for her, her dead mother followed. The harsh illumination of the flashlight accentuated the death pallor and threw tiny shadows beside each of the staples across Marjory Nelson's forehead.

Her feet continued moving for a moment before Vicki realized she wasn't going any farther, that the distance between them was closing. The cold metal curve of the isolation box pressed into the small of her back. *Go around!* she thought, but she couldn't remember how. She couldn't take her eyes off the approaching figure. Nor could she turn the light away in the hope that it would disappear in the darkness.

"Stop!"

Vicki jerked, the sound slapping at her.

The dead woman, who had been Marjory Nelson, dragged herself forward one more step, then had to obey.

"Stay!" Catherine, with number nine following close behind her, entered the lab, squinted as she crossed the beam of light, and glared around. "Just look at this place. It'll take days to get it all cleared up." She kicked at a fractured bit of circuit board and turned on Vicki, her movements nearly as jerky as her companion's. "Who are you?"

Who am I? Her glasses were sliding down her nose. She bent her head until she could push them up with the index finger of her injured hand. Who was she? She swallowed, trying to wet her mouth. "Nelson. Vicki Nelson."

"Vicki Nelson?" Catherine repeated, coming closer.

The tone sent a knife blade down Vicki's spine, although the grad student was still outside the boundary of her vision. *This person is insane.* Crazy just wasn't a strong enough word for the fractures in Catherine's voice.

Leaving number nine in the shadows, Catherine crossed into the cone of light and stopped just in front of where Marjory Nelson strained against the compulsion holding her in place. "Dr. Burke told me about *you*. You wouldn't stop snooping around." The pointed chin rose and the pale blue eyes narrowed. "She wouldn't have tried to terminate the experiments if it wasn't for you. This is all your fault!" The last word became a curse and she threw herself forward, fingers curved to claws, claws reaching for Vicki's throat.

Self-preservation broke the paralysis. Vicki threw herself sideways, knowing she wasn't going to be fast enough. She felt fingertips catch at her collar, had a sudden look into the pit of madness as, for an instant, Catherine's contorted face filled her vision, then all at once, found herself staggering back, no longer under attack. Sagging against the support of the box, she raised the light, searching for an explanation.

Catherine dangled from her mother's hands then was tossed, with no apparent effort, to one side.

It was the sort of rescue that small children implicitly believed their mothers could perform. In spite of everything, Vicki found herself smiling.

"Way to go, Mom," she muttered, trying to catch her breath.

Number nine had not understood what the other who was like him was about to do.

Then he heard *her* cry out as she struck the floor.

She was hurt.

He remembered anger.

Number nine's first blow shattered ribs, the crack of breaking bone gunshot loud, splinters driven into the chest cavity.

That first blow would have killed her, had she not already been dead. She staggered under the impact but managed to remain standing. The second blow knocked uplifted arms aside, the third threw her halfway across the lab.

Vicki struggled to keep the battle in sight, bracing herself on the box and playing the flashlight beam over the room like some kind of demented spotlight operator at a production more macabre than anything modern theater had to offer.

Nutrient fluid dripped from the ruin of number nine's hands, violence having finished what rot had begun. Glistening curves of bone showed through the destruction of his wrists. He used his forearms like clubs, smashing them down again and again.

Vicki watched as her mother's body slammed into a metal shelving unit, shelves and contents crashing to the floor. A number of the glass containers seemed to explode on contact with the floor, spewing chemical vapor into the air to mix with the smell of decay. As number nine lurched forward, Vicki could stand it no longer.

"For chrissakes, Mom!" she screamed. "Hit the bastard back!"

Her mother turned, head lolling on a neck no longer capable of support, met her daughter's gaze for a moment, then bent and ripped free one of the shelves' flat metal struts. Holding it like a baseball bat, she straightened and swung.

The ragged end of the steel bar caught number nine in the temple, shearing through the thin bone and into the brain. Gold gleamed for a second as the neural net tore loose, then number nine reeled back and collapsed.

The bar rang against the tile. Marjory Nelson swayed and crumpled, as though invisible strings had been cut.

"MOM!" Vicki stumbled forward and threw herself to her knees. She couldn't hold her mother and the flashlight both, so she shoved the latter in under her sling and dragged the limp body up onto her lap. The diffuse light, shining through the thin cotton of Henry's shirt, wiped away all the changes that death and science had made and gave her back her mother.

"Mom? Don't be dead. Oh, please, don't be dead. Not again. . . ."

Too much damage. She could feel the binding letting go.

But there was something she had to do.

"Mom? God*damn*it, Mom . . ." Pale gray eyes, so

like her own, flickered open and Vicki forgot how to breathe. She shouldn't have been able to see their expression, but she could, could see it clearly, felt it wrap around her and for one long moment keep her safe from the world.

". . . love you . . . Vic . . . ki . . ."

Tears pooled under the edge of her glasses and spilled down her cheeks. "I love you, too, Mom." Her vision blurred and when it cleared she was alone. "Mom?" But the gray eyes stared up at nothing and the body she held was empty. Very, very carefully, she slid it off her lap and stroked the eyes closed.

Her mother was dead.

She started to shake. The pressure grew, closing her throat, twisting her muscles into knots, tossing her back and forth where she knelt. The first sob ripped huge burning holes in her heart and held as much anger as grief. It hurt so much that she surrendered to the second, curled around the pain, and cried.

Cried for her mother.

Cried for herself.

Number nine lay where he had fallen. The anger was gone. Although he had no way of knowing that the neural net had stopped functioning, he dimly understood that the part that was body and the part that was *him* were now separate.

He stared up at the ceiling, wanting . . .

. . . wanting . . .

Then the view shifted and *she* was there.

Catherine gently turned number nine's head to face her.

"I can't fix you," she whispered, drawing her finger softly around the curve of his jaw, alternately tracing flesh and bone. "You were going to stay with me forever. I wouldn't have let her shut you down." She smiled and tenderly pushed a flap of skin back into place.

"You were," she told him, voice catching in her throat, "the very best experiment I ever did."

He wanted her to smile.
He liked it when she smiled.
Then she was gone.
He wanted her to come back.

Slowly, every movement precisely performed, Catherine got to her feet. Every step carefully planned, she advanced across the lab. She paused at the jagged length of steel, still lying where it had been dropped, bent, and lifted it from the floor.

The end torn from the shelf gleamed, polished and pointed by the force that had ripped it free.

She held it up and smiled at it.

The flat metal bar cracked across Vicki's bent shoulders and smashed her to the floor. The world tilted and instinct took over as, gasping in pain, she managed to squirm around to face the assault, shoving her glasses back into place.

The flashlight twisted in the folds of cloth and somehow finished pointed straight up, a miniature searchlight. It lit the gleaming end of steel descending toward Vicki. But not in time.

Sixteen

Henry heard the pounding as he raced down the corridor leading to the lab, heard it and would have ignored it had it not been accompanied by a fine libretto of Italian profanity. He rocked to a stop in front of an old paneled door, saw that the doorknob had been bent down in such a way as to render it nonfunctional, and solved the problem by bracing one hand against the wall and yanking the entire mechanism out of the wood.

The door crashed back and Celluci exploded out into the hall, the force of his exit throwing him to his knees.

Grabbing him by the collar, Henry hauled him to his feet, blocking the resulting flurry of blows with his other arm.

Celluci's snarled challenge broke off as he finally recognized the vampire. ''Where the hell were you?'' he demanded.

''Finding my way back,'' Henry answered coldly. ''What were you doing in there?''

''Trying to get out.'' The tone matched exactly. ''I heard Vicki scream.''

''So did I.''

Together they turned and ran toward the lab.

As they raced through the doorway, the bloodscent hit Henry an almost solid blow, too close now to be masked by either decay or the alcohol vapor still seeping into the air. Far from replete, the Hunger rose. For Vicki's sake Henry held it, and forced it back; he couldn't help her if he lost control. While he struggled to maintain reason, Celluci pulled ahead.

It seemed there were bodies all over the room, but Celluci only saw one that mattered. Sprawled on her back to one side of the isolation box, Vicki lay motionless except for the purely kinetic jerk that occurred when a blow landed. He saw the steel bar go up and come down, then, howling in inarticulate rage, he grabbed the pale-haired woman by the shoulders and flung her behind him.

"Your fault, too!" Catherine screamed, launching herself back, the jagged end of the bar dripping crimson.

There was no time for Celluci to prepare himself for the attack. Then, all at once, there was no attack.

His arm darting out faster than mortal eye could follow, Henry caught Catherine by the back of the neck, wrapped his other hand around the top of her head, and twisted.

The pale eyes rolled up. For the second time that night the metal strut rang against the tile as it fell from fingers suddenly slack.

Tossing the body aside, Henry threw himself to his knees, his hands joining Celluci's as they frantically searched for the wounds below Vicki's blood-soaked clothing.

The iron bar had torn a chunk of flesh from her left shoulder and had scored the right side of her ribs in two places. Ugly wounds, all three, but hardly fatal.

Then they lifted her fingers out of the puddle between hip and thigh.

"Jesus!" Henry pressed his hand down on the spot and met Celluci's wild gaze. "Arterial," he said quietly and strained to hear her heart above the painful pounding of his own.

The blood spattered across the flashlight lens made Rorschach patterns on the ceiling.

* * *

Number nine lay, head to one side as she had left him, waiting for her to come back.

And then she was there.

But she didn't see him and she didn't smile.

"Fifteen minutes. It takes fifteen minutes to bleed to death from that kind of wound."

"I know that!" Henry snapped. He had her heartbeat now, but it was frighteningly faint.

"Of course you do." His fingers trembling, Celluci looped the arm of her glasses back over the curve of her ear. "You're a fucking vampire. You know bleeding. So do something about it!"

Henry glared at him. There was no way to do a tourniquet in the joining of torso and leg. No way but direct pressure to stop the bleeding and he was already doing that, even if he did it too late. "Do what?" he demanded, sure there was nothing else he could do.

"How the fuck should I know! You're the fucking . . . Jesus!"

Pulled by the intensity of Celluci's terrified stare, Henry twisted around. Across the lab, by the wall of boarded up windows, one of the bodies rose slowly to its feet.

One of them had killed her.

Killed her dead.

The anger number nine had known before was less than nothing in comparison to what he felt now.

My gun? Where the hell is my gun? Swatting aside panic, Celluci scanned the floor and finally spotted it almost under the cavader's feet. *Fucking great . . .*

Scrambling to his feet, he launched himself forward, dove, got both hands around the weapon, rolled, and pulled the trigger at almost point-blank range.

The bullet plowed through the putrefying tissue with almost no loss of velocity and rang against the brass casing of the oxygen tank directly behind. It ricocheted up the curve, hit the next tank, and sprayed bits of the valve across the room. Oxygen began to hiss free.

"Jesus H. Christ!" Still on the floor, Celluci crabbed back. Although pus and fluid and God-knew-what poured from the hole, the dead man continued to shuffle forward. "What the fuck do you think this is? A fucking James Cameron movie?" His hands were shaking too hard to try a head shot. He watched his second round blow a chunk from the outside curve of the thing's thigh without any noticeable effect. "Goddamnit, stay dead!"

The third round passed through the abdomen again, rang against brass and sparked.

All hell broke loose.

Henry threw himself over Vicki.

Celluci flattened.

The explosion sent chunks of the oxygen tank flying through the air like shrapnel. Several of the larger chunks slammed into number nine, cutting him into pieces.

He remembered dying.

The last time, she had been there when it was over.

He hoped she'd be there again.

With a whoosh, the alcohol vapor in the air ignited, then the alcohol, then the desk.

Then the emergency light shut off.

Celluci picked his way back to Vicki's side. "Fucking place is on fire. At least we can still see." He squinted at Henry, the pale skin of the vampire's face and chest just barely visible in the flickering light. "You okay?"

"Yes."

"Vicki?"

Henry hesitated, praying he'd hear something different, knowing he wouldn't. "She's dying."

"Fuck that!" Ripping off jacket and shoulder hol-

ster, Celluci yanked his shirt over his head, ignoring
the buttons. Folding most of the fabric into a rough
pad, sleeves dangling, he shoved it at Henry. "She
said your saliva causes clotting."

"Yes, but . . ."

"Spit on this and tie that wound off. We're practically on top of a fucking hospital. You get the bleeding
stopped and we move her."

"It's too . . ."

"Do it!"

Although he knew it would make no difference,
Henry took the shirt and bent over the jagged hole.
Michael Celluci had lived less than forty years and still
thought death could be fought. Four and a half centuries had taught a different lesson. In a battle between
love and death, death always won. He could feel
Vicki's life ebbing, knew that nothing they could do
would change that.

His fingers maintaining pressure, he covered the still
bleeding gash with his mouth. At least when she died,
he would have contact with her blood. He pulled the
touch, the taste, the scent of her into memory. *You are
mortal, my love. I always knew you'd die, but I never
dreamed we'd have so little time . . .*

Suddenly, Celluci's fingers were in his hair and the
contact broken.

"I said wrap it, Goddamnit. Not fucking take what
she has left!"

Henry drew bloodstained lips back off his teeth.
"Get your hands off me, mortal!"

The explosion had jerked Vicki back out of the twi-
light zone of pain and darkness she'd sunk into. She
hadn't thought it was possible to hurt so much and still
be alive. She could hear the two men arguing and
fought against the weight hanging from her tongue.

"Mi . . ."

"Vicki?" Henry forgotten in the sound of her voice,
Celluci twisted around and cupped her face in his

hands. The fire licked at the plywood over the windows. Celluci ignored it. The high ceiling drew the smoke up and away. The path to the door remained clear. As long as the fire posed no immediate danger, it could be ignored for more important concerns. The highly polished metal of the isolation box reflected the orange glow of the flames out into the room. In its light, Celluci saw Vicki's eyelids flicker, once, twice. "Hang on, we're going to get you to the hospital."

The hospital? She wanted to tell him there wasn't any point but couldn't figure out how.

"Michael." The pain in the detective's voice damped Henry's anger and drew his own grief to the fore. With one hand still foolishly, hopelessly holding pressure on Vicki's leg, he gently grasped Celluci's shoulder with the other. "There isn't enough time."

"No."

"She'll be dead even before you get her out of this building."

"No!"

"I can feel her life ebbing."

"I said, NO!"

Listen to him, Mike. He's right. She thought she was still breathing but she couldn't be certain. *I'm still here, I must be breathing.*

"Damn it, Vicki, don't die!"

Oh, God, Mike, don't cry. She'd thought it couldn't hurt anymore. She'd been wrong.

"There has to be *something* we can do!"

Henry felt a vise close round his heart and squeeze. "No." One word, two letters, somehow carried all he felt.

Pulled by the sound of suffering as great as his own, Celluci looked up and met hazel eyes washed almost gold by the firelight. They held a truth too bitter to deny. Vicki was dying.

I'm cold. And it's dark. And it isn't fair. I could tell you I love you now. Could tell both of you. Love was enough to bring my mother back. I guess I'm not as strong. Her body didn't seem to be a part of her anymore. The flesh wrapped around her like a badly fitting suit of clothes. *Oh, shit. I can't feel anything. This sucks. This really sucks. I DON'T WANT TO DIE!*

Her eyes snapped open. She could see a familiar shadow bending over her. Her fingers trembled, aching to brush the curl of hair back from his face.

"Vicki?"

She pulled enough strength from him to form a single word. "Hen . . . ry."

The name pierced into Celluci's soul and ripped it to shreds with barbed hooks. She wanted Henry. Not him. Wanted to die in Henry's arms. He bit his lip to keep from crying out and tried to jerk his head away. He couldn't. Something in her eyes held him. Something that insisted he understand.

She saw the sudden white slash of his smile and carried it with her into darkness. She'd done what she could. Now it was up to him.

Henry had heard his name and was bending forward when Celluci lifted his head. He froze. He'd expected to see on the other man's face the pain of Vicki's choice written over the pain of her dying. He hadn't expected to see a wild and insane hope.

"Change her!"

Henry felt his jaw drop. "What?"

"You heard me!" Celluci reached across Vicki's body and grabbed a fistful of leather coat. "Change her!"

Change her. He'd fed from her deeply only a short time before. And fed from her the night before that. His blood held enough of the elements of hers that her system might accept it, especially as she had so little blood of her own left to replace. But considering his condition, did *he* have enough for them both?

Change her. If he changed her, he'd lose her. They'd have a little over a year but no more before her new nature drove them apart.

"Do it," Celluci begged. "It's her only chance."

Henry suddenly realized that Celluci had no idea of what the change would mean. That he, in fact, believed the exact opposite of the truth. Believed that if Vicki changed she was lost to him. Henry could read the knowledge of that loss in the other man's face. Could read how he was willing to surrender everything to another for Vicki's sake.

You think I've won, mortal. You're so very wrong. If she dies, we both lose her. If she changes, I lose her alone.

"Henry. Please."

And if you can give her up for love, wondered Henry Fitzroy, vampire, bastard son of Henry VIII, *can I do any less?* His heart would allow only one answer.

Lifting his own wrist to his mouth, Henry opened a vein. "It might not work," he said as he pressed this smaller wound into the hole in her leg, forcing the flow of his blood to act as a barrier for hers. A moment later, he lifted his arm and threw Celluci back his shirt, the motion flinging a single crimson drop across the room like a discarded ruby. "Bind it. Tightly. This could still kill her in spite of everything I do."

Celluci did as instructed, lifting his eyes in time to see Henry open a vein over his heart with Vicki's Swiss army knife. Even with so prosaic a tool, it held the shadow of ancient ritual and he watched, unable to look away, as blood welled out of the cut, appearing almost black against the alabaster skin.

Sliding his arm behind Vicki's shoulders, Henry lifted her and pressed her mouth to his breast. Her life had dropped away to a murmur in the distance; not dead, not yet, but very, very close.

"Drink, Vicki." He made it a command, threw all he was into it, breathed it against the soft cap of her hair. "Drink to live."

He was afraid for a moment that she could not obey him even if she wanted to; then her lips parted and she swallowed. The intensity of his reaction took him completely by surprise. He could vaguely remember how it had felt when Christina had fed from him. It was in no way comparable to the near ecstasy he felt now. He swayed, wrapped his other arm around her body, and closed his eyes. This rapture wasn't enough to make up for the eventual loss of her, but, by God, it was close.

Celluci tied off the makeshift pressure bandage, his hands operating independently of conscious direction. There was something both so blatantly sensual and so extraordinarily innocent about the scene that he couldn't have looked away had he wanted to. Not that he wanted to. He wanted every second of Vicki he could have before he had to face the rest of his life without her.

The firelight turned Vicki's hair the color of spilled honey, danced orange highlights down the black leather enveloping her, and reflected crimson in the puddles of her blood spilled on the floor.

Jesus H. Christ! The fire! All at once, as though it had been waiting to be remembered, he could feel the heat licking against his back. He turned. The entire wall of boarded windows was aflame. The smoke had a greenish tinge and an unpleasant taste—spilled chemicals or burning plastic, it was irrelevent at the moment. They had to get out.

"Fitzroy!"

The voice seemed to come from a long way away, but it held an urgency difficult to ignore. Henry opened his eyes.

"We've got to get out of here before this whole place goes up! Can you move her?"

It took a moment for Henry's eyes to clear, but gradually he, too, became aware of the danger. He glanced down at Vicki, still nuzzling like a blind kitten at his breast, and pulled free enough to find his voice. "I've never done this before, Detective." He had no energy left for anything but the truth and the touch of her life was still so tenuous. "She's dying slower than she was, but she's still dying."

"Christ! What more will it take!"

"More, I'm afraid, than I have right now to give." He swayed, Vicki's head rising and falling with the motion. "I told you it might not work."

Fucking great. Vicki was still dying, Fitzroy looked like hell, and the building was burning down around them. He coughed and scrubbed his forearm across his face. *God-damned cup's not half empty if I say it's half full.* Grabbing jacket and holster and gun up off the floor, Celluci stood. "If she's still dying, she's not dead. Let's try to keep it that way. Come on!"

Shifting his grip, cradling Vicki in his arms as though she were a child, Henry tried to stand. The room tilted.

Eyes streaming from the smoke, Celluci shoved his free hand into a leather-covered armpit and helped heave Henry and his burden off the floor. "Can you hold her?"

"Yes." He didn't actually think he could let her go but he didn't have enough strength for the explanation. Henry leaned on the larger man's strength as his knees threatened to buckle and, together, they staggered toward the door. Unable to see where he was placing his feet, he stumbled over a piece of something wet— he didn't want to know what—and nearly fell.

"Oh, no, you don't." Muscles popping, sweat streaming down his chest, Celluci somehow kept all three of them up and moving. "After everything we've been through tonight, we aren't fucking quitting yet."

Arms locked around Vicki, holding her life with his own, Henry dredged up the ghost of a smile. "Never say die, Detective?"

Celluci tossed the curl of hair back off his face and led the way out of the lab. "Fucking right," he growled.

As they disappeared down the hall, the door to the

storeroom slowly swung open and, coughing, Dr. Burke stumbled out into the lab.

"Now that," she declared, "was a most edi . . . fying evening. Who says eaves . . . droppers never hear anything good?" She wiped her streaming eyes and nose on her sleeve and picked her way carefully through the smoke and debris toward the door.

From the sound of it, Marjory Nelson's daughter and her companions had problems of their own. Problems that could easily be used to convince them that Dr. Aline Burke might be better left alone, that her involvement in this whole sordid affair was nothing more than chance.

Donald was dead. She didn't want Donald to be dead, but upon consideration there wasn't anything she could do about it. Why should she suffer just because Donald was dead?

Catherine was dead, too, and therefore a convenient, nonprotesting scapegoat.

"I had no idea what was going on, your honor." She started to giggle and gagged instead. Whatever chemicals were burning were undeniably toxic. "Go ahead, burn!" she commanded. "Let's give Catherine and her friends a fine Viking send-off and in the pro-shess . . ." A fit of coughing doubled her over. She staggered to the isolation box and sagged against it, stomach heaving.

"And in the proshess," she repeated when she'd caught her breath and swallowed a mouthful of bile, "destroy as much evidence as possible. A little vampiric blackmail, a little—what's the word?—con . . . fla . . . gration and I'll be out of this with no major career damage done." Her flame-bordered reflection appeared smugly satisfied and she smiled down at it, patting herself on the cheek. The box was becoming warm to the touch and the skin of her face and hands was beginning to tighten in the growing heat. Time to go.

Head lowered to avoid the worst of the smoke now

billowing down from the ceiling, coughing almost continually, she started for the door, lifting her feet with alcohol exaggerated caution over bodies and parts of bodies.

Then she spotted the disk. Spilled half out of Catherine's lab coat pocket, very blue against the blood-stained white, it could contain only one thing: the copies of the tests made that afternoon on the vampire. What else would be important enough for Catherine to carry around with her?

Only this afternoon. Seems so long ago. With one hand resting against the end of the isolation box, her balance not being exactly stable, Dr. Burke bent to pick it up. It didn't seem to be damaged. Having been sheltered in the curve of Catherine's body, it didn't even seem to be very hot. She shoved it into her own pocket, suddenly realizing that not only would she come out of this with her career essentially undamaged, but with information the scientific community would award high honors for.

A few simple experiments, she thought, grinning broadly, *and that Nobel prize is . . .*

One of the oxygen tanks had remained amazingly undamaged after the earlier explosion had flung it out into the lab. It had lain, partially under the far side of the isolation box, safely away from the main heat of the fire. But temperatures were rising. The plastic valve finally began to melt. The metal collar below it expanded a very, very small amount. It was enough.

The blast slammed Dr. Burke to the floor where she watched in horror as a giant, invisible hand lifted the isolation box and dropped it to fall, impossibly slowly, across her legs. She heard bones shatter, felt the pain a moment later, and slid into darkness.

When the light returned, it was the orange-red of the approaching fire and almost no time had passed. She couldn't feel what was left of her legs.

"That's all right. Don't need legs."

Catherine's extended hand had begun to sizzle.

"Don't need legs. Need to get out of here." The isolation box was on its side. The curve would give her a little room. If she could just push against it, she could pull her legs free and crawl out of the room. Crawl away from the flames. She didn't need legs.

Dragging herself up into a sitting position, she shoved at the box. Nestled on an uneven surface, it rocked. Something squelched beneath it but that didn't matter.

The flames were licking at the sleeve of Catherine's lab coat. Over the stink of chemical-laden smoke, came the smell of roasting pork.

Swallowing saliva, she pounded at the box.

It rocked again.

The latch that number nine had partially turned, gave way.

The lid fell open, knocking Dr. Burke back to the floor as it rose into the air on silent hinges, spilling the body thrown up against it by the explosion onto her lap.

The naked, empty shell of Donald Li rolled once and came to rest in the circle of her arms, his head tucked back so that it seemed his face stared up into hers.

The flames stopped the screaming when they finally came.

"Christ on crutches!" Detective Fergusson ducked behind his car as the explosion flung pieces of burning wood and heated metal out into the street. "Next time I investigate drunken confessions in the fucking morning!" Snatching up his radio, he ignored the panicked shouts of the approaching security guards and called in the fire with a calm professionalism he was far from feeling.

". . . *and* an ambulance!"

He thought he could hear screaming. He hoped like hell he was wrong.

* * *

"Now what."

"It's just after two. I need to feed. In about an hour, if she's still alive, I need to feed her. And then I need to get her back to Toronto before dawn."

"Why Toronto? Why can't she just stay here?"

Henry sank down onto the end of the bed. His head felt almost too heavy to lift. "Because if she changes, I need to have her in a place I know is secure." He waved a weary, bloodstained arm at the apartment. "This isn't. And if she . . . if she . . ."

"Dies," Celluci said emotionlessly, staring down at Vicki's unconscious form. He felt as though the world had skewed a few degrees sideways and he had no choice but to try to keep his balance on the slope.

"Yes." Henry matched the detective's lack of expression. If the facade cracked now, it would sweep them all away. "If she dies, I'll need to dispose of the body. I'll need to be in a city I know in order to do that."

"Dispose of the body?"

"Her death is going to be a little difficult to explain if I don't, don't you think? There'll be an autopsy, an inquest, and questions you don't have the answer to will be asked."

"So she just disappears . . ."

"Yes. Yet another unsolved mystery."

"And I'll have to act as though I have no idea if she's dead or alive."

Henry lifted his head and allowed a hint of power to touch his voice. "Mourn her as dead, Detective."

Celluci didn't bother to pretend that he misunderstood. He jerked his gaze from Vicki and recklessly met the vampire's eyes. "Mourn her regardless? Fuck you. You tell me what happens, Fitzroy. If she disappears because she's dead, I'll mourn her. If she disappears into the night with you, I'll . . ." A muscle jumped in his jaw. "I'll miss her like I'd miss a part of myself but I won't mourn her if she isn't any more dead than you are."

Since they'd found her dying in the lab, Henry had

been measuring time by Vicki's heartbeat. He let three go by while he studied Mike Celluci's soul. "You really mean that," he said at last. He found it difficult to believe. Found it impossible not to believe.

"Yeah." The word caught in Celluci's throat. "I really mean it." He swallowed and fought for control. Then his eyes widened. "What do you mean, you have to feed?"

"You should know what means by now."

"On who?"

"I could hunt." Except that he was so incredibly tired. The night had already lasted longer than any night he could remember. It seemed a pity to hunt when there was . . . He allowed the power to rise a little more.

"Stop it. I know what you're trying." With an effort, Celluci wrenched his gaze away and back to the woman on the bed. She was still alive. All that really mattered was keeping her that way. He'd made that decision back in the lab. He'd stand by it now. "If it includes anything but sucking blood, you can fucking well order takeout."

Astounded by the offer, Henry felt his brows rise. "It needn't include anything but sucking blood, Detective. It's not nourishment I need so much as refueling."

"All right, then." Celluci shrugged out of his jacket, dropping it carefully inside out so as not to stain the carpet, and began to roll up his sleeve. "Wrist, right?"

"Yes." Henry shook his head, wonder and respect about equally mixed in his voice. "You know, in four and a half centuries, I've never met a man quite like you. In spite of everything, you offer me your blood?"

"Yeah. In spite of everything." With one last look at Vicki, he turned and lowered himself onto the end of the bed. "At the risk of offending, after what went down tonight," he sighed, "this doesn't seem like much. Besides, I'm doing it for her. Right now, as far as I'm concerned, you're just a primitive branch of the Red Cross. Get on with it.''

Henry lifted the offered arm, then looked up at Celluci, his eyes dark, the smallest hint of a smile brushing against the outside corners of his lips. ''You know, it's a shame there's so much between us, Detective.''

Celluci felt the heat and tossed the curl of hair back off his forehead. ''Don't press your luck, you undead son of a bitch.''

As he carried her out the door, her life still balanced on the razor's edge, Henry paused. ''Doesn't it gnaw at you,'' he asked at last, unable to leave with knowing, ''that at the end she chose me?''

Celluci reached out and gently tucked her glasses into the pocket of her coat. Her purse and her suitcase had already been loaded in Henry's car.

''She didn't choose you,'' he said, stepping back and rubbing at the bandage on his wrist. ''She chose the one chance she had to live. I refuse to feel bad about that.''

''She could still die.''

''See that she doesn't.''

A thousand thoughts between one faltering heartbeat and the next. ''I'll do my best.''

Celluci nodded, acknowledging truth; then he bent forward and kissed her gently on lips that felt less warm than they had.

''Good-bye, Vicki.''

And there wasn't anything more he could say.

He dealt with Detective Fergusson. Explained Vicki had had a bit of a breakdown, perfectly understandable under the circumstances, and gone back to Toronto with a friend. ''I'll let her know what happened . . .''

He dealt with the contents of her mother's apartment, calling an estate auctioneer and putting everything in his hands. ''Just sell it. The money goes to the lawyer until the will clears probate, so what's the problem."

He dealt with Mr. Delgado.

"I saw her leave in his car; through my window." The old man looked up at him and shook his head. "What happened?"

Just for a moment, Celluci wanted to tell him—just for a moment, because he desperately needed to tell somebody. Fortunately, the moment passed. "There's an old saying, Mr. Delgado, 'if you love something, let it go.' "

"I know this saying. I read it on a T-shirt once. It's bullshit, if you'll excuse my language." His head continued to shake like it was the only moving part of an ancient clockwork. "So she made her choice."

"We all made a choice."

He dealt with driving back to Toronto not knowing. He wouldn't call Fitzroy. He'd bent as far as he could. Let Fitzroy call him.

He dealt with the message when it finally came and thanked God he only had to deal with Fitzroy's voice on the machine. Even that was disturbing enough. He tried to be happy she was still alive. Tried very hard. Almost managed it.

He found out what was happening next by accident. He hadn't intended to walk by her apartment. It was stupid. Ghoulish. He knew she wasn't there. He'd gone in once, the night he'd arrived from Kingston, cleared out his stuff, and without knowing why, had taken a picture of the two of them that he hated off her dresser. When he got home, he shoved it up on the shelf in his hall closet and never looked at it again. But he had it.

"Hey, Sarge." A slender shadow detached itself from the broad base of the old chestnut tree and sauntered out onto the sidewalk. "There's no point in going in, her stuff's all gone. New tenants coming next week, I expect."

"What are you doing here, Tony?"

The young man shrugged. "I was dropping off the

key and I saw you coming around the corner, so I figured I'd wait. Save me a trip later. I got a message for you.''

"A message," he repeated, because he couldn't ask who from.

"Yeah. Henry said I was to tell you that you were one of the most honorable men he ever met and that he wished things could've been different.''

"Different. Yeah. Well.''

Tony shot the detective a glance out of the corner of his eye and hid his disappointment. Henry wouldn't tell him what he meant by *different,* if he meant with Vicki or what, and now it looked like Celluci was going to be just as closedmouthed. Although he'd been given the overall story behind that last night in Kingston, he had none of the details and curiosity was almost killing him. "Henry also wanted me to tell you that a year is a small slice of eternity.''

Celluci snorted and started walking down Huron Street, needing the distraction of movement. "What the hell does *that* mean?" he asked as Tony fell into step beside him.

"Beats me," Tony admitted. "But that's what he wanted me to tell you. He said you'd understand later.''

Celluci snorted again. "Fucking romance writer.''

"Yeah. Well.'' When they reached the corner at Cecil Street, and the detective hadn't spoke again, Tony sighed. "Mostly she sleeps," he said.

"Who sleeps?" A muscle jumped in Celluci's jaw.

"Victory. Henry's still pretty worried about her, but he thinks things are going to be all right now that the hole in her leg finally healed up. We're moving to Vancouver.''

"We?''

"Yeah. She's pretty helpless right now. They need someone who can deal with the sun. And . . .''

"Never mind.'' Vancouver. All the way across the country. "Why? For the sea air?''

"Nah. So nobody recognizes her when she starts to hunt. Apparently they're pretty messy at first."

They'd eaten a thousand meals together. Maybe two thousand. "Tell him she's not likely to get a lot neater."

Tony snickered. "I'll tell him. Anything you want me to tell her?"

"Tell her . . ." His voice trailed off and he seemed to be staring at something Tony couldn't see. Then his face twisted and, lips pressed into a thin, white line, he spun on one heel and strode away.

Tony stood and watched him for a moment, then he nodded. "Don't worry, man," he said softly. "I'll tell her."

He dealt with everything until Detective Fergusson called from Kingston about the inquest.

"Look, she's moved to Vancouver, all right. Other than that, I don't know where the fuck she is."

Detective Fergusson jumped to the obvious conclusion. "Dumped you, eh?"

In answer, Celluci ripped the phone off his kitchen wall and threw it out the back door. A few days later, after he'd been brought in by a couple of uniforms for racing a jet down the runway at the Downsview Airport, the backseat of his car rattling with empties, the police psychologist suggested that he was suppressing strong emotions.

Still painfully hung over, Celluci barely resisted the urge to suppress the police psychologist.

"I hope she's worth you flushing your career down the toilet, because that's what you're doing." Inspector Cantree's chair screeched a protest as he leaned back and glared at Celluci. "You know what I've got here?" One huge hand slapped down on the file folder centered on his blotter. "Never mind. I'll tell you. I've got a report from the department shrink that suggests you're dangerously unstable and that you shouldn't be allowed out on the street carrying a gun."

Lips compressed into a thin, white line, Celluci started to shrug out of his shoulder holster.

"Put that the fuck back on!" Cantree snapped. "If I was going to listen to the pompous quack, I'd have had your badge days ago."

Celluci shoved the curl of hair back off his face and tried to ignore how much the motion reminded him of her. "I'm fine," he growled.

"Bullshit! You want to tell me what's wrong?"

"Nothing's wrong." His tone dared Cantree to argue the point and Cantree's expression did just that. Celluci had heard the rumors making the rounds about ex-Detective Vicki Nelson's hasty relocation to the West Coast—although he'd heard them second or third hand because no one had the guts to speculate to his face. Obviously, Cantree had heard them, too. "It's personal."

"Not when it affects your job, it isn't." The Inspector leaned forward and held Celluci's gaze with his. "So here's what you're going to do. You're going to take a leave of absence for at least a month and you're going to get out of the city and you're going to find wherever it is you've left your brains and then you're going to come back and have another little talk with Dr. Freud-enstein."

"What if I don't want to go?" Celluci muttered.

Cantree smiled. "If you don't take a leave of absence, I'll suspend you for a month without pay. Either way, you're out of here."

Betting in headquarters had three to one odds that Mike Celluci's leave of absence would begin on the first available flight to Vancouver. Several people lost some serious money.

A week after the interview in Cantree's office, Celluci found himself escorting his ancient grandmother onto a plane bound for Italy and a family reunion.

* * *

"Jesus, Mike it's good to have you back." Dave Graham's grin threatened to dislodge the entire lower half of his face. "I mean, one more temporary partner like the last one and *I'd* have taken six weeks off."

"Who the fuck left coffee rings all over my desk!"

"On the other hand," Dave continued thoughtfully as Celluci began accusing coworkers of messing with his stuff, "it *was* a lot quieter while you were gone."

"You buying one of those, Mike?"

"What?" Celluci looked up from the paperback book display and scowled at his partner.

"Well, you've been staring at it for the last five minutes. I thought that maybe you were in the mood for a little light reading." Dave reached past his head at the blond giant cradling a half-naked brunette on the cover. "*Sail into Destiny* by Elizabeth Fitzroy. Looks like a winner. You think you know a guy . . ." He flipped the book over ". . . think you know his tastes, and then you find out about something like this. You figure Captain Roxborough and this Veronica babe are going to get together in the end or is that a given?"

"Jesus H. Christ, we're in a mall! Someone might see you." Celluci grabbed the book and shoved it back on the shelf.

"Hey, you were the one who stopped to browse," Dave protested as the two detectives started walking again. "You were the one . . ."

"I know the author, all right? Now drop it."

"You know an author? I didn't even think you knew how to read." They watched a crowd of teenage boys saunter past and into a sports store. "So what's she like? Does she live in Toronto?"

He's a vampire. He lives in Vancouver. "I said, drop it."

There were bits of Vicki scattered all over the city and whenever he ran into one—her old neighborhood, her favorite coffee shop, a hooker she'd busted—it gouged the scabs off his ability to cope. Now, he was finding bits of Fitzroy as well and every copy of the book he saw ground salt into the wounds. Fortunately, he'd gotten better at hiding the pain.

He'd even convinced the police psychologist that he was fine.

". . . and the Stanley Park murders continue in Vancouver. Another known drug dealer has been found by the teahouse at Ferguson Point. As in the three previous cases, the head appears to have been ripped from the body and sources in the Coroner's Office report that, once again, the body has been drained of blood."

Celluci's grip tightened around the aluminum beer can, crushing the thin metal. His attention locked on the television, he didn't notice the liquid dripping over his hand and onto the carpet.

"The police remain baffled and one of the officers staking out the teahouse during the time the murder occurred freely admitted having seen nothing. Speculation in the press ranges from the likelihood of a powerful new gang arriving in the Vancouver area and removing competition, to the possibility of an enraged sasquatch roaming the park.

"In Edmonton . . ."

Drained of blood. Celluci shut off the sound and stared unblinkingly at the CBC news anchor who silently continued the National without him. *Not a sasquatch. A vampire.* A new, young vampire learning to feed. Rip off the heads to hide the first frenzied teeth marks. Fitzroy was strong enough. Leave dead drug dealers in the park to make a point. He could see Vicki all over that.

"God-damned vampire vigilantes," he muttered through teeth clenched so tightly his temples ached. Back before Fitzroy, Vicki had realized that law was one of the few concepts holding chaos at bay. As much as she might have wanted to behead a few of the cockroaches that walked on two legs in the city's gutters, she'd never have taken matters into her own hands. Fitzroy had changed that even before he'd changed her.

Vicki was alive, but what had she become? And why didn't he care?

Celluci didn't want to face the answer to either question. The TV continued to flicker silently in the corner as he cracked open a bottle of Scotch and methodically set about searching for oblivion.

Time passed but only because there was nothing to stop it.

She stood outside for a while and watched his shadow move against the blinds. There was a tightness in her chest and, if she didn't know herself better, she'd say she was frightened. "Which is ridiculous."

Wiping her palms against the thighs of her jeans, the movement dictated no longer by need but by habit, she started up the driveway. Waiting would only make it worse.

Her knock, harder than she'd intended for she still didn't have complete control of her strength, echoed up and down the quiet street. She listened to him approach the door, counted his heartbeats as he turned the knob, and tried not to flinch back from the sudden spill of light.

"Vicki."

She felt as though she hadn't heard her name spoken for a very long time and couldn't hear his reaction over the sound of her own. With an effort, she kept her voice more or less even. "You don't seem especially surprised to see me."

"I heard about what happened last night to Gowan and Mallard."

"No more than they deserved. No more than I owed them."

"The paper says they'll both live."

The night flashed for an instant in her smile. "Good.

I want them to live with it.'' She rubbed her palms against her jeans again, this time wiping clean old debts. ''Can I come in?''

Celluci stepped back from the door. She was thinner, paler, and her hair was different. It took a moment for the most obvious change to sink in.

''Your glasses?''

''I don't need them anymore.'' This smile was the smile he remembered. ''Good thing, too.''

Closing the door behind her, he felt like an amputee who'd woken up to find his legs had grown back. He couldn't seem to catch his breath and it took a moment to identify the strange sense of loss he was feeling with an absence of pain. He almost heard the click as the piece that had been gouged from his life slid back into place.

''You know the potential problems with the RP never even occurred to me that night in the lab,'' she continued, leading the way into the kitchen. ''Can you imagine a vampire with no night sight? Biting by braille—God, what a mess that would be.''

''You're babbling,'' he said shortly as she turned to face him. •

''I know. Sorry.''

They stared at each other for a long moment and a number of things that needed to be said were discussed in the silence.

''Henry owes you an apology,'' Vicki told him at last. ''He never mentioned to you that vampires can't stay together after the change is complete.''

''It's been fourteen months.''

She spread her hands. ''Sorry. I got off to a slow start.''

Celluci frowned. ''I'm not sure I understand. You *can't* ever see him again?''

''He says I won't want to. That we won't want to.''

''The bastard could've told me.'' He dragged a hand up through his hair. *''Henry wanted me to tell you that a year is a small slice of eternity.''* Taking a deep breath, he wondered what he would've done had their positions been reversed. "Never mind. Henry doesn't owe me anything. And the son of a bitch already apologized."

Vicki looked doubtful. "Yeah? Well, I'm not buying into his tragic separation bullshit even if we can't share a territory." Brave words, but she wasn't so sure that they meant anything, that her new nature would allow a bond to remain without the blood.

"I'm not giving you up without a fight."

Henry turned away from the lights of a new city and sadly shook his head. "You'll be fighting yourself, Vicki. Fighting what you are. What we are."

"So?" Her chin rose. "I don't surrender, Henry. Not to anything."

"He's got a cellular phone and he just bought a fax machine, for chrissake; I think we'll manage to stay in touch."

"Really?" Celluci propped one hip on the counter and crossed his arms over his chest. "You never called *me*."

"I wasn't able to until just recently—things were a little chaotic at first. And then . . ." She rubbed a pale finger along the edge of his kitchen table, glad she'd lost the ability to blush. "And then, I was afraid."

He'd never heard her admit to being afraid of anything before. "Afraid of what?"

She looked up and he found his answer in the desperate question in her eyes.

"Vicki . . ." He made her name a gentle accusation. *Couldn't you trust me?*

"Well, I'm *different* now and . . . What are you laughing at?"

How long had it been since he laughed like that? About fourteen months, he suspected. "If *that's* all you're worried about; Vicki, you've *always* been different."

The question faded, replaced by hope. "So you don't mind?"

"I'd be lying if I said it won't take getting used to, but, no, I don't mind." Mind? There wasn't much he couldn't get used to if it meant having her back beside him.

"It won't be the same."

"No shit."

"Henry says it can be better."

"I don't care what Henry says."

"It won't be settling down and raising a family like you wanted."

He slid off the counter. "Don't tell me what I wanted. I wanted you."

She opened her arms, her teeth a very white invitation against the curve of her mouth.

He met her halfway.

They hit the floor together.

Two hours and twenty-three minutes later, Vicki pillowed her head on his shoulder and stared up at the kitchen ceiling. She'd thought that over the last fourteen months she'd come to terms with what she'd become—vampire, child of darkness, nightwalker—but she hadn't, not really, not until her teeth had met through a fold of Mike Celluci's skin and she'd drawn his life back into hers. She licked at a drop of sweat and could feel his breath, warm against the top of her head, his scent wrapped around her.

"What're you thinking of?" he asked sleepily.

Vampire. Child of Darkness. Nightwalker.

Reaching up, she brushed the curl of hair back off his forehead and smiled. "I was just thinking about the next four hundred and fifty years."

TANYA HUFF
VALOR'S CHOICE

"Readers who enjoy military SF will love Tanya Huff's
VALOR'S CHOICE. Howlingly funny and very
suspenseful. I enjoyed every word."
—*scifi.com*

Staff Sergeant Torin Kerr was a battle-hardened professional.
So when she and those in her platoon who'd survived the last
deadly encounter with the Others were yanked from a well-
deserved leave for what was supposed to be "easy" duty as
the honor guard for a diplomatic mission to the non-Confedera-
tion world of the Silsviss, she was ready for anything. Sure,
there'd been rumors of the Others being spotted in this sector
of space. But there were always rumors. Everything seemed
to be going perfectly. Maybe too perfectly. . . .

0-88677-896-4 $6.99

Prices slightly higher in Canada **DAW: 149**

FIONA PATTON

"Rousing adventure, full of color and spectacular magic"—*Locus*

In the kingdom of Branion, the hereditary royal line is blessed—or cursed—with the power of the Flame, a magic against which no one can stand. But when used by one not strong enough to control it, the power of the Flame can just as easily consume its human vessel, as destroy whatever foe it had been unleased against. . . .

☐ **THE STONE PRINCE**   UE2735—$6.99

☐ **THE PAINTER KNIGHT**   UE2780—$6.99

☐ **THE GRANITE SHIELD**   UE2842—$6.99

Michelle West

The Sun Sword:

☐ **THE BROKEN CROWN**   UE2740—$6.99

☐ **THE UNCROWNED KING**   UE2801—$6.99

☐ **THE SHINING COURT**   UE2837—$6.99

In the Dominion, those allied with the demons of the Shining Court fear the bargain they've made, for to the *kialli* betrayal was a way of life. And as the Festival of the Moon approaches, demon kin begin to prey upon those in the Tor Leonne. But even more frightening than their presence was their "gift" for the Festival, masks created not by human craftsmen but by the *kialli*. . . .

The Sacred Hunt:

☐ **HUNTER'S OATH**   UE2681—$5.50

☐ **HUNTER'S DEATH**   UE2706—$5.99